The child Lina is carrying
belongs to Webb Harper. Or so he claims.
But how can that be if she's never met the
man...and never imagined the courts
would be involved when she realized
her heart's desire to become a mother?

THIS CHILD IS MINE
by Janice Kaiser

Anna Rose Palmer figures the gossips may
finally leave her alone when she introduces
Britt Cameron as her fiancé. Unfortunately, the
fact that the would-be groom has been accused of
murder gives the gossips even more to talk about!

CAMERON
by Beverly Barton

Janice Kaiser, a former lawyer and college instructor, now has to her credit over forty novels—translated into twenty languages—and a worldwide following. She turned to writing in 1985 after marrying her husband, Ronn, who is also a writer. She and Ronn have also collaborated on women's fiction for MIRA Books. They make their home in Northern California, although Janice's fascination with exotic locales has taken her to over forty different countries.

Beverly Barton has been in love with romance since her grandfather gave her an illustrated copy of *Beauty and the Beast.* An avid reader since childhood, she began writing at the age of nine and wrote short stories, poetry, plays and novels through high school and college. After a stint as a full-time wife and mother of two, she joined Romance Writers of America in 1987, and realized her lifelong dream of becoming a published writer. The author of over thirty books, Beverly has won numerous awards, and her books have placed on both the Waldenbooks and *USA Today* bestseller lists.

Janice Kaiser
Beverly Barton

Special Deliveries

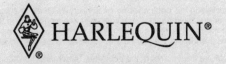

HARLEQUIN®

TORONTO • NEW YORK • LONDON
AMSTERDAM • PARIS • SYDNEY • HAMBURG
STOCKHOLM • ATHENS • TOKYO • MILAN • MADRID
PRAGUE • WARSAW • BUDAPEST • AUCKLAND

HARLEQUIN BOOKS

by Request—SPECIAL DELIVERIES

Copyright © 2001 by Harlequin Books S.A.

ISBN 0-373-21717-X

The publisher acknowledges the copyright holders
of the individual works as follows:
THIS CHILD IS MINE
Copyright © 1997 by Belles-Lettres, Inc.
CAMERON
Copyright © 1993 by Beverly Beaver

This edition published by arrangement with Harlequin Books S.A.

Visit us at www.eHarlequin.com

Printed in U.S.A.

CONTENTS

This Child Is Mine
by Janice Kaiser

CHAPTER ONE

WEBB HARPER LOVED Mary dearly, but he couldn't come to her house without his stomach getting all twisted in knots. She'd told him to make himself comfortable while she went for the money, but he hadn't sat down for long. Instead he paced, running his fingers through his shaggy hair, feeling jumpy as a heifer carrying her first calf.

Part of him wanted to call out to her in the other room, tell her to forget the money. But borrowing wasn't the only thing that made him uneasy. Seeing all the reminders of his wife and child was enough to make him want to bolt for home.

Mary had pictures of Karen and Robbie on every table. And the prize pieces from Karen's doll collection were stuck in the glass trophy case, along with her baton-twirling awards and the ribbons from the beauty contests she'd won. Even Robbie's baby shoes and silver cup were there.

Webb glanced at a huge framed photo of the contestants in the Miss Colorado pageant that hung over the fireplace. From clear across the room he could pick out Karen in the front row, third runner-up, but the one with the best legs, far and away. He would know. In his younger days, he had been a true connoisseur of women. He'd cut a pretty wide swath through central Colorado. But once he'd met Karen Carson, everything had changed.

As far as he was concerned, there wasn't a prettier girl in the state—not even the three who'd come in ahead of her in the pageant. He had told her that eleven years ago, and he'd felt that way until the day she'd died.

Karen's losing the contest had had a big impact on their lives. Since she wasn't going to Atlantic City, she'd decided she wanted to marry right away.

"I'm the booby prize, eh?" he'd teased.

"If I had to pick one or the other, I'd have married you, Webb," she'd told him, driving home after the contest in his battered old pickup. "As you know damned well."

"Convenient you say that now," he'd said, rolling his tongue around his cheek.

She'd given him a violent pinch and told him he was cruel, hitting her while she was down. Webb pulled off the highway, kissed her and told her to set the date.

To Karen's credit, she'd always made him feel as if he were what she wanted most in life. "Queen for a day is fine," she'd say, "but a lifetime with you is a better deal by far."

They'd been so happy. Webb couldn't think about her without his gut wrenching. Losing Karen had been the worst experience of his life. Even so, wallowing in self-pity was not his way of dealing with problems. Maybe, as Mary said, he'd been hiding from his sorrow, avoiding his grief. But everybody had to deal with these things in his own way. One picture of Karen holding Robbie, and a swatch of satin from the hem of her wedding dress stuck in the corner of the frame was all he'd kept out. The rest he'd given to Mary or stuck in a box in the closet.

His mother-in-law, on the other hand, had turned her house into a virtual museum commemorating her only child and grandson. That was what made coming to Mary's so hard. Karen and Robbie were everywhere. It was like the funeral all over again.

Finally the pressure got to be too much. "Mary," he called to her. "On second thought, let's forget the money. I'd feel better solving my problem some other way."

"We've been through that, Webb," she called back from her bedroom. "There is no other way. And I'm not going to let you lose everything."

"There's no point in you and me both going down," he replied. "It was a dumb idea, me coming here. I don't know what I was thinking. You aren't a bank. You're living on social security and your sewing money."

"Cord Stewart wants his rent money and he won't give you any more extensions. You know that," Mary responded.

"Best thing is for me to sell my herd, get current with the rent and start over."

Mary appeared at the door, an envelope in hand. She was sixty-five, and though she'd put on some extra pounds in recent years, she was still a handsome woman. "Webb," she said, "that's foolish and you know it. With the price of beef what it is, you'll lose big. It'll set you back years, even if you're lucky enough to hang on through the winter, which is doubtful."

"That's the risk a man takes trying to run a ranch with no capital," he said. "I threw the dice and I lost. Simple as that. Accepting charity's the only thing I know that's worse."

She walked over to where he stood and extended the envelope. "I'm not offering charity. I'm expecting to be paid back."

"I can't take your money. Don't care what you say."

"Stop it," she said, stuffing the envelope into his jacket pocket and taking his hands in hers. "All that money's good for is to pay the nursing home when I need one, and they'll take me in whether I have it or not. This twenty-five hundred will do you more good than it'll do me."

"Mary…"

She gave him a stern look. "Listen to me, son. I wouldn't let Karen and Robbie get pitched into the street, so why should I let you? Don't fight me on this, please."

He hated gambling with other people's money, but Webb knew the chances were fair that beef prices would firm up. If spring calving went well, he'd be dollars ahead. The problem, though, was getting from fall to spring. Cord Stewart stood to gain from Webb's plight. If Webb defaulted on the lease, Cord could get possession of the land, as well as title.

"Leasin' at that price was the sorriest mistake I ever made," Cord had said when Webb tried to negotiate with him. "I'll forgive the back rent if you abandon. Plus, I'll throw in a thousand cash."

Webb refused to give up so easily—not when he'd once owned the place and had been forced to sell after losing an entire herd of beef cattle to disease. His dream had been to buy land, not sell it. He had wanted a respectable spread to pass on to Robbie. But fate had intervened. First he'd lost his wife and child to a drugged-out trucker. Then he'd lost his land. In just over two months he had been transformed from a married land owner to a widowed renter.

"If I had my way," Mary told him, "I'd just give you the twenty-five hundred outright. But you're a man, and a man has his pride to contend with, so I'll agree to make it a loan. Bank rates."

Webb sighed, hating this. Noticing he was standing on Mary's carpet in his dusty boots, he self-consciously rubbed the toes against the backs of his legs. "You'd rather I hate myself, wouldn't you?"

"Karen said your only fault was you were stubborn as a mule. Well, I got news for you, Webb—she was right."

She looked at him with Karen's soft brown eyes. And she had that expression on her face that women got when they weren't going to be dissuaded, no matter what. He wished he hadn't come. Then he wouldn't have had to face the problem.

"Don't make me beg you," she said. "I've got my pride, too."

"I don't know why this is so hard," he said.

"I'll tell you. Because you're confusing good luck with manhood. Accepting my help makes you no less a man. People born with money never think twice about taking what's handed to them—they figure it's their due. A fellow like you, who grew up an orphan and never was given a darned thing but a pair of pants and a clean shirt, assumes if he didn't earn it with the sweat of his brow, he doesn't deserve it."

"You're probably right."

"Damned right I'm right. Now let's not hear another word about it."

Webb shifted uneasily. "This is really decent of you, Mary," he muttered.

"There's five extra hundred-dollar bills in there," she said. "It only seems logical you should eat between now and spring."

"I won't take extra," he said, opening the envelope.

Mary clamped her hands on his and looked him dead in the eye. "Webb, I don't want you going under, physically or financially."

"I'm fine. I'm not going hungry. Beans and corn bread are more healthy than a beefsteak, anyway."

"I won't take no for an answer."

He shook his head, his eyes getting glossy. He couldn't look at Mary without seeing Karen. They both had the same goodness of heart.

"I've got something else for you," Mary said, turning and heading for the kitchen. "I baked myself a pie this morning and, while I was at it, I figured I might as well make one for you." She disappeared into the kitchen.

Webb looked inside the envelope. It was stuffed with one-hundred-dollar bills. Shaking his head again, he folded it and shoved it into his jacket pocket. Mary returned with the pie in a box.

"You can set this on the seat next to you and it won't spill."

Webb took the box and kissed Mary's cheek. "I'd like to think I deserve you," he said, picking up the sweat-stained Stetson on the little table by the door.

"In ten years you're going to own half of this valley," she said. "Mark my words."

He smiled. It was good knowing someone believed in him. Pressing the hat down over his browny blond hair, he went out the door of Mary Carson's modest frame house. After the closeness indoors, the afternoon air seemed especially crisp.

The sun shone bright in the cloudless sky. It felt warm, despite the mild temperature. The mountains to the south and southeast, toward Aspen, were dusted with snow, but in the valley there were no signs of winter. He went down the steps.

"Webb," Mary called after him.

He turned.

"Why don't you take twenty out of that money and go to the Friday-night dance in Glenwood Springs?"

"You trying to play matchmaker again, Mary?"

"Half the girls in the valley past high-school age would kill to go out with you. There's no reason to spend every night alone."

"I've gone to the dance a time or two."

"Did you dance?"

"When I was asked."

She shook her head. "Webb, it wouldn't hurt to be your old self for a little while—the one this country knew before Karen came along."

He laughed. "Just when folks are thinking it's safe to let their daughters out of the house again?" He shook his head. "No, Mary, those days are behind me. I'm doing fine. Don't worry."

Webb climbed into his pickup, setting the box with the

pie on the seat beside him. Looking up through the windshield, he saw Mary leaning against the door frame in the sunshine. Karen used to do the same thing, waving goodbye, when he'd come courting her.

Webb put the image from his mind and started the engine. It took several turns. The battery was getting low and wouldn't last the winter. There was another fifty or sixty bucks he'd have to shell out.

Mary waved as he backed down the drive. Webb waved back. Once he was on the highway and headed into Carbondale, he rolled up the window. The smell of apple pie filled the truck. He'd go home, have a piece of pie, then call Cord Stewart and tell him he would be coming over with the rent money. Webb was a bit relieved, but sad, as well. Mary's generosity didn't change the facts.

He was glad she hadn't mentioned that a good part of his financial problems—the reason he'd lost the ranch in the first place—was because he and Karen had spent all his working capital trying to have a child. Robbie had been an in vitro baby, their biological child, but conceived with the help of the doctors in the laboratory.

"The least fun way to have a baby known to man," Webb had told Karen on many occasions during the two years they'd gone to the fertility clinic in Denver.

"We still have our fun," she'd replied, "so don't complain."

Webb hadn't complained. Not even about the money. He'd have given everything he owned so that Karen could have a baby. It meant more than anything to her. And she had been so proud when Robbie was finally born.

Ironically, she was on her way back from the clinic where she'd gone for an exam in preparation for a second pregnancy when the accident occurred. Karen had dropped Mary off only ten minutes earlier, or her mother would have been killed, too.

Just past Carbondale, Route 133 intersected with Route

82. Webb turned east, following the route Karen had taken that night. After a mile or so he came to Road 103, where the accident had occurred. It was a terrible thing to have to pass the spot whenever he went into town, but he told himself over and over that death was part of life, even if it didn't help much.

Webb let up on the accelerator as he approached the intersection. He always slowed, as though by reducing his speed he could reduce the pain. He glanced at the ditch on the south side of the highway where Karen's crushed car had landed. The berm had been repaired and the grass was growing naturally, as though nothing had ever happened.

Whoosh, his pickup passed the spot and he was able to relax. Webb took a deep breath. His mind slowly went back to the apple pie. He realized he was hungry. Maybe it was because he hadn't eaten since breakfast. Mary was right. He had to take care of himself. After all, he had a hell of a lot of work ahead if he was going to own half the valley in ten years' time.

Smiling to himself, Webb turned on the radio. It crackled some, but the station finally came in. The music made him think of Mary's suggestion that he socialize. He had, more than she realized. Trouble was, if he took a woman out to a movie, she started talking about marriage. He'd kissed Amy Coulton once, and the next night she was on his doorstep, wanting to fix him a four-course meal, her overnight case in the car.

Twelve, fifteen years ago, he'd have laughed at the thought of beating them off with a stick, let alone actually doing it. Before Karen, any girl who gave him a come-hither smile had better have been prepared to hang on to her bonnet. That was a time when he took no prisoners and made no apologies. But that was then.

Now, if he had to choose between going out with a woman he didn't truly care about and reading a good book, he'd take the book every time. The old Webb Harper barely made it through high school, but the new Webb Harper had earned thirty-six college credits taking correspondence courses through the University of Colorado extension program. There wasn't a soul who knew about it, not even Mary Carson.

The radio crackled loudly, then went dead. He tried to get it again, but couldn't. He patted the dash of the truck he'd had for more than fifteen years, having bought it used to begin with. "I know you're tired, Nelly," he said, "but give me another year or two, then you can go out to pasture."

Glancing at the dash, Webb noticed he was low on gas. Duggan's Market was at the crossroads where Road 100 intersected the highway. He could stop there for a couple of bucks of gas. That's all he had in his wallet, except for Mary's hundreds. If he used one of them, folks might think he'd robbed a bank. There wasn't a soul in the valley who didn't know he was on the edge.

There was no other vehicle at the pump when Webb got to Duggan's. He put in exactly two dollars' worth, then went inside to pay.

Harriet Duggan was at the register. The wall behind her was lined with packages of cigarettes and candy, chips, pretzels and dusty boxes of Kodak film. "Hi, Webb," she said, taking the two bills he extended.

"Hello, Harriet."

"Those folks ever find you?"

"What folks?"

"A couple, a man and a woman. Middle-aged. Stopped here maybe twenty minutes ago, asking for directions to your place. I told 'em how to get there."

"I've been out, Harriet."

"If you skedaddle on home you might catch them, then."

"Who was it, anyway?"

"Nobody I ever seen before," the woman said. "They

had a city smell about 'em. A new Toyota. Colorado plates. Maybe from Denver.''

Webb nodded and left the store. He couldn't imagine who'd be coming to see him from Denver. Everybody who knew him well enough to care lived here in the valley.

He started the engine, trying to remember if he'd passed a new Toyota in the past five minutes. He'd have to keep an eye out. But then, he wasn't sure flagging someone down would be such a good idea. About the only stranger he could imagine wanting to see him was a process server, though the description Harriet had given didn't sound like somebody serving legal papers. Maybe the thing to do was leave well enough alone. If more trouble was coming, he'd find out soon enough.

LINA PRESCOTT REFOLDED all the sweaters on the display table, then checked the sleepers in the antique armoire, arranging them by size. She hadn't had many customers that afternoon, but the few she'd had managed to mess things up just the same. That was the life of a retailer. Yawning, she retreated to her spot behind the counter to wait until closing time.

She was tired and hadn't had a good night's sleep in weeks, which certainly didn't help with the morning sickness. And her usual orderly life seemed to be on the verge of falling apart. At thirty-five, she'd felt ready for single parenthood. Lina had a beautiful home, a business, financial security, supportive friends and a deep, abiding desire for a child. But she hadn't anticipated that someone might contest her rights to the baby even before she gave birth.

Sitting on the stool behind the counter, Lina stared out the window of her shop at the sparse crowds in the streets of Aspen. It was a beautiful day—not that she'd been able to appreciate it as she should. But she had been trying to improve her state of mind any way she could. Getting out and enjoying the crisp autumn air was one thing she'd like to do. Walking was her chief form of exercise these days. Work—or any activity requiring concentration—had become a challenge. Just that morning she'd tried to give someone change for a hundred-dollar bill when they'd given her a twenty. If she kept that up, she wouldn't be in business long.

Lina checked her watch. She'd close shop soon and head over to Zara Hamilton's office to learn the latest developments in her legal problems with the clinic. Appropriately enough, whenever she thought of Dr. Walsh, she'd get nauseous. If it weren't so infuriating, it'd be funny. But then, her emotions had been so unpredictable of late. She'd found herself breaking into tears for the slightest reason—like that morning when a customer came in, carrying a newborn. Lina had looked down at the sweet little thing and suddenly lost it. The poor mother didn't know what to think.

Rousing herself from her stool, she headed for the door. A young couple was standing outside, looking at the window display. Lina didn't want to put up the Closed sign in their faces, so she waited until they moved on before flipping it over and locking the door. On her way to the back room where her office was located, she stopped to straighten the Belgian lace christening gowns and antique sterling rattles. She pondered the empty space where the crib she'd sold over the weekend had been, deciding she had to find something to replace it. She carried the best selection of Italian baby furniture in the state, but her stock was low at the moment, and the shipment of her last order had been delayed in customs.

Grabbing her down vest from the coatrack in her office, Lina turned off the lights. Cash receipts for the day were minimal, so she'd wait until morning to go to the bank. She'd already locked the credit vouchers in her desk, leaving nothing to do but be on her way. She walked through the darkened shop and let herself out, locking the door behind her. Turning, she started up the street, inhaling the autumn-scented air.

October was one of her favorite months. The summer tourist season was behind them and ski season was still over a month away. The weather was nice, the trees were full of color and the town belonged to the residents. Of course, without the out-of-town crowds, business was slower, but the change of pace had its appeal, as well. Most of the retailers used the respite to restock and prepare for the winter season. Lina carried some seasonal items, but much of her stock was available year-round.

She had a reputation as a capable merchandiser, probably because she'd managed to thrive even though many people, including some friends in the Chamber of Commerce, had said Aspen was not a good place for an upscale baby shop and children's clothing store. She'd surprised the skeptics, including her father, who, though he knew nothing about retailing, was certain she'd made a mistake. Morgan Prescott's millions did not give him infallible knowledge, but they certainly gave him the courage of his convictions.

What Lina had not yet done was tell her father about the baby. She'd rationalized her procrastination, telling herself she hadn't found the right occasion yet. But the truth was, she was being a coward. The conversation was not one she was looking forward to. She hadn't made a public announcement about being pregnant, but the time was coming when she wouldn't be able to hide her stomach from her father or anyone else.

As she walked, Lina glanced at her reflection in the plate glass windows of the shops, searching for telltale signs of her condition. So far, so good. She remained the tall, slender brunette she'd been since adolescence. Long, jean-clad legs, flat stomach, smooth raven-colored hair and the same vigorous, yet feminine and graceful demeanor.

Unless someone were to see her naked, they wouldn't be able to tell she was pregnant. And yet she was—with a baby nourished by her body but biologically the offspring of a couple she didn't know and had never met. The donors of the fertilized egg were, according to her agreement, to remain anonymous. But Lina had little doubt she'd be hearing from them or their attorney soon—assuming that nurse who'd called her was telling the truth about the egg having been stolen.

No sooner had the thought gone through her mind than she teared up. "The best laid plans of mice and men," she muttered to herself. Maybe that's what a woman got when she started messing with nature. More than once over the past few months she'd heard her father's voice as he pontificated in her imagination: "Why in God's green earth didn't you find yourself a husband like any normal woman?" he'd say, or, "What are you trying to prove—that men are irrelevant?"

In fairness, Morgan Prescott probably wouldn't have been quite so direct, but he'd have found a way to get that message across. He'd never forgiven her for divorcing Kyle Girard, the son-in-law he'd virtually handpicked. Lina had cared for Kyle, but she'd allowed herself to be talked into marriage by her father and her friends.

Kyle had proposed as she was finishing college. She'd lost her mother two years earlier and was emotionally vulnerable. He was considered a good catch by everyone, so the logic of the situation was hard to refute. How could she say no to an opportunity like that? Her father made it plain she couldn't.

Kyle came from a prominent Denver family, he was good-looking, charming, but in truth, the poor guy lacked real substance and character. He was his family's creation, content to be the person and live the life his parents had designed for him. He was shallow and soulless and cared for her for all the wrong reasons—mainly because of whose daughter she was.

Lina crossed the street and admonished herself not to

dwell on the past; she had more pressing problems to worry about. She had already resolved that she wasn't going to run to her father for help, though it was tempting. After all, she'd gotten into the mess on her own. She was going to handle it on her own.

The worst part of the ordeal had been the first week or so after that call from the nurse at the clinic. Zara Hamilton, her lawyer, had been vacationing in the Caribbean, so the timing couldn't be worse. Zara was a good friend, too—and the only person other than her doctor and the people at the clinic who knew about the pregnancy. She had been supportive of Lina's decision from the start.

"Maybe it's because Arianna and I were raised by our grandmother after our parents died," Zara had said, "but I know that mothers can come in all forms. You don't have to grow up in a traditional family to have a good home life."

"And can give birth and still not be a biological parent," Lina had added. Even now she was amazed that such a terrific idea had turned into a nightmare.

"Maybe the usual father-mother-baby thing is best," Zara had said before leaving on her trip, "but you have a lot to offer, Lina. You'd make a wonderful mother, and just because you don't have a man in your life doesn't mean you shouldn't bring a baby into the world."

Of course, Lina felt that way as well, but the timing was prompted partially by her age, and partially by the fact that she couldn't have a child of her own. When her doctor had told her the only way she'd be able to give birth was with a donated egg, she had decided the time to do it was now, before a man came into her life and she'd have that complication to deal with.

She'd also considered adoption. But there was a long waiting list for children, and single parents were not as likely to get a baby as a couple. And, since she had a burning desire to experience both pregnancy and birth if at all possible, Lina had decided to go to the fertility clinic. Later on, if she felt emotionally prepared to have a second child, she would probably try to adopt an older one.

Zara's office was on East Main in a three-story brick building, second floor. Lina climbed the stairs instead of taking the elevator. When she entered the suite, Zara came out to greet her wearing a green cotton sweater and slacks. They embraced.

"So, what's the word?" Lina asked, her voice shaking with emotion. "Did you talk to the clinic?"

Zara shepherded her into her private office and closed the door. "Yes," she said, leading Lina to the sofa against the wall opposite her desk, "but I don't have much concrete to report."

"What did they say?" Lina asked, dropping onto the edge of the cushion.

Zara sat next to her. "Dr. Walsh referred me to the director, who referred me to the clinic's attorney."

"You got the runaround, in other words."

"Sort of. I spoke with the attorney, and she assured me that the clinic follows its procedures scrupulously. All consents are systematically obtained. I asked if she's sure they were in this case, and she said she was confident that they were but that she would verify that and get back to me. That was three days ago."

"Have you heard from her since?"

"This morning. She didn't actually admit that there were irregularities, but I could tell by the qualification in her voice that she'd turned up something of concern. The official line was that they're doing a thorough audit, complicated by the fact that Dr. Walsh unexpectedly had to leave town."

"Oh, Lord," Lina said with a groan. She pushed her dark hair back over her ear and looked questioningly into Zara's eyes. "It's true, isn't it? They implanted a stolen egg into my womb?"

"I can't say for sure, Lina, but it appears that something questionable is going on. I asked for copies of the consent forms signed by the donors of your baby and the attorney said she couldn't provide them. She was hiding behind their contract, but I have a feeling she couldn't produce them if she wanted to."

Lina closed her eyes, her heart fluttering. A wave of nausea passed over her. For a moment she thought she might be sick, then she recovered. She took a fortifying breath. "So, what do we do next?"

"I'm going to keep the pressure up. If necessary we can sue, perhaps have their documentation examined by a court. But the real problem we face is the donors. If they accept the situation, and we can come to some sort of accommodation with them, you'll be all right."

"And if they fight me?"

Zara put her hand on Lina's arm. "We cross that bridge when we come to it, honey."

Lina's deep blue eyes filled with moisture and she had to dig into her purse for a tissue. "I can't believe how emotional I've been. I don't think I've cried in ten years. Now it seems like the tears start flowing every five minutes."

"Probably hormones," Zara said.

"I'd like to think I haven't turned into a wimp," Lina said, trying to smile. She blew her nose.

"Listen," Zara said. "Why don't you have dinner with Alec and me tonight and we can talk some more? I've got a settlement conference to attend over at Charlie Albright's office in a few minutes."

"I wouldn't want to interfere, Zara. I know this is a special time for you. A month ago we were both spinsters. Now you've found the love of your life, and he's a fabulous cook to boot!"

Zara blushed. "I am awfully happy."

"It shows, believe me." Lina checked her watch. "I

know you've got to go, so I'll get out of your hair." She rose. "But don't bother with dinner. You and Alec go on and have a good time."

"No, Lina," Zara said, "I insist. Alec loves to cook, and besides, he told me he's very fond of pregnant women."

Lina laughed. "And you didn't go running off? It must be true love!"

"He *is* adorable," Zara said wistfully. "Sometimes I have to stop and pinch myself."

Lina grinned, happy for her friend.

"Oh, I almost forgot!" Zara said, her blue-green eyes growing round. "I have something for you. It's in my purse." Zara went and got her purse from the large drawer in her desk. "It's not much," she said, "but it could mean a whole lot to you, depending. What I mean is, it's kind of silly, but maybe important."

Lina was amused by Zara's odd comment. Usually she sounded so reasonable and, well, lawyerlike, especially in her office. But now she almost sounded like a giddy schoolgirl.

Zara sat back down on the sofa and opened her purse. After rummaging through it, she removed something wrapped in a paper napkin. "When I was in New York," she said, "Arianna had me go to this Chinese restaurant called Destiny House. Madame Wu, the proprietor, has sort of become a cult figure. It's like you go to Destiny House and the fortune you get comes true."

"You've got to be kidding," Lina said.

"Nope. I know, it sounds dumb. But I sort of became a believer when my fortune said I'd find romance in an exotic place."

Lina eyed her friend. "And you went to the Caribbean and met Alec."

"Right," Zara said. "Who can argue with success like that?"

"And you brought me a fortune cookie from the place."

Zara nodded, pushing a strawberry blond curl back off her face. She handed the napkin to Lina. "It's been in my purse for over a week, so I'm afraid it's a bit the worse for wear."

Lina smiled, biting her lip. "You don't really believe in this, though?"

"No," Zara said, "of course not. But after my trip to Martinique, I don't make fun of it, either."

"You're hedging your bets, in other words."

"Yeah, I guess."

Lina looked down at the napkin and began unwrapping it. Strangely, she was nervous. Just like the time she'd bought an annual horoscope book—the year she'd divorced Kyle. There'd been a prediction of a major change in her family life, which of course could have meant anything, but she chose to interpret astrology as prescient. After that she'd decided she didn't want to know anything in advance and had never read her horoscope again.

A corner had broken off the cookie, and it was lying in two pieces; the larger portion still contained the fortune. Lina glanced up at Zara as a little wave of nausea went through her.

"I'm not sure I want to read it," she said.

"You don't have to."

Lina thought for a moment, then on impulse, broke the cookie open and extracted the fortune. She read it, pondered for a moment, then handed it to Zara, who read it aloud.

"Pain can be the midwife of joy." Zara looked at her. "That's not bad. And the word *midwife* is kind of apropos, don't you think?"

"Yeah, but it says 'can be.' That's no guarantee."

"Nothing in life is guaranteed." Zara handed her back the slip of paper.

Lina thought for a moment as she studied it. "This isn't a setup, is it?"

"No, Madame Wu picked it out herself. That, they say, is the key."

"So do you think I'll get to keep my baby?"

"If I have anything to say about it, you will."

They looked at each other, exchanging tearful smiles. Lina wiped her eyes and sighed. "You have work to do. I'll get out of your hair."

"See you at dinner, then," Zara said. "Why don't you be at my place at...shall we say seven?"

"You're sure you want me?"

"Positive."

Lina leaned over and hugged the tiny lawyer. "Thanks for being my friend."

CHAPTER TWO

WEBB HAD DRIVEN all the way to Coulter Creek and still hadn't seen a sign of the Toyota. At Road 113, he turned east toward Shippees Draw. Three quarters of a mile farther, at the fork in the road, he spotted the strangers Harriet had told him about. He waved them down, stopping next to the Toyota.

The driver was a pudgy man with thinning hair and bifocals. He rolled down his window. Webb greeted him.

"I'm Webb Harper," he said. "You the folks who're looking for me?"

"Yes," the man said, looking relieved. "My wife would like to speak with you."

Sitting in the cab of his pickup, Webb was too high up to see in the passenger side of the car, so he couldn't tell if he knew the woman or not. "Concerning what?"

"A problem at the Colorado Fertility Clinic," the man said cryptically.

Webb frowned. "What kind of problem?"

"I think it'd be best if we went somewhere to talk," the man said. "We drove up from Denver so my wife could inform you of something very important."

Webb couldn't imagine what it could be about, but he saw no harm in finding out. "We can go back to my place, I guess. I assume that's where you've been."

"Right."

"Well, follow me."

Webb put the pickup in gear and continued up the road.

A mile past Shippees Draw, he turned onto the side road that led to his ranch. The Toyota stayed right behind him, though when they got to the gravel section, it did drop back some so as not to eat his dust.

The ranch house was set on a low bluff in a stand of pine. The barn and other outbuildings were on lower ground. He had just under a thousand acres in all, about half of which was good for grazing, especially the bottom land down along East Coulter Creek. The higher ground, up toward Van Springs Reservoir, was rocky and more heavily wooded—good for riding and hiking.

He brought the pickup to a stop in front of the freestanding garage, which he used for storage. The Toyota stopped at the top of the drive. Webb climbed out, pulling his hat squarely onto his head. Curious about what this mysterious news from the clinic could be, he ambled back toward the car, the box with the pie under his arm.

The woman was vaguely familiar, but Webb couldn't say he knew her. She was about fifty, round-faced without being fat. She and her husband seemed to belong together, something Webb had gotten into the habit of looking for in a couple. Folks always said he and Karen looked as if they were married—the handsome young cattleman and his beauty-queen wife.

The woman seemed unusually dour for someone who'd come calling uninvited. She scarcely looked Webb in the eye.

"You folks seem to know me," he said, "but I don't know that I've had the pleasure."

"I'm Carl Lindstrom," the man said. "My wife, Joan, works at the clinic."

Webb shook hands with the man and nodded at his wife, who did not appear happy. "You sort of look familiar, ma'am," he told her. "Could be I saw you at the clinic. My wife and I spent quite a bit of time there a few years back."

"Yes, Mr. Harper, I know." The comment was veiled, her tone enigmatic.

"Well, why don't we go on inside?" Webb suggested. "No sense standing around in the sun."

He led the way.

"You'll have to forgive the house," he said, climbing the steps to the porch. "My wife died a couple of years back and I'm not much of a housekeeper."

Webb pushed the door open and stood aside for the Lindstroms to enter. Seeing the sofa was covered with books, he put the box with the pie down on the table and quickly cleared the couch.

"Make yourselves at home," he said, stacking his books by the huge bookcase that covered an entire wall. He removed his hat and put it next to the pie. "Anybody want coffee? I've got instant, if that's okay. And fresh-baked apple pie. I can have some water boiling in two shakes of a lamb's tail." He grinned, knowing he wasn't much of a host and never would be.

"No thanks," the man said, speaking for both of them. "Joan has something to tell you, as I mentioned. She'd like to get it over with if you don't mind, Mr. Harper."

Webb heard the solemnity in the man's tone. Judging by the lady's demeanor, whatever she had to say, it wasn't pleasant. Webb dropped into the easy chair. "I'm listening."

Joan Lindstrom moved to the edge of her seat. She seemed to have trouble looking at him. Finally, she cleared her throat. "My husband told you I work at the clinic where you and your wife had the in vitro insemination."

"Yes..."

She gave her husband a furtive look. "Something has been going on there that I think you need to know about." She took a deep breath, hesitated, then plunged ahead. "One of your wife's fertilized eggs was implanted in another woman."

For a second Webb didn't speak. He wasn't sure what she was telling him. "One of *Karen's* fertilized eggs?"

"Yes, you and Mrs. Harper wanted more than one child. The doctor took several eggs in the initial procedure and, after they were fertilized with your sperm, they were frozen for future implantation."

"Right. I remember. And you're saying they gave one of the leftover ones to another woman?"

"Yes, Mr. Harper. Your child—the embryo that is—was transplanted without your permission. My understanding is that you didn't authorize the procedure. Or am I wrong?"

"Authorize it? Hell, I'd forgotten there were more eggs. Once Karen died..." Only then did the full implications start to sink in. "Wait a minute, you're telling me that Karen's and my kid is out there somewhere, that some woman gave birth to it?"

"No. Not yet. The donee is pregnant. Just over two months pregnant. The baby hasn't been born."

"Good Lord," Webb said, falling back in his chair. He was stunned.

"I asked Dr. Walsh if it was proper, and he assured me that since your wife was deceased it didn't matter. But I was pretty sure that wasn't true. He was taking a shortcut because there wasn't a suitable donor egg available. For weeks I kept my mouth shut, then I spoke to Dr. Walsh again, telling him I was disturbed by what had happened. That baby is biologically your child, Mr. Harper—yours and your wife's. I told him it wasn't right to keep the truth from you. And it wasn't fair to the donee, either."

The woman paused, biting her lip. Webb could see she was about to cry. She dug into her purse for a handkerchief and began dabbing at her eyes.

"The fact is," her husband said, "Joan's risking her career to come and tell you this. She's been sick with worry, knowing what was happening was wrong, and she couldn't stand silently by any longer."

"I called the donee a while ago to let her know. And I tried to call you, but the phone company indicated the number was temporarily disconnected."

"Oh, yeah, well, the phone company and I were having this disagreement, but it's taken care of now," he said, embarrassed.

"In any case, I thought you should know," she said tearfully. "What you do about it is your business, but I've done my duty telling you."

"We'd like you to recognize the sacrifice Joan made to come here," her husband said. "We know you'll have to do whatever you feel is right, but any trouble you can spare her would be appreciated."

"Carl..." his wife said.

Webb didn't know what to think. His first impulse was to say that the whole thing sounded like medical high jinks to him, flimflam by some doctor, but when Joan Lindstrom had said this was Karen's baby—his and Karen's—a shiver went through him. They were talking about Robbie's little brother or sister.

"I appreciate this," Webb assured them. "I really do. But I'm not sure I understand. This other woman who has our baby. She's not the natural mother, I know, but if she gives birth to it, does that mean it's hers?"

"Not if you didn't give your permission," Joan Lindstrom replied. "I don't know what her legal rights are. I don't know if anybody knows. Nothing like this has happened before, at least not at the clinic."

Webb ran his fingers through his hair. Suddenly it felt hot in the house, though he knew it wasn't. "Who's the woman?"

"She lives not far from here, actually. In Aspen."

"Aspen." Webb didn't say so out loud, but that was a whole different world, full of rich, influential people—unless this surrogate mother was one of the ski bums who paid for their lift tickets waiting on tables. That struck him as unlikely, though.

"All I know is her name," Joan Lindstrom said weakly. "Carolina Prescott."

The name meant nothing to him. "Was she in on it? Getting our baby without permission, I mean?"

"No, she was very upset when I told her."

"I guess she would be," Webb acknowledged, rubbing his jaw. "It's sort of like adopting a baby that's been kidnapped."

"Exactly. That's why I've felt so bad," the woman said. "I didn't want to agonize over this the rest of my life. Someday that fetus will be a person. Its father ought to at least know that it exists."

"You've given me a hell of a jolt. I can't tell you what it means to me, knowing that Karen and I...well, have...another baby. I lost Robbie, our first, when I lost Karen."

"I don't know what any of this means or where it will lead," Joan Lindstrom said, wiping her eyes. "The only thing I was sure of is that I had to tell you."

Webb nodded. "Thank you."

Joan patted her husband's knee. "I think we should go."

The couple got up. Webb did, as well. He went with them to the door. They shook hands.

"What was the name of the woman who...has our baby, again?"

"Carolina Prescott."

"Oh, right. Prescott. Aspen's not that big. I should be able to find her."

Joan Lindstrom bit her lip. Nodding, she turned and headed for the Toyota, her husband following.

Webb stood at the door watching until the car headed down the drive and disappeared from sight. With the sun lower in the sky, the air had gotten chilly. He went inside and took off his coat, hanging it on the back of a chair.

Then he carried the pie into the kitchen, pushing aside the mess on the counter to set it down. He thought about cutting a piece until he realized he'd lost his appetite. He went to the table and dropped wearily onto a kitchen chair instead.

Webb stared at the stove, thinking of the meals Karen had cooked, the hours she'd labored in the kitchen for Robbie and him. He remembered slipping up behind her and putting his arms around her and giving her a kiss. She never complained, even when he was dirty and sweaty.

"Karen, honey," he said aloud, as he so often did when he was alone in the house, missing her, "what the hell do I do about this?"

His eyes moved over the invisible image of her at the stove. In his mind's eye he saw her turn. He saw her pretty, sad smile. "It's our baby, Webb," he heard her say.

Webb Harper allowed that it was true. That baby was Karen in a way all the dolls, trophies and photos in the world could never be. Carolina Prescott's baby was theirs—Karen's and his.

LINA HAD JUST gotten out of the shower when the telephone rang. Putting on her cashmere robe, she went off to answer it.

"Has my beautiful daughter had dinner yet?" came her father's familiar voice over the line.

"Daddy!" she said, surprised. "Are you in town?"

"I will be shortly. I'm in the plane, over Independence Pass at the moment. George is flying me to the ranch and I got to thinking about dinner and all those good restaurants in Aspen. So I said to myself, 'Hell, it's been a while since I've seen my daughter. Why not stop in Aspen and kill two birds with one stone?'"

Lina had to smile. That was her father. If Morgan Prescott had a whim, he wasn't one to deny himself. It was an eccentricity she found amusing, if sometimes inconvenient.

But then it occurred to her that fate might be trying to tell her something. She'd agonized over telling him about her pregnancy, and maybe this was the opportunity she needed.

"As a matter of fact I do have plans for dinner," she said, "but they can be changed. Nothing pressing."

"Don't want to interfere, Carolina, especially if there's a gentleman involved."

"There's a gentleman involved, but it's Zara Hamilton's fiancé. I was planning on dinner with the two of them."

"Zara's that little girl who's the lawyer, isn't she? The tiger in kitten's clothing."

"Yes, that's the one."

Lina had to laugh at her father's characterization. He had the heart of a chauvinist, but of the benign variety. Her father really liked women. He'd been a good husband to her mother; her death had been a severe blow to him, but he'd rallied after a year and reentered the social whirl. A number of widows had set their sights on him, but Morgan Prescott had managed to "elude capture," as he put it. Lina had never said anything, but she was sure part of him was afraid of another commitment. For all his bluster, the man had a vulnerable side.

Heaven knew the two of them had had their differences over the years. As a child she'd definitely been Daddy's little girl. But during her adolescence, she'd been very close to her mother and it seemed as if she and her father were always arguing. When her mother had died, she and her father hadn't grown closer, as one would have expected. In a moment of candor, Morgan had admitted he didn't want to make Lina her mother's emotional replacement because that wouldn't have been fair. "I can be a demanding SOB," he'd confessed. "Better we keep a cordial distance."

And so they did, though they'd get together for holidays, and Lina would go to see him whenever she was in Denver.

Morgan didn't come to Aspen often, but he did spend more and more time at the family ranch in western Colorado.

"Did you say the girl's engaged?" her father asked. "I thought you two vowed never to marry."

"Zara broke ranks. She met this wonderful guy in Martinique and brought him home with her. Alec's thinking of opening a restaurant here in town."

"A restaurant?"

"Zara says he's a fabulous cook."

"But is he a businessman?" Morgan said. "That's where most eating places fail."

"Maybe you and Alec ought to talk sometime," Lina said. "I'm sure he'd profit from your insights."

"Well, not tonight, sweetheart. I won't take you from your friends. George and I can grab a bite in town."

"No, Daddy, I'd like to talk to you. Really. I've been meaning to drive down to Denver so we could have lunch or something."

"You've met somebody, too," he said.

"Hardly. Just the opposite."

"Well, if it's advice about men you want, Carolina, you've heard what I have to say already."

"No, it's not that. We'll talk when you get here. How far away are you?"

"We're making our approach now."

"Yikes! I'd better get dressed or you'll have to wait."

"Don't bother, sweetheart. George has some things he wants to do in town, so we'll rent a car and he can drop me off at your place. See you in twenty minutes or so."

Lina hung up. She was in for an emotional evening, but telling her father about the baby was something she had to do. It was better to get it behind her. But she would have to phone Zara. She dialed her friend's number.

"Why not bring him with you?" Zara suggested when Lina told her why she had to beg off.

"I wouldn't want to burden you and Alec with my family, as well as my problems," she replied.

"Nonsense," Zara said. "Your father's a hoot. Besides, it might make it easier for you if other people are around. Just tell him about the baby before you get here. He can't be too rough on you in front of us."

"Daddy will do what he wants, as you well know," Lina said. "But if you really don't mind…"

"Of course not. Alec's cooking plenty of food, so it's not a problem."

"Shall I bring a white wine? I can't have any, but I might as well bring what you'd like."

"That would be fine."

"Thanks, Zara."

"Hey, what are friends for?"

"I owe you one," Lina told her. "Baby-sitting for a year when you and Alec start your family. How's that?"

"If you think you're up to it after coping with your own," Zara said, "then sure."

"Assuming I'll get to raise my baby," she said as the reality of her situation swept over her again.

"Lina, of course you will. I promise."

"Is that Zara my friend speaking, or Zara my lawyer?"

"At the moment, it's your friend. But your lawyer's doing everything possible to make sure that's the way it turns out."

"Yes," Lina said, swallowing back tears. "I know you will."

LINA LOOKED ACROSS her living room from the wet bar where she was pouring some Scotch for her father. Morgan Prescott was slumped in her leather easy chair, looking tired, older. He'd spent the morning negotiating the sale of one of his office buildings near the Denver Tech Center. "I used to love business the way I love hunting," he told her, "but each year it loses some of its charm. Maybe it's time I retire, though I don't exactly have a herd of grand-children to keep me busy, do I?''

The comment was ironic, considering. Lina carried the drink to him. He looked her over. She'd worn a clingy electric blue knit dress that emphasized her slenderness. She wasn't sure why she'd picked it, unless it was to belie her news.

Morgan took the drink from her. "Aren't you having one, honey?''

"No, Daddy.''

Morgan was a tall, broad-shouldered man whose girth had grown some in recent years. His silver hair was thinning, but he looked robust despite his heart trouble that had plagued him for years. He had a dominating presence. By his own account, he was a doer—a man who came from the land, an empire builder. Yet he was also modern and attuned to the ways of the world.

Though he was most at home on the Prescott ranch, an accumulation of tracts occupying many thousands of acres, most of his time was still spent in Denver, where he could more easily manage his portfolio of investments, many in the high-tech realm. Boots and a cowboy hat were his native attire, but he knew how to wear a tuxedo and "hobnob with the opera sissies,'' as he liked to say to the ranchers out west, whom he still counted as his best friends. Morgan Prescott had adjusted to the world of computers, but he loved riding the range and shooting an occasional antelope or pheasant.

"You never did drink much,'' he said to Lina, "but as I recall you'd have a glass of wine with me to be sociable.'' He glanced at her figure. "Can't be worried about gaining weight. You're thin as a rail.''

"Not for long, I'm afraid.''

Morgan gave her a slow double take. "Sis?'' he said, using the pet name she'd scarcely heard since she was ten.

"Dad,'' she said, using the sternest, most businesslike

voice she had, "I want you to know that I'm going to have a baby."

His expression was blank then became quizzical, uncertain, and bemused in turn. "You're joking, of course."

"No, Father, I'm not. The baby's due next May."

"You're *serious?*"

"Yes."

He hesitated. "Well, is that all?"

"Isn't it enough?"

Morgan scratched his head. "Wait a minute. I thought you were doubtful you'd be able to have children."

"I *am* sterile, Dad. I went to a clinic and got impregnated with a fertilized egg. I'm the birth mother for another couple's biological child."

"You mean you're doing this as a public service, one of these humanitarian things?"

"No. At least that wasn't my intent. I wanted this baby for myself, but there's a problem. The egg might have been used without the couple's consent. And there may be a legal battle over it. We're waiting to see."

"Good Lord," Morgan said, taking another gulp of Scotch. He held out the glass. "Get me another, would you? This isn't exactly the way I expected to learn I was going to be a grandfather."

She took his glass and returned to the wet bar. Morgan got to his feet and ambled over, still an imposing figure in his alligator boots.

"How the devil did you get mixed up in a deal like this?" he asked. "Beautiful girl like you. There's no shortage of men who'd marry you."

"My problem has nothing to do with being single." She poured more Scotch into his glass. "It'd be the same if I had a husband. It's the donors we're concerned about."

"Well, who are these folks?"

"That's just it," she said, handing him back his glass. "We don't know. Everything is supposed to be completely confidential. At the moment the clinic's denying there's a problem, but Zara's pretty sure something's going on.''

"What makes you think the egg was stolen?"

Lina told him about the anonymous calls, Dr. Walsh's disappearance and the waffling of the clinic's attorney.

"Well, don't fret, sweetheart. I'll get my attorneys on this right away." Morgan knocked back another whiskey. "We'll take that clinic apart board by board and brick by brick if we have to."

Lina reached out and took his hand. "Dad, your attorneys are going to do no such thing. I got myself into this and I'll deal with it. I'm not your little girl anymore."

"Then why did you have me come over?"

"You called up and invited yourself, remember?" She patted his hand. "But I'm glad you did, because I figured it was time you learned you're going to be a grandfather."

Morgan Prescott shook his head. "I guess I know now. But I'm telling you, Lina, it was the last thing I expected to hear from you."

"Sometimes I have to pinch myself to make sure it's true, that I didn't just imagine it."

"I take it you're happy," he said.

"I was until that nurse called."

"Maybe the Good Lord's trying to..." His voice faded off.

"Trying to what?" she said.

"Oh, nothing," he said, waving her off. "I was just mumbling out loud."

Lina had a fairly good idea what he'd planned to say— either that she shouldn't be messing with nature or that she should have stuck with Kyle. To his credit, though, her father bit his tongue. In fact, he had taken everything better than she'd expected.

She checked her watch. "We should get over to Zara's. The way Alec cooks, you won't want to miss this meal."

"What's his background? You said Zara met him on a trip?" her father asked.

"Alec's from New York originally. He was a cop. But the last few years he's been the captain of a charter sailboat in the Caribbean."

Morgan chuckled. "That's quite a combination. But I guess a regular guy would never have appealed to Zara enough to make her want to give up her independence."

"Alec's special in a lot of ways. He's very nice and very good-looking."

Lina turned off some of the lights. They moved toward the door. Morgan picked up his Stetson from the hall table.

"I guess one of these days you'll be bringing a fella like that to meet me." He opened the door for her. "It'd be too much to expect somebody more or less normal, like Kyle."

Lina rolled her eyes. She'd known Kyle would make his way into the conversation sooner or later. She decided not to take the bait. "The first fella I'll be bringing to meet you will be your grandson, Daddy."

They went out the door. "Do you know it's going to be a boy?"

"No, but I have a hunch."

"This is one area where women's intuition doesn't work very well. Your mother was sure as sin you were going to be a boy. Fortunately, I didn't bite."

"Fortunately?" she said, going down the stairs. "You wanted a boy?"

"Sweetheart, I got the strong-willed, independent-minded, businessperson I wanted. It just happened to turn out she's a girl."

"Liar."

As they moved toward Lina's BMW parked in the driveway, Morgan put his arm around her waist. "So tell me, sugar, have we picked out any names for this critter?"

At the passenger side of the car, she stopped and turned to face him. "Thank you for being so understanding and supportive," she said, her eyes welling up with tears. "I was afraid you'd be…"

"Be what?"

"I don't know…unpleasant."

"Well, you did throw me for a loop," he replied. "The only thing you said I didn't like much was that you wouldn't let me help sort the mess out."

"It's my baby, Dad."

"Yeah, but it's my grandbaby." He wagged his finger at her. "Someday you'll be in my shoes and some whippersnapper's going to tell you to get back in line. You won't like it, either."

Lina kept her mouth shut and smiled sweetly. But she could see the handwriting on the wall. Sooner or later her father just might try to dig in his heels on this. It simply wasn't in his nature to sit back passively. Oddly enough, a part of her was secretly glad. If she was in for a long battle, it might be good to have all the help she could muster.

CHAPTER THREE

LINA HAD AWAKENED before dawn again, though she knew her body would have preferred to sleep in. The trouble was, her mind wouldn't cooperate. Ever since she'd gotten the call from the nurse, she'd been in turmoil. Her obstetrician had told her eating right, getting lots of rest and moderate exercise were essential to a healthy pregnancy. The resting part had already become a problem.

Of course, it would be different once she was no longer in doubt about what would happen. Even if the court ruled she couldn't keep the baby, she would find a way to live with that—she wouldn't really have a choice. It was the not knowing that got to her, gnawed at her and made her afraid to hope. Part of her had already given her heart to the baby; she had begun to plan, to dream about their life together. Now she had to keep reminding herself to hold back, at least a little, so that the pain would be less if she lost him in the end.

Zara hadn't said so, but Lina knew enough about the law to realize that legal battles could drag on forever. How would she learn to live with the uncertainty if things went on indefinitely? How could she give birth to a child, love and nurture it, and then turn it over to someone else to raise? Lina didn't know how surrogate mothers could be so loving, so unselfish. Of course, they had the benefit of making that decision of their own free will. She had been blindsided.

Lina sighed. At least she hadn't had to rattle around in

the house alone that morning. Her father, who probably had seen the sun rise every day of his life, was stirring in the guest room when she went downstairs. He appeared in the kitchen before the coffee was ready. They'd chatted amiably while she made him scrambled eggs, and he'd tried hard to be upbeat, talking about the pony he'd buy for his grandson and the fishing trips he'd take him on. What Morgan Prescott hadn't realized was that such talk actually depressed her.

When George came by to take him to the airport, Lina and her father had their most emotional farewell in years. Morgan held her for an extra long time, assuring her he'd see to it that everything was fine. What he'd really wanted to say, he'd said to Zara the night before. "Listen, little lady," he'd told her, "I know you're a sharp cookie—undoubtedly the best lawyer in Aspen—but you're going to be up against at least one high-powered Denver law firm, so don't you hesitate to call on my legal eagles if you need help."

Zara had assured him that her client's interests always came first, even if it meant giving up the case. Morgan had said he didn't want her doing that, but he wanted her to have all the resources she needed.

Once her father had had his say, the atmosphere had become more relaxed. He and Alec had a nice conversation about the Caribbean and sailing and the restaurant business, and Lina had talked to Zara enough to confirm that her new relationship was for real. "If anything, it's even better than when we were in Martinique," Zara told her while they cleared the dishes.

On their way back to Lina's place, her father told her how much he liked both Zara and Alec. "Nice young couple," he'd said. "Zara is cute as a button and bright, but she's got nothing on you, Carolina. You'd have yourself a man if you'd give one a chance."

That had been her father's only flub in an otherwise positive evening. She'd responded in a resolute and confident manner, informing him that finding a man was not high on her list of priorities. "I have nothing against them," she assured him, "but this pregnancy is all I can handle at the moment."

Lina checked the time. She had to leave for the shop soon, but she toyed with the idea of having another cup of coffee first. The doctor had told her to cut down on caffeine, so she'd been drinking an awful lot of herbal tea the past month, but she had a strong urge to give in to temptation just this once. So she poured the rich, dark liquid into her mug, telling herself that one more cup wouldn't be the end of the world. But then, the mug poised at her lips, she thought of the baby. Every sip of caffeine or alcohol, every aspirin tablet or antihistamine capsule she took, her baby took, too.

Her hand shaking, Lina dumped the coffee into the sink. Lord, it wasn't even her baby—it belonged to some people who'd probably try to take it away from her—and still she couldn't drink a cup of coffee without feeling guilty!

For the first—and certainly not the last—time that day, she cried over the terrible mess she'd made of her life. It was getting tiresome, but she just didn't seem to be able to help herself. She knew it was dangerous to allow herself to slip into a "victim" mentality and that she had to get a grip on her emotions.

Wiping her eyes, she went to the refrigerator to get a glass of juice. It was then she noticed the fortune from the cookie Zara had given her. Lina had stuck it under a magnet on the front of the fridge. "Pain can be the midwife of joy," she read. Wouldn't a little joy be nice, though?

It was then she heard the sound of a vehicle. The engine sounded rough, like a truck needing a tune-up. Lina left the kitchen area of her great room, which included the living and dining area, den and kitchen, all in one large open-beamed space. She peered out the front window. There was an old pickup in her drive. The driver was just climbing out.

She wasn't expecting a delivery, but it occurred to her it was probably someone soliciting orders for firewood or Christmas wreaths. This was the time of year when people stocked up on wood and began preparing for the holidays.

Lina watched the guy make his way up the driveway. He was wearing a cowboy hat and boots, jeans and a sheepskin jacket that had seen plenty of use. A working man, by all appearances.

Lina was inclined not to answer the door. Aspen was comparatively safe, but there was a lot more wealth around than was normal for a town of its size, and people wanting to prey on it drifted through from time to time.

As the stranger climbed the steps to the front door, Lina moved away from the window. The doorbell sounded, but she ignored it, returning to the kitchen area instead. The bell rang again and there was loud knock on the door.

Given his insistence, it occurred to her the man might not be soliciting. She went back across the great room to the front door. Since she was alone, Lina used the intercom her father had insisted she install.

"Yes?" she said. "Who is it?"

"My name's Webb Harper, ma'am," he shouted through the door.

Lina smiled. Obviously he wasn't versed in electronic gadgetry. "What do you want?" she said into the intercom.

"I'd like to talk to a Mrs. Prescott," came the muffled reply.

"Please use the intercom," she said.

She couldn't make out the grumbling response, but she pictured him fumbling to make the contraption work.

"Push the button and speak into the intercom," she said.

"Hello?" His voice came through the system more loudly than necessary.

"What is it you want?" she repeated.

"To talk to a Mrs. Prescott," he said.

"About what?"

"Well, it's personal, ma'am. Are you Mrs. Prescott?"

"Yes. But I'm afraid I don't open the door to strangers."

"This is something you definitely want to talk about," he said insistently. "It has to do with your baby."

Lina's heart nearly stopped. Had she heard right? "My baby?"

"Yes, ma'am."

She couldn't imagine how a complete stranger would even know about her being pregnant. She'd told a few close friends, but it certainly wasn't common knowledge.

Turning the dead bolt, Lina opened the door a crack. The man immediately removed his hat. He was older than she'd thought at first—probably in his late thirties. He was ruggedly handsome with a tanned, weathered face and a square jaw. His flinty gray eyes somehow managed to look unthreatening. His mouth was generous, yet stubborn. Sexy. Lina blinked, bowled over first by what he'd said and second by his appearance.

"I'm sorry to come here uninvited, Mrs. Prescott," he said, his voice sober without being hostile, "but there's something I've got to ask you."

She opened the door a bit wider. "How do you know I'm pregnant?"

He glanced at the road as though concerned they would be overheard. Lina could see the hat marks in his hair and a thin line of dried blood on his jaw—probably a razor cut. He smelled like pine and earth and fresh air.

"It's a long story," he said, turning his attention back to her. He inched his fingers around the brim of his hat, looking ill at ease. "I think it'd be better if we discussed this privately."

Lina didn't know if she wanted to allow him in the house or not. It could be some sort of ruse. "What's your name again?"

"Harper," he replied. "Webb Harper."

"Before I discuss anything with you, Mr. Harper, I want to know how you found out I was pregnant."

He seemed displeased by her insistence. "I found out from the Colorado Fertility Clinic in Denver."

"Why would they tell you?"

"I'll answer that in a minute, but first I want to know if they've told you who the father and mother are."

His eyes were harder now, demanding. This was no joke, she could tell. She had a terrible, ominous feeling. This man couldn't be the… "I think you'd better come in," she said abruptly, stepping back and opening the door.

As he entered, she could see that he was checking her out, a hint of surprise on his face. She wore black leather pants and a violet silk blouse under a violet cashmere sweater. The sweater was loose, but not because she had anything to hide yet. She liked casual styles, spending much of the time in sweats and ski sweaters.

Stepping to the side, he glanced around the great room before turning his attention back to her. Lina closed the door but wasn't inclined just yet to invite him to sit down. She was wary and shaken.

"Why do you want to know about the parents of my baby?" she asked, determined to get to the bottom of things.

Webb squinted at her, still turning the brim of his hat round and round. He seemed every bit as uncomfortable as she, a fact she took solace in though she didn't exactly know why.

"I guess what I'm really asking, ma'am, is if they told you the names of the parents or showed you a consent form."

She knew then who he was. Shaking her head, she said, "No, they didn't."

He stroked his jaw. "Hmm. That's not good."

"You're the father, aren't you?"

"Well, ma'am, it appears I may be."

Lina felt as if she'd been kicked in the stomach. She closed her eyes, groaning.

"The embryo they implanted belonged to me. That is, the egg was my wife's, Karen's. And they didn't get my permission, so that sort of makes the whole thing illegal…if you get my drift."

Lina felt dizzy. Even though she'd sensed this was coming, his words tore at her heart and confirmed her worst fears. "Then it's really true," she murmured.

"You knew?"

"I had an anonymous call."

"Sounds like we're sort of in the same boat," he said.

Lina felt ill and knew she had to get off her feet. "Take off your coat and come sit down, Mr. Harper," she said. Without waiting for a reply, she led the way to the sitting area.

She dropped onto one of her matching custom-made taupe suede sofas and looked up at him morosely. Webb had slipped off his coat. He was broad-shouldered and wore an off-white Western-style shirt. It was clean and freshly pressed, though there appeared to be faint scorch marks on the sleeve.

Webb glanced up at the soaring ceiling before dropping his coat on the floor by a chair. He sat down, sinking into the soft suede cushion. "Quite a place you've got here."

"Thank you."

Folding his large hands on his lap, he looked at her as though trying to divine her state of mind. It was obvious to her that he was no more pleased than she.

"Have you spoken to Dr. Walsh?" she asked.

"No, ma'am. I was going to, then I thought maybe I should get your side of the story first. It occurred to me there might even be a mistake."

"I wish there was, but I'm beginning to doubt it. How

this happened, though, I don't know. The clinic assured me everything was in order. I signed papers.''

"But I didn't, Mrs. Prescott. That's the point. Karen and I did not agree to donate an egg to you or anybody else. It seems Dr. Walsh pulled a fast one.''

Yes, she thought, in all probability that was true. But, given the fact, what did the Harpers intend to do about it? That's what she wanted to know. "Let's get right to the bottom line,'' she said. "You want money. That's why you're here, isn't it?''

"No,'' he said, visibly annoyed. "I don't want money. If you think that's why I came here, you're dead wrong.''

"Then why did you come?''

"To find out what you're thinking. To see if maybe you knew something I didn't.''

Lina squeezed the bridge of her nose, knowing she was going to have to live this nightmare whether she wanted to or not. "You seem to know as much or more than I do,'' she said.

"That's what I was afraid of.''

She drew a long breath, shuddering. "Why couldn't this have been a mistake?''

"I wish it was, Mrs. Prescott.''

"I'm not Mrs. Prescott,'' she snapped irritably. "I'm not married.''

"Oh. Begging your pardon, ma'am.''

Lina sighed. "I'm sorry if I was abrupt. I'm upset and I don't know what to think.''

"Forget it.''

The hard look that had been in his eyes had softened some, and Lina decided he might be a decent person. At least he wasn't pushy and demanding. But that didn't tell her what he was going to do about this. It seemed, for the moment anyway, that he wasn't sure himself. But the time for a decision would come eventually. He'd said himself he'd come to get a reading on her thinking.

"Assuming Dr. Walsh has pulled a fast one," she said, "what are your feelings about me carrying your child?"

"That's the problem, isn't it? I mean, you can't very well give our baby back, can you? Not as if it were kidnapped or something."

His words hit home. "There's not much room for compromise, is there?"

"I hate to sound negative, Miss Prescott, but no, I don't see any obvious compromise."

Lina sensed she was dealing with a man who was more shrewd than he let on. The open-faced innocence had probably been intended to draw her out. But the real question was, could he be bought? "How does your wife feel about this?" she asked.

"Karen and our son died in an auto accident a couple of years ago. I believe that's why Dr. Walsh figured he could get away with giving you our baby."

"It wasn't a baby, Mr. Harper," she quickly rejoined. "I was implanted with an embryo, a tiny smear of cells. Even now, the fetus isn't as big as my thumb."

"All due respect, ma'am, that's true of any one of us. We're nothing until our father and mother make us."

"And each of us has to grow into a viable child and be born. They haven't yet made machines to replace mothers." Lina's eyes flashed and her voice became brittle.

Webb Harper frowned. "I didn't mean to turn this into an argument...."

"No, don't apologize," she said, realizing she'd let her fears carry her away. "You're right. I was the one who got emotional."

"It's understandable. It's not like you were expecting me to walk in and dump this on you."

Unable to sit still, Lina got to her feet. She knew she was revealing her anxiety, but she couldn't help herself. She paced, trying to compose her thoughts.

Webb watched her, his eyes moving up and down her

leather-clad legs. It was hard to tell if he was thinking about his baby or her. God knew, she was no stranger to cowboys. They had fascinated her from the time she first noticed boys, though her father had always ensured there was a polite distance between her and the ranch hands. If some young buck ever got too friendly, he found himself looking for another job. But being spirited and independent, Lina had still found ways to have a little illicit fun.

Nevertheless, given the circumstances, Webb Harper's scrutiny was disconcerting. She abruptly returned to the sofa and sat, self-consciously crossing her legs. It was odd to think the child growing inside her was the product of his body. She gazed at him, taking in the shaggy blond hair, the square jaw, the even features. Would her baby look like this man?

Of course she'd known there was a father somewhere, but so long as he was faceless, anonymous, he was irrelevant. But this man was real. He was flesh and blood and impossible to ignore. In fact, now that she'd met him, she saw that Webb Harper was not the type of man anyone could ignore.

The mere thought of having to negotiate with him sent shivers up and down her spine. The whole point of going to the clinic in the first place had been to make certain everything would be impersonal.

"Forgive me for stating the obvious, Mr. Harper," she said, "but it's in both our interests to resolve this as quickly and efficiently as possible. I mean, it's going to get worked out eventually, so we may as well spare ourselves unnecessary heartache by finding a solution we both can live with now."

"If you've got a solution, Miss Prescott, I'll listen."

"Obviously I don't have an answer at my fingertips, but there are certainly avenues to be explored." She checked her watch. "Can I get you coffee or something? No point in being unsociable while we deal with this."

Webb Harper shook his head. "I really don't care for anything, thanks."

"Would you mind if I got myself a cup of tea?"

"No, ma'am."

Lina turned and headed for the kitchen area. She had no ideas, but her intuition told her it was important not to allow things to get hostile. Her father had taught her never to negotiate when she was angry. Adverse interests were enough for people to contend with; adverse emotions only made solutions more difficult.

As she put a kettle on to boil, she looked across the room at Webb Harper. He was watching her, his expression solemn. God knew what he was thinking. She could only hope it was constructive.

She moved about the kitchen, noticing his eyes following her. Once again she wondered what he *really* wanted. Her father had told her that everybody wants something. The trick in dealing with a person was figuring out what motivated them. Sometimes the person knew and sometimes they didn't. Sometimes the way to resolve a dispute was to help them figure it out.

It occurred to her it would be strange if Webb Harper was wondering the same thing about her. Or was he thinking about the baby inside her body, knowing it was his? She shivered, suddenly feeling as if she'd been invaded by a stranger.

WEBB RAN HIS FINGERS through his hair as he turned his attention from Carolina Prescott and glanced around the room. Karen used to cut out pictures of places like this from magazines and paste them in her dream scrapbook. And she'd make him watch that TV show, "Lifestyles of the Rich and Famous." "Why watch a bunch of superrich folks prancing around like they had more money than sense?" he'd ask her. "There's probably not a one who's ever worked a day of his life."

"There's nothing wrong with dreaming," Karen would say. "That's the way to change your life. Everything starts with a dream."

"I'd say hard work," he'd reply.

And then she'd kiss him and rub his chest and tell him it didn't serve him to carry a chip on his shoulder. Karen was probably right. In that respect, if no other, his upbringing hadn't served him well. The only men he truly respected where those who made what they had with their own hands.

How Carolina Prescott had come by her money he didn't know, but she was obviously loaded. A fella could buy a hell of a spread with the kind of money one of these Aspen mansions cost, even the small ones. If he had to guess, this one was worth at least triple what he could get for his whole ranch—house, barn and land included. She might have earned the money, but it was more likely she'd inherited it. Not that it mattered a hill of beans to him as long as she didn't try throwing it in his face. Except for that one remark implying that he intended to shake her down, she hadn't been hostile or played the rich bitch. So his instinct was to give her the benefit of the doubt.

For his part, Webb had been careful not to come in with both guns blazing. What *she* was thinking, he had no idea, though it was clear she was afraid. But then, that was natural under the circumstances. And, of course, pregnancy wasn't easy at the best of times. He remembered how Karen had seemed like a completely different person when she was carrying Robbie.

Pregnancy aside, Carolina Prescott was still hard to read. In a way, he found her surprising. He couldn't exactly say she was sweet-tempered, but she seemed sincere. And she was damned good-looking—slim with a real nice body, glossy black hair, bright blue eyes and the face of a china doll. What really had thrown him for a loop, though, was the fact that she was single. She hadn't said a word about why she was doing this, nor did it seem as if she were particularly eager to talk about it. But if it was his kid in her body, it shouldn't be all that unreasonable to ask her why she wanted a baby when she didn't have a husband.

When she returned to the sitting area with a mug of tea in hand, Webb decided he'd jump right in. "I don't mean to stick my nose in your business, Miss Prescott," he said, "but if you're single, why are you even having this baby?"

He saw the color rise in her neck, but she kept her cool. "You *are* sticking your nose into my business, Mr. Harper."

"It just seems to me that if we're going to sort this out, it'd help if we each knew where the other was coming from."

She sipped her tea, looking at him over the rim of the mug. Her expression was distant, untrusting. "Maybe you have a point," she said mildly. "I'm thirty-five and have to begin having my children soon if I want them. Since there isn't a man in my life, I either have a baby on my own or I don't have one at all."

"Of course, you can never have one completely on your own," he said.

"True. In this case I got some help from you."

"From me and Karen."

"That's right. I needed a fertilized egg because I'm sterile. But tell me, Mr. Harper, if your wife is deceased, why were you keeping the embryos?"

"I'll be honest with you. I'd forgotten they had extras. Karen was working on her second baby when she was killed. The whole thing just went out of my head when I lost her."

Carolina's eyes grew glossy. "I'm sorry," she said. "That must have been very difficult."

"It was."

She took a long sip of tea. "Mind if I ask what you do, Mr. Harper?"

"I ranch. Got a little spread northeast of Carbondale. Run a few head of cattle, nothing fancy."

"My father's a rancher," she said.

"Oh?"

"His place is over in Montrose County, near Cimarron."

"Oh, yeah. Pretty country down that way."

Webb had an idea she wasn't talking about a couple of hundred acres. The ranches tended to be huge in that part of the country. Carolina Prescott had a rich daddy, just as he'd suspected.

"And how about you, Miss Prescott? What do you do?"

"I have a store here in town. A baby boutique."

"No kidding," he said. If he had to bet, he'd guess her daddy bought it for her. "You seem partial to babies, professionally *and* personally."

"I've always loved children. Especially babies."

"Karen was the same."

"And she needed help from the doctors, too."

Webb nodded. "Funny how that works, people craving what they can't have." He studied her as she fell silent. In the course of talking to her, he'd found that she'd become a person, not just the carrier of his and Karen's baby. When he'd first arrived, he hadn't known what to expect, and had simply tried to get a read of the situation. While not exactly relaxed, the mood was becoming less tense, and that made things easier.

"I'm going to have to leave soon, Mr. Harper," she said after they'd sat quietly for a time. "But I hate to part company without having some idea of what happens next. Do you have any inclinations at all?"

He rubbed his jaw, knowing she was trying to lure him into making the first move. The irony was, he didn't know what he wanted. "Seems to me we're in one of those situations where we both have to think on it," he said. "Maybe we should take a day or two to ruminate about this, then talk again. Frankly, I don't even know where to begin.''

"I'm at a loss myself," she said. "I guess I should be thankful you didn't come here with a list of demands.''

"I take no pleasure in this, I assure you. At the same time, it seems honesty is called for.''

"I agree.''

Webb sighed. "I suppose the thing for me to do is put myself in my wife's shoes and treat this as though she were here with me.''

Carolina's expression turned wary again. "Do you know what she'd say?''

He thought for a moment, deciding that since he'd come this far, he might as well go the rest of the way. "I believe so, Miss Prescott.''

"Tell me.''

"All due respect, ma'am. She'd want her baby back.''

CHAPTER FOUR

WEBB SPENT THE MORNING riding the fence line and looking for sick cattle. He spent more time upland than was necessary, but it had been Karen's favorite place to ride and he went there whenever he wanted to feel close to her. There was one spot where they used to picnic. It was a rocky outcropping shaded by a stand of pines offering a view of the valley and Snowmass Mountain to the south. It was a good place to sit and think.

Three days had passed since he'd gone to Aspen. Carolina had called him yesterday to ask if they could get together to discuss their problem further. He'd offered to drive back to Aspen or meet her in Carbondale, but she said a return visit was only fair—whatever that meant. Webb decided she wanted to deal and wondered if he wasn't being set up. He couldn't say why, but it was something he felt in his gut.

His mistake had probably been in not discussing the situation with Mary before going to Aspen—she might have had some good advice. But he'd reasoned she couldn't possibly be an impartial observer. That baby Carolina Prescott was carrying was Mary's grandchild, her only link to Karen. Once it was born, it would be her only living relative.

When he'd finally told Mary about the Lindstroms' visit and his trip to Aspen, she had been as dumbfounded as everyone else. But to his surprise, she wasn't as possessive about the baby as he'd expected.

"There's no way the poor woman can change anything now," Mary had said.

"So are you saying I ought to walk away and let her have it?"

"No, of course not, Webb. All I'm suggesting is that she's in a tough spot, too."

"Everybody's agreed it's a mess," Webb said. "I guess the question is, what happens after the baby's born?"

Mary had no suggestions.

He picked up a pinecone and tossed it down the slope, watching it tumble. A chipmunk admonished him for disrupting the universe without cause, and Webb's horse stomped the ground under the trees where he was tethered. Everyone, it seemed, had an opinion, but nobody an answer.

He checked his watch. In a few minutes he'd have to head back if he was going to get cleaned up before Lina was due to arrive. Fortunately, the house was in good shape.

He'd spent the previous day getting the place ready. Mary had lent him a hand, chastising him for allowing things to get so bad. He'd kept the kitchen and bath sanitary, but the rest of the house was, as Mary put it, a "holy mess." While she scrubbed, she told him to fix up the yard, and so he'd raked and trimmed and swept. He'd even done some touch-up painting on the trim.

After they'd finished, he and Mary sat at the kitchen table having a beer.

"So, what does Miss Carolina Prescott look like, Webb?" she'd asked.

"Pretty. She's pretty."

"How pretty?"

"Well...real pretty, Mary. Very pretty."

She'd laughed.

"Come on," he said, "what do you want me to say?"

Mary drew on her beer. "The way you've been fussing

and bustling, I figured as much. Men get real strange when there's an attractive woman in the picture.''

"Hell, that's the last thing on my mind."

"Oh yeah?"

"Yeah."

"Could have fooled me."

"Mary, you know how I've been since Karen. A woman could crawl in my bed naked and I'd be annoyed."

"That's nothing to brag about, Webb."

He looked at her in surprise. "Whose side are you on, anyway?"

"Yours, knucklehead. That's the point, Webb. Which is exactly what I've been trying to tell you for the past six months. God knows, I loved my daughter, but I don't want you wasting your life like those women in India who...what do you call it when they jump in the fire?"

"Suttee."

"Yeah, that's it." Mary scratched her head. "How is it a dumb cowboy like you knows so much?"

"Books. I read books."

"Karen used to say your head was always full of ideas and that if she'd let you, you'd have more books than the library."

"Some guys spend money on guns, some on fishing tackle. Me, it's something to read."

"A man could have worse habits, I guess," Mary said, absently drumming her fingers on the table.

She took a drink of beer. Webb did, as well. He wiped his mouth with the back of his hand and glanced around the kitchen.

"So, are we ready for inspection?"

"The house is. You could use a haircut."

He chuckled. "I'm trying to work out an accommodation with this lady, Mary, not ask her to the prom."

His mother-in-law had pondered that for a moment or

vo, her expression growing serious. "I guess only you
now what you want concerning this baby."

"That's the hell of it," he said, shaking his head. "I
on't. At least not yet. To tell you the truth, I don't have
e slightest idea what's right and fair."

And so he'd struggled, in the end doing what he usually
id when he felt anxious—he retreated into his memories
f Karen. That was why he'd ridden to their spot.

His wife had been a crutch much more in death than in
fe. When she was alive, Karen had given him balance.
ince her passing he'd withdrawn into work. He worked,
ad and took his courses. And he had long, imaginary con-
ersations with her.

Karen would have wanted him to get their baby back no
atter what. But Karen didn't know Carolina Prescott. Car-
lina was a good and decent woman. She hadn't asked for
is problem any more than he had.

The worst of it was that even though he knew what
aren would have wanted, he still didn't know what to do.
a Aspen, he'd gone off half-cocked, he knew that. But
hat did a man who spent his days working with horses
nd cattle know about telling a woman she was carrying a
olen baby?

Besides, pregnancy was a sensitive issue for him. While
aren was carrying Robbie, sometimes he'd gotten a little
range himself. His mother had died when he was born,
nd he hadn't even had a father to forgive him. Being an
rphan wasn't easy, even an adult orphan.

It had taken him a while to get used to the idea of having
nother child. But he *was* going to be a father again, and
e baby was his and Karen's—albeit with some help from
arolina Prescott. She, of course, looked at the situation
st the other way around, which was what made it so con-
ounded impossible.

And if a tug-of-war over the baby wasn't enough, Webb
ad found himself lying awake at night thinking about Car-

olina herself. Much as he wished it weren't so, he realized he was strongly attracted to the woman. Most people would have found it strange that a guy would have to think about a thing like that before he managed to figure it out. But most people hadn't been in his shoes. For more than two years other women hadn't existed as far as he was concerned. None of his attempts to get involved with someone after Karen's death had worked. His heart had a will of its own.

Maybe that was why he'd sort of popped Carolina's balloon when he'd told her he knew Karen would want her baby back. It had been his way of pushing her off, of keeping her at arm's length. Maybe he was just a damn coward, afraid to take responsibility for his feelings.

To her credit, Carolina Prescott hadn't blown her cool. He knew she had to be churning inside, but after a moment or two she'd calmly asked if that was why he'd come—to get the baby back. He'd told her he didn't know, he hadn't made up his mind. And so, it had been left at that. They both agreed to think about it.

God knew, he'd been thinking about it, all right. But his problem was, he couldn't separate Carolina from the baby. One minute he'd be picturing her pretty face, the next he'd remember she was pregnant with his and Karen's child. Inside her body, she was carrying his past life—his love for his wife. What, he asked himself, would he feel for her if she were plain or ugly? Would he be able to separate her from the baby then?

It was a hell of a mess. That's about all Webb could say for sure.

Before he'd left her house they'd exchanged phone numbers and promised to stay in touch. She had walked with him down to his truck. The last thing he'd said to her was that he was sorry to spoil her happiness. "I know this baby means a lot to you," he'd said. "You went to a hell of a lot of trouble to get it."

Her eyes had gotten all shimmery and she'd said, "Thanks for not being a bastard about it."

Webb had tipped his hat and watched her walk back up the driveway, those black leather pants gleaming in the sun. Halfway up, she stopped and turned around.

"I'll call you, Mr. Harper," she said.

"If you're going to call me, it might as well be Webb."

She smiled at that, but only nodded in response. He waited, his eyes on her, until she'd gone back inside. And then he'd left.

Webb took a long, last look at Snowmass Mountain, liking the cool caress of the rising breeze. The time for ruminating was over. She'd be arriving before long. And he had a hunch that by the time she left, they'd both know where things stood.

LINA, HER ELBOWS RESTING on the fence, watched the wheels of her father's plane touch down with a little puff of smoke. In a minute or two the Cessna would be at the tie-down area and Morgan Prescott would disembark, walking toward her in that quick, purposeful stride of his, his jaw set.

Whenever she saw him getting out his plane, Lina couldn't help but think of him as Zeus, the sky god, paying a visit to all the wretched mortals on earth. It wasn't until she'd studied mythology in college that Lina realized how Zeusian her father really was.

The Cessna arrived at the tie-down area and, as it swung around, the backwash from its props swept over her, blowing her hair. Lina clutched her suede jacket at the throat for protection against the cold air and squinted behind her sunglasses. The pilot killed the engines and the door on the side of the craft opened almost immediately.

Morgan appeared, perching his Stetson on his head as soon as he'd cleared the doorway. Descending the wing, he took the large step to the ground with the agility of a much younger man. He struck her as more fit and robust than he had just a few nights earlier when he'd allowed the years to show. It wasn't hard to guess why. He'd joined the battle on her behalf and, if her father loved anything, it was a good fight.

Morgan was not without his health concerns. He had a "faulty ticker," as he called it, but insisted it was more an annoyance than a genuine concern, though she suspected he gave his problem a good deal more credence when talking with his doctor. But there was a challenge at hand and he was in his glory. Any other concerns he might have could wait.

Lina had brought him back into the problem reluctantly. After Webb Harper had left, she'd gone to her shop, but except for waiting on the few customers who happened in, she'd spent the morning and much of the afternoon wondering what she should do. If Webb was proving hard to get a handle on, it was probably because she didn't understand the cowboy mentality as well as she thought. That was what had finally convinced her to call on her father for help. If there was anyone suited to take an independent-minded cowboy in hand, it was Morgan Prescott.

"Calling me was the right thing to do, sweetheart," he'd said when she'd phoned him at the ranch. "Harper sounds like he's right down my alley. By this time tomorrow I'll know everything there is to know about the son of a gun, right down to the brand of underwear he prefers."

"Dad," she'd protested, "Webb's not the enemy. He's a victim in this thing, just like me."

"Carolina," he'd said, "this has nothing to do with friends, enemies or victims. It has to do with two people wanting the same thing. When there's a drought and the cattle business goes to hell, all the cattlemen are victims, but that's not the point. The point is, some will survive and some won't. In a down market, there's only so much room. It's as simple as that."

She didn't care for that outlook on life but figured Webb Harper was probably looking at the situation the same way. And though he might not understand her language, he'd certainly understand her father's. Truth be known, Webb probably would appreciate being able to take this thing on man-to-man. Even if Morgan Prescott was a formidable foe, it'd be a fight Webb could understand. That was how she'd rationalized it, anyway.

Her father strode toward her, looking as happy as could be. Oddly, she had the clearest understanding ever of why men anguished over a clash of feelings but embraced battle. It had to be the testosterone.

"Afternoon, sweetheart," he said, kissing her on the cheek and putting a protective arm around her shoulders as they made their way toward her BMW. "Hear any more from your wild-assed cowboy friend?"

"Daddy, he's not wild-assed. Actually, he seems like a very nice person."

"You don't know the man, Carolina."

"And you do?"

"A lot better than you. Especially since I've checked him out."

Lina went around the car. Morgan got in the passenger side.

"So what did you find out?" she asked. "That your grandchild's biological father is a bank robber, an ex-con, what?"

"For starters, he's a nobody, Lina."

"I already knew he wasn't rich and famous," she said. "That's not news."

"Well, he's got problems."

"Pray tell, what kind of problems?"

"According to my sources, Webster Harper is on the brink of bankruptcy. The man doesn't have two nickels to rub together. He sold his spread to cover his debts and is leasing back the land. Barely makes enough to cover the rent.''

"That doesn't exactly sound immoral."

"No, but it's obvious he's after money. *Your* money, sweetheart. Chance brought him a fat hog and he plans to butcher it.''

The man her father was describing didn't sound like the man who'd come to her house. "What makes you so sure?"

"Lina, the man's desperate. I've talked to the fella who bought his place, a man named Cord Stewart, and also to a banker I know in Glenwood Springs. Harper's spread himself too thin and now he's got his back to the wall.''

"Sounds a little like that rodeo cowboy from Montrose who got himself in a real financial bind back in the fifties. As I recall, he actually did file for bankruptcy. Had to start over without a thing to his name but a hat, a pair of boots and a saddle. You remember him, don't you? Fellow named Morgan Prescott, I believe.''

"Very funny, Lina.''

"Am I wrong?"

"I never went after a rich man's daughter and I paid back every cent I owed, plus interest. Didn't have to, but I did.''

"Before we hang Webb Harper, Daddy, why don't we wait for him to commit his crime." She started the engine. "It somehow seems more civilized.''

"To be forewarned is to be forearmed," Morgan said.

"I'm not taking anything for granted," she said, putting the car in gear, "but I believe in giving people the benefit of the doubt.''

"Well, I only told you part of the story.''

"Oh, really? He has other skeletons in his closet?"

"Yes, but before I get into it, why don't you give me your impression of him first. How did he strike you?"

"After that, I can hardly say anything positive.''

"The important thing is, you didn't cut a deal without checking up on him first. Half of being a good businessman is knowing how to read people. The other half is knowing when to question your own judgment," he replied. "But, come on. Give. How did Mr. Harper strike you?"

"Well, I was so shook up I didn't pay a whole lot of attention to the man. But my impression was that he's sincere, earnest and considerate." She stopped at the highway and waited for traffic to clear. "So what are you going to tell me? That he's a registered sex offender?"

"Not quite. But he has a reputation as a real ladies' man. Left a trail of broken hearts a mile wide, according to my information. A regular Don Juan in chaps."

"He's a widower. He told me his wife died a couple of years ago."

"Yes, but since then he's had every single woman in three counties after him."

When there was a break in the traffic, Lina turned west on Route 82, toward Carbondale. "Webb Harper sort of sounds like that fellow from Montrose we were talking about. Only that guy has every single woman in three *states* after him—at least every one over forty."

"I don't take advantage of women and you know it, Lina."

"What I'm trying to say is, you're assuming the worst about Webb without giving him a chance."

"If I didn't know better, Carolina, I'd say the varmint has already duped you. If you're convinced he's such a wonderful guy, why did you call me in to take care of him for you?"

"I don't think he's a wonderful guy. I don't even know him. But I don't see any reason to assume the worst. And as far as calling you in, I did it for Webb as much as myself. I thought you could speak his language better than me."

"That part you got right, Lina."

"What, exactly, do you plan to do?"

"The first message he's going to get is that he's not up against a woman alone. I'm going to make it clear you've got family who's looking out for you and that you aren't ripe for the plucking. That alone may sober him up."

"And if it doesn't?"

"I'm prepared to take off my gloves."

"Oh, Daddy, I think you want to bloody his nose just for the sport of it."

"I didn't go looking for him, Carolina. He came to *my* daughter, telling her he might want her baby. You can't expect me to ignore that."

"Let's get something clear. Webb didn't make a demand. He told me he doesn't know what he wants to do. All he said was that his wife would want her baby back."

"He was testing you, sweetheart, don't you see? I bet you dollars to donuts he's already got a figure in mind. Common sense tells you that. What's a cowboy whose sport is chasing skirts going to do with a baby except sell it? And in you he's got a willing buyer. Trust me on that, Lina."

"Fine, but I think you should go into this with an open mind. Don't forget, I've met him and you haven't."

Morgan Prescott grinned. He reached over and patted her hand. "One thing I know about this fella—he sure can turn a girl's eye."

"If you weren't my father, Mr. Prescott, I'd take offense at that," she returned. "In fact, maybe I will anyway."

Morgan laughed. "No offense, honey. Believe me, I'm relieved to know you're interested. Never have felt comfortable with the notion of you going through life alone. As you well know, I think you made a mistake dumping Kyle."

"Please, Dad, let's not get into that. And as for Webb Harper, yes, he's attractive, but I outgrew cowboys a long time ago. Besides, I'm pregnant and have a baby to worry about. The only reason we're even having this conversation is because Mr. Harper happens to be the father of the child I'm carrying.''

"I can promise you this, Lina. He knows fate couldn't have picked him a better woman. I'm sure he thinks he's got the world by the tail right about now. In his shoes, I would!"

Lina gripped the steering wheel tighter. She hated to admit it, but that was the most telling remark of all!

AS THE TIME FOR Carolina Prescott's arrival neared, Webb paced back and forth, growing more and more anxious. He'd been vacillating, but in his heart he knew he had to decide what he wanted to do, what was right. The hardest part was knowing that his feelings weren't the only issue. He had a responsibility to Karen. This was her baby just as much as if she'd given birth to it.

Of course, Karen could never have anticipated this would happen, but if she had known, Webb was positive how she'd have felt. Those embryos were to be her children. She wouldn't have wanted them put out for adoption. A mother's feelings went beyond life. Webb had no doubt that his own mother had anguished over him even as she took her last breath.

Looking out the front window, he saw the plume of dust coming over the rise and figured it was Lina. The car wasn't moving fast, but to him it was coming with a sense of purpose. Undoubtedly she'd have a proposal of some sort. He just didn't know what.

Webb wasn't going to stand on ceremony. He stepped out onto the porch as the BMW neared, coming to a stop at the top of the drive. It was then he realized Lina was not alone. There was a man in the car.

His first thought was that she'd brought a lawyer. The possibility of a legal battle had been lurking in the back of his mind. It was a prospect he didn't relish. He didn't like lawyers—even good ones who were on his side, like Harv

Cooper, who had handled his wrongful death claim against the trucker who'd killed Karen and Robbie. It hadn't been Harv's fault that the trucker's insurance had lapsed or that he'd had virtually no assets. In the end, neither of them had come out of the suit with much—Harv might even have lost on it.

Webb had found the entire experience disgusting. He couldn't have been happy about taking money for the loss of his wife and son, whether it was millions or only a few thousand, as it had turned out. He'd never have bothered filing suit in the first place, but Harv had convinced him, and he had always trusted his judgment. But certain kinds of victories could never be victories. Webb had known that all along, of course, but he had been so grief-stricken at the time that he'd forgotten it.

Lina Prescott climbed out of the car and waved. Webb waved back, but he sensed false friendliness in her gesture. How could they be friendly when they were after the same thing?

"Hi," she called. "Hope we're not too late."

"No, right on time."

Webb felt his heart pick up its beat as he noticed her shiny hair in the sunlight. Lina was wearing a moss green cashmere sweater, brown wool skirt and brown suede jacket. But his eyes didn't linger on her long. He turned his attention to the older man who was in the process of getting out of the car.

The gentleman was in Western business attire, a crisp off-white Stetson on his head. His demeanor said he was substantial, confident, in control. The man had the look of someone who knew what he was doing—an expert horseman who'd come to check out the livestock before an auction. In this case, the livestock was him.

Second-guessing himself, Webb decided this man wasn't a lawyer, after all. His manner was all wrong. The other possibility was almost as problematical. It could be her father. The man, whoever he was, certainly fit the image of a big-time rancher.

"Webb," Carolina said as they approached the house, "this is my father, Morgan Prescott. I asked him to join us. I hope you don't mind."

"Don't let her fool you, son," Morgan said. "I twisted Lina's arm to make her let her old man feel useful." He reached out and gave Webb's hand an aggressive shake, winking as he did so.

Webb congratulated himself on figuring out what was about to hit him. He wasn't sure what difference it would make, other than the fact that he wouldn't be dealing with Lina.

"Pleased to meet you, Mr. Prescott," he said, looking directly into the man's eyes and seeing steel.

Webb turned his attention to Lina, offering her his hand. "Good to see you again, ma'am."

She seemed surprised by his gesture but showed no reluctance. Her hand was cool and soft and felt good to him. She was a lady, there was no disputing that. Very feminine, lovely. As cool, soft and slender as her hand. The pretty face was the one he'd faced the past couple of nights as he'd lain awake in his bed.

"Come on inside, folks," he said, stepping back so they could enter.

Lina glanced around the tidy but spartan living room as Webb closed the door. He checked out her shapely legs. Catching her father's look of disapproval, he motioned for them to sit, embarrassed. At least his place looked decent. He had nothing to be ashamed of in that regard.

"Make yourselves at home," he said.

The Prescotts sat side by side on the sofa, Morgan placing his Stetson on the floor next to him. Webb dropped into his easy chair, not quite sure what to expect.

"Looks like you have a nice tidy little spread here, son," Morgan said without ceremony.

Webb knew Prescott was wondering about the size but was constrained by cattle country etiquette from coming right out and asking. Webb wasn't about to duck the issue, though. "It provides a living, Mr. Prescott. I've got just under a thousand acres."

"Does it run up into the timber?"

"Yes, sir. I've got some good grazing land in the bottom along the creek and summer pasture in the higher ground. Enough to support several hundred head. But I'm running a little thin right now," Webb said, knowing the next question in Prescott's mind. "The herd's mostly young bred heifers."

"That's the way to build, all right. With any luck, you'll be looking at a better market next year."

"Yes, sir. That's what I'm hoping."

"Don't we all."

Webb noticed Lina look down. She seemed uncomfortable. What he couldn't tell was whether it was because of him or her father. Morgan didn't take his eyes off him, his gaze steady.

"You must be a rancher yourself, Mr. Prescott," Webb said after a brief silence.

"I've got a place over in Montrose and Ouray Counties."

"Straddle the county line, do you?"

"Yep."

Lina shifted uneasily and glanced at her father. She seemed not to like the conversation. Webb didn't understand why, except that it might be boring. Admittedly he'd rather talk to her, but he couldn't ignore her father. So, even though he could have stared at her all day, he turned his attention back to Morgan.

"You been ranching long, Mr. Prescott?"

"Better part of fifty years. The main ranch runs fifty-five thousand acres. I've got a somewhat smaller chunk up in Delta County, but the cattle operation's just a shadow of what it once was, when I had leases on big pieces of Federal grazing land. We're down to about thirty thousand head now. I like to keep my finger in, if you know what I mean.''

Webb could see right there what he was up against and suspected he'd just gotten the message Morgan Prescott wanted him to have. He could just as easily have said, ''I'm not a man to fool with, son.''

''I must have heard of your spread, Mr. Prescott. What do you call it?''

''The Double C Ranch. Named it that because it stretches from Cimarron to Colona and because I had a wife and daughter named Carole and Carolina. The answer I give depends on who I'm talking to,'' Morgan told him with a laugh. He patted his daughter's knee. ''This one spent the first fifteen years of her life on the Double C, Mr. Harper. She was a country girl until I sent her off to get citified.''

''Don't listen to his bluster, Webb,'' Lina said. ''Daddy's a city boy himself now. Has trouble dragging himself away from the comforts of Denver.''

''You believe that, son,'' Morgan said, ''then I've got some swampland I want to show you. As I'm sure you know, a man of the land can't ever get ranching out of his blood.'' He laughed heartily.

Webb and Lina exchanged looks. He sensed she was uncomfortable and could only assume it was because of the circumstances.

''I'm not being much of a host,'' he said, looking away. ''I've got coffee on the stove. Can I interest anybody in a cup?''

''That sounds fine,'' Morgan said, speaking for both of them, ''but I'd sort of like to stretch my legs first if you don't mind.'' He put his hand on his daughter's knee again. ''Sweetheart, you don't mind if Mr. Harper and I go out to look at his heifers, do you? I know you wouldn't want to get mud on those pretty shoes of yours.''

"Do whatever you want," she said, glancing at Webb. "I've known my whole life you've never seen a cow you didn't want to meet."

"See what happens, Mr. Harper, when you indulge a daughter? They get right uppity and spoiled as two-week-old milk."

The way Lina smiled, Webb could tell Morgan Prescott wasn't being completely facetious.

"Let me get you a cup of coffee, Lina," Webb offered, getting up. He headed for the kitchen without waiting for an answer. "Take anything in it?" he called over his shoulder.

"A little milk if you have it."

He entered the kitchen, which, thanks to Mary, was gleaming. "Powdered okay?" he called back, embarrassed that he didn't have any fresh milk.

"Fine."

Webb got a mug down from the cupboard. He selected the one Karen had used all the time, but which he'd hardly touched since her death. But then he thought better of it and exchanged it for another.

"Can I help?" It was Lina in the doorway.

Webb blushed for no good reason apart from what had been going through his mind. "There's not much to do. Unless you'd like some cookies or something."

He took down a bag of cookies that had been on the shelf for a couple of weeks, wondering if they were stale. Why hadn't he thought about getting something to serve?

Lina came up next to him and took the bag from his hand. He liked the way she smelled. He turned and looked at her face, noticing again her long dark lashes and the creamy smoothness of her pale skin. She opened the bag of cookies.

"Thank you for indulging my father," she said under her breath. "He's a take-charge sort of person."

"I reckon he's earned it."

Lina glanced up at him. "I suppose he has," she said.

Webb got her a plate for the cookies and the box of powdered milk. Changing his mind, he got down Karen's mug and set it on the counter. Then he got the coffeepot and filled it. Lina had put half a dozen cookies on the plate. She faced him, leaning against the counter. They regarded each other.

Webb had no idea what she was thinking—whether it was about him, the baby, her father or the situation. His own thoughts were completely unambiguous. He had a strong desire to take her face in his hands and kiss her. It was one of those forbidden impulses that no man in his right mind would act on. And so he didn't.

Whatever was going through her mind obviously made her anxious. She looked down and fiddled with the plate. Webb broke the tension by picking up the mug. "You'd probably be more comfortable in the front room," he said.

Lina followed him back into the living room, where they found Morgan Prescott staring out the window across the valley. He turned.

"Let's have a look at that stock," he said in what Webb was beginning to see as his characteristic directness.

Morgan retrieved his hat from the floor as Webb put the mug and plate of cookies on the coffee table, then got his own hat from the hook next to the door. Morgan was already on his way out when Webb turned to Lina, who was taking off her jacket. He realized he should have invited her to take it off earlier. At times like this he wished he weren't such an inept host. Reading novels about people with manners didn't necessarily translate into social graces.

He was glad Lina had grown up on a ranch, though. That meant that for all her sophistication, she'd at least understand him, if not appreciate his awkward behavior.

"Make yourself at home," he said earnestly.

Lina smiled faintly as she sat on the edge of the sofa cushion, her knees pressed together, her hands clasped.

"Would you mind if I browsed through your bookcase?" she said, gesturing.

"Be my guest." Giving her a last long look, he went out the door, only to find himself face-to-face with Morgan Prescott, who'd been listening from the porch.

"Lina's a good girl." Morgan's tone was weighty, full of implication.

"Yes, sir. She seems like a very nice person."

They went down the steps, then strode along the path leading toward the barn and other outbuildings.

"I'm sure I don't have to tell you, Harper, that my daughter's in a vulnerable position."

"No, sir, I realize that."

"Even the strongest of women are affected by being pregnant. Maybe it's hormones.... Point is, menfolk look after their women when they're carrying a child."

Webb wasn't sure what Prescott was getting at, but he was sure it was leading up to the real reason they'd left the house. "I understand."

"And since Lina doesn't have a husband, I feel a special responsibility," Morgan said. They walked along for several steps before he continued. "Harper, I'm a man of few words, and the ones I say tend to be direct."

"I tend to be the same, Mr. Prescott."

"My question to you is, what're you asking to sign off on that baby of hers?"

"Sir?"

"No need to be cagey. You obviously have some claim to that child she's carrying, though my lawyers tell me the matter is totally unsettled, that medical science has outrun the law. What it means—bottom line—is that this is probably best handled man-to-man. So, what's your price to give up your rights to the baby?"

Webb stopped dead in his tracks. Morgan took a few more steps, then he, too, stopped, slowly turning around.

They faced each other like a couple of old-time gunfighters squaring off.

"You want to buy the baby."

"I don't know that I'd put it so crudely, son."

"But that's what it amounts to, Mr. Prescott."

"Define it any way you please. Point is, I want to buy Carolina's way out of this with the least pain and inconvenience possible."

"The least pain for her."

"The least pain for everybody, Harper. You must be smart enough to realize that if this becomes a fight, I'll outlast you. Besides, mothers end up with the kids. That's the way the system works."

"My wife, Karen, is the mother, Mr. Prescott. That's the point."

Morgan slipped his hands into his pockets, completely unperturbed. Webb stood his ground as calmly as he could. He, too, had a woman to defend—or more accurately, the memory of one—and a child that was his, his and his wife's.

"This is no different than a couple of cowboys coming across an unbranded calf on the open range, Harper. Each of us thinks it's his. Now it seems to me we can tear each other apart or we can deal."

"All due respect, sir, I'm not dealing on this. The baby's not for sale."

"I'll give you Cord Stewart's deed to this place, Harper. And I'll buy any stock you want to sell at the highest market price for the year and give you all the replacement heifers your land can handle. The deed'll be in escrow in a week along with my lawyer's papers giving Lina full rights over the baby."

Webb was dumbfounded. "You talked to Cord?"

"I know you're hanging on by your fingernails, son. But I'm not going to take advantage of that. Stewart gave me his price. When the title's in your name, the lease lapses, of course, so you've got the place free and clear, plus the operating capital and stock you need to start over. What more could you ask for?'' Morgan reached inside his jacket pocket and produced a checkbook. ''To show my good faith, I'll give you a check right now for five thousand in exchange for your handshake on the deal.''

''Put away your checkbook, Mr. Prescott. My baby's not for sale. At any price.''

Morgan looked surprised. Then he stared at him hard, his eyes turning steely. ''Are you stubborn or stupid, Harper? I frankly can't tell which.''

''If I had money and offered to buy your daughter's claim to the baby, I don't believe there'd be an amount large enough for you to agree. Some things can't be replaced. Karen's and my flesh and blood is one.''

''You're right, I wouldn't sell. But then, I'm in a position where I don't have to.''

''Same as me.''

''Not quite, son. Cord Stewart can put my name on that deed. Then this place becomes mine. It'll be me you have to make your lease payments to.''

''You do what you have to do, Mr. Prescott.''

''The deed, the stock and a hundred thousand in cash in escrow by next Friday. That's my final offer.''

''Sorry, sir, but you might as well save your breath.''

For the first time Morgan Prescott turned red. ''I'll end up with your ranch *and* the baby. You realize that, don't you?''

''For the moment, the place is still mine, sir. All due respect, I think maybe you should leave while things are still civil. Neither of us is going to put a brand on this calf today. That much is clear.''

''And this is the last time you'll be able to say it,'' Morgan said, brushing past him and heading back to the house. He went a dozen steps and stopped. He turned, a smile on his face. "I'm not a man who holds grudges, Harper. If you come to your senses, call me."

"Good afternoon, Mr. Prescott."

Morgan strode off to the house, and Webb stuck his hands in his hip pockets and faced Snowmass Mountain, its frosted peak rising in the crystalline air as solid and immovable as Webb's own determination.

For the first time his head and his heart were in perfect harmony. He knew where he stood and what he had to do. Webb's sole regret was that he'd have to hurt that pretty woman who was about to get bad news from her father. Losing her goodwill—and what little bit of friendship they'd forged—was a sad loss. A tragedy. But he was used to tragedy. And there was no escaping the fact that this offer for the baby couldn't have happened without her concurrence.

A few moments later he heard the front door close for a second time. He turned to see Morgan Prescott descending the steps, followed by Lina. She stopped and looked in Webb's direction. He swallowed hard, feeling the pain of his disillusionment and regret.

He'd been too stupid to realize what this visit was really about. True, she'd let her father do the dirty work, but her desires were clear. No wonder she'd been embarrassed. Webb was embarrassed himself for having been so easily fooled. Even her conspiratorial little smiles had been fraudulent.

But whatever was going through Lina Prescott's head, she apparently abandoned any intent she might have had to express it. She silently followed her father to her car. Webb waited until they were out of sight before returning to the house.

The only evidence of their visit was the half-empty mug of coffee and the plate of cookies. Picking up the mug, he carried it to the kitchen and dumped what was left of the coffee into the sink. Then he carefully washed the mug and put it back on the shelf, resolving never to take it down again.

CHAPTER FIVE

LINA STOPPED THE CAR at the fence opposite her father's plane and turned off the engine. It had been a tense ride from Carbondale. She was heartsick, but she couldn't really blame her father. He'd done what he thought was best. Besides, she'd agreed to let him handle it, so she had to take at least partial responsibility.

"I know you're angry, Lina," her father said after several moments of silence. "I failed you and you have every right to be upset."

"Dad, you didn't fail me. Webb didn't want to sell his baby. It's as simple as that."

"You won't like hearing this," he said, "but that was only a skirmish, not the war. Harper talks tough, but he has nothing to back him up. Eventually, he'll have to fold because I'll milk him dry. When I finish with him, he'll have nothing."

"Wonderful," she said. "What good will that do? I take no pleasure from hurting him."

"I don't, either. Just the opposite. I tried to make it as painless for him as possible. I was willing to all but set him up for life. All he had to do was let you have your baby."

"Obviously, he considers it *his* baby."

"Well, he's stubborn *and* wrong."

"I'm not so sure about that, Daddy."

"What?"

"Webb and I both have an interest in this baby. I can

see that now. True, one of us will probably end up with it, and it may well be me, but at what price?''

"Carolina, are you going soft?'' her father said, his tone disapproving. "Harper's no wimp, I'll grant you. He's not afraid. But he can be beaten. So unless you want him to walk away with the booty, you'd better be prepared to step up and fight. The weak never win the battles of life.''

It wasn't the first time she'd heard her father say that. In fact, she'd heard it her whole life. There was truth to it, she knew that, too, but Lina yearned for a rosier view of human nature. "I'm not sure Webb wants to win at any cost. I think he cares about the baby, and for his wife's sake he can't turn his back and walk away. That's to be admired, in my opinion.''

Morgan Prescott shook his head with disappointment. "All you're doing, Lina, is proving the man's reputation with women is well deserved.''

"Dad, I'm trying to convince myself that Webb Harper is a decent human being.''

"You think if you're nice to him, he'll let you have the baby?''

"Right now I've got nothing to lose, do I?''

Morgan shrugged. "I guess I'm in no position to criticize, and my credibility's shot. But personally, I think time's on your side. Let him think about it for a while, let me turn the screws a little. Eventually he'll realize discretion is the better part of valor. He might even be hoping I'll up the ante.''

"Please, Dad, just let me handle this from here on out.''

"Well,'' her father said with a sigh, "it's your life. But if your approach doesn't work, don't hesitate to give me a call. The man can't hold out forever. And I've got a very large club.''

"Thank you,'' she said, leaning over and giving him a kiss on the cheek. "I'll remember that.''

Morgan had gotten out of the car and strode to his plane

then. He hadn't had quite the bounce in his step he'd had when he arrived a few hours earlier, but then, she was sure Webb Harper wasn't doing a victory dance, either. That was the trouble in this type of situation—there usually weren't any clear-cut winners.

Once her father was inside his plane and the pilot fired the engines, Lina started the car. During the drive back to Aspen, she'd been weighing her options. Her first instinct was to contact Zara, but on reflection, she decided that at this point it wasn't a legal question she faced so much as it was a human one. She wanted to undo whatever hard feelings her father might have caused, and the only way she could see to do that was to apologize to Webb. Morgan Prescott would quail at the thought, but that was a man's way of thinking. She'd come to realize she was dealing with Webb's wife as much as she was with him, as strange as that seemed.

MARY CARSON SAT on the stoop in front of Webb's house, smoking one of the five daily cigarettes she'd been allowing herself since the doctor had ordered her to cut back. She probably would have skipped it altogether, but she was upset, and it was hard to be upset and crave a cigarette at the same time. If Webb hadn't bolted from the house so angrily—if he'd stayed and talked to her instead—she might not have felt the need to smoke. But he had, and here she was.

The sun had gone down, but that didn't mean she'd be seeing Webb anytime soon. He was fully capable of riding all night, or at least until the wee small hours. Karen had said he liked riding when he was upset and sometimes would go out in the middle of the night. What worried Mary was that he was upset with her.

"What do you mean, consider their offer?" he'd roared when she'd tried to help him find a solution. "You want me to sell them your grandchild, Mary? Is that what you're saying?''

''No, not sell it. Of course not. There must be some kind of middle ground that would be acceptable, though. You can't beat them in court, if only because they can afford the fight and you can't. So get what you can. Take part of the deal they offered but demand the right to see the baby regularly.''

''You mean like a divorced father?''

''Why not? The way things are now, you'll be ruined and lose the baby, both.''

''I'm not going to give in to blackmail, Mary, and I'm surprised to hear you, of all people, suggesting it. Karen would die before she'd let some stranger take a child of ours and you know it.''

''Webb, Karen's dead. She's not here to fight this fight.''

''But I am!'' he said, his face red with anger. ''Don't I count?''

''Of course you count. All I'm trying to do is to get you to be realistic.''

''*You're* not being realistic, Mary. You've let them buffalo you.''

''Webb, suppose you did fight it out. Say by some miracle you even ended up with the baby. And say by some crazy act of grace Mr. Prescott didn't strip you of everything you own. Even with all that luck, how are you going to raise a child? You're a cattleman, Webb, with a job that demands more time than you've got. That baby's not going to come home from the hospital and climb on a horse and help his old man herd cattle. I would help in every way I could, but children aren't livestock. They need full-time care, at least the first few years.''

He'd given her a long hard look, shaking his head. ''Karen wouldn't run from this, Mary, and I'm not going to, either. Now, if you'll excuse me, I'm going to get some air.''

He'd left the house then, slamming the front door behind him. Mary had felt terrible, as if she'd let him down. But she knew she was talking sense. Webb simply couldn't see that because he was blind with emotion. He was in the grip of Karen's ghost. Mary understood that because she'd been clinging to her memories, too. But her situation was different. She didn't have many alternatives. Webb still had a life to live. She only had one to remember.

Stamping out the last of her cigarette, Mary sprinkled the last shreds of tobacco in the flowerbed. Then she stuck the paper and filter in the pocket of her apron. She didn't want to leave any butts around. She was in the middle of trying to decide whether to go home or give Webb a little more time to return—maybe fix him dinner—when she saw a plume of dust coming over the rise. She couldn't imagine who it might be unless one of Webb's friends was dropping by. Then she saw that the vehicle was a shiny new foreign car. That wouldn't be any of Webb's friends, not the usual ones anyway.

When the car stopped at the top of the drive, Mary stood. As the trailing dust cleared, she saw that the driver was a woman. Mary wondered if she was about to meet Carolina Prescott. The woman emerging from the vehicle was tall, well-dressed and had shiny black hair. Mary walked toward her, meeting her halfway between the car and the house.

"Hello," the woman said, clearly perplexed at seeing Mary. "I'm Lina Prescott. Is Webb inside?"

"No, he's off riding. I was hoping he'd be back before now, but it looks like he decided on a nice long ride. I'm Mary Carson, by the way, Karen's mom."

"Then you're Webb's mother-in-law," Lina said, extending her hand.

Mary took it. "Former mother-in-law, I guess."

Lina looked off across the valley as though she were hoping to see Webb. She had a disconcerted expression. She turned her electric blue eyes on Mary. "Is he angry?"

"That's probably as good a word as any," Mary said.

Lina gnawed on her lip, looking very anxious. "I figured he would be. My father gave him a bad time. I don't know if he told you."

"Yes, me and Webb are pretty close."

Lina contemplated her, a question in her eyes and a lot of uncertainty. "It's your daughter's embryo they implanted in me, Mrs. Carson. How do you feel about this whole business?"

"To my mind, it's tragic for everybody concerned. Including you, Miss Prescott. And I'm sure Webb feels no ill will toward you."

"He can't be very pleased with me after what happened this afternoon. And I won't pretend it was all my father's doing. I agreed to let him handle it man-to-man."

"You let a man loose and he does seem to find a way to bungle things," Mary said with a laugh. "At least when there's family issues involved."

Lina smiled, looking a bit more at ease and not quite as anxious as when she first arrived. And in spite of everything, Mary decided that she liked Lina Prescott. Lord knew, there were a million far less desirable women that fate could have picked to bring Karen and Webb's little one into the world.

"I can't tell you how long it'll be before Webb's likely to return," Mary told her, "but if you want to wait, we might as well go inside."

"I probably shouldn't have come, but I didn't want things left on a bitter note," Lina said as she began walking alongside Mary. "I wanted Webb to know I was willing to work out a solution we could both live with."

"Funny thing," Mary said, "but I was urging Webb to think that same way."

"Were you really?"

Mary could see Lina's relief and happiness at her words. It made her feel good, too. It was nice they saw things the same. In a funny way it made her feel close to the woman. And if Carolina Prescott was going to have Karen and Webb's baby, it would help if they were friends—or at least pulling in the same direction.

"How did he react?" Lina asked.

"You don't want to know. Webb can be pretty stubborn when he puts his mind to it. That can be good or bad, depending on what you're trying to accomplish and how you go about it. My mama used to tell me it's fine to go after a rat until you kill it, just don't burn your house down in the process."

"In other words, he's willing to go down with the ship."

"He's got it in his head Karen wouldn't give an inch, so he won't."

"Would she, Mrs. Carson?"

"This might sound coldhearted coming from a mother, but I'm not all that sure it matters, Miss Prescott. Webb's got to get it into his head it's his life he's living now, not *theirs*."

"That's a very enlightened view," Lina said.

They went up the steps. Mary opened the door, letting Lina Prescott in. As she stepped past her, Mary took a good look at the way Lina was dressed. Though she hardly considered herself an authority on such things, she knew enough to know the woman had taste as well as money.

Mary offered to fix some coffee, but Lina told her she was avoiding caffeine, having had her quota for the day. They went into the kitchen.

"I don't reckon Webb has any herbal tea around here," Mary said, peeking in a cabinet or two. "He sticks pretty close to basics."

"That's all right. I don't need anything," Lina said.

Mary checked to make sure there was water in the tea-kettle, then turned on the burner. "It's instant, but I think I'll have a cup. Sit down," she said, pointing to the table. "Unless you'd be more comfortable in the front room."

"This is fine."

Lina sat while Mary found the coffee jar and got a mug down from the cupboard, then turned to face the woman who was to be the surrogate mother of her grandchild. She'd allowed that was exactly what Carolina Prescott was.

"Tell me, Mrs. Carson," Lina said, "since you and I both seem to be reasonable people, what would you recommend I do?"

Mary considered the question, knowing there was no easy answer. "I wish I could say, Miss Prescott, but Webb's not an easy one. He's more complicated than he seems. The average person would look at him and say he's just another dumb cowboy, but it's not true. He's smart as a whip, and even though he hasn't had a lot of education, he knows an awful lot."

"Yes, I was looking at his books this afternoon."

"Lord, does the man like to read. And he remembers what's in the books, too. I guess you could say he was self-educated."

"It's admirable to do something like that on your own."

Mary nodded and checked the water. It wasn't quite boiling, but she decided it was close enough. She fixed her coffee and invited Lina to join her in the front room. Before sitting, she went to the window to see if Webb might be coming up from the barn, but he wasn't.

Mary sat in her favorite chair and picked up the plastic shopping bag she always carried her sewing in. Before going out for her cigarette she'd been knitting. Taking the piece she'd been working on from the sack, she began to knit again.

"You're into needlework, I see," Lina said.

"I've knitted and done needlepoint all my life. I cross-stitch, crochet, sew clothes. My grandmother was a wiz and taught me everything I know."

"Would you mind if I have a look?"

Mary handed her the piece.

"You do lovely work," Lina said, examining it. "Have you ever done things for babies?"

"Lord, I must have made fifteen or twenty pieces for Robbie before he was even born—tiny little sweaters, a stocking cap, blankets, booties, you name it. There wasn't a lot Karen and Webb had to buy."

"Have you ever sold any of your needlework?"

"All the time. But just to friends and neighbors, and I mainly charge for the materials. I mostly do it because I love it. I like to keep busy."

"Would you be interested in doing a few pieces for my shop? I run a baby boutique in Aspen."

"Webb told me. But you wouldn't really sell any of my stuff, would you?"

Lina handed the piece back to her. "If this is any indication of what you can do, I'd say I'd be lucky to have it. Of course, items for babies can be tricky, both in the making and marketing. I'm sometimes surprised by what moves and what doesn't."

"I've never thought of putting my things in a real shop before."

"We'd have to agree on pricing, design and so on, but you wouldn't be doing it for free."

"I'm so flattered, Miss Prescott, I don't know what to say."

"I've never carried anything by local artisans before—except for a woman who did a little custom embroidery to personalize items—and I think it'd be a nice addition to my line. Do you have some things you could show me?"

"I have most of the things I made for Robbie. Webb said he'd rather I have them than throw them in some old box. He had trouble going through Karen and the boy's belongings afterward. I ended up doing most of it. Karen said he was tough as nails except when it came to family things."

"I guess men are entitled to some weaknesses."

Mary nodded and continued to knit, her fingers moving at lightning speed. Lina watched her.

"Tell me about your daughter, Mrs. Carson," Lina said as Mary's fingers continued to fly.

It was not something she was frequently asked to do—talk about Karen—even by Webb. But Mary could see how Lina would be curious. "Karen was a beautiful girl," she said. "She had the prettiest honey blond hair and the sweetest disposition. But what mother doesn't think of her child as special?"

"I imagine you had good reason."

"I like to think Karen was unique. Needless to say, she adored Webb. And it was mutual. They were a beautiful young couple, Miss Prescott, they really were." Mary had to fight back her emotion. Then something occurred to her. "You've never seen a picture of her, have you?"

"No."

"Webb's got one in his room. It's the only picture he keeps out. Would you like to see it?"

"Sure."

Mary put down her knitting and went off, leaving Lina to wonder about this family she'd been drawn into by a strange twist of fate. Mary had already revealed a good deal about herself and her daughter, and Lina was getting a better feel for Webb. They seemed like good, decent, hard-working, salt-of-the-earth people. A lot worse could be said about a family.

It sounded as if Karen had been a lovely person. And about the worst thing she'd heard about Webb was how stubborn he was. That particular trait hadn't been so obvious in her conversations with him, though underneath his soft-spoken, polite veneer, she'd sensed tenacity. Despite the fact that they'd been forced into adversarial positions from the very beginning, Webb had piqued her curiosity. His rugged good looks were a part of it, but mostly it was knowing she was carrying his child. There was also a little nostalgia on her part, as well.

There'd been a period during her teen years when she'd romanticized cowboys, finding their independence, swagger and barely restrained wildness a turn-on. It was her mother who'd first tempered her enthusiasm for that kind of danger. "If you're going to kiss a cowboy in a downpour," she'd said, "you gotta make sure there's room under his hat for the both of you. And believe me, Lina, there aren't many of them with a big enough hat."

She'd outgrown her fascination with cowboys in time. Once she was living in the larger world, wild young firebrands lost their appeal. She'd dated a variety of men, guys who were teachers or in business or government. Since her divorce she'd gone with a plumbing contractor and a man who owned a local bookstore. None of them had had the edge of the sexy young cowboys from her youth, but all of them had been genuine, good people.

Mary Carson returned, carrying a framed photograph. "This is a picture of Karen and Robbie when he was two," she said. "Webb keeps it on his chest of drawers." She handed the photo to Lina.

The young woman in the photo was lovely—blond and with a happy smile. This was the person Mary had described, the perfect mate for Webb Harper. And the little boy was adorable. Karen's love for her son came through clearly in the picture. It wasn't surprising that this was the way Webb wanted to remember them.

"That little swatch of cloth in the corner is from Karen's wedding dress," Mary said. "She was such a pretty bride, you can't imagine. And I don't think there was a prouder man on earth that day than Webb."

Lina could see it all in her mind's eye, plain as could be—the pretty young woman with the sweet disposition on the arm of the cowboy she adored. They had their home, their child, then tragedy struck. Tears came to Lina's eyes just thinking about it. Poor Webb. She knew he'd been through a terrible and tragic ordeal because he'd told her so, but she hadn't felt the sting of his loss as profoundly as now, with his wife's picture in her hands. This was the woman he loved, the one with whom he'd created the embryo she was carrying.

"She's lovely, Mary," Lina said, wiping her eyes. "And the little boy, too. It must have been terribly painful for both you and Webb."

She returned the photograph, and Mary looked down at it fondly, her brow furrowing slightly as she relived her pain. Sighing, she carried the picture back into the bedroom. Lina shook her head sadly. Webb's reaction to her father's threats made even more sense to her than before.

Mary returned and sat heavily in her chair. "I try not to let myself get all morose about what happened," she said, her tone surprisingly philosophical, "but Karen and her family were a big part of what I lived for." She smiled sadly and picked up her knitting. "That's not good, I know. And a person's got to find their happiness inside, not in somebody else. They say you don't have much future if you spend all your time living in the past, but knowing it and living accordingly are two different things."

"I know," Lina said.

Mary took another long breath, then looked into Lina's eyes, her smile a little warmer. "I've been going on about my woes like they were all that matters, when you've got much happier things to think about. Like that baby."

"I'm not so sure *happy* is the right word, Mrs. Carson. When I signed up for this, I thought it was going to be a wonderful experience. Now I'm not so sure."

"I wish you wouldn't feel that way. Webb'll come around and the two of you'll get things worked out."

"Do you believe that or is it wishful thinking?" Lina asked.

Mary groaned. "I hate seeing more suffering on top of what we've already been through."

"I like to be optimistic, too, but I truly don't know where this is headed."

"I don't mean to poke my nose where I've got no business," Mary said, pulling on her ball of yarn, "but why'd you choose to have a baby this way?"

"Webb asked me the same question. The reason is, I can't have children normally because I'm sterile. But I'm able to carry a baby and give birth. I think that makes me a mother in the ways that really matter. The woman who nourishes the baby and brings it into the world is not just incidental. The genetic material may not have been mine, but everything else is. And this baby would never be more than a smear of cells in a test tube if I hadn't done what I did."

"I wouldn't criticize you for the world. Just the opposite. I think what you're doing is a wonderful thing."

"My father thinks it's scandalous—especially because I'm single."

"It's the way of the modern world, I guess."

"I'm not having this baby for anyone but myself," Lina said defensively, feeling the need to justify herself. "But it seems to me if I have the love to give a baby and the resources to raise it, that ought to be enough. I dearly love children, and I intend to try my best to be a good mother. This was not a decision I made lightly."

"I'm sure you'd have a lot more to give it than some couples," Mary said.

"It's not selfish to want a child of your own to love," she said, her eyes welling up.

"Of course it's not."

"Your daughter needed to go to the clinic to have a baby," Lina said, choking back her tears. "If she'd been single, her desire to be a mother wouldn't have been any less pure or worthwhile."

"No, it wouldn't. And I'd have supported her," Mary said.

"Which is worse," Lina said, her emotion growing out of control, "a child being raised by a single mother or never coming into the world to begin with? Isn't the gift of life worth something?"

Lina wasn't sure who she was arguing with or against. It wasn't Mary Carson. But she'd fallen into the grip of emotion, a deep frustration and pain that seemed to rise out of nowhere. Normally she wasn't like this, but ever since she'd gotten pregnant—and especially since she'd gotten that call from the nurse at the clinic—her emotions were hardly her own. Unable to help herself, she began to sob into her hands.

Mary got up from her chair and sat on the sofa next to her, putting a comforting arm around her shoulders. Lina scarcely knew the woman. She was Webb's ally, not hers. But except for Zara and one or two other friends, Mary was the first woman Lina had bared her soul to—certainly the first older woman, the first mother figure. Turning, she sobbed on Mary's shoulder as the woman rubbed her back. After a minute or so Lina regained control of herself.

"I'm sorry, Mrs. Carson," she said, taking a tissue from her purse. "I'm not myself anymore."

Mary patted her cheek. "You're under a lot of stress, honey. And you're alone. I know what that's like."

Lina blew her nose. "My mother died when I was in college," she said. "The last time I cried on anybody's shoulder was when I went to see her at the hospital." She sniffled. "It's been fifteen years."

"It's been a while since I had a girl to cry on this shoulder of mine," Mary said, her own eyes shimmering.

"My tears aren't Karen's, Mrs. Carson, but I do appreciate you lending your shoulder."

The woman reached out and took Lina in her arms and the two of them hugged—virtual strangers, but united by a series of tragedies. "I'd appreciate it if you called me Mary," the older woman murmured.

"And you call me Lina."

The front door flew open just then. Both women turned to see Webb standing in the doorway. There was consternation and surprise on his face, which began to soften when he saw Lina dab her eyes.

"I saw your car out front," he said, glancing around the room. "Did you come back alone?"

Lina sat upright, summoning her dignity, embarrassed at having been caught crying. "Yes," she said. "After dropping my father off at the airport, I decided there were some things I needed to say. So I came back."

"Your father did a pretty thorough job of stating your case. I know exactly where you're coming from. I don't think there was any point in your returning."

"Dad overstated my case," she replied. "I didn't intend for it to get confrontational."

Webb took off his hat and closed the door. He hung his hat on the peg, then took off his jacket, hanging it up, as well. He sauntered over and dropped into the chair opposite them. His cheeks were rosy from riding in the cool evening air and he smelled of the outdoors—of pine and earth and horse. He gave Lina a long, level look that was part disbelieving and part challenging.

"Are you saying he wasn't speaking for you?" he asked.

"No, I knew generally what he intended. I guess I wasn't expecting him to be so heavy-handed."

"Don't you mean you expected me to buckle under the pressure, and when you saw I couldn't be bought or threatened, you had second thoughts?"

"Webb," Mary said, interjecting, "Lina's come here to smooth over hard feelings. The least you can do is hear her out."

"No, that's all right, Mary," Lina said. "He's got a right to be angry. I would be in his shoes."

"Well, that's something, I guess," Webb said. "When I saw your car out front, I thought maybe you'd come back to throw a new pickup into the deal. I'm glad it's to apologize, because I'd have thrown you out of here on your ear."

"Webb!" Mary said.

"Mary," he said, his voice growing stern, "I know you're good-hearted and a peacemaker, but I think I can handle this alone."

Lina noticed Mary bristle, but the last thing she wanted was to be the cause of ill will between them. She quickly jumped in. "I came to apologize," she told him. "And not just for my father, but for myself. I allowed it to happen and take full responsibility. After talking to Mary I'm aware of the depth of your feelings and I regret the threats and insults."

"Apology accepted. And I want to apologize to you both for coming in here loaded for bear. It didn't help matters."

"Everybody has good intentions now," Mary said. "That's a first step for solving any problem."

Webb nodded, his blue eyes resting on Lina. She could see he was still skeptical, but he appeared less hostile than when he first arrived. He rubbed his jaw.

"So, what are you proposing to do?" he asked.

Lina lowered her eyes. "I don't know," she said, wringing her hands unconsciously. "It seems to me we ought to be able to work out something we can both live with. I understand how you'd feel possessive of a baby you and Karen made. But it's also important you realize I'm not the bad guy in this," she said, her voice more imploring than she intended. "I thought I was being impregnated with the embryo of a willing donor."

"Yes," he said, "I'm aware of that."

"My point is, we both have equities."

"I can see that, too. But what does it mean? That we cut the baby in half?"

The pain of anguish went through her, though now it wasn't so much because of his hostility as because of his frustration and pain—feelings she could easily identify with. What she was really seeing was her own hopelessness reflected in his expression.

There was an uncomfortable silence. Mary, next to her, was holding her tongue. Webb was censoring his thoughts. Lina almost felt as though she'd explode. But this stalemate couldn't go on forever.

"Though you probably don't like looking at it this way, Webb," she said, "I'm the baby's birth mother. It certainly won't be aware of any biological distinction."

"So?"

"So it clearly will be dependent on me, the same as any other baby on its mother."

"Surrogate mothers have babies and turn them over to the people who are going to raise them," he said.

"I am *not* a surrogate mother!" she snapped. "And please don't try to characterize me that way. I did not get pregnant with the idea of giving this baby up. And you might as well know I have no intention of doing so!"

"All right, then," he returned, his voice equally firm, "let's get right to the point. What *are* you proposing? Visitation rights?"

"Is that so unreasonable?"

"What are we talking? Once a week for an hour? Once a month? A week each summer?"

"I don't know!" she cried. "I haven't gotten that far."

"Well, it makes a hell of a difference," he said, getting to his feet. He began pacing. "Put the shoe on the other foot. Say *I* take the baby home from the hospital and *you* get to see it once a week or once a month. Is that the kind of compromise you have in mind?"

Lina was so angry she was again on the verge of tears, though mostly out of frustration. "You know damned well it isn't,'' she said through her teeth, fighting to restrain herself. ''That isn't what I signed up for.''

''Well, I didn't sign up for anything! That baby was intended for my wife and my wife alone!''

Lina began shaking she was so angry. Mary rubbed her shoulder.

''Webb,'' she said, ''there's no need to raise your voice. It isn't Lina's fault. Don't you see she's just as anxious and upset as you are?''

Lina sniffled despite herself. She quickly dabbed her eyes and looked over at Webb, who was squeezing the bridge of his nose, his head lowered.

''I'm sorry,'' he said in a low voice. ''This seems to be going from bad to worse.''

It was an impossible situation. Taking her purse, Lina stood up. ''I don't think there's anything we can accomplish today,'' she said. ''We're obviously too emotional about it. I don't know if that'll ever change, but I don't see any point in putting us through more of this now.''

''Look, I'm really sorry,'' he said.

''No, don't apologize. We both have honest feelings. We're both innocent. And we're not really enemies. We just happen to want the same thing.'' She looked down at Mary and extended her hand. ''Thank you for being understanding,'' she said. ''If it's convenient, drop by my shop sometime. I'd love to see more of your work.''

''I will,'' Mary said.

''My shop's called Bébé, and it's located in the Hyman Avenue Mall, a couple of blocks above Main.''

''I know where that is,'' Mary replied.

''I'm there almost all the time.''

Mary nodded.

Webb had moved near the door and was looking down, rubbing the side of his face as she approached.

''I'm sorry about this,'' she said. ''I guess I did more harm than good by coming back.''

"No, that's not true."

"Well, I don't know what's left to do but think some more. Let me know if you get any bright ideas."

She reached for the door handle and Webb took her arm, stopping her. He engaged her eyes, his own intense, more determined than hard. "I admire you for coming back here," he said. "It took guts."

"I'm not brave," she said, her voice low like his. "I just care about this baby."

Her eyes began to fill again and she bit her lip, hating this consuming emotion that seemed to control her completely. She again tried to reach for the door handle, but Webb hadn't yet let go of her.

"We'll find a way," he said.

She looked into his eyes, deciding his words were prompted more by a desire to be constructive than out of a conviction that there was a solution. Still, she appreciated any sign of goodwill. "I hope so," she said.

"Webb," Mary called to him, "it's getting dark out. Maybe you'd better walk Lina to her car. There's no lighting to speak of and we don't want her falling."

"I'll be okay," Lina told her.

"Webb, walk her to the car," Mary insisted.

He took his jacket and hat from their hooks. Then he flipped on the porch light and they went outside. There was some light in the western sky, but stars were already shining and the path leading to the BMW was in deep shadow. Webb took her elbow as they moved over the uneven ground.

They'd gone a ways and he still hadn't spoken. She felt the need to say something.

"Mary's awfully nice."

"The two of you seemed to hit it off," he said.

"We have something in common. I lost a mother and she lost a daughter." She'd said it before thinking, afraid the comment might somehow hurt Webb.

"Since you and I met, I've been thinking about Karen more than I have in months," he said.

Lina wasn't sure she understood his point. "I suppose that's natural," she said. "All the talk about the baby is bound to bring back memories."

Webb was silent, but he still had a firm grip on her elbow. When she made a misstep, stumbling slightly, his strong hand supported her. A bit farther on, they came to the car.

"It's not because of the talk about the baby," he said.

Lina turned to face him. There was just enough light that she could see his handsome face under the brim of his hat. Her mother's quip about a cowboy's hat came to mind. Webb Harper's hat seemed awfully large to her just then.

"It's you," he said.

Lina didn't know what he meant. "Me?"

"It's not the baby, it's you," he added. "And that's a compliment."

He opened the car door for her and she climbed in. He didn't close it right away, though.

"I don't go to Aspen often," he said. "But I thought I might head that way sometime later in the week. If I do, can I come by your shop and see you?"

"Sure."

"Maybe if it's around lunchtime, we can have a bite to eat."

"That would be good."

She waited, but Webb seemed not to want to close the door.

"You take care of that baby now, you hear?" he finally said.

Lina nodded. Webb surprised her then by reaching out and brushing her cheek with the back of his fingers. Then he slammed the door shut and took a step back. The shadows were deep enough now that she could only make out the contours of his face, but she could imagine his expression easily enough. He wasn't smiling—of that she was quite certain.

She started the engine, backed the car around, then headed down the drive. The last time she glanced in the mirror, Webb Harper was still standing there, as immutable as a mountain.

CHAPTER SIX

WEBB LAY IN BED, staring at the darkness. The last time he'd checked the luminous dial on the clock it was nearly three in the morning. Wakefulness in the night was nothing new; he'd never been a very good sleeper, especially when he was carrying burdens.

Of late his sleeplessness had seemed more onerous, though he hadn't dealt with it well for a long, long time. When Karen was still with him and he'd lain awake like this—worrying about money or how a late winter storm would affect his stock—her soft breathing would be a comfort. Sometimes he'd put his foot against the bottom of hers or lay his hand on her thigh, just to make a connection with her—one that wouldn't wake her but would still give him a measure of peace.

Karen's baby was a worry to him, but so was Lina Prescott. In fact, the woman made him anxious. He was strongly attracted to her, but he wasn't sure if it was because of the baby or because of her. Whatever the reason, it left him uncomfortable, perhaps because he didn't understand what was happening.

Growing tired of tossing and turning, he finally climbed out of bed and went to the kitchen to warm some milk in hopes that would help him sleep. Karen would sometimes awaken in the night and find him at the kitchen table reading, or at the window, looking at the moon, and she'd fix him a cup of warm milk and take him back to bed. Oh, how he wished she were here now. When they were together, he'd never doubted anything. His feelings were always unambiguous.

As he stood at the stove, stirring the milk with a wooden spoon, he heard a sound behind him and he turned, expecting, for some inexplicable reason, to see Karen in her nightgown. But there was no one. Perhaps the house had creaked in the wind or he'd been visited by Karen's spirit, if only in his imagination. "What should I do, honey?" he said aloud. "That's our baby. Yours and mine."

To Webb, a piece of Karen was alive in that child. There was no way he could abandon it. Ever. That had to be what Karen was telling him, what she wanted. But how would he accomplish it? And what did he do about Carolina Prescott?

Webb walked around the house while he drank his milk. His mind kept turning. One moment he'd be in conversation with Karen, the next he'd be debating with himself. Then he'd be talking to Lina.

The feel of her cheek when he'd brushed it with his fingers was burned into his brain. He remembered the way she'd looked up at him, vulnerable and uncertain, in the final moment before he'd closed the door and sent her on her way.

When he'd finished his milk, he returned to his bed and the single pillow. For a few weeks after Karen had died, he'd kept her pillow in the bed, unable to part with it because it still smelled of her. But finally he'd put it away. That was the way he'd let go of her—one little piece at a time.

Webb was relieved when sleep finally crept up on him, but he couldn't let go of Karen and Lina. They were both right there, following him into sleep—Karen his silent companion, Lina the beauty with the china doll face and coal black hair. Lina, the woman with his baby in her body.

Some hours later he awakened from a sexy dream and found himself in his bed alone, his heart tripping, the first light of dawn coming in the window. Only moments earlier he'd been at that spot in the woods where he and Karen used to go, but he hadn't been with her this time, he'd been with Carolina Prescott, making love on one of Mary's hand-sewn quilts.

Lina's skin had been so smooth and soft that he'd been afraid to touch it with his rough hands. But she'd excited him and he'd taken her enthusiastically, though he had sensed her reluctance and fear. She hadn't resisted him, but she did keep calling out Karen's name. And then he woke up, both anxious and sexually aroused.

No interpretation of the dream was necessary. It had been about conflict and guilt and it left him feeling just terrible. Yet, nowhere in the dream had he felt Karen's wrath or disappointment. Lina was his problem, not hers. Karen was silent and absent, though the dream was full of reminders of her. It had happened at their place in the woods, on Mary's quilt, with Lina calling Karen's name. Curiously, it had been a call for help, as though Lina expected Karen to come to her rescue.

Webb got up and went to put water for coffee on the stove to boil. He wanted to forget the dream and worry about his day. There was plenty to keep him busy without adding Lina Prescott to the list.

LINA HAD SLEPT IN LATE, having gotten her first good sleep in weeks, and was about to climb into the shower when the phone rang. Quickly wrapping a towel around her, she went back into her bedroom and grabbed the phone. It was her father, calling from the ranch. He'd already been out for his morning ride and had breakfast when he decided to see how things had gone with Webb. She gave him an abbreviated account.

"I'm sure he was nice about it, Lina," her father said. "The longer he's able to keep you at bay, the better for him. He's going to play you for the fool if he possibly can."

"Oh, Daddy, why do you have to see everything as a battle? Hasn't it once occurred to you that Webb might want to resolve this amicably as much as I do?"

"Sure he does, as long as it's on his terms."

Lina rolled her eyes. "You may be right," she said, "but I'd rather be optimistic. I'm going to give him the benefit of the doubt, and I'm also going to work to find a mutually acceptable solution."

"I wish you luck, sweetheart, but I don't think it's going to happen. I got a feel for the man yesterday, had a good look at his heart. He's determined."

"He was determined not to let you blow him out of the saddle," she said. "But that was your doing as much as his. I'd like to think he's going to react positively to my constructive approach."

"Carolina," Morgan said, "nothing would please me more than if I was dead wrong about the man."

"I appreciate your saying that, Dad. So let's leave it at that, shall we? I'll keep you posted, but there's no need for you to concern yourself anymore."

"I get your message," he said.

Morgan Prescott sounded more compliant than was usual for him. Lina wanted to think it was a result of the maturing of their relationship, but with her father, she could never be sure.

"Oh, by the way," Morgan said, "I got a rather surprising call last evening, one you'd find interesting."

"Really? From who?"

"Kyle Girard."

"Kyle?" Lina was surprised. Her father rarely mentioned her former husband, though she was aware that the two of them had stayed in contact. "He phoned from London, did he?"

"No, from Denver. He's in town on family business and

wanted to see if I'd have dinner with him. Tracked me down here at the ranch."

"That's nice," she said casually. "I know how fond you always were of him."

"We haven't seen much of each other lately, but I see no reason why we shouldn't."

"Of course not," Lina said. "You certainly don't need permission from me."

"I assume then that you have no problem with the fact I updated Kyle on things going on in your life," Morgan said.

Lina was beginning to smell a rat. "You mean like the fact that I'm pregnant?"

"For example."

"I don't care what you told him as long as you don't plan to involve me," she said. "As you know, I haven't seen Kyle since the divorce and I have no desire to do so now...just in case you're getting any ideas."

"Hmm," Morgan said.

Lina could tell by his reaction that something was afoot. "All right," she said, "out with it. What have you done?"

"Nothing to get your dander up about, sweetheart. Kyle and I had a nice chat, mostly about business. Then we got to talking about family and he asked me how you were doing. It was natural enough and polite all around."

"And so you told him I was pregnant."

"Well, yes. It's true, isn't it? If you'd gotten married, or broken your leg, I'd have mentioned that, too."

"Is there a point to this story?" she asked, getting a bit annoyed.

"Some of it will be of interest to you, the rest won't," Morgan replied. "I invited Kyle up to the ranch to go fishing with me."

"That part's not of interest to me," she said. "Get to the other part."

"Well, he's driving up, so I suggested he swing by Aspen and say hello to you. I figured since he's going to be in the neighborhood, why not?''

"Daddy, you didn't!''

"Yes, I did. What's the harm?''

"The harm is I have no desire to see Kyle Girard. He's not in my life for a reason. I think that ought to be obvious, even to you!''

"Hold on, young lady. Before you go off half-cocked, you might as well hear the rest. Kyle and his second wife have been separated for a year and they recently decided to go through with the divorce.''

"Oh, great,'' she said. "That's even worse. It was always a relief to me that he'd remarried.''

Lina began pacing, adjusting the towel at her breasts. She had no doubt that Kyle and her father had worked out an elaborate plan, probably based on the fact that she was in a vulnerable situation. What could be better? Little Lina is pregnant, doesn't have a husband and is being manipulated by this unscrupulous, fortune-hunting cowboy.

"I fail to see why you're so upset,'' her father said. "Surely you aren't afraid of Kyle. It's not like there was a lot of bad blood between you, even during the divorce. As I recall, you both behaved like mature adults.''

"Yes, but I have no desire to see him. Don't you see, when a part of your life is over, dead and buried, it makes no sense to resurrect it.''

"Even for old times' sake?''

"*Especially* for old times' sake.''

"Well, what's done is done,'' her father said, sounding disgusted. "When Kyle shows up this afternoon, you can politely tell him to get lost. I'm sure he can take it.''

Lina was not at all pleased. Her father knew damned well she wouldn't be rude. She could only hope that Kyle would have the sense to see she had no interest in socializing with him. With luck, she might get through it with no greater inconvenience than a few minutes of polite conversation. With luck!

"I'm glad you at least warned me," she said. "It would have been very annoying if he'd just showed up."

"Kyle specifically asked me to warn you. He's really a decent fella, Lina. And if you kept an open mind, you might find he's not as objectionable as he used to be. You've both grown up and lived some. You might even like him."

"Daddy, that's enough. You've had your little victory. I'll say hello to Kyle and that's that. But I want your promise you won't do this again. It's really very inconsiderate."

"All right, I promise."

"I honestly don't know how Mother put up with you all those years. I wish she'd told me her secret before she died."

"Your mother figured out early on that the best way to deal with me is to let me have my way—most of the time. She'd put her foot down on certain issues, but not many."

"Modern women aren't so indulgent," she said.

"And they wonder why there's so much divorce. That's the reason, Lina. The way to be happy is to find a good man and let him take care of you."

"That's *your* formula for happiness, Dad. In the past women didn't have a lot of choice."

"What good's choice if you end up alone?"

"Dad, I think we're on the verge of an argument and I don't have time. I've got to get to the shop."

"I didn't mean to be contentious, sweetheart. Maybe I'm feeling a little frustration myself. Things have been a little slow for me of late."

"What? Morgan Prescott doesn't have them knocking down his door? What's this world coming to?"

"There are plenty of gals out there in love with my money, Lina. But there just aren't many good old-fashioned ones left who appreciate a man for what he is."

Lina suddenly had an idea. "Well, I happen to have an

acquaintance, a widow, who's really very decent and sweet and would probably find a gruff old bear like you a tolerable date—if you think you're serious about finding an old-fashioned girl.''

"Who?"

"A lady I met recently. She may do some needlework for my shop. She's not the type you take to the opera, but she's an attractive country girl of sixty-something with a good heart.''

"Hmm. I'm having trouble picturing my daughter fixing me up.''

"Well, give it some thought and sometime when you're in town maybe I'll invite her over for coffee and cake.''

"I suppose after you agreeing to see Kyle it's the least I can do.''

"Goodbye, Father. I'm getting into the shower.''

Lina hung up, then hurried back to the bath. Despite the bomb her father had dropped, it had been a reasonably successful phone call. It was one of the most adult-to-adult conversations they'd had in years. And she was happy to have thought about fixing him up with Mary Carson, though she had doubts he'd care much for a real down-home type of woman anymore. But if her dad had any sense, he'd see that somebody like Mary would understand the rancher mentality, unlike the forty-five and fifty-year-old socialites who only understood his bank account.

As she shampooed her hair, she groaned at the thought of having to indulge Kyle. He should have known better than to agree to such a thing, though it could have been that her father had twisted his arm a little, too. She could only hope he wasn't coming to gloat. "So, Lina, I understand you have opted for artificial insemination. I trust that's a commentary on the quality of the male population around here, not on you. From what I can see you still have your charms.'' Kyle Girard was prone to be glib and even sarcastic when it suited him, but she couldn't believe his intent was to give her a bad time. When he'd married that Englishwoman with the title, he'd made sure the word got back to Denver, so it was hard to tell what he had in mind. One thing was certain, though—she wouldn't cut him much slack.

After rinsing off with the hand spray, Lina stepped out of the shower stall and dried herself with the big fluffy bath sheet. Turning sideways, she checked her tummy in the mirror. No easily discernable signs of pregnancy, though her nipples were definitely different. The doctor said she could often tell if a patient was pregnant just by examining her nipples.

Sighing, Lina got out the hair dryer and ran a comb through her hair, examining her face. Her cheeks were rosy, but that could have been from her shower as much as from the healthy glow of pregnancy.

Her pregnancy. Funny, but it almost didn't seem hers anymore. What had begun as such a joyful experience now made her apprehensive and uncertain. And Webb Harper had her completely confused. One minute he seemed ready to take her scalp, and the next, the compassion he showed bordered on tenderness. She'd thought a lot about the way he'd touched her cheek and told her it was a compliment that she made him think of his wife. Considering the way he apparently felt about Karen, it *was* a compliment. But surely he didn't mean to say he was thinking of her in the same terms. It had to be that because she was carrying Karen's baby, he felt a special tenderness toward her.

Checking the clock, Lina saw that she was going to be late. It wouldn't be the end of the world if the shop didn't open on time, but she tried to be conscientious. She was, after all, a serious businesswoman. A businesswoman who, at the moment, just happened to be pregnant and mixed up in a crazy custody battle with a handsome cowboy who had her befuddled and confused. Not to mention the fact that her ex-husband was about to pay her an unwelcome visit. Other than that, life was grand!

WEBB HAD SPENT four hours cleaning the barn. He'd stripped off his shirt; he was hot and had been perspiring heavily. He'd worked hard, going at it like a demon, getting a blister or two under his calluses in the process. Stretching his sore back, he lifted the wheelbarrow and ran out the last load of manure, dumping it on the pile. Then he went back inside the barn and filled his drinking cup with water from the spigot. He gulped it down. Filling the cup again, he dumped the water over his head, splashing more water on his face. Then he went outside, dropping down on the rickety bench against the side of the barn. He sat there, his face turned up to the warm sun, catching his breath.

Every once in a while he'd get possessed like this and throw himself into a job until he was sweating blood, ready to collapse. It had happened the day after Karen had told him she was pregnant, and also the day he'd sold the place to Cord Stewart. What had set him off now was the imbroglio he'd gotten into with Carolina Prescott.

This time Webb wasn't completely sure what he was running from or running to, but as he had worked, he'd been fighting back recollections of that dream of his, hating himself for having it, and alternately wanting to embrace Lina Prescott and admonish her for confusing his feelings.

He thought about the way Mary was always saying that he needed to find himself a woman. Then, the next minute, he'd be resenting Lina for tempting him. As the hours had worn on, he'd come to realize he didn't so much fear Lina because she was a woman and he desired her, but rather because she was resurrecting a life he'd already buried.

As he'd raked and shoveled and tossed bales of hay, his mind spinning like a top, Webb had gradually come to realize that he couldn't deny his attraction to Lina Prescott. He had to accept it as a fact and he had to find a way to let her know how he felt. Unless he did that, their relationship would remain confused and there'd be no way they could ever sort out the mess they were in.

Webb was the type who, once he'd made up his mind about a thing, wanted to act on it. He wasn't going to wait any longer; he was going to get into his truck and drive to Aspen and tell her what he thought.

Grabbing his shirt from the fence, Webb headed to the house. Squinting up at the sun, he saw that it was approaching its zenith. That meant he'd make it into Aspen by one or so. Too late to take her to lunch, but he could still talk to her.

Walking with purposeful strides, his fatigue half forgotten, Webb was amazed at how lighthearted he felt. That was the funny thing about taking action—the agonizing beforehand, making the decision, was always the hardest part. Doing the thing could almost seem easy.

CHAPTER SEVEN

IT HAD BEEN A slow morning. Lina managed to get the storage room straightened and only had to come out to help customers four or five times. The good news was, she'd gotten a lot of work done in back. The bad news was she'd only made two sales, though one was a $160 bassinet.

The mail had come a few minutes earlier, and Lina was going through it when the front door opened and she looked up to see Kyle Girard. True, she had been forewarned, but a wave of discomfort—the remembrance of things unpleasant—went through her just the same. Kyle was the symbol of a largely unhappy period in her life, a reminder of the person she'd once been and didn't much like. Kyle, the man to whom she'd once pledged her love, only to discover he was empty and shallow and alien, had returned.

"Lina, darling, how are you?" he greeted her as he made his way to the back of the shop, his voice faintly accented by the years he'd spent in Britain. He wore wool trousers, a long-sleeve dress shirt with an ascot and carried a tweed sport coat over his arm.

"Hello, Kyle," she said, coming round the counter to greet him.

Lina offered her hand, but Kyle, presumptuous as ever, brushed past it. Taking her shoulders, he kissed her cheek. He smelled of cologne and pipe tobacco. He was flushed, probably from the afternoon heat, and there was a light sheen of perspiration on his brow and lip. "Terribly good to see you," he said. "I trust Morgan told you I was coming."

"Yes, Daddy called this morning to say you were on the way."

Kyle stepped back and looked at her. "I'm so glad you didn't object, but I told Morgan if there was any reluctance on your part, I wouldn't come."

Lina smiled thinly. Her father hadn't mentioned she had an option, but that was like him, too, presenting people with a fait accompli whenever possible. "I saw no harm in saying hello," she said, straining to be gracious.

Kyle was looking her over. He still had a lean, angular handsome demeanor that—because of his years in Europe probably—seemed even more affected than when he was just the golden son of one of Colorado's wealthier families. Now he was Oxford rather than Dartmouth, Saville Row rather than Barney's in New York.

"Oh, but don't you look marvelous, Lina," he observed. "The picture of health. And for good reason, as I understand it."

"As good a reason as there is, I suppose," she replied with a laugh.

"Well, good for you. I couldn't be happier for you!" He beamed. "Truly!" With that, he stepped forward and gathered her in his arms like an elder brother, catching Lina completely off guard.

Just then the bell on the front door jingled again. Lina and Kyle both turned to see a cowboy filling the door frame, his hat pulled down over eyes that were full of surprise. It was Webb Harper and he didn't look pleased.

"Hello, Webb," Lina said, stepping clear of Kyle's embrace. She moved toward the door, where Webb stood motionless. It was obvious he thought he'd walked in on an intimate moment.

"Sorry to interrupt," he mumbled in a low voice that

wasn't particularly apologetic. "I'll catch you another time."

"No, don't go, I want you to meet someone."

He looked past her at Kyle. "No, really, I just happened to be in town and thought I'd say hello."

Lina didn't want him to leave with the impression she knew he had and she was determined that he stay. She took his arm. "Then come say hello to my former husband."

Webb peered back at Kyle again. "Husband?"

"My ex."

She started dragging him toward Kyle, who'd somehow gotten a jaunty expression on his face and struck a pose. "Kyle," she said as they approached, "meet Webb Harper." Then, to Webb, "My former husband, Kyle Girard, presently of London, England. It still is London, isn't it, Kyle?"

"We...that is I...have a house in Surrey, actually. But it's just outside of London. How do you do, Mr. Harper?" he said, taking Webb's hand.

"Nice to meet you," Webb grumbled. He'd taken off his hat and stood holding it in front of him, looking very uncomfortable, much as he had that first day he'd come to her house.

"Webb's the father of my child, Kyle," she told him cheerfully. "Though I didn't realize it at the time, it turns out he lives just down the road a ways."

"Oh, really?" Kyle said.

He was retaining his aplomb, though she knew he'd been thrown completely off balance by Webb's unexpected arrival. Lina realized she was glad and hoped it might deflate Kyle a little.

"How terribly modern," Kyle commented, giving them both a supercilious look. "I didn't know it was done that way."

"It isn't normally," she said, taking Webb's arm, "but we met and now we're friends."

Kyle arched a brow. "Smashing.... Um, I mean, that's great."

"You're sounding awfully British, Kyle," she said. "Is it intentional or are you trying not to?"

"Sorry," he replied, smiling sheepishly. "It's habit. After seven years abroad and being married to an Englishwoman it's not easily avoided.... But I expect after a fortnight...um...that is, a couple of weeks here in Colorado, I'll sound as genuine as Mr. Harper."

Lina chuckled but Webb shifted uncomfortably. She squeezed his arm.

"I never recall seeing you in a Stetson, Kyle," she said. "Have you ever owned one?"

Kyle Girard frowned, looking uncomfortable. "Perhaps as a boy." He fiddled with his ascot, running his finger under it. Finally he loosened it and pulled it off his neck altogether, stuffing it in the pocket of his jacket. "I'd forgotten how bloody hot it could get here," he muttered, his pasty skin turning red, "even up in the Rockies."

"A few days of fishing with Dad and you'll get acclimated again," she said. Lina turned to Webb. "Kyle's on his way to my father's ranch to do a little fishing."

Kyle grinned. "I told Morgan the fly fishing in Scotland was incomparable, and he insisted I visit a few of my father's favorite spots with him before rushing judgment." Then, arching a brow, he asked, "Do you fish, Mr. Harper?"

"I have," Webb replied.

"Webb is a reader," Lina told him. "He has quite an impressive library."

"Ah," Kyle said. "You collect, then, do you, Mr. Harper?"

"Sort of. I specialize in paperbacks from the secondhand bookstore."

Kyle grinned. "Charming." He glanced around the shop, then turned his attention back to them. "I'd only just ar-

rived when you did, Mr. Harper. My intention was to invite
Carolina to have lunch with me. Perhaps you'd care to join
us."

"Well, I..."

"You see, Kyle," Lina said, jumping in, "Webb and I
already had plans for lunch. He's come by so we can discuss arrangements for the baby. I don't know whether
Daddy mentioned it, but there were some paperwork snafus
at the clinic and we're having to sort them out."

"I believe Morgan mentioned there were anomalies."

"That's putting it mildly. But maybe we can do lunch
another trip. Do you expect to be coming back to Colorado
very often?"

"Only as family business requires. The bulk of our business is in Europe these days, which means I'll spend most
of my time there. However, this is a combination holiday
and business trip and I will be around awhile longer. Perhaps..."

"You know, Kyle," she interrupted, "I'll be blunt. I
really think we'd both be better off looking ahead instead
of back."

Kyle appeared a bit stunned but smoothly recovered. "I
take your point, Lina. Well, it seems you and Mr. Harper
have business to attend to, and I still have quite a drive
ahead of me. Perhaps I'll be shoving off."

"It was nice that you came by to say hello," Lina said.
She offered him her hand.

Kyle shook it self-consciously. Then he shook hands
with Webb. Kyle put on his jacket. "All the best to you
both, and good luck with the little nipper!"

"Catch a lot of fish," Lina said.

Kyle nodded, then beat a hasty retreat toward the door.
Lina didn't let go of Webb's arm until her former husband
was out of sight. "Whew!" she said. "That was tedious.
Thanks for coming along when you did."

"You were really married to that guy?" Webb asked.

"In a previous life. But Kyle wasn't quite so stuffy in those days. He was just as much of a bore, though. Give me credit, Webb. I *did* divorce him." Lina stepped over to the counter and leaned against it, facing him.

Webb was all cleaned up, like the first time she'd seen him. There was a little nick on his chin from shaving, though in a different spot from before. If his expression was sober, it was more ponderous than critical. His eyes did look tired, but his slightly rumpled good looks affected her more powerfully than ever. A little shiver went through her as his eyes deliberately slid down her body.

Expecting Kyle, but not Webb, she'd dressed more plainly, but the father of her child did not look disappointed by what he saw. If anything, he appeared as though he might like to touch her cheek again.

"So," Lina said when he hadn't spoken, "can I take you to lunch?"

"You haven't eaten? I thought you said that to get rid of Kyle."

"I did want to get rid of him. And I did have a yogurt and snack bar around eleven-thirty. But these days I seem to be able to eat at the drop of a hat. I'm eating for two, don't forget."

Webb's eyes got glossy, and she could tell he was wrestling with some demon. He was there—his eyes focused on her—but at the same time he seemed to be somewhere else. Maybe, as she'd surmised, he was struggling with his memories of his wife.

"I wanted to talk to you about something," he said.

"Okay. Is over lunch all right?"

"If I can pay."

"No, Webb, this is *my* town. When you visit here, you're my guest. When we meet in your neck of the woods, it can be your treat."

He did not look pleased.

"Come on," she said. "Don't be grumpy. If we're going

to talk about the baby, which is what I assume you're here for, we've got to be in a positive frame of mind. Just let me close the shop.''

Without waiting for a reply, she went back to turn off the lights and get her purse. Webb wandered toward the door, pausing as he went to look at some of the baby things on the display tables. Lina watched him from the back of the shop, realizing once again that he was a man of tremendous passion, a passion she found mesmerizing.

WEBB STOOD IN THE SHADE of the tree-lined mall, resting his booted foot on a bench as he waited for Lina to finish with the customer who'd come in just as they were about to leave. Behind him, water babbled in the tiny brook that meandered along what had once been the middle of Hyman Avenue. Most of the mall was already in shadow and the air had begun to cool. That was the thing about altitude— once you were out of the sun, the ambient temperature could quickly drop.

A group of tourists strolled by, three couples in their late thirties or early forties, wearing shorts, sweatshirts from eastern colleges and shiny white athletic shoes. They glanced at him, probably wondering whether he was for real or in costume. What they couldn't know was that he didn't have much of anything else to wear. The one suit he owned was so badly out of style that he looked like a hick in it, and the clothes he'd bought since the onset of his financial problems had to be work clothes—either that, or he'd have ended up pitching hay in a polo shirt.

He hadn't known what to make of Kyle Girard. Lina no more looked like she belonged with him than with the man in the moon—which was probably why they wound up getting divorced. As for the uncommon friendliness she'd showed toward him, Webb figured it was calculated to be a message to Kyle. But he didn't mind being used that way if it helped her out, though he'd rather her friendliness was real.

The worst thing about Girard being there was it had thrown Webb off his game. Opening the door to her shop, he was all but ready to tell her he was deeply attracted to her—maybe even enough to eventually fall in love with her—before reality had intervened. Kyle Girard might have been an oddity, a snob who sounded more British than a real Englishman, but Lina had once been married to a toned-down version of the same guy. Webb knew her old man had a jillion bucks and that she'd been to college. Maybe he was kidding himself by thinking they had anything in common—apart from the baby, that is.

Webb waved his hand at a swarm of gnats and began to reconsider what he was going to say to Lina. He didn't like feeling unsure of himself, but he'd found that living a solitary life—going days at a time without talking to another living soul—a person's view of things could get sort of twisted. Maybe he'd lost all perspective. Maybe if he were smart he'd climb back into his truck and get his butt back to the ranch. But just then, Lina and her customer came out the door of the shop. The two women said goodbye and, while Lina locked the door, Webb ambled over to her.

"I'm sorry about that, Webb," she said as they started walking east along the brick walk. "Liz Nelson's a long-time customer with enough children and grandchildren to single-handedly keep me in clover."

"Oh, I understand," he said. "Business is business."

"Is Rudy's okay for lunch?" she asked. "It's not very elegant, I know, but I've been having this terrible craving for pizza lately."

Webb chuckled. "Karen had a craving for pizza when she was pregnant, too."

"Normally, I'm not big on pizza," she admitted.

"Same with her."

"How funny. Do you suppose we've made some kind of breakthrough in genetics?" she quipped.

Webb shrugged. "Could be. Have any other cravings?"

"This sounds terrible," she answered, "but sauerkraut, kiwi fruit and bananas."

He shook his head. "No, with Karen it was blueberry pie and cranberry sauce."

"Actually, blueberry pie sounds good," she said with a laugh.

"Maybe you're carrying a girl instead of a boy like Karen was," Webb mused, getting into the spirit of the conversation.

"Maybe so."

Webb worried that quipping about her pregnancy might have been the wrong thing to do—considering it had been such a problem between them. When she looked up at the blue sky and changed the subject, he realized he was right.

"Pretty autumn day, isn't it?" she observed.

"Yeah, sure is."

"Much as I love to ski, I think I still like fall best."

"And summers," Webb said.

They walked along in silence for a while.

He searched for something upbeat to say. "You seem in good spirits today. Was it seeing your ex?"

"Lord no. Just the opposite. If I feel good, it's because he's gone. My father—who will rot in hell for it—set the thing up. I'm just glad you came along when you did."

Webb reflected. "You get credit for divorcing him, but what I don't understand is why you married him in the first place—not that he wouldn't be right for some girl, somewhere. Maybe what I'm saying is, since I can't see it, is it me?"

They'd come to Galena Street and turned right, heading up the hill.

"No, it's not you, Webb. Picture a girl of twenty-one being asked to marry one of the most eligible, wealthiest young men in Colorado. And Kyle wasn't the only one who wanted us to marry—my father, his father, all our friends were for it. They expected it.''

"I guess I don't move in those kinds of circles."

"To be fair, Kyle had his charms, though I know it was hard to see them when he was doing his Prince Charles routine. He had what I thought at the time was a good sense of humor. And I took his glibness to be maturity.''

"Erase the past. If you had it to do over again…"

"I'm afraid I'd tell him to go to hell.''

"Which is sort of what you did today,'' he said.

"Better late than never,'' she said with a laugh.

They fell into another self-conscious silence, then Lina surprised him by taking his arm again. "Tell the truth, Webb, did you just happen to be in town and drop by to say hello?''

"No, I came specifically to see you.''

They turned onto Cooper Avenue.

"Dare I ask why?''

"Since yesterday I've done a lot of thinking about you and the baby.''

"And?''

"I don't have any proposals or anything,'' he said. "But I think you're a very nice person. I like you a whole lot, and I felt kind of bad about how things have gone till now. I'd really like to work this out.''

"That's a very sweet thing to say.''

"I'm not just trying to be diplomatic, Lina,'' he confessed, feeling a well of emotion. They'd come to Rudy's and stopped on the sidewalk as a couple of in-line skaters zipped past. "I haven't had much to do with women since Karen and…well…I feel different about you.''

"I'm carrying your baby, Webb.''

"That's part of it, probably, but it's not all.''

She was looking up at him, and he got the same feeling he'd had when they'd said goodbye the night before. She had such a soft, delicate beauty. And today, after seeing her with Kyle Girard, he understood her appeal better. She was a princess, whether she'd rejected Prince Charles or not. It was no mystery why Kyle wanted her. Or why *he* did. The woman touched his soul.

"What's the other part?" she asked, waiting.

A kid on a bicycle came flying by, followed by a skateboarder, who hit a bump in the walk and went flying just as he reached them. He was a small kid, not more than ten, but at that speed he was a missile. When his shoulder caught Lina in the arm, he almost knocked her over. Webb reached out, catching her.

The boy went tumbling and landed in a heap. As he slowly got to his feet, his face contorted in pain, it was apparent he'd scraped his arm and leg. Webb started to go over to help him up, but the kid, sensing he was in hot water, grabbed his skateboard and hobbled up the street. Webb started to holler after him to watch where the hell he was going because there were old people, small children and pregnant women everywhere, but he realized it would do no good. Instead, he went back to Lina, who was shaken but otherwise seemed all right.

"You okay?" he asked with concern.

"I'm fine."

Webb searched her eyes to satisfy himself it was true.

"And so's the baby," she said with a little laugh, "so don't look so worried."

Webb ducked his head. "I'm concerned for you both."

Lina took a deep breath. "Smell that pizza, Webb? If you don't want me going delirious with hunger, you'd better get me inside so I can order some."

"Suppose they have any kiwi fruit?" he asked, taking her arm.

"I have a hunch I'm going to have to make do with pizza."

LINA RETURNED FROM the bathroom to find Webb had already drunk half his mug of beer. He still wore that intense expression that hovered midway between engrossed and preoccupied. She'd never known a man like Webb Harper and certainly never felt such energies so profoundly directed at her. She still wasn't entirely sure why he'd come to see her and what it was he had to say, but she chose to take the fact that he was there as a good sign. A compliment of sorts.

"Still no pizza?" she said.

"No. I almost told them the well-being of a woman and a baby was riding on this, but I figured it wouldn't help."

"Pizza making, like pregnancy, moves at its own pace," she said.

He smiled broadly, revealing strong white teeth. Smiling was something he didn't do enough as far as Lina was concerned. He needed to relax more. It would help his disposition. And hers.

"Are you always so serious?" she asked him.

"Fate toughened me up when I was still in the cradle," he replied, drawing on his beer. "Orphans, they say, aren't as jolly as most folks."

"You didn't know your parents at all?"

Webb pushed his hat onto the back of his head. "Nope. Never laid eyes on either one of them."

"What happened to your father?"

"He was a high stepper passing through town. About all my mother knew about him was that his name was Wes Harper and he was from Nevada—assuming he gave her the right information."

"Have you ever tried to find him?"

"I made a halfhearted attempt when I was sixteen, but decided it was more painful than was justified."

"Did he even know you exist?"

"I don't know. My guess is not."

Lina could see it was a history that helped define the

man. And considering what had happened to his own wife and child, he'd certainly had his share of tragedy. Maybe it was a miracle he was as normal as he was.

She sipped the Diet Pepsi she'd ordered and looked into Webb Harper's eyes. She'd learned what his married life was like from Mary, but she'd seen no evidence of that portrait of the wild cowboy her father had painted, apart from Webb's native appeal. It was hard to tell whether it was something she could ask him about, though.

"I hope that's not pity I see in your eyes," he said.

Lina shook her head. "No. Just the opposite, I was wondering about the secret Webb Harper, the one you keep carefully hidden."

"There is no secret Webb Harper," he said. "The one you see is the one that exists."

"Oh, I'm not so sure about that. My spies tell me you're quite the ladies' man, having left a trail of broken hearts all across central Colorado."

A little smile curved the corner of his mouth, and he gave her the look of a man habituated to leaving broken hearts in his wake. "Your spies are still living in the era of the Cold War. I admit to a reputation, but it was all earned in my bachelor days."

"It's all past tense, in other words?"

"Ancient history," he said.

"I hear the ladies don't regard you with the same disdain you apparently have for them."

"A reputation's not easy to live down."

"You once cut a pretty wide swath, then."

Webb turned his beer glass in his hand. "I started out as my father's son, Lina. Let's put it that way."

"I can see why," she said, feeling brave. "You have your qualities."

"I'm more content with the new Webb Harper," he stated.

"The one that protects pregnant women from roaming bands of skateboarders?"

"For example."

"You have the soul of a protector. You must have been an awfully good husband and father."

"I tried," he said, his eyes shimmering.

Their pizza came, and for Lina it was none too soon, though she'd found their conversation very revealing. She immediately tore off a piece, and Webb watched with pleasure as she chewed it happily. He was smiling again, and she liked that. What she didn't know was if he was seeing her or Karen. That was the great imponderable. She suspected Webb was as confused about it as she.

"Can I ask you a blunt question?" she said between bites.

He shrugged as if to say, why not?

"If I weren't pregnant with your kid and we'd met someplace, say here at Rudy's, would you have looked at me twice?"

"Looked at you? Of course. You're a beautiful woman, Lina. Losing Karen didn't make me a eunuch."

"Would you have asked me out if we'd gotten acquainted?"

"You're talking now, not in my bachelor days."

"Yeah, right now."

He looked deep into her eyes, his head canted inquiringly. He seemed to be honoring her question with serious consideration. "I'd like to say yes," he finally murmured.

"But you aren't sure."

"I know you differently, Lina."

She took another bite of pizza, chewing deliberately as she gazed back at him with the same intensity with which he gazed at her. "I admire your honesty, even if it's not entirely flattering."

"Let me turn the question around," he said. "Would the woman who was once married to that lord-of-the-manor chap who dropped by today have given this two-bit cowboy the time of day?''

"You mean if I weren't pregnant with your child and we happened to meet?''

"Yeah. Say you were sitting here having pizza and I slid right into the booth with you, half a glass of beer in my hand and said, 'Hi, sugar, what's up?' ''

"Well, if that was your opening line, I'd probably have asked you to leave.''

"I've got news for you, Lina. The most clever line in the world wouldn't have made a difference.''

"How can you be so sure?'' she asked.

"What would be the point? You aren't a party girl.''

"That's true. So what do you think I am?''

"A regular, decent person. A grown-up woman.''

"And you don't think a person like that would be interested in you?'' she said.

He contemplated her. For a long time. "What are you trying to say, Lina?''

She lowered her eyes, embarrassed. "I guess what I'm getting at is that it would be nice if we could relate to each other as people and not as parents in competition for the same kid.'' That was only part of what she was feeling, but it was the part she could safely say aloud.

Webb took an extralong draw on his beer, nearly finishing the glass. "You're right,'' he agreed. "It would be nice.''

Lina took another piece of pizza, insisting that Webb have some. He reluctantly took a piece and ate without enthusiasm. He seemed once again to have withdrawn into himself. She worried that maybe she'd been too forward. After all, Webb was a man with deep scars.

When she'd finished the last of the pizza, Lina picked up the check and they went to the cashier. Webb seemed uncomfortable as she paid the bill. His pride was obviously hurt.

"You have to realize that modern women are independent," she said as they went out the door. "They invite men to lunch and they pay. The days of guys doing everything are over."

"I guess I'm behind the times, then," he said.

"Maybe you're behind the times in a lot of respects."

"Could be."

Lina sensed that an air of caution had returned to their relationship. She wasn't sure why, exactly, unless it was that their mutual expressions of goodwill hadn't really changed anything. They were willing to cooperate with each other, true, but they were essentially right back where they'd begun. Neither spoke until they'd reached Hyman Mall.

"So where do you think we are, Webb?" she asked.

"That's still the problem, isn't it?"

It was a cryptic comment, but it told her he'd come to the same conclusion. They were still circling the airport, but eventually they would run out of fuel. Hard decisions would have to be made.

When they came to her shop, they stopped. Lina felt self-conscious, and she could see that Webb did, as well. She got her key ring out of her purse.

"I think the next step is for one of us to come up with a formal proposal," she suggested. "If you like, I can discuss it with my attorney. Maybe if we got something down on paper for you to look at..."

"That would be fine," he said.

"I'm sure you have someone you could take it to."

He nodded. "Yeah."

"I'd like to think that two people of goodwill can come up with a mutually acceptable solution."

"Perhaps," he answered.

Webb had been looking at the ground more than at her. Lina couldn't be sure what the hitch was, unless he'd come to the conclusion that they had an insurmountable problem.

She was determined, though, to leave things on a positive note.

"Thanks for coming, Webb," she said. "And thanks for rescuing me from Kyle."

That quirky smile touched his lips, though it was a watered-down version. "Just happened to be in the right place at the right time."

Lina reached out and touched his shoulder as she might a friend's. Then, on an impulse, she stepped forward and kissed him on the cheek. Webb seemed taken by surprise at her gesture but was clearly pleased.

"I'll be in touch," she said.

"'Bye, Lina."

Webb turned and ambled up the street. She watched him for a moment or two, then, sighing, went inside. First, she turned on the lights, then went to the counter with the cash register, noticing that she hadn't finished going through the mail. She'd been opening it when Kyle had arrived.

Sitting on the stool behind the counter, she shuffled through the remaining pieces until she came across a letter from the director of the clinic in Denver. She hastily tore the envelope open. It stated that errors had been made in the administrative process in connection with her pregnancy, that the proper permission forms had not been obtained from the donors of the embryo. Without admitting liability, the clinic proposed to remedy the situation by performing an abortion on her fetus and, at a subsequent time, performing as many embryo implantation procedures as necessary to ensure a successful pregnancy and the delivery of a healthy child, all at no expense. She would receive damages in the amount of a hundred thousand dollars for her suffering and inconvenience.

Lina was astounded. Abort her baby? What did they think it was, a mechanical toy? And what about Webb? For a moment she considered running after him, but then she decided nothing was to be gained. The first thing she

needed to do was take the letter to Zara. The legal intri-
cacies she didn't understand, but it was becoming clear that
even if she and Webb were having trouble getting off the
dime, the clinic might end up forcing their hand.

CHAPTER EIGHT

MARY CARSON AWOKE EARLY, had her usual breakfast of toast and coffee, then searched her closet for her most businesslike attire, finally settling on the tailored black dress she usually wore to funerals. The symbolism didn't particularly appeal to her, but she wanted to look as professional as she could when she drove into Aspen to see Lina.

Mary had tried not to get too excited about Lina's invitation to bring samples of her needlework by the shop, because she knew it could lead to nothing. But in truth, she had thought of little else. As soon as she got home from Webb's the afternoon she had met Lina, she'd dug through her cedar chest, where she'd kept Robbie's things, in search of baby clothes that were representative of her work.

The items that were worn she'd had to eliminate, but she'd found four pieces that were presentable, yet showed a range of style and design. She included an embroidered smocked dress she'd recently made for a friend's granddaughter. The items had been laid out on her dining room table since the night before, and she'd carefully looked them over twice that morning, worrying that they wouldn't be up to Lina's standards.

Mary had spent most of the previous day sketching items she had either made in the past or planned to make, reasoning that would give Lina more to choose from—if she felt the workmanship was adequate. Of course, she knew it was possible Lina would decide against ordering anything at all. And, though that would be a disappointment, she had prepared herself for the eventuality. It was flattering, she told herself, just to be asked to bring her work in. If things didn't pan out...well, nothing ventured, nothing gained.

Mary wasn't sure whether to phone first or just drop in. She finally decided to drop in, as it seemed less eager. The last thing she wanted was to make Lina worry about disappointing her. Good relations between them were important, if only for Webb's sake.

Once she'd had her bath and dressed, Mary got a large department store box she'd used for keepsakes down from the shelf in her closet, emptied the contents onto the bed and took it to the dining table. Then, using tissue paper, she carefully wrapped each of the five items and placed them in the box. She had no idea how a professional handicraft person would display her wares, but this seemed a reasonable method.

Having packed the box, she tied it up with some bright red cord, got her purse and checked to make sure she had her car keys. Then she got her wool coat from the closet. According to the weather report, the Indian summer they'd been enjoying was about to end and a cold front was due to move in. Mary had noticed the house was quite cold when she'd gotten up that morning and, though it wasn't the first time she'd had the heat on that fall, it seemed to take a lot longer to get the temperature up to seventy where she liked it.

After putting on her coat and turning off the heat, Mary headed for her car. She put her box in the back seat, then got in. Just as she started backing out of the drive, she saw Webb's pickup coming down the road.

Mary knew he was coming to see her, so she turned off the engine. Webb stopped his truck on the shoulder of the road out front, then walked up the drive. He was wearing his sheepskin coat. Mary rolled down her window.

"Morning, Webb. What brings you to town this time of day?"

"I wanted your advice," he said, looking morose. "I guess I should have called before coming over. Are you headed for the store?"

"No, I'm driving up to Aspen to show Lina my needlework. Remember, she wanted to see it and maybe sell some pieces in her shop."

"Oh, yeah."

"Well, what is it you want advice about?"

Webb stared off in the distance, over the roof of the car. He rubbed his chin. "I got a letter from the clinic offering to settle."

"You mean they've admitted they screwed things up?"

"Yeah, I guess. But if you're in a hurry, I won't keep you."

"Don't be silly, Webb. This is more important. Get in the car."

Webb climbed in the passenger side, removing his hat so he'd fit. He looked glum. Mary had no idea what to expect.

"So, what did they say?"

He reached inside his coat and removed an envelope, handing it to her. Mary took out the letter and read.

"Five hundred thousand dollars," she said. "They want to give you five hundred thousand dollars?"

"If I'll either release my rights to the baby or let them off the hook," he said.

"Dear God. That's a lot of money, Webb."

He turned, looking at her with surprise. "You saying I should take their money and give up Karen's baby?"

"No, I'm not saying what you should do. I'm just saying that's a lot of money."

"I don't give a hang about money, Mary. What's got me confused is what this is really about."

"What do you mean?"

"I'm wondering if Lina put them up to this."

"Lina?"

"Or her old man."

"Why would they do such a thing?"

"To let the clinic buy the baby for them."

"But if you wouldn't take their money, why would you take the clinic's money? And besides, the letter says they'd pay you just to let them off the hook. That won't do Lina any good, will it?"

"That's what's got me confused," he said.

"Could be this has nothing to do with her. Maybe the clinic knows they got caught with their pants down and are trying to buy their way out of it quick and clean as they can."

"That's what I thought at first, but why would they want me to give up my rights to the baby if it weren't to help Lina?"

"I don't know," Mary admitted. "Seems to me, this may be over our heads. Maybe what you need to do is see a lawyer."

Webb nodded. "I've been thinking I probably should anyway. Lina's talking to her lawyer about it."

"How do you know?"

"I saw her yesterday. She's thinking of making some kind of formal settlement offer."

"I see."

The two of them sat pondering the situation, watching a couple of hay trucks pass by. Mary was beginning to see Webb's problem had even broader implications than she'd thought.

"Hold on," he said. "I think I know why they asked for a release on the baby. If I sign the papers, then Lina's got no complaint against them and they won't have to worry about her suing. That's what they'd really like—to get us both off their back at the same time."

"So maybe she's not mixed up in their offer after all," Mary said.

"Maybe."

"What are you going to do?"

"I think you're right about the lawyer. I'm going to give Harv Cooper a call."

"What about Lina?"

"If you're going to see her, maybe you can check out the situation for me," he said. "Tell her you understand I got a letter from the clinic and see how she reacts."

"I don't mind conveying a message," Mary said, "but I think you really should talk to her yourself."

Webb stroked his jaw. "You're probably right."

"Want to drive to Aspen with me?"

"No, I've got things to do. And besides, I was just there yesterday."

"I've got an idea," Mary said. "Why don't I invite her to dinner sometime soon? You can come, too."

He pondered that. "You think?"

"That would be a sociable way to handle it."

"You wouldn't mind, Mary?"

"Of course not. I'm fond of you both." She reached over and patted his hand. "The Lord sure does move in mysterious ways. Be honest, Webb. A month ago if I told you you'd be getting a letter from somebody who wanted to give you half a million dollars because of something you didn't even know had happened, wouldn't you have said I was crazy?"

"Sure I would."

"Lord knows where this business will end."

"There's one thing I know for sure, Mary. It won't end with me selling Karen's baby. There isn't enough money in the world for that. No way."

ZARA HAMILTON PUT DOWN the letter and took a sip of her iced tea. "The plot thickens," she said.

Lina stared at her friend, nodding.

They were in the dining room of the Hotel Jerome, one of the fine old historic buildings in Aspen. During ski season the place would be teaming with guests from all over the world, but in the tranquil period between summer and winter the atmosphere was actually serene. Spring and fall were the only times Lina ever ventured into the Jerome.

The day before, when Lina had gotten the letter from the clinic, Zara was in Boulder, so this was the first opportunity they'd had to discuss it. Lunch was the only free time Zara had the whole day.

"What do you make of it?" Lina asked.

"If you agreed to an abortion," Zara said, "it would make your conflict with Webb a moot issue. The clinic can satisfy you with another baby and give some cash for your trouble, thereby taking care of any liability they have to you."

"What about Webb?"

"That's an entirely different issue," Zara said. "They would be liable to him for damages caused by any negligence or wrongdoing in connection with the embryo. But that's not your problem. My guess is they fired off a letter to him with a settlement offer the same time they sent this. It's a smart move. Pay everybody off and move on. Besides, the abortion option won't be available forever."

"I'm not getting an abortion. We can put that one to rest right now. It's not as if I were buying a car and the first one was a lemon."

"That, of course, is entirely up to you, Lina."

"What about Webb?"

"If you mean concerning the abortion, the courts have been fairly clear that the father has no rights either to force an abortion or prevent one. It's the mother's body and her choice."

"But once my baby is born, all that goes out the window."

Zara nodded. "Strange as it may seem, after birth the father's rights are, generally speaking, equal to the mother's."

"And it doesn't matter that this baby is not genetically mine?"

A grimace crossed Zara's pretty face. "I've been researching the issue and I still haven't come up with a definitive answer. The question of the comparative rights of a birth mother without a genetic connection to a baby to those of a genetic parent have never come up before. In the surrogate mother cases, the birth mother is usually a genetic parent. And don't forget, surrogate mothers sign a contract. They go into the pregnancy knowing in advance that they are going to give up the baby. It can be argued that your situation is more like an adoption. You got pregnant with the expectation of keeping the child and rearing it as your own, just as an adoptive parent would."

"Never mind all the legal gobbledygook, Zara. Who would the court give my baby to if it came down to a legal battle?"

"The answer is, I don't know, because the issue has never been decided. But I've got to be honest with you, Lina. There tends to be a preference in the law for the genetic parent. Whether that holds up against a birth mother who's genetically unrelated, I just don't know. If we went to court, I'd argue that the woman who gives birth to a baby has greater equities than just an adoptive parent, but what the outcome would be is anybody's guess."

"You're saying if Webb and I ended up in court, he might win."

"I think it's a close case, but I might have to give him the edge. Keep in mind, though, that's based on preliminary research. That could change if I manage to turn something up in one of the surrogate mother cases I'm checking out."

Lina shivered with frustration. "Zara, no offense, but why is it that when we're talking law you insist on sounding like a lawyer?"

Zara smiled. "The answer speaks for itself. Law has its own language. And nothing in law—just as nothing in life—is an absolute certainty. Anyway, Lina, you know lawyers always cover their butts, even when talking to their friends.''

The waiter came with their lunches. Lina had ordered a fruit plate, pastries, a banana, blueberry pie and milk. Zara ordered a roast beef sandwich. She eyed the strange mélange of food in front of Lina.

"You're really going to eat all that stuff?''

"I get cravings," Lina told her. "Your time will come. Trust me.''

They ate for a while without conversation. Then Zara said, "I hate to sound like a lawyer while you're eating, but it occurs to me that the letter from the clinic might give you some leverage with Webb.''

"What do you mean?''

"You have the abortion option…''

"Zara, I could never even threaten such a thing. No, I wouldn't do that to Webb under any circumstances. He'd die.''

"Well, it's my responsibility to present all your options.''

"Let's put that one in the round file.''

"Okay.''

Lina was pleased that there was some kiwi fruit in the assortment on her plate. She happily munched on her banana while contemplating the blueberry pie. "I'll say one thing about pregnancy—every meal's an adventure," she said.

"Yeah," Zara replied. "You never know when you're going to get sick and throw up!''

"Very funny, Miss Hamilton.''

Zara pushed her strawberry blond hair back off her face, chuckling. Lina was glad she had someone she could confide in, but she wished she could be similarly helpful to Zara.

"You know," she said, "we're always talking about my

problems. I think you're entitled to equal time. I trust you and Alec are still on cloud nine.''

"Lina, I can't tell you how wonderful it's been. Believe it or not, we're already thinking about marriage.''

"He's asked you?''

"No, and I haven't asked him, either. But we've both made it clear we consider it a possibility. In a few days he's flying back to Martinique to make arrangements for his boat. Then he's returning to spend the holidays with me. He's already started exploring the possibility of opening a restaurant. We've looked at sites and he's meeting a banker today to discuss financing. It's preliminary, but that's the way things are headed.''

"Zara, that's wonderful! I couldn't be happier for you!''

The lawyer sighed. "Of course, it seems too good to be true, but there haven't been any rude awakenings. Alec's a dream." She smiled. "To be honest, I'm looking forward to our first argument so we can get it behind us.''

Lina laughed. "That's a good one! I'll have to remember that.''

"I'm not without my worries, though.''

"Oh?''

"My sister. I got a note saying she'd be dropping out of sight for a while, but I still haven't heard from her. I have no idea where she is or what she's doing. I've tried to reach her former fiancé a couple of times, but Mark has dropped out of sight, too. I'm kind of worried about them both. Alec thinks I should call her boss at the publishing house, but knowing Arianna, she'd hate to have me interfere.''

"You can't ignore the situation forever.''

"I know," Zara said. "That little taste of the Mafia I got in the Caribbean was enough to scare the you know what out of me. I hate to think Ari's going through anything like that.''

"At least you ended up with Alec.''

"I think Ari would rather find the book that made her career than the man of her dreams."

"Well," Lina said, "to each her own."

Zara smiled. "I guess if I'm going to worry, it should be about you. At least I have some control over what happens in your life."

"If you could figure out what's going on in that crazy cowboy's head, I'd be eternally grateful," Lina said.

Zara regarded her, an odd expression on her face. Finally she spoke. "You kind of like him, don't you?"

Lina munched on a pastry as she reflected. "In the abstract, Webb and I have nothing in common. Our backgrounds are very different, except for the fact that I grew up on a ranch. And there are similarities between Webb and my father, so it's not as if the guy's from outer space or anything."

"That's not all bad."

"It's not a question of good or bad. The point is, even with the problems we're facing, when I'm with him, I'm drawn to him. It's as if we connect at some fundamental level."

"You're obviously attracted to him."

"It's more than that, Zara. It's his heart, his spirit, his passion. In one respect he's just a cowboy, but at the same time he's so much more. Have you ever felt that way about anyone?"

Zara gave her a quizzical look.

"Silly question," Lina said. "It must be that way with Alec."

"Sometimes it seems magical."

Lina pushed her other plates away and pulled the blueberry pie in front of her. "You know where Webb and I are now?" she said. "We're both wondering how we'd feel about each other if the baby weren't a factor. We even talked about it in a roundabout way. If you can believe it, we were actually speculating on whether we'd have been friends if we'd met under normal circumstances.''

"You sound like two people who want each other," Zara said.

"The chemistry's there, no doubt about it."

Zara gave her a knowing look. "Maybe you've stumbled on a solution to your legal problem."

Lina chuckled. "If you're talking about a serious relationship, we're a long way from that."

"Don't laugh," Zara said. "Love has a way of sneaking up on you. Alec and I can attest to that."

Lina shivered. "I don't need that on top of everything else. Please, Zara, one thing at a time."

"*Au contraire,* Miss Prescott. Look at it from a practical standpoint. Why sue somebody if you can marry her?"

Lina, who was taking a drink of milk, nearly choked. She put down her glass and dabbed at her mouth with her napkin. "One more remark like that, counselor, and you're fired!"

As LINA MADE HER WAY the two short blocks from the Hotel Jerome to her shop, she zipped her parka up to her neck. It was amazing how in the course of hours, let alone days, the temperature could change so radically. Just yesterday people were running around town in shorts, and today the top of Aspen Mountain was dusted with snow and the biting wind was hinting at winter.

When Lina reached the Wheeler Opera House, she cut across the street to the west end of the open mall where Bébé was located. As she approached the shop, she spotted a customer standing under the sign, holding a big box. That usually meant a return. But then, when she got closer, she saw that it was Mary Carson.

"Mary," she said as she hurried up to her. "How good to see you!"

The woman looked relieved. "Guess I picked a bad time. I never thought about you being at lunch."

"During the slower seasons I just close up," Lina explained, taking her keys from her purse, "but during the busy season I have one or two extra salespeople and we take turns eating. It's amazing how many sales you can miss in an hour when the streets are full of potential customers."

"I bet."

Lina got the door open and they went inside. "Are those your samples?" she asked.

"Yes. I took you at your word."

"Oh, I'm thrilled you've come. I'm eager to see them."

Lina led the way back through the shop.

"I hope you aren't expecting too much," Mary said, sounding a little afraid.

"I know you do lovely work. The only question is if it's right for my shop. Why don't you put what you've got on the counter here," Lina said as she went past it. "I'll get the lights and turn the heat up a bit."

"It's gotten mighty chilly, hasn't it?"

Lina went into the back room. "They say we could have snow by the weekend."

"A real storm from what I hear."

Lina took off her parka and hung it up. She was wearing jeans and a sweater, but she still felt cold. Returning to the shop area, she rubbed her hands together. Mary had opened her box and lifted out a tiny green sweater trimmed with red. It had a hood. Lina examined it, oohing and aahing.

"Mary, this is gorgeous! Just darling!"

Next Mary unwrapped a blue-and-white crocheted baby blanket. Laying it on the counter, she ran her fingers over it lightly. Lina glanced at her and saw a stirring of emotion. Mary was clearly remembering.

"Karen loved this so much she didn't want to use it,"

she said, her voice trembling slightly. "They took it to Robbie's christening and that was it."

"I can see why. It's a lovely piece. Beautiful."

Mary continued to stare down at the blanket. "You know, sometimes it seems like they can't be gone. I look at this blanket and that day is so very clear. I can see the smile on Karen's face like it was just ten minutes ago."

Lina touched Mary's arm.

"Sorry," Mary said. "I usually don't do that."

The next item was a tiny yellow sweater with a matching cap. It only brought a sigh from Mary.

"Oh, can't you see this on a little one for his first ski season?" Lina exclaimed. "Adorable."

Mary handed her a white smocked dress with tiny pine-cones and holly embroidery. "I made this for a friend's grandbaby."

Lina gasped. "Oh, my," she gasped, examining the work closely. "Oh, Mary. I have to have this! I want it for my-self. This is precious." She held it, turning it front to back. "If you don't do another thing for me, make me one of these. You have to. I'll pay you right now!"

Mary laughed, her pensiveness gone. "You're convinced you're having a girl, are you?"

"No, actually I think it's a boy, but this is too delicious to pass up."

Mary Carson was clearly pleased.

"You do fabulous work, Mary. There's not a thing here I wouldn't proudly sell. The question is, how much can you do for me, how fast and at what price?"

Mary chuckled, now fully recovered. "Well, I can work fast when I put my mind to it. I suppose I could do two or three sweaters a week. The embroidery only takes an hour or two, depending on how elaborate it is. I can make a blanket in two or three days, depending."

"Hmm," Lina said, thinking. "There are various ways to do this. Sweaters like this made from top-grade imported yarns I can sell for between a $125 and $200. My markup's about fifty percent, give or take. If you didn't want to invest in materials, I could buy the yarn and pay you, say, fifty to sixty dollars for the work, depending on the item.''

''For a tiny little sweater like this?''

''You do beautiful work, Mary.''

''I had no idea.''

''There's less profit potential in the embroidery and crocheted items. I already carry some plain smocked dresses that I buy at a very reasonable price. I doubt it would be worth your while to compete. You *could* do the embroidery on the pieces I have, though. For something like this one with the pinecones and holly I could pay, say, $20 to $25.''

''That's two hours' work.''

''The question is, would ten to twelve dollars an hour be worth your trouble?''

''When you've done it for next to nothing your whole life, Lina, that sounds like a whole lot of money.''

''What do you think?''

''I'm ready to go to work!'' Mary said.

''Would you like me to provide the yarn?''

''That way you can pick the colors.''

''Let's start out that way, then,'' Lina said.

Mary showed Lina some drawings she'd done, and they spent some time discussing design and color. Lina wanted the first several items to be holiday-oriented. She got the plain white smocked dresses she had in stock and discussed how they might be embroidered. In addition to the pinecones and holly, they settled on a candy cane design that Mary sketched out.

Mary told her she was ignorant of how business was done, so Lina wrote out a price list and what they had agreed on for the various items and type of work. She also put down that she'd provide the yarn and the finished smocked dresses that were to be embroidered. Lina explained that Mary would be working as an independent contractor, which meant she was responsible for her own taxes and so forth.

"You'll want to keep records of your income and expenses," Lina told her.

"I can get Webb to help me with that," Mary said. "He was always good at the paperwork side of the ranching business." She laughed. "He always said his problem was income, not organization."

"Webb has had a lot of bad luck, hasn't he?" Lina asked.

"If ever there was a young man entitled to a good turn, it's him."

"There's an old Chinese saying—'Pain can be the midwife of joy.'"

"Don't believe I've ever heard that one before," Mary said.

"I just heard it recently. It was in a fortune cookie a friend gave me, as a matter of fact."

"That could apply to you and Webb both."

Lina nodded, thinking about her conversation with Webb the day before. She had been thinking about him a great deal. And unfortunately, her thoughts and emotions were always conflicted. "Webb's a very complex person, isn't he?" she said to Mary.

"There's a lot more to him than meets the eye," Mary allowed. "He sure is worrying about this baby. Suffering."

"How well I know the feeling."

"Situation's gotten messier, too. Just today he came by the house and showed me a letter he got from the clinic."

"Oh?"

"They want to buy him out. That's as good a way to put it as any, I guess. I told him he ought to discuss it with you, since you're both affected."

"What did Webb say to that?" Lina asked.

"He's willing. To be truthful, I think a goodly part of Webb's torment over this is you, Lina."

"Me? Really?"

"He knows you're in a tight spot, same as him. You might be on different sides in one way, but you're on the same side in another. You both care about that baby."

Lina nodded, remembering Zara's remark about marriage being an alternative to a lawsuit. She'd made it in jest, but fate did seem to be pushing her and Webb together in the strangest sort of way.

"In fact, I was thinking," Mary said. "If you see it in your interest to discuss what the clinic's up to, maybe the two of you could come to my place for dinner this weekend. You've been kind to me, Lina, and well, you know how fond I am of Webb."

"It's very sweet of you to offer."

As Mary refolded the samples, Lina thought of the letter she'd received from the clinic and wondered if it was something she should share with Webb. If Mary was able to speak for him—and Lina suspected she already had—he seemed willing to share. Maybe that was the tact to take.

"How's Saturday?" Mary said, placing the items back in the box. "You have any plans for Saturday night?"

Lina, who was still deep in thought, hadn't heard her. "Pardon? I'm sorry."

Mary repeated her invitation.

"Saturday's fine, Mary. I don't have any plans, no."

"Now isn't that a sad commentary," Mary said. "Two lovely young people like you and Webb and nothing to do on a Saturday night."

"Webb's in mourning and I'm pregnant."

"Sorry, but that's no excuse."

"I think Webb and I have too much on our minds to be concerned about socializing."

"You might be coming to discuss business, but I don't see how it would hurt to enjoy yourselves."

Lina reached out and put her hand on Mary's. "Mary

Carson, you aren't thinking of becoming a matchmaker, are you?''

The woman turned bright red. "Well," she sputtered, "not like you're thinkin'."

"How *are* you thinking?"

"I just like to see people happy," Mary said.

"You have a good heart."

"When it comes to other people, I reckon I'm an optimist."

"With a whole new career before you," Lina said, gesturing around the shop, "I think you have reason to be optimistic about yourself, as well."

Mary beamed. "I gotta admit, it's pretty exciting, Lina."

"I've got an idea! Why don't I see if I can get that yarn and bring it with me Saturday?"

"That would be great!"

"And if you like, you can take some of these smocked dresses now."

"I could have a couple finished to bring back with you!" Mary enthused.

Lina chuckled. "I think we're on the verge of a budding partnership."

Mary nodded happily. "Now if we can just get Webb on track…"

The door jingled and a couple of customers came in. Lina gave Mary a telling look. "If you're going to twist Webb's arm, discourage him from trying to take my baby away from me." With that, she went off to wait on her customers.

CHAPTER NINE

JUST SITTING IN Harv Cooper's law office brought back memories that Webb would prefer to forget. The lawyer had insisted on following through on the lawsuit against the trucker who'd killed Karen and Robbie, even after it looked as if there would be no money in it for him. "At some point it becomes a matter of principle," he'd said.

Webb himself had never had the heart for it, even when there was a prospect of collecting a substantial amount. Trying to put a value on what he'd lost almost seemed sacrilegious. Just the same, he'd gone through the miserable experience like a zombie, sitting in this very office, listening to Harv explain the law and try to get his agreement on a strategy or a decision. As often as not Webb had said, "Do what you think's best, Harv. I don't really care."

At the moment, the lawyer was leafing through some big legal book he'd taken off the shelf, his glasses pushed up in his white hair, his unshaven jaw frosted white. It was strange seeing Harv in a plaid wool shirt, but it was Saturday, and Harv never wore a coat and tie on Saturday, no matter what. The fact that he'd agreed to come in at all was testament to the importance he placed on the letter from the clinic. Webb had read it to him over the phone when he called him earlier in the week.

Webb glanced over at the lit gun case where Harv kept his prize collection. The walls were covered with hunting trophies, antlers, fish and other memorabilia from the lawyer's sporting life. "You'd better hope the animal rights folks never come to you for representation,'' Webb had once joked. "They might start out by suing their lawyer.'' Harv Cooper was definitely old-line, a throwback.

He closed the big book in front of him and leaned back in his chair. "According to Martindale-Hubble, Wilbur Hands, the attorney the clinic cc'd in their letter, is a partner in one of the big Denver firms, which is exactly what I suspected,'' Harv said. "This is no amateur production. If I had to guess, the carrier for their malpractice insurance is in on it, too. My nose tells me they're all lying in the bushes, waiting to see what happens.''

"Translate that into English, Harv.''

"They're offering half a million for a quick settlement, hoping you'll grab it and run. What it probably means is that they'll go to a million pretty damn quick and make you work hard for more than that.''

"Doesn't matter how high they go. I'm not giving away the baby.''

"The way I read this letter,'' Harv told him, "they're willing to settle with you even if you won't help them out with the woman.''

"She's the one I've got to settle with,'' Webb said. "The clinic's got no say on which of us gets the baby.''

"True,'' the lawyer agreed. "But they're holding the resources that could help decide the outcome.''

"What do you mean?''

Harv leaned back in his big maroon leather chair, folding his hands over his prominent stomach. "The woman's got family money. She's Morgan Prescott's daughter, right?''

"That's right.''

"Well, to beat 'em you need the law on your side and the money to buy the justice you're entitled to. A principal with a bank account always has an advantage in a protracted litigation. What I'm sayin', Webb, is that with a million bucks in your jeans, you're a different adversary.''

"You're saying I settle with the clinic and use the money to fight it out with the Prescotts if it comes to that."

"If it's the baby you want."

"It is."

"That's your strategy, then, son."

"I'm hoping Lina and I can work something out."

"Morgan Prescott's more likely to counsel compromise if he knows you have the resources for a fight. But if you're litigating with your Visa card, you're in trouble."

"Harv, they took my Visa card away years ago."

"You can bet the Prescotts know that."

Webb stroked his chin. He didn't want to think it would come to a fight, and he'd been encouraged by Lina's attitude, but if he'd learned anything in life, it was that it was better to prepare for a storm and hope it didn't hit than to get hit and wish you'd been prepared. "Tell, you what, Harv. Write the clinic and see if you can get the million in exchange for letting them off the hook. If I can put that much in the bank, then, as you say, I can deal with Morgan Prescott."

"I think that's a sound approach."

"Meanwhile, I'll do what I can to come to terms with Lina."

"It might not hurt for me to do a little research on that, as well. It'd be nice to know we've got a case."

"A court wouldn't give her the baby just because she's a woman, would it, Harv?"

"Those days are over, my friend, though I'm no expert on family law. However, I've got a niece in Denver who happens to be one of the state's leading experts on child custody matters. I'll give Gwen a call."

"Good, Harv." Webb slapped his knee and rose to his feet. "Well, I've got to get the hell out of here. There's a storm coming down from Canada and I've still got some strays up in the woods, not to mention a couple of heifers about to calve."

The lawyer grinned. "You had a bull jump the fence?"

"Pretty as you please, Harv."

"You seem to be suffering from a plague of unwanted pregnancies," the lawyer said, chortling.

"Hell of a sad tale," Webb agreed, putting on his sheepskin coat. "Especially for a man who hasn't so much as been on a date in six months."

"Maybe a million bucks will help ease the pain."

Webb put his hat on his head. "Only if it helps me keep that baby."

MARY CARSON GOT UP early and finished the last of the little smocked dresses. She'd done an extracareful job, wanting to make a good impression. She had worked on ten dresses altogether, and had averaged close to three hours on each. That meant she'd made less on an hourly basis than she'd planned, but considering she'd mostly worked for free or for a cake or pie in the past, any sort of paycheck would be welcome.

Lina had called Friday to say that she'd located top-quality yarn and that she'd be bringing it with her to dinner. Mary was thrilled. She was eager to start work.

Dinner was well in hand. She'd baked an apple pie and had marinated the pork roast with green peppercorns, garlic and rosemary. That left the vegetables and mashed potatoes, but she'd cook those last. Everything was in readiness except touch-up dusting and getting dressed. That meant she had three or four hours to kill.

Mary was nervous about having Lina over. Not that Lina had any pretensions or looked down her nose at her—on the contrary, she'd been very sweet. Mary felt a real warmth toward her. But no matter how much she tried to focus on their new business relationship, she couldn't forget that Lina was carrying her grandchild, her last link with Karen. And there was something else going on, too. But she was having trouble putting her finger on it.

As she sat in her favorite chair in her tidy little front room, listening to the rising wind whistling through the eaves of the house, she examined her feelings. There was the nervousness and excitement and something she hadn't felt in a long time—expectation. She was actually looking forward to something!

In recent years she'd spent most of her time looking to the past—back to a time when her daughter and grandson were living. Mary gazed at the case full of Karen's trophies and at the dozens of photos spread around the room. She had known for a long time that Webb didn't much like coming here because of all the mementos. She'd thought it was Webb who had the problem. But over the course of the past week, she'd come to realize that she was living in a shrine as much as a home. She wanted to have Karen and Robbie constantly around her, because that was all she had.

Mary had a friend, Jenny Carpenter, who had lost her son in a military training accident about the same time she'd lost Karen. They'd grieved together some, if only because they understood each other's pain. Jenny kept photos of Roy in her house, but she had long since put away his athletic trophies and the other personal memorabilia. Jenny still had her husband, and Mary had assumed that was the reason they "remembered" their dead children differently, but she was beginning to question that rationale. Maybe the real difference was that Jenny was looking ahead, not back.

Seeing Karen's pretty face in every direction she turned, Mary got all teary. For the first time, she felt herself pushing her child away—not with bitterness or resentment, simply with acceptance of the finality of death. She would love her daughter forever, but the truth was, Karen was gone.

When Mary looked at the room through Lina Prescott's eyes, she didn't see the image she wanted to project. She didn't want to invite Lina into her past, but rather into her present. Mary realized it was time to bury her daughter.

Mary spent the next few hours removing Karen's trophies and photographs and packing them away carefully in cardboard boxes she got from the attic. Even though it was long overdue, the task was not easy. She cried much of the time, sometimes sobbing when an item sparked a particularly poignant memory. And yet the exercise brought her a curious sense of peace. It almost seemed as though Karen herself was thanking her.

"Goodbye, baby," she muttered as she kissed a photo of Karen as a bride, then wrapped it in newspaper before placing it in the carton. "Oh, but how I remember that day," she said, sniffling.

There were four photos that Mary decided to keep out— Karen's high school graduation picture, a photograph of Karen and Webb on their wedding day, a picture of Robbie and a family photo of Karen, Webb and Robbie taken the Christmas before the accident. The baton twirling and beauty pageant trophies all went into boxes, except for the one Karen had gotten for being a finalist in the Miss Colorado contest. Mary filled the empty display case with the collection of crystal figurines she'd had in it before Karen and Robbie had been killed.

Once she'd finished, Mary glanced around the room. It looked as it had when she'd been living her own life— when she still had a future. And although it had been painful, Mary knew she'd done the right thing. Now she had a responsibility to help Webb make the same transformation. He was living with a ghost, and that wasn't right. True, he'd dealt with Karen's passing in a very different way than she had, but he still had not put the past behind him. Worse, this baby of his and Karen's might be doing him more harm than good, if only because it made him cling to Karen all the more.

The bright ray of hope was Carolina Prescott. In Lina, Mary had found a friend, a business partner and a sort of adoptive daughter. Of course it was a new relationship, but even if it ended in a week, Mary knew she'd benefited from it. The unknown was how Lina was affecting Webb. Mary sensed an affinity between them, but she knew Webb was fighting it. He'd deal with Lina the hard way. Like a stallion that didn't want to be broken, he'd fight to the end. That was his nature.

BY LATE AFTERNOON, when the first snow flurries had begun, Webb had completed the day's work. He'd scoured the high country and chased another dozen head of cattle down from the woods, including another pregnant heifer, bringing the total calving out of season to three. He found the carcass of a fourth that had died giving birth sometime during the past week. For a man whose herd was marginal to begin with, that was a painful loss. He couldn't help wondering if it could have been prevented if he'd spent more time in the saddle than running all over creation trying to straighten out the mess that damned clinic had gotten him into.

Although he couldn't blame Lina for what had happened, his feelings about her had figured prominently into the problem. He didn't want to be attracted to her, but he was. And she wasn't easy to put from his mind, though he tried that, too. Her physical appeal and the fact she was carrying Karen's baby was an explosive combination.

Once Webb got the strays into the fenced pasture in the bottom land, he counted the herd and came up with 372 head, three less than he'd had at the beginning of summer. He'd found the carcass of a heifer at the beginning of August and there was the one he'd spotted today. That left one unaccounted for. Either it had died in the brush or he had miscounted. All in all he was entering winter in decent shape, but he could hardly claim to be a serious cattleman. Three hundred-seventy head was fine for a hobbyist, but he needed double that to gross the fifty or sixty thousand a year he needed to survive. And that was assuming prices rebounded.

A reasonable man in his shoes would sell off and buy himself a truck tractor or something of the kind. Trucking was a hell of a life, but what would it matter if he was always on the road? There was nobody at home. That would be giving up, though, and Webb was not one to give up. As long as there was a valley to conquer and land to buy, he'd stay in the saddle until they pulled him down.

The million bucks Harv had talked about had been going through his mind as he'd ridden that afternoon, but Webb had already decided not to allow himself to be tempted by it. If he ever did collect the money—and experience had taught him to be a skeptic—he'd decided to earmark it for the baby, either by spending it to settle his differences with the Prescotts or to give the child a good life. That could include building up his holdings to have something to pass on, but the first order of business was to win.

To protect his feelings, if for no other reason, Webb had already discounted the offer Lina intended to bring him. He couldn't fathom her giving him more than some kind of visitation rights. And what could he offer her? Nothing she'd want. That was why as the week had progressed he'd gotten more pessimistic. True, there always seemed to be good vibrations when they were together, but that was only because they were both decent people. What the world didn't seem to understand was that his hands were tied by his obligation to Karen. It was, after all, her baby.

The last thing Webb needed to do before he went in and got cleaned up was take the pregnant heifer up to the barn with the other two. Getting them through calving and the winter was not going to be an easy task, but doing it right would mean six more head of cattle come spring.

After getting the heifer into the barn, Webb unsaddled his horse, brushed him down and cleaned the rocks and mud from Jake's shoes. Horses more than any other kind of livestock seemed to sense winter coming. All day, it was as though Jake had known this would be the last full day of work before spring and that he would have oats and a warm barn for the duration.

If Webb had made a shrewd business move that year, it had been the price he'd paid for his winter supply of hay. In September he had happened across a hay farmer on the highway with a broken-down semi. They'd made a deal on the spot for cash and Webb's agreement to unload right off the flatbed. It had taken a day of backbreaking labor and his rent money, but he'd gotten a hell of a deal. With Mary's influx of capital, he was good until spring calving. From there on, things were in the hands of fate.

LINA DIDN'T KNOW Carbondale. She'd passed the town on Route 82 numerous times, but in her mind it had never been more than an inconsequential cluster of buildings half a mile off the highway.

There'd been snow flurries most of the afternoon, but it had begun to snow in earnest shortly before she left. The weather report indicated they were in for a sizable storm but that the brunt of it wouldn't hit until midnight. She'd had her snow tires installed during the week and was confident the accumulation wouldn't be severe enough to pose a problem before she got home. Besides, the highway people were good about keeping 82 open—it was the only route of consequence in and out of town.

It was dark by the time Lina reached the outskirts of Carbondale. She'd already passed the turnoff to Webb's ranch, but since she'd allowed a margin for error, she'd be right on time—assuming Mary's place was as easy to find as it sounded from her directions.

When she reached the turnoff for Route 133, Lina exited the main highway, following the road into town. There wasn't much to see, but the modest houses looked warm and hospitable in the falling snow. She continued on as instructed, checking her odometer at the market so she could measure the six-tenths of a mile she had to go to Mary's place.

Slowing as she neared the half-mile mark, Lina looked for lights, finally spotting some coming from a little bungalow on the right, sitting a hundred feet or so off the road. She entered the drive as Mary had told her, stopping the BMW behind the old car parked near the house. There was no sign of Webb's pickup, so Lina figured she was the first to arrive. She hoped Mary would forgive her for not being fashionably late.

Climbing out of the BMW, Lina flipped up the hood of her red wool coat and went to the rear of the car. Opening the trunk, she removed the large basket of imported yarns, checking to make sure that the bottle of Chardonnay she'd tucked in a corner was okay. Closing the trunk, she made her way through the thin layer of snow to the porch. Just as she climbed the cement steps, the door opened. Mary Carson, a wide smile on her face, greeted her.

"Lina, honey, I'm so glad you're here. I've been worrying, with all the snow."

"The highway was clear. It wasn't bad at all."

"Here, let me take that," Mary said.

She took the basket and stepped back inside. Lina followed, closing the door.

"My land, look at all this beautiful yarn!" Mary exclaimed. "And what a pretty basket."

"The basket and the wine are a gift for you," Lina said.

"Aren't you sweet. Thank you."

"The yarn you have to turn into beautiful baby things."

"And it'll be a joy, believe me."

Mary put the basket down on a chair and told Lina to take off her coat.

"Don't you look cute in that!"

Lina smiled happily. "My Little Red Riding Hood look, Mary."

She put her purse down and slipped off the coat. Mary took it and admired her openly.

"Oh, you look so lovely."

Lina had done her hair in a French twist. She was wearing a black turtleneck, long-sleeve cashmere dress and knee-high black leather boots. Her only jewelry was a thin gold tank watch and gold hoop earrings.

It was one of her better days. Checking herself in the mirror before she'd left home, she'd seen that healthy glow people associated with pregnancy and she'd felt radiant. Her anticipation at seeing Webb had been building all week. Not that she knew what she expected, but she'd come to realize she had a very special feeling when she was with him. She wanted to know him better at the very least.

"Turn around so I can see you," Mary instructed.

Lina, beaming, did a model's turn, to Mary's delight. With Lina's red coat over her arm, she pressed her hands together prayerfully.

"It's so nice to have a beautiful young woman in my house again."

"You look pretty spiffy yourself," Lina said. "Is that a new outfit?"

Mary glanced down at her navy wool skirt and white satin blouse trimmed with fagoting. "Heavens, no. The blouse is eight or nine years old if it's a day. Karen was still living at home when I bought it. She was with me."

"You look pretty, Mary. I may be doing you no favors by mentioning this, but I've been thinking I'd like to introduce you to my father. Be warned, he fancies himself a real ladies' man—and in ways I suppose he is—but what he really needs for a friend is a nice lady like you."

"Aren't you sweet to say so," Mary said. "I'm flattered, Lina. I truly am."

They exchanged smiles.

"I'll just hang up your coat. Sit down. Make yourself at home."

Lina looked around the room. It was old-fashioned and homey. Actually it reminded her of the home of her father's longtime ranch foreman, Ben James, and his wife, Ella. There was a time during her difficult teens when Lina had been sent to Ella for lessons in the domestic arts. Her mother, the daughter of a prominent physician, had never been much for sewing, cooking, flower arranging and the like, and she had hoped that some of Ella's talents might rub off on Lina. The experiment had been a partial success.

Mary's framed photographs caught her eye. "Do you mind if I look at your pictures?"

"No, not at all."

Lina went to the long shelf where the pictures were arranged. The first was a photo of Karen, probably a high school graduation picture. She was exceedingly pretty, wholesome, bright-eyed, the perfect homecoming queen— a sparkling blonde with perfect white teeth, heart-shaped mouth and round, innocent brown eyes. The little locket around her neck said it all.

Lina moved on to the other pictures, lingering over the wedding photo of Webb and Karen. They looked very young, very happy and, of course, oblivious to the tragedy awaiting them. But instead of the brooding passion she associated with Webb, she saw a certain brashness. He'd married the prettiest girl within a hundred miles and he knew it.

Mary joined her. "Until this afternoon I had thirty or more pictures out. The room was crammed full of mementos of Karen and Robbie."

"You took them down?"

"Yep."

"Why, Mary?"

"Truthfully?"

Lina nodded.

"Because of you," Mary said.

"Me?"

"Because you got me to thinking about the future. I realized I'd been living in the past for too long. It was time to let Karen go, but I've been hanging on because I didn't know what else to do. This baby, and the work I'm going to be doing for you, changed things."

Mary's words touched her, and Lina got a lump in her throat. "I hope for the better," she croaked.

"Sometimes all it takes is a smiling face or a kind word to change a person's life. You've made a difference."

Lina couldn't help herself. She gave Mary a hug. They both got misty-eyed, holding hands as they looked at each other.

"Oh, I nearly forgot," Mary said. "I've got some little dresses to show you!"

"You do?"

Mary led her back into the bedroom, where she had the dresses spread out on the big, high double bed. Lina exclaimed at the work as she looked them over.

"These are perfect, just perfect. I know they're going to sell."

"I had a little extra time," Mary said, "so I made something for you." Going to the dresser, she took a small tissue-paper-wrapped bundle from the drawer and handed it to Lina.

"What's this?"

"Something you said you wanted."

Lina unwrapped it and found an embroidered dress identical to the one Mary had brought to the shop as a sample. "Oh, my!" Lina exclaimed. Then she gave Mary a hug. "Oh, thank you, thank you. It's adorable. Now I *have* to have a little girl."

Mary Carson beamed.

Lina held up the tiny garment, admiring it. She couldn't help wondering what Webb might think of Mary's gift, considering it made it seem as if his former mother-in-law were endorsing her claim to the baby. Lina wasn't about to comment on it, though. Mary had probably been thinking with her heart, not making a statement.

Lina hugged the little dress to her breast. "I just love it, Mary."

"Why don't I get these dresses boxed up so you can take them home with you?" Mary said.

"That would be great."

As Mary got a box, Lina glanced around the small room, noticing a photograph of a nice-looking man of fifty on the bedstand. She picked it up.

"Is this your husband?"

"Yes, that's Will. He passed on when Karen was in high school."

"What did he do?"

"Worked for the railroad for years. The last five he was a dispatcher with the power company. Honest man who cared for his family. Will enjoyed his beer and an occasional cigar, but he didn't have any serious vices. We had a good life together."

Lina put the photograph back on the bedstand. Mary went to work packing the dresses. Lina noticed the care with which she moved and her reverence for her work. She wondered if her father would appreciate the woman. As she watched Mary carefully folding the dresses, there was the sound of a vehicle out front.

"That'll be Webb," Mary said. "Would you mind letting him in, honey?"

Lina felt her heart bump. She'd been looking forward to this for several days, though with as much trepidation as expectation. The thing about Webb Harper was, she never knew quite what to expect.

The little dress still in her hand, she left the bedroom and got to the front door just as Webb knocked. Opening it, she found him on the porch, the collar of his sheepskin coat up around his ears, his hands thrust in his pockets, his hat pulled down over his eyes, the snow swirling around him.

Webb seemed stunned at the sight of her, though he had to know she was there, because her car was in the driveway. He took her in with one long, languorous look. Finally he mumbled something. It sounded like ''My God.''

CHAPTER TEN

SHE WAS THE MOST glamorous creature he'd ever seen, and he was so taken aback by the vision, he was stunned.

"Hi, Webb," she said.

He somehow managed to nod.

She canted her head. "Well, aren't you going to come in?"

"Yeah.... Hi, Lina." He stepped inside, removing his hat. He checked her out again, noticing she smelled wonderful, too. "You look nice," he said. "Real nice."

"Thank you."

Webb took off his coat.

"Can I take that for you?"

"No, I've got it," he said. "But thanks." He went to the closet and hung up his coat, wedging his hat in a corner. Then he turned, taking her in again, liking the sensuous curve of her hips, her long, booted legs.

Lina was sexy as hell in the dress, but in a refined way. Not blatant. With her hair up she looked elegant, but also younger, more vulnerable or something.

"I'd have dressed up more if I'd known you were going to get so...fixed up," he said. He had on clean jeans, his best boots and a freshly pressed Western dress shirt with pearlized buttons.

"You look fine, Webb. When a handsome man is cleaned up and neat it's ninety percent of the battle. Women aren't so lucky."

"That dress looks terrific," he said. "And I like your

hair that way. But you'd look good no matter what you had on.''

Lina smiled. "My, but aren't you full of compliments."

"Guess I've had myself for company too long," he said. "Sorry if I'm gushing."

"Go ahead and gush."

He grinned. It was only then he noticed something in her hand. "What's that you've got?"

Lina held up a little baby dress. "Mary made it for my...*our* baby."

They were just simple words, not offensive, not even a slip, really. But they were a sudden and pointed reminder of who the two of them were and what was between them. He nodded, trying not to look grim. "It's nice."

Lina hugged the little dress to her bosom as though she'd read his thoughts, heard the qualification in his voice, and taken exception. "It's adorable," she said.

"Where's Mary?"

"In her room. She'll be right out."

Webb glanced around, noticing that all the mementos and memorabilia were gone. "What's happened to the place?" he said.

"Mary said she'd done some rearranging."

"Rearranging? Hell, she's cleaned the place out."

Lina peered around the room. "You don't approve?"

"I don't know. I guess I'm just surprised. Never thought I'd see this."

"I figured it was time to let go, Webb." It was Mary. She was at the door, a big box in her arms.

Webb nodded. "I guess you have. A sudden hankering to put Karen behind you?"

"I reckon it's been building," she said, walking past them, across the room. "You never liked my mausoleum anyway." She put the box on the chair by the door.

"You didn't do this for my sake," he said.

"No, I expect I didn't."

Webb wasn't sure why he was disappointed—if disappointment was what he was feeling. Maybe he just didn't like change. Mary had always been predictable. They had chided each other some at the way the other had dealt with the loss of Karen and Robbie, but Webb had always considered it supportive concern on both their parts. Maybe this struck him as rash. Or maybe he didn't like it that Mary had made the baby dress for Lina.

"Well," Mary said, ending the uncomfortable silence, "why don't we sit down? No sense acting like strangers in a bus station. You sit there in the big chair, Lina."

"No, that looks more like a chair for Papa Bear," she said. "I'll sit on the sofa." She passed behind him, touching his arm as she went.

Webb stood there watching her, his arm tingling from her touch. She sat on the sofa, crossing her legs. Gawking the way he was, he felt like a rube, especially when she looked up and gave him a bemused smile.

"I'll get everyone a drink," Mary said. "Sit down, Webb. What can I get you, Lina?"

"You have any fruit juice?"

Webb sat in the big armchair.

"Apple," Mary said. "Or I can mix up some orange if you like that better."

"Apple's fine."

"Webb?"

He rubbed his jaw. "Beer…if you've got it."

"Lina brought a nice bottle of wine," Mary said. "I thought I'd have a glass, but I don't want to open it just for myself."

"Okay, then," he said, trying not to be annoyed, "I'll have a glass of wine."

"You can have beer if that's what you'd prefer."

"The wine's fine, Mary."

She started to respond, but thought better of it. After she'd gone Webb looked over at Lina, who was sitting up straight, yet still managed to look comfortable. He sat a little straighter himself. Lina had a pleasant smile on her face, and had smoothed the little dress over her knee. She glanced down at it as though the baby were there on her lap.

"Funny how women ask you what you want," he said, "but always end up telling what they would rather you have."

"I think it's because we want to please but we're smart enough to know that the only way we'll ever get what *we* want is to say what it is."

"Wouldn't it be easier just to say so in the first place instead of beating around the bush?"

"If we did that, we'd be accused of being bossy. This way it becomes a discussion with options. Mary would have brought you a beer if you'd insisted."

"And I'd have been insensitive and selfish if I'd let her."

She gave him a coy smile. "This way you can be a martyr, Webb."

"For somebody who wasn't married long, you've got men pretty well figured out, don't you?"

"I understood what Mary was thinking and why she said what she did. What it boiled down to was she wanted you to have a glass of wine with her. Didn't Karen ever do that?"

"I reckon so," he grumbled, not wanting to get into that. Webb realized he was in a testy mood, probably because he felt threatened. He sensed something in the air. A conspiracy, maybe. "You seem to be in pretty good spirits, Lina," he said, switching to the offensive. "What's happening with you?"

"I don't know. I've been in a good mood all day. Sometimes you just have good ones."

"Or bad."

"Yours has been rough, I gather."

Webb hadn't intended to get right into it, but his instinct

for male directness took over. "Today I lost a heifer and I talked to my attorney," he said. "For a cattleman, those are the makings of a bad day."

She hesitated as a thought crossed her mind. "You evidently didn't see the attorney about the heifer."

He shook his head. "No, it was about you."

"That explains your depression."

"No, Lina, what I meant was, I saw him about our problem. Mary told you I got a letter from the clinic offering to settle, didn't she?"

"Yes."

"Well, that's what I talked to Harv about."

Lina sighed, staring off. "I got a letter from the clinic myself."

"Oh?"

"Yes, I brought it thinking you might like to have a look at it. It's in my purse."

She set the baby dress aside and got up to retrieve her purse from the floor. Mary came in with a tray and three wineglasses. Lina got the letter and returned to the sofa. Mary held out the tray for her.

"This must be the apple juice," Lina observed, taking the glass that was darker in color.

Webb took one of the two remaining glasses. Mary took the last.

"Well," she said, "I propose we drink to this baby who's brought us together."

Webb and Lina exchanged glances, then lifted their glasses. Everybody drank.

"Good wine," Mary said. "Now if you two think you can find something to talk about, I'm going to finish getting dinner ready. We should eat in about twenty minutes."

She left. Lina handed Webb an envelope. Putting down his glass, he took out the letter and began to read.

LINA WATCHED NERVOUSLY as his eyes moved across the page. He read deliberately, the only indication of consternation a slight frown. When he'd finished, he handed back the letter and peered questioningly at her, as though what he wanted to know was obvious.

"I'm not having an abortion," she said. "And I'm not going to use it as a threat to exact concessions."

He seemed relieved. "I appreciate that."

"Webb," she said, "I've been giving this a lot of thought. I'd intended to come with a written proposal prepared by my lawyer—and I can still do that if you'd rather be formal about it—but I thought instead I'd run some ideas past you."

"Okay."

She drew a nervous breath, surprising herself at how tense she felt. "Say a few months ago we'd met at that pizza parlor in Aspen and I took you home with me and I ended up getting pregnant. Say it was just a fling and it didn't mean anything to either of us, but when I told you I was pregnant you said you were really into children and wanted to be in the baby's life." She looked into his eyes. "It seems to me the fairest way to resolve a situation like that is to split the expense and the time fifty-fifty, taking account of our respective ability to pay and of the needs and welfare of the child. Little babies, babies nursing, for example, need to be with their mothers more. As they get older, the time can be divided more equally."

"Is that what you're proposing, Lina?"

"Doesn't it make sense?"

"Lina, this baby is not the result of a one-night stand."

"I know. It's the result of a third party's mistake. And, understandably, you think of it as Karen's baby. I don't want to take that away from you. All I'm trying to do is be practical. If the problem had been dumped in our laps as a result of too much beer, we'd have to sweep fault and blame aside and find a solution."

Webb picked up his wineglass and took a drink. He

stared off, pondering. She waited. He continued to reflect. He took another sip of wine.

"Webb, you're being quiet and that's making me very nervous."

"I don't want to respond to your proposal," he said. "You make some good points and I admit you're trying to be fair. You're not playing games. I respect that."

"But you don't like the idea."

"No, that's not what I'm saying."

"What are you saying? Just spit it out. Please."

Webb drew in a long breath. "I'd like to think about it. I'd like to try it on for size and wear it for a while."

"Oh, great," she said, feeling deflated. "How long?"

"A week or two."

Lina considered that. She'd been hoping that he'd accept her offer in principle. What could be more fair than fifty-fifty? After all, she'd gone into this expecting to have one hundred percent of her child. "A week or two won't kill me, I suppose."

"I promise you I'll either accept your offer or have one of my own for you to consider."

She nodded. "That's fair." She took a big gulp of apple juice. "So, what did the clinic offer you, Webb?"

"Half a million dollars."

Lina's brows rose. "To take a hike?"

"Basically."

"I take it you've rejected the offer."

"I haven't accepted it," he said. "And I don't intend to."

He'd answered carefully, if without hesitation. The merchandiser in her said there was more to this bargain than she'd heard thus far. Webb hadn't said there was no deal he'd accept, just that he didn't intend to accept this one. That probably meant he was in negotiation—or at least exploring his options. Unless he had a fool for a lawyer, that's what he would have to be doing.

Lina picked up the little dress Mary had made for her and smoothed it on her lap, straightening the fabric with care. She could almost see a plump little two- or three-month-old baby in it, a little girl with a bow taped to her bald head, the way her mother had taped a bow her to her head in the first months of her life. The thought made her eyes shimmer, but when she looked up at Webb, she managed a pleasant smile.

"You aren't going to make me go through nine months of dreaming, then take her away from me, are you?"

He shook his head. "No."

"Really?"

"Really."

"That's something, I guess," she said with a laugh that was part sob.

Webb offered no further assurances. He seemed lost in his own thoughts and his own misery. It was as if they were condemned to a tug-of-war between trust and distrust, hope and despair. The struggle wouldn't be easy. It might even be disastrous.

WEBB DID HIS BEST to make nice the rest of the evening, but he'd never been very good at that sort of thing. Mostly he listened to Lina and Mary, though they both endeavored to include him in the conversation. There was a lot of talk about the baby and, without Mary actually saying so, Webb got the impression his former mother-in-law had signed on to Lina's plan.

He also discovered that the two of them had gotten pretty thick in the baby clothes business, which explained a lot. Not that Mary had sold out but, like Lina, she was taking a practical approach. Webb, though, had trouble seeing the problem in practical terms. There was principle involved, and there were feelings. And it was in the area of feelings that he had the most trouble. The baby, and the obligation he felt toward Karen, were complicated by the fact that he had feelings for Lina, too.

The attraction he felt toward her was nothing new, but the wrench in his gut that night was the strongest yet. Her beauty, her softness, got to him. He wanted to fight his feelings, but he couldn't deny them, couldn't control them—all of which added to his frustration.

"Webb," Mary said as they were having their coffee after dinner, "what's gotten into you? I might be boring, but I know Lina isn't."

"I'm just tired, Mary. I don't mean to be dull."

"I hope all that time you spend alone hasn't made you strange. The company's got to be an improvement over what you're used to, even if the food isn't."

"There's not a thing wrong with the food or the company," he said, glancing at Lina. "Two of the prettiest women I've seen in an age, and the best pie since the last one of yours I ate."

"You see, Lina," Mary said with a laugh, "you prod them and they eventually come around."

"Webb's got a lot on his mind," Lina said. "So do I. In fact, I've been worrying about the storm and the drive back to Aspen. I hate to eat and run, but maybe I should start on home before the roads get too bad."

"I hate to see you go, Lina, but I understand. And I expect you'll be worrying about your cattle, Webb."

"Yes, I should go, too."

Lina got up to clear the table. Webb started to get up to help, as well.

"You stay seated, honey," Mary told him. "You worked hard today. Besides, the kitchen's small and you'll just get in the way."

So Webb stayed at the table, sipped his lukewarm coffee and watched Lina in that knit dress moving around the kitchen. When she came back to the dining room for something, she favored him with a word or a smile, but mostly she was aloof.

He was coming to realize he was in torment over her, mainly because she was the first woman he'd wanted since Karen. He wanted to put his hands on her body and kiss her mouth. He wanted to feel her softness. He wanted to possess her.

When she and Mary returned for the last time, Webb went into the front room to get his coat and hat. Mary seemed a bit surprised at his abruptness, but he was through socializing, tired of feeling closed in. He needed some air, and the quickest way to get it was to leave.

"The red coat's mine," Lina said as he was removing his coat from the hanger, "if you wouldn't mind getting it for me."

Webb carried it to her, and when she turned her back to him, he helped her put it on. She and Mary were chatting as he put on his own coat and hat.

"Webb," Mary directed, "maybe you could carry this box of dresses to Lina's car for her."

"Sure."

Lina had that little baby dress in her hand and was thanking Mary for it, managing in the process to make him feel uncomfortable.

Impatient, Webb opened the door and picked up the box. "You want this in the back seat or the trunk?"

"The trunk's fine."

"Let me have your keys and you won't have to be out in the snow any longer than necessary."

Lina got her keys from her purse and handed them to him.

"Thanks for the evening, Mary," he said.

She came over and gave him a kiss on his cheek, then Webb went outside, letting Mary close the door behind him. The sting of the cold air in his lungs felt good, clearing his wine-numbed brain. In the few hours since he'd arrived, there'd been a fair accumulation of snow. It was soft and wet and didn't look to be much of a driving hazard as yet. He was sure 82 would be in good shape and Lina wouldn't have any trouble getting home. The back roads he'd have to travel would be a little more tricky, but he knew the way like the back of his hand.

He put the box in the trunk of the BMW and carried the keys back to the house. Lina came out right away, pausing only to give Mary a hug goodbye. She took his arm as she went down the steps. As they went toward the car she gazed up at the swirling snow.

"The first heavy snowfall of the season's always pretty, isn't it?" she remarked.

"Yep."

They came to the car and Webb unlocked the door for her, then put the keys in her hand. He brushed the snow off her windshield, dusting his hands before turning back to her. Lina looked up at him from under her hood.

"Guess I'll be hearing from you in a week or two," she said.

"Yes, that's what I promised."

"Be constructive, Webb."

He looked into her eyes. "I will."

Then, like the last time, she pulled down his head and gave him an affectionate kiss on the cheek, letting her face linger near his long enough for her scent to spice the chilly air. He resisted the temptation to take her into his arms.

"Good night, Webb." Lina opened the car door, and he held it for her as she climbed in.

"The road's not bad, but if you like, you can follow my tracks back through town and over to 82. I go about four miles east on it before I turn off. You shouldn't have any trouble from there on."

"I'm sure not. Thanks, Webb."

He nodded and closed the door. Then he went down the drive to his truck, brushed the snow off the windshield and climbed inside. It took several tries before he got it to start. Once it was running smoothly, he backed into the road and waited for Lina. She came up behind him and he headed back into Carbondale, the headlights of the BMW in his rearview mirror.

Webb drove slowly, feeling tormented. He didn't like their parting because he did not want to part with her. He didn't want to brood for a week or two over her and the baby. He didn't want to think about that at all. He wanted to think about the woman in the soft clingy dress.

They encountered no traffic until they reached Highway 82, and even there it wasn't heavy—just enough to wear ruts in the snow. It was coming down harder now and the wind seemed to pick up.

Webb turned east, driving a little faster than before. Lina followed. He stewed in his frustration, knowing that what he wanted was to take her home. He wanted to return her kiss with one of his own.

A mile from his turnoff, Webb gazed anxiously into his rearview mirror, fighting his demons. Finally, in exasperation, he put on his blinker and pulled over to the side of the road, watching to make sure Lina followed. Then, jumping out of his truck, he strode back to the BMW in the blowing snow. She lowered her window and looked up at him.

"What's wrong?" she said.

Webb looked back down the highway at an approaching semi, not responding until it rolled past, kicking up slushy snow. He set his hat lower on his brow. "I'd like for you to come to my place with me."

"Webb, the snow's not that bad."

"I'm not thinking of the snow."

Despite the darkness, he could see the question in her eyes.

"I think we need to be together," he said. It was as honest as he could say it.

She thought for a long moment, probably considering the obvious questions. She had to know her response would be momentous. In the end, she elected to answer as directly as he'd asked. "Do you want me to follow you?"

"No, you could slide into a ditch. Duggan's store is up ahead at the crossroads. You can leave your car there and ride with me."

She nodded and he went back to the truck. Climbing in, he pulled back onto the highway, amazed at how relieved he felt. Maybe the cause of most of his torment had been the internal struggle. Having said what he wanted, having faced it honestly, much of the burden was gone.

Coming to Road 100, he pulled into Duggan's lot. The store was closed. One other vehicle, covered with three or four inches of snow, sat under the solitary yard light. Webb rolled down his window and gestured to Lina to park next to it. She pulled into the space and he got out to help her out of the car, offering his hand. Lina silently looked up at him from under the hood of her red coat. Taking her chin, he kissed her tenderly on the mouth, relishing the feel, the taste of her soft lips. Then, taking her keys, he locked the door for her and led her to his truck.

Opening the door, he helped her up, then went around and climbed in behind the steering wheel. Glancing over, he found her looking at him, a serious expression on her face.

"I just have one question," she said. "Is this about the baby or about us?"

"It's about us," he said, putting the transmission in gear.

She said nothing more.

CHAPTER ELEVEN

LINA WASN'T A HUNDRED percent sure how she felt about
going with Webb. All she could be certain of was that she
was willing.

In a funny sort of way they'd changed places. At Mary's,
she'd been the sociable one. Now she was prone to brooding silence and Webb was doing the talking. As they made
their way along nearly invisible roadways, Webb commented on road conditions or previous experiences with
weather. He was obviously trying to put her at ease.

The snowfall was getting heavier by the minute. It almost
seemed as if they were on the verge of a whiteout, but
Webb managed to pick his way along the roads, making
turns at places where she wouldn't have known there was
an option. As they moved to higher ground the road seemed
to get more slippery, but Webb was a skilled driver and
managed to get them to the entrance of his ranch without
incident.

There was a question that had been going through her
mind, and so, as they made their way up the long drive,
she spoke. "What made you ask me to come with you,
Webb?"

He only hesitated a moment. "I realized it's what I
wanted and that I'd been kidding myself that I didn't."

"A part of you doesn't want to, though, right?"

"Any new thing can be frightening, Lina. You must feel
the same."

"I just want you to realize that this isn't easy for me."

"So, why did you come?" he asked.

"The same reason. Because I wanted to."

Lina could honestly say she didn't understand her motives better than that. She'd been attracted to Webb Harper from the beginning. There'd been a certain inevitability about being with him. They'd simply recognized the same thing at the same time.

Webb stopped the truck near the house at the point where the drive ran on to the barn. They both got out.

The wind was stronger and cut deeper than it had down in the valley. The storm had intensified. Webb took her hand and they slogged through the foot of snow on the ground. By the time they got to the porch, Lina was chilled. She was glad they didn't have farther to go. He let her in the house and turned on a light.

She shivered as she looked around the stark room, recalling the circumstances of her last visit. More than that, she felt Karen's presence, remembering the picture Mary had brought from Webb's room. A sudden feeling of desperation went through her, and she didn't know what had put it in her mind to come.

Webb had taken off his hat and coat and was turning up the heat. She hugged herself, rubbing her arms as her wariness grew.

"This is a night for a fire if there ever was one," he said, going to the small stone fireplace.

As she watched from the middle of the room, he laid a fire. Webb glanced over his shoulder at her. "Sit down and make yourself at home. It'll be warm in here in no time."

"Webb," she said, "should we be doing this?"

Again he turned. "Doing what?"

"Should I be here?"

"I thought you wanted to come."

"I did. I mean, that's what I thought I wanted."

"Well, you haven't sold yourself into white slavery, Lina."

"I'm serious."

"So am I," he returned. "By coming here you haven't agreed to anything. Not even to having a cup of coffee, though I can put some water on, if you'd like some."

She appreciated his lighthearted tone, but she still agonized. As he struck a match to the paper he'd stuck under the kindling, she paced. Once Webb had the fire going, he stood up and came to where she was standing.

He first took her by the shoulders, then took her face in his hands. "The only problem we have is that the storm makes it tough to run you back down the hill to the highway, so we can't just change our minds all that easily. Now that's not to say it's too late to salvage your virtue. When I said I wanted us to be together, I didn't necessarily mean in bed. It's not like there aren't other ways to be friendly."

Lina realized how silly the situation was and couldn't help smiling. "I don't mean to sound like a blushing virgin, Webb. I'm sure you're a gentleman."

He grinned and tweaked her nose. "So how about if I go in and make us a cup of coffee while you warm yourself by the fire?"

She gave him a long, appraising look. "You're a sweet man," she said.

"I never claimed otherwise," he drawled, his lip curling with amusement.

He went off to the kitchen and Lina made her way to the fire. Webb had managed to quell her panic. Maybe she'd just needed reassurance. And the fire did cheer her. She was no longer so chilled.

"It appears I've got some cocoa here, too, Lina," he called from the kitchen. "Would you rather have some hot chocolate?"

"That sounds good, actually."

Lina stared into the fire, feeling much better for the warmth and Webb's kindness. After a minute she unbuttoned her coat and went to the kitchen door. He was at the stove, stirring the pot.

"What do you know about white slavery, anyway?" she said.

"Nothing firsthand. Only what I've read."

"And what's that?"

"That in days gone by it was not uncommon for *chhoti sahibahs* to disappear into the subcontinent or the Arabian deserts to become concubines to some prince or sheik, never to be seen again by their families."

"Cho...what?"

"*Chhoti sahibahs*. Young ladies, usually European. They became white slaves when they were kidnapped or strayed too far from the family bosom. In some cultures women are fair game when unprotected, you know."

"A favorite subject of yours?"

"India interests me a lot."

"Webb Harper, you're a very unusual man. You keep surprising me."

"If a fella doesn't care much for television, what else is he going to do on a winter night besides curl up by the fire with a good book?"

"Just so you don't mistake me for a *chhoti sahibah*."

"Don't worry, I only look like a sheik."

Lina laughed and Webb decided the hot chocolate was ready. He filled a mug for her and they went back into the front room to sit by the fire. She sat on the oval braided rag rug in front of the fireplace, her legs curled under her. Webb added a log to the fire, then sat opposite her.

With her fingers wrapped around the cup, soaking up the warmth of the blazing logs, she marveled that she was with the father of the child she would bear. After she'd gazed into the fire for a long time, she glanced over and saw that Webb was staring at her. "What are you thinking?" she asked.

"That you're very beautiful and that I didn't have a chance."

"A chance for what?"

"When you opened the door at Mary's tonight and I saw you in that dress, I knew it was all over."

Lina sipped her hot chocolate. "I don't want to be a pessimist, but I still wonder if this is a good idea," she said.

"I can only tell you what I feel, Lina," he replied. "This night would have been a loss if it hadn't ended like this."

"Like this?"

"With us together."

"You're suggesting we forget our problems, everything that's going on around us, that we just pretend that..."

"We're holed up by a cozy fire, riding out a winter storm."

"In addition to being well-read, you're very clever, Mr. Harper."

Smiling, he crawled the few feet separating them and gave her an affectionate little kiss. Lina looked into his eyes, and Webb took her mug from her and set it on the hearth. Then he kissed her again, this time more deeply, taking her breath away and making her heart race. Afterward, he pressed his forehead to hers.

"Why don't I make it a little more comfortable here?" he said.

Then, getting up, he left the room, returning after a few moments with an armload of blankets and a big fluffy pillow. After he turned off the overhead light, they spread the blankets out on the rug, making a nice soft pallet. Lina sat on the corner near the fire as she had before. Webb took off his boots and stretched out on his side, facing her, his head propped on his hand.

"I think I could lie here for days just looking at you," he said.

Lina felt the color rising in her cheeks. "I might even like that."

Webb reached out and took her hand, caressing her fingers. His hands were warm and strong, yet gentle. "Are you this pretty when you aren't pregnant?" he asked.

She chuckled. "I'm not sure it's made a difference," she answered lightly. "Maybe my cheeks are rosier."

"It's only going to get better," he said. "Pregnant women are beautiful and sexy."

"I'm glad my condition pleases you, Webb."

He kissed her fingers. "Come lie down here with me," he suggested. "I'll give you half the pillow."

Lina complied, stretching out on her side, facing him, her head on one end of the pillow, his on the other. She wanted to touch him, so she reached out and ran her index finger along his jaw. She saw that intensity in his eyes, but it was softer and less threatening than before.

Being with Webb like this was a curious experience. She'd been with other men, but the intimacy always seemed mechanical, somehow. Perfunctory. Maybe because she hadn't been with anyone special, anyone she really cared for. Physical attraction, even combined with friendship, never seemed quite enough.

Lina had wondered if the problem was her—that her expectations were too great or her standards too high. Every man she had met somehow fell short. So what was it about Webb Harper that made him so much more?

Her feelings for him had been growing, but she hadn't trusted them. She was sure she'd been romanticizing him. Maybe that's why she'd come home with him—to find out.

"That pensive look on your face is kind of scary," he said.

Lina smiled. "I was just thinking about you."

"What about me?"

"I'm trying to figure out why you intrigue me. You're not the first sexy cowboy who's crossed my path."

"Really?"

"Growing up on the ranch, there were dozens of cow-hands who drifted through. And some of our neighbors had sons the right age for me."

"Maybe I'm a pleasant reminder," he mused.

She pushed a tawny lock of hair off his forehead. "I don't think so."

Webb caressed her cheek with the back of his fingers. "That's good. I'd rather think I'm one of a kind."

"That you are, Mr. Harper."

He moved closer, putting his arm around her waist. They were just inches apart. He kissed her lower lip, his rich, manly scent filling her lungs. His breath washed over her and she felt the heat of his body. When the wind gusted, rattling the windows, she shivered. Webb ran the flat of his hand up and down her back. His jean-clad legs touched her thighs, sending tremors through her. Then he pulled her close, pressing her full, tender breasts against his chest.

They began kissing, their lips hungry for each other. Lina had been holding back, testing both her feelings and the situation, but now she felt herself let go with a rush. The same thing seemed to happen to Webb. He kissed her eagerly, further sparking her desire, her yearning for him.

As he kissed her, he moved his hands over her, feeling her flesh through the fabric of her dress. They were soon deeply aroused. Webb found the zipper at the back of her neck and ran it down to her waist. He slipped his hand under the opening and ran it over her skin, pulling the soft cashmere off her shoulder.

Lina moaned. After he kissed her deeply one more time, he sat up and, taking one of her feet, removed her boot. Then he took off the second one. She pulled her dress off. Webb took it from her and tossed it onto a chair.

Turning his attention back to her, he grasped her jaw and kissed her forcefully. Lina fell back on the pillow. Webb was nearly on top of her, his hand exploring her half-naked body.

Her heart was chugging heavily and her breathing was uneven. She wanted him. She was very sure of that, even if her body had gotten ahead of her.

Webb helped her strip off her panty hose, then he removed her bra. Before his tongue touched her breasts, her nipples were taut and throbbing, but when he gently sucked on them and ran the tip of his tongue around the nub, she arched against him. And when he touched her mound, she began to throb. Her lips quivered as she looked into his shadowed eyes.

Then he slipped her panties off and pressed his face against the soft flesh of her stomach. The kisses were tender, affectionate, worshipful.

Lina held his head against her stomach, in awe that it was his baby she carried. Her sole regret was that he hadn't given it to her in love. But Webb was loving her now. When he ran his hand over her breasts, caressing the nipples, a surge of excitement went through her.

"Oh, Webb," she said, rolling her head on the pillow.

Kneeling over her, he kissed the soft undersides of her breasts. He was making her warm and creamy. She wondered if she might have an orgasm simply from being kissed.

Lina wanted him to make love with her, but she worried about the baby. The doctor had told her she could have sex, but that it shouldn't be too rough. Webb wanted her, she could tell, but would he be careful?

"Will you be gentle?" she asked, taking his face in her hands.

"Of course I will, sugar. I wouldn't hurt you."

She knew he meant it. Webb cared too much not to be careful.

Kneeling, he removed his shirt, his muscular, downy chest manly and inviting. He took off his jeans, then kissed

her until she was so aroused that she had to have him inside
her. Webb read her desire. Moving between her legs, he
gently entered her, making her gasp as he inched deeper
and deeper into her core.

She clung to him, digging her fingers into his skin as he
began to undulate, sliding in and out of her with measured
strokes. Soon she got lost in the sensation. She moved
harder against him, encouraging the rhythm of their lovemaking to quicken.

Her excitement built quickly. Webb accommodated her,
holding back a little, not loosening the full fury of his own
excitement. But Lina couldn't help herself. Her body took
over. When she finally came, she cried out, writhing under
him, making him come, sending a spike of excitement
through her. She lay spent, shocked at how long and intense
her orgasm was.

Webb settled on her, breathing hard. They were both
perspiring and she was exhausted. But it was a good exhaustion. She ran her fingers through his hair, amazed that
she'd gotten so caught up in her excitement.

"Good heavens," she said, still breathing hard, "was it
you, or does this become more intense when you're pregnant?"

"I was trying to be gentle," he replied, kissing her neck,
"but you wouldn't let me."

She let her arms fall to her sides. "I expected to feel
tentative," she said. "It must have been you, Webb. Or it
was all pent up in me and you pushed the right button."

"We just made love, Lina," he murmured, nuzzling her.
"The fact that you enjoyed it doesn't have to be explained."

He was right, of course. But she was amazed just the
same. Sex hadn't ever been that good before. It was especially surprising, considering her condition. But once he'd
aroused her, she'd hardly thought of the baby. Webb hadn't
forgotten, though.

Recovering, he took his weight off her. Pulling his face back so he could see her, he kissed her chin. "You all right?"

"I'm fine. Couldn't be better."

"I shouldn't lie on you too long," he said, easing away. Grabbing the corner of the top blanket, he pulled it over her glistening body and dropped down beside her. Then he took her hand, intertwining their fingers. Lina pulled the blanket over her breasts. They lay like that, savoring the closeness and staring at the firelight playing on the ceiling.

She realized that in the course of those last few minutes their relationship had been transformed. They had been intimate—which would have meant something in ordinary circumstances. But these circumstances weren't normal. In spite of the loving, the sharing, the give-and-take, they were still competitors. They both wanted the baby. As wonderful as the lovemaking had been, it couldn't change that fact.

"So what do you think now, Webb?" she asked.

"I think you're fabulous."

"The sex was good, I agree. But that isn't what I meant."

He turned his head toward her. "What *did* you mean?"

Lina took a long breath. "We didn't just meet at the pizza parlor tonight."

"No, that's true," he said. "You are still pregnant with my child."

"That makes it a little different, don't you think?"

He rolled onto his side, facing her. He touched her lower lip with his finger, then caressed her cheek. "Yes. It was different. Special. Doubly special because of the baby. It seems more...ours, I guess."

"*Ours?* Really ours, Webb?"

He sighed. "Don't you feel that way?"

She wanted to ask, "Has anything changed or is everything just the same?" But what could have changed? Except that the sexual tension was over now. Lina took a deep breath, suddenly realizing what had happened. They'd had sex. Just sex. Webb had made her feel good. He really seemed to care, but how much of it was for her and how much of it was for the baby?

Under the blanket, he ran his hand over her stomach. She knew what he was doing. He was loving the baby. And why not? she asked herself. She did the same.

"I think I want a shower, Webb. Could I take one?"

"Sure. There should be plenty of hot water. Do you want to get up now?"

"Yes, if you don't mind."

"Let me get you a robe and some towels. Stay here by the fire where it's warm."

He got up and, taking his clothes, went off to the bedroom.

"Well, that's unfortunate," she heard him call from the other room. "The power seems to be off."

"Does that mean no heat?"

"You got it. But the water in the tank will still be hot. You can have your shower. Just let me find my flashlight and I'll get things set up."

Lina rolled onto her side and watched the flames dancing over the burning logs. A terrible, lonely feeling went through her.

After a couple of minutes Webb returned to the front room. He was wearing a purple robe and carrying a candle. Over his arm was another garment.

"Would it bother you to wear Karen's robe?" he asked. "There were a few of her things still in the closet. This terry robe was one. It's practically new."

Lina looked up at him, the utter truth of her recent thoughts confirmed. Who was she kidding? What had she been thinking? But it was too late to undo things now. She had taken the short view when she'd consented to make love with him. Now it was time to take the long view.

"Of course it wouldn't bother me," she said, struggling

to keep her voice even. "I'm carrying her baby, why shouldn't I wear her clothes?"

Webb put down the candle and held the garment open for her. She got to her feet, quickly slipping into the robe. Thankfully, it didn't smell of another woman. That might have been a little much.

Taking her shoulders, Webb turned her around and folded her tenderly into his arms. Lina looked over his shoulder at the fire as he rubbed her back. Tears welled in her eyes. She felt so lost. She couldn't even be sure who or what was in his mind. Karen? The baby? Both?

Ironically, she couldn't blame him for clinging to what he held dear. Deep down, he wasn't over his wife. Lina's role was very clear and very well-defined. She was an incubator, albeit a pretty one that had turned him on and fed his fantasy. For all she knew, she hadn't even been the one he'd made love with. Not in his heart.

When he let go of her, she turned her head away so that he wouldn't see her tears. There was a way to deal with this situation, she decided. It was to be cheerful and put up a brave front. After all, she had desires of her own, and they transcended Webb Harper. This baby was not only in her womb, but it was also in her heart, even before he knew it existed.

CHAPTER TWELVE

WEBB DAMNED NEAR couldn't get the truck started, but the engine had finally turned over. He'd managed to drive it through the blowing snow down to the hay barn, where he'd put chains on the tires. Then he'd loaded the truck with bales of hay and driven it to the fenced pasture. There was no way he could get into the middle of the field, so he'd backed to the fence and pitched some hay over the barbed wire, repeating the process a couple of times at other locations so that more cattle could get to it. When he'd gotten enough feed over the fence to get the herd through the storm, he drove back to the main barn. While he was there, he checked the pregnant heifers. One looked as if she were getting close to giving birth. It would be a good idea to check back during the day.

After feeding Jake and the heifers, Webb started slogging his way through the drifts back to the house. When he'd climbed out of bed that morning, Lina was still sleeping. It had seemed so strange to see her dark hair on the pillow in the place where Karen's—and only Karen's—had ever been.

He'd liked sleeping with Lina, even if she had gotten a little strange when they'd gone to bed. He'd given her a sweatshirt, a pair of long johns and some sweat socks to wear, assuring her it would get quite cold before morning. He'd piled the extra blankets on, since they'd probably have to go the night without heat, but when he tried to snuggle up to her, she'd been a little distant, saying she wasn't used to sleeping with anyone and would prefer some space. And so he'd kept to his side of the bed until they'd both fallen asleep. Like Karen, though, as the temperature dropped, Lina had come after him like a heat-seeking missile.

While he was awake during the night he'd pondered his feelings for her, amazed that it should seem so natural to be with her. Their lovemaking had been wonderful, but it hadn't seemed to register on her until afterward. He suspected that she'd had misgivings, which explained why she'd pulled back later. What exactly was bothering her, he didn't know, but if she needed to say something, he was sure she would.

By the time Webb reached the house, he was really looking forward to the fire. He'd built a big one before leaving and figured Lina would know to throw more wood on.

Stepping inside, he found the fire roaring and Lina sitting in front of it huddled in a blanket. She turned at the sound of the door.

"Where have you been?" she asked, sounding annoyed.

"Feeding the cattle."

Her expression softened. "Oh, I should have thought of that. I was afraid you'd wandered off in the storm."

Webb took off his gloves, hat and the scarf he'd tied around his ears. Then he removed his coat, hanging everything on the pegs next to the door.

"By the way," she said, "your phone's out of order."

He made his way to the fire and squatted down to warm his icy hands. "What did you do, try and call out for pizza?"

"No, I tried to call home to check my messages."

The way she was wrapped up in the blanket, not much more than her face showed, but it was a welcome sight. "You're as pretty in the morning as you are at night," he said.

She didn't look thrilled by his comment. "Don't, Webb, it only makes things worse."

Her words caught him by surprise. "Is there a problem?"

"Yes, I think we crossed a line we shouldn't have crossed. All we accomplished was to complicate the situation with the baby."

"What do you mean, complicate?" He stood and let the fire warm the backs of his legs.

"I made you an offer and, before I got your answer, I went to bed with you."

"Lina, I told you last night that was about us, not the baby."

"I don't believe you."

He glared.

"I'm not saying you're lying," she amended. "You might even have believed it when you said it, but you can't divorce the baby from the things we do."

He gave her a look. "It's nice to know you place such trust in me."

"What I feel has nothing to do with trust."

"Maybe that's the problem," he grumbled.

"Look, Webb, it's obvious what happened. Why can't you see it?"

"Since you seem to have it all figured out, maybe you should explain."

She closed her eyes, gnawing her lip. "I'm not trying to pick a fight," she said.

"I'm not, either," he returned. "You're saying I can't see what happened and I'd like to know what you mean."

Lina set her jaw. "That wasn't me you made love to last night."

"Oh?"

"That's right. And if you were honest, you'd admit it."

"Lina, why don't you just spit it out? We're talking about Karen, aren't we?"

Lina lowered her eyes. "I can't blame you for thinking

about her. I'm sure I would in your shoes. But it puts me in an awkward position—one of my own making, I admit. The point is, I want to undo what I've done and get back to the way things were before. I want to be your friend, Webb, not your lover.''

"Life isn't a videotape that can be rewound or erased,'' he objected. "Besides, I think you've got this whole thing blown out of proportion. And you've misunderstood.''

"What have I misunderstood?''

"For starters, last night I made love with you and you alone. If you can't accept that, it's not because of anything I've said or done. I know what I was feeling and you don't.''

"Please don't make this difficult for me,'' she said, once again lowering her eyes.

Webb was frustrated. This made absolutely no sense. He didn't know if Lina was really having second thoughts or if she was being paranoid. "All right,'' he said, "tell me what it is you want.''

"I want you to take me to my car.''

"That's easier said than done. There's a blizzard out there if you haven't noticed.''

"When do you think I can leave?''

"When I can dig us out. If it stops snowing soon, maybe this afternoon. More likely it'll be tomorrow. Or the day after.''

"Oh, great. I've got to open my shop tomorrow.''

The backs of Webb's legs were getting warm, and so he moved away from the fire. "Well, good luck.''

She turned, glaring at him. "Well, you don't have to be so damned glad,'' she groused.

"Look, if you're going to be this way, I'd be glad to take you to your car. Hell, I'd drive you home, if that's what it took, because I don't want you here against your will. White slavery is not my idea of fun, Lina. Believe it or not." He went to the kitchen door and peered in. "I take it you haven't had breakfast."

"No."

"What do you want?"

"You can't cook without electricity."

"I've got a propane stove."

"I don't need anything," she argued. "I'm fine."

"No, you should eat."

"That's right, your baby. I forgot."

"Lina, I was thinking of *you*. And if you weren't so damned defensive and paranoid, you'd notice that I do happen to care about you. There's not a thing I've said to indicate otherwise. So far everything negative has come right out of your head." With that, he left the room.

It was a lot cooler in the kitchen, since the only heat in the house was coming from the fireplace in the living room. But he was so pissed off that he didn't mind the cold. In fact, he was glad to get away from Lina, if only so that he wouldn't really blow up.

The first thing he did was get the propane stove out from one of the lower cupboards. Then he put water on to boil. Next he got eggs out of the fridge and a mixing bowl and whisk from the utensil drawer. As he was putting all the stuff on the counter, he noticed Lina at the door, still wrapped in the blanket.

"Webb," she began, "I apologize for upsetting you. I wasn't at all diplomatic."

"Your diplomacy isn't the issue," he returned. "What I took offense at is what you said, not the way you said it."

"I don't think you really understood what I was trying to say. I'm not criticizing you. To the contrary, I think I owe you an apology. Last night I deceived myself, and in so doing, I deceived you."

"Oh, great," he muttered, "that makes me feel wonderful."

"No, that's not what I mean. I wanted to be with you,

but just because you want something doesn't mean it's all right.''

He didn't like what he was hearing. Lina could tell. She came into the kitchen, making her way to where he stood. She held the blanket closed at her throat with one hand, and with the other, reached out and took his hand, looking up at him from under her sooty lashes.

"Webb," she said, "I wish it had been just us last night. I really do."

"It *was* just us."

She shook her head. "Help me with this," she pleaded. "I'm trying very hard because I know what this baby means to us both, and I haven't done a very good job keeping things separated. I like you an awful lot and I do want us to be friends."

Webb gazed into her eyes. "Forgive me for bringing up my wife, but you know what this reminds me of? Karen's last beauty pageant. It was her shot at being Miss Colorado. She could have me for fifty years—or so she thought—and the contest was her one chance at being something that really set her apart, something she cared about."

"What are you trying to say, that you don't like playing second fiddle?"

"I mean I don't like having my life determined by how something else turns out. If Karen had won, I would have had to wait a year for her. And now I have to wait for you to give birth because you're convinced you can't be pregnant and sleep with me at the same time."

"It's not being pregnant, Webb, it's having everything up in the air and pretending otherwise. Surely you understand." Her tone was pleading.

It came to him then and he slowly nodded. "Yeah, maybe I do. Maybe I was being so damned selfish, I didn't even see the issue. But there is one thing you're dead wrong about. The woman I made love to last night was you and nobody else." Taking her face in his hands, he kissed her.

"And if you don't like that...well, it's too damned bad."
He let go of her. "Now, how do you like your eggs?"

WHEN DARKNESS CAME the power was still off, the phone
was down and the storm had been howling and blowing all
day except for a couple of brief lulls. By midafternoon Lina
had resigned herself to another night with Webb.

He hadn't liked it that she'd gotten a runny nose and
sneezed a few times, certain she was getting sick, but she
assured him cold air always did that to her and that she felt
just fine. Still, he'd gotten the mattress off the bed and
dragged it in by the fire. Then he'd closed off the rest of
the house and built up the blaze so that after a while the
front room was actually cozy. The only remaining source
of real discomfort was the bathroom. It was almost as bad
as a winter trip to the privy.

Lina had agonized over what was happening between
them, though she hadn't backed down from her position.
And Webb, except for that kiss at breakfast, had accommodated her. He'd treated her solicitously and with respect.

Webb had spent a couple of hours working on his business accounts and trying to set up some books for Mary.
Just before dark he'd gone down to the barn to check on
the heifer that was ready to calf. In twenty minutes he was
back, reporting no change. "The first calf is kind of frightening for these young cows," he said.

"Are you sure you aren't projecting a little?" she'd
asked him.

Webb allowed that maybe he was.

Once he'd gotten warmed up again he'd picked up a
book and stretched out on the mattress, reading by the light
of the fire. Lina curled up in an armchair, watching the
flames.

"What are you reading?" she'd asked when the silence
began to wear on her.

"It's a book on mythology from various cultures."

"Which do you like the best?"

"I guess I know Greek mythology the best," he said.

"Have a favorite god?"

"Apollo, maybe."

"How about goddess?" she asked.

"Artemis and Athena."

"Why them?"

"They appeal to me for some of the same reasons you do."

"Me?"

"Yes, I've decided you're not so much regal as divine, a goddesslike creature rather than a princess."

"Lord, after this morning, I'd have thought you'd have said witch."

"Even the gods have their dark sides, Lina."

He went back to his reading and she to her contemplative silence. She wasn't sure if it was the fire, the darkness or being alone with him, but romantic thoughts and desires were again entering her mind. Of course, after all she'd said, she couldn't permit things to get romantic. But she was tempted.

Webb read like an earnest schoolboy. There was something endearing about that, and she had to fight the temptation to get down next to him and give him a hug.

"How about if I make dinner tonight?" she offered after a while.

"You getting hungry?"

She wasn't particularly, but she was restless and wanting a change, so she said yes. Webb observed that the kitchen would be cold and that maybe it was better if he cooked. He'd bring her dinner into the front room and they could eat by the fire.

"You're determined to pamper me, aren't you?" she accused. "Me and your heifers."

"Maybe I am."

"Well, I'm not fragile and I want to be useful, so how about if I help?"

Webb admitted that would be fine, and so they went to the kitchen to see what they could rustle up. There was enough food in the house that they could easily last a week if necessary, but fresh food was in short supply. Canned soups, stews, rice, beans and pastas, plus eggs and some cheese were what they were limited to. For dinner they elected to have soup, some beef jerky Webb found in the cupboard, the last of the bread and canned peaches.

"This is as good as I ever had growing up."

As they sat eating by the fire, sitting cross-legged and side by side on the mattress, Lina asked about his childhood. Webb told stories about the orphanage and the foster families he'd lived with—some were sad, some funny, some heartwarming. Mostly his life was a story about persevering.

"You're surprisingly normal," she said.

"You think so?"

"Yes. I admire you."

Webb put aside his dishes and lay back on the mattress. "I think I've had enough false love and rejection in my life to know my feelings—to know when I really care for someone and why."

"Are you talking about you and me?"

Webb nodded. Lina put aside her dishes, too, and lay back on her elbows beside him. They both held their stockinged feet to the fire.

"It shouldn't be a surprise to you," she said, "that if I let myself, I could easily make love with you again."

"But you want me to refuse and let you off the hook."

"That would make it easier for me," she agreed.

"Okay, whatever you want."

He was being compliant, but he didn't mean it, she could tell. What he was doing was tweaking her nose, daring her to undo everything. "It's better if we don't give in to temptation," she said.

Webb nodded, but he did run the top of his foot under her sole. "Fine."

She had a terrible urge to roll right over on top of him, to kiss him, to bite his lip and tell him he was a bastard for tempting her, for making her say the things she was, for being so enticing, for making her grovel and feel like a fool. There was a long silence, the only sounds the crackling of the fire and the howling of the wind.

"You know," she continued, "before last night it had been almost a year since I'd slept with a man."

"Oh?"

"And I didn't miss it all that much. Women can go without sex much easier than men."

"Is that a fact?" he said.

He was playing with her and she wanted to punch him in the stomach, but she kept her control. She rubbed the top of his foot with hers. "So why is it do you suppose I keep thinking about having sex with you?" she asked.

Webb shrugged. "I suppose because you told yourself you won't. It's human nature to want what's forbidden, you know."

"Is that a fact?" she remarked, smiling.

"That's what they say."

After another long silence, Webb put some more wood on the fire, then he lay back down beside her. Neither said anything. Lina fought her temptation but she felt herself slipping.

"So if we had sex one more time, just for the hell of it," she mused, "could we treat it for what it is—just a physical thing, just attraction and affection and nothing more?"

"You're asking if I'm willing to get laid and not make a big deal out of it," he said.

"Isn't that kind of a crude way to put it?"

"How would you put it, Lina?"

She saw she'd made a big mistake. She'd let her desire get the best of her. She'd sent Webb the wrong message. "Oh, never mind. Just forget I said anything."

"No," he replied, "I'd like to hear what you were proposing."

She sighed with exasperation. "I thought maybe we could pretend, like we did last night. I thought that for a couple of hours we could forget who we were, but it was a dumb idea and I'm embarrassed I said anything. Attribute it to your sex appeal, Webb."

"The making love I have no trouble with. The playing games I don't want any part of."

"Hey, if you thought I was playing games," she objected, "you're dead wrong."

"Then what's wrong with just making love? With doing it without discounting it, denying it or pretending it meant something other than it did? What's wrong with being with each other and letting the chips fall where they may?"

"But isn't that a form of denial, too?"

"It's honest."

"Lust is honest," she said.

"So what are you feeling, lust?"

Lina gave him a whack on the stomach, catching him off guard. "Bastard," she muttered under her breath as he doubled up, half laughing, half wincing in pain.

It took him a moment to catch his breath. "You afraid to answer the question, Lina?" he challenged.

She studied him. "Sure, I feel lust. And I happen to like you, you turkey. But you're still sort of the enemy. And I don't want to screw things up."

Webb caressed her cheek. "I promise I won't hold it over your head. I promise to treat you exactly as I would otherwise. I promise this has nothing to do with anything except you and me."

"Will you promise to take me home tomorrow and forget this happened?" she asked.

"No, I won't promise that."

"Why?"

"Because I don't want to forget. The most you can get out of me is no expectations for the future."

Lina closed her eyes and sighed. "You're really a tough man to get to bed."

He gave her a wry smile. "Hey, I've got a reputation to maintain."

She knew it was wrong; she knew it was stupid; she knew it was the last thing in the world she should do. But Lina simply couldn't help herself. Reaching over, she began to unbutton his shirt. And as Webb folded her into his embrace, she mumbled a silent prayer that she wasn't making another mistake.

CHAPTER THIRTEEN

THE FURY AND POWER of nature had always given Lina a profound respect for the grit and resiliency of the pioneers. Washing the dishes in ice water was only one small example of the hardship of winter without electricity. By morning, the storm had pretty well blown over but had left them with the task of digging themselves out. Webb said he'd never seen so much snow come down in such a short period of time, especially that early in the season. While he went out to tend to his herd, Lina kept the fire going.

From the front window she was able to see him down in the snowy pasture on horseback, doing what he could to feed his cattle. He'd come back to the house around mid-morning to warm himself by the fire and get a cup of coffee, telling her that one of the heifers had calved during the night. "So, unless I lost some head in the blizzard, the herd is growing."

Their second morning had been less tense than the first. Lina had managed to accept what was happening for what it was. Webb seemed to have things in perspective, too. They'd wanted to make love, so they had. The implications—the future—were not a topic of discussion. They would worry about that another day.

Which wasn't to say that in private Lina didn't speculate on how their intimacy might affect their relationship. It couldn't be ignored. But could it be discounted? She suspected not, but she also knew that as new issues came along, the past could be seen in a different light. Men, especially, had a knack for living in the moment.

Not that she didn't deserve her share of the responsibility. If anything, their lovemaking had been more her doing. Yet she had no regrets, even knowing she'd complicated the situation considerably.

Their second night together had been different from the first, though no less pleasurable. They'd made love twice, the first time more quietly and tenderly than the night before, with the passion of lovers who were no longer strangers. The second time was hours later. They'd slept naked in each other's arms. She'd awakened with Webb behind her, hugging her and kissing the nape of her neck.

Perhaps she'd dreamed of him making love to her, because she'd awoken aroused. He'd caressed her breasts and kissed her shoulder. Lina had pressed her backside against his erection and he'd entered her from behind, one large hand clamped over her belly, the other cupping her breasts as he undulated against her.

Webb was a skilled lover, but even more than the things he did to her, it was the mood he created—the way he made her feel about being in his bed and in his arms that made it special. He was masterful, but his power was in the way he enabled her to submit as much as his ability to dominate. Webb made her want to be his woman.

Was it the psychological aspect of sexuality, she wondered, or was it something more? Was this love she felt? She didn't know, though she was certain that it was more than lust. She cared for Webb. She liked him, she respected him. But had she let the fact she was carrying his child blow things out of proportion?

As she watched from the window, Webb made his way toward the barn. Except for a brief visit to the house, he'd been out in the cold for hours. She figured that once he had his horse unsaddled and stabled in the barn, he'd come inside. She'd have hot coffee waiting and some soup, as well.

It wasn't that she was all that domestic and relished the thought of taking care of a man, but they were in survival mode. Webb had given her shelter and he was struggling to save his herd. She wanted to help.

When she'd volunteered to help him feed the cattle, he'd refused. "I'm as strong as I've ever been," she'd protested. But Webb wouldn't hear of it. "I don't want you to get sick or hurt yourself," he'd replied. "Maybe I get kind of spooky about pregnancy, but I don't want anything to happen. I'd as soon lose the entire herd as have you come down with something that could cause you to lose the baby."

Lina allowed that it was nice to feel protected. Things were a little different when you were pregnant and becoming more vulnerable by the day. Even so, she felt Webb was overdoing it. There was no point in arguing, however. The easiest thing was to do dishes, make the bed and keep the fire going.

Being pampered by Webb did make her think how nice it would be to be looked after when she had a baby at her breast. From the first, she'd thought in terms of going it alone. Until now, she hadn't fully appreciated the advantages of having a man to help out and make her feel safe and protected. That—more even than the fact they'd become lovers—made her wonder if they might not have a future together, a relationship that transcended the baby.

Lina knew that was a dangerous train of thought. She'd always been self-sufficient. Had that not been the case, she'd never have considered having this baby alone. She reminded herself that if she let herself cling to Webb emotionally, she'd be asking for trouble if things didn't work out. No, she had to look on this as a romantic interlude. If Webb looked at it the same way, then they should be fine.

He was out of sight, so Lina put on her coat and went into the kitchen, where the temperature was like the inside

of a refrigerator. She put water on the propane stove to boil
for coffee. Next she got a can of soup from the cupboard
and opened it, putting the contents in a saucepan. She put
that on the other burner. Then, as she was getting a bowl
for Webb's soup from the dish rack, she heard the sound
of an engine in the distance. She wondered if Webb had
decided to bring his truck through the snowbanks after all.

Turning the burner under the soup on low, she returned
to the window in the front room. There was no sign of the
pickup in the direction of the barn or, for that matter, any
sign of Webb. But she distinctly heard the motor, and it
was getting louder. Then she saw a spray of snow in the
direction of the road, followed by a snowplow. It was making its way up the drive. That was a surprise. Webb hadn't
mentioned that anyone would be coming, and he certainly
couldn't have called for help, because the phone was still
out.

The plow was actually a dump truck with a huge blade,
and it continued to the top of the drive, where it stopped.
As Lina watched, the door on the passenger side opened
and a man got out. He had on a Western hat and, as he
came tromping toward the house, wading through the hip-
deep snow, she realized it was her father. She was shocked.

She continued watching him work his way toward the
house, her surprise replaced first by dismay, then anger and
humiliation. What in the hell was he doing here?

When he neared the porch, Lina went to the door, embarrassed at how ridiculous she looked in Webb's sweats
and her red coat, knowing there was no way to hide what
had been going on. She pulled open the door just as Morgan
reached the top step.

"Daddy!" she said indignantly. "What are you doing
here?"

"Well, thank God you're alive," he said.

"What do you mean, alive?"

"Carolina, you were last seen leaving Carbondale on

Saturday night. You never made it home. For two days
nobody's seen or heard from you. There's been no trace of
you until the state police found your car last night, abandoned at a store down on Route 82. And you wonder why
I'm relieved you're alive."

"I came by Webb's to have a cup of coffee and ended
up getting trapped by the storm. That's certainly no crime,"
she snapped.

"I didn't say it was a crime. I said I was glad to find
you alive. I think a father's entitled to feel that way about
his daughter."

"Honestly, you're making a mountain out of a molehill.
I can't imagine how you knew I didn't get home, let alone
why you organized a search party. God, you'd think I was
still seventeen!"

Morgan Prescott gave her a stern, very displeased look.
"Do you want me to leave? Is that what you're saying?"

Lina started shivering. The house was filling with cold
air. "I don't want to stand here in the cold arguing with
you, so you might as well come in."

"Where's Harper?"

"Down at the barn. Come on in."

Morgan Prescott stepped inside, removing his hat. He
glanced around, seeing the mattress on the floor in front of
the fire. His expression changed slightly, but he didn't say
anything. Lina closed the door.

"Listen, Lina, my intent was not to intrude, but if you
were fifty and missing, I'd still be worried."

"What made you think I was missing?"

"I called to see how the storm was affecting you and
never got an answer. Sunday morning I telephoned the
Hamilton girl and asked if she knew where you were, thinking she'd know if you'd left town. She told me you'd gone
to dinner at a friend's and was fairly certain you intended
to come home."

"I did intend to go home."

"Yes, but when you didn't return my messages, naturally I worried. That certainly wasn't unreasonable, Lina."

She could see that her father meant well and that his intrusion was more a result of circumstances than meddling, even if he was being a bit overprotective. "There wouldn't have been a problem except that Webb's phone was out. If it hadn't been, I would have gotten your messages and I'd have called."

"So I'm not the bad guy after all," Morgan said.

"When you found out where I left my car, you must have figured out where I was. Do you think it was really necessary for you to come up here?"

"I tried calling and discovered the phone was out of order. And, yes, I admit I knew the odds were that you were here. But it was also possible you and Harper had ended up in a ditch or that you were here and didn't want to be. Not everybody who gets snowed in with someone is pleased about it, you know."

Lina could see he was goading her. And he had also crossed the line. He was playing the role of jealous father, thinking he was protecting her from some unscrupulous cowboy bent on taking advantage of her. For all his explanations, that was really what this was all about.

"Since you went to all the trouble to find out what happened to me, I'll tell you what the situation is. I'm here voluntarily, though I didn't intend to stay. Webb has been a gentleman and was prepared to take me to my car as soon as conditions allowed. I appreciate your concern, but I'm safe and well and capable of looking after myself. If you don't mind me saying so, Daddy, I think it's time you let go."

"Lina, be honest. Have I interfered in your life since you and Kyle split up? Have I been overly protective?"

"Well, I suppose not."

"So this is not a pattern."

"Dad, what's your point?"

"Maybe it's *you* who's changed, Lina. I mean, let's look at the facts. First, you decide to have a kid without bothering to find a husband. Second, you fall under the spell of some fortune-hunting cowpuncher with a couple of head of cattle and a few acres of leased land. And third, you lose all your common sense and judgment, thinking you can charm your way out of hot water. So look what happens," he said, gesturing toward the mattress. "You end up being the one charmed, being taken advantage of. Don't you think it's obvious what's been going on here?"

"And it's also none of your damned business!"

His eyes narrowed. Then he said in a low voice, "Yes, you're right. You're of age. But you also happen to be pregnant, Lina. It's plain to anyone who knows you that you aren't yourself. You aren't thinking clearly—your hormones or whatever are out of balance and you've lost your judgment."

"I can't believe this!" she said, throwing up her hands as the door flew open. Lina glanced over to see Webb with a stunned expression on his face. In the brief moment she took a breath, Webb and her father exchanged looks. "Is it all men, or just you two?" she said. "Just because a woman's pregnant, it doesn't mean she's lost her brain! I'm not suddenly frail and stupid and helpless and incompetent just because I'm carrying a baby! The truth is, I need to be left alone to make my own decisions, not coddled and cajoled and patronized by a couple of men who think I'm suddenly helpless without them to do my thinking for me!"

She stomped over and got her dress and her purse and her boots while the men stood there, dumbstruck. She buttoned her coat and pulled her hood up.

"That snowplow came along at the right time," she went on. "I'm going to catch a ride back to my car. If it's all right, Webb, I'll send your sweats to you after I get home. Thanks for the hospitality. Your soup's on the stove—you'd better go stir it." She turned to her father. "And you, Mr. Prescott, I don't care what you do. As far as I'm concerned, you can stay here with Webb and exchange war stories about pregnant women and pregnant cows! Goodbye, gentlemen. Have a nice day.''

With that, she went out the door, slamming it behind her.

LINA WAS NEVER so happy to get home in her life. Her father showing up at Webb's like that was one of the more embarrassing experiences ever. She'd been so mad at him that when she'd gotten to the truck, she'd told the driver to take her to her car at the highway. He could come back for her father later.

She had no idea what had happened after she left, and almost didn't care. Webb wasn't really to blame, but while she was there, he *had* gotten a little proprietary and...well, he was a man! Even though he had treated her well, the whole business was still a tug-of-war, and he'd been pulling on the rope along with everyone else. Besides, it wouldn't hurt to make him wonder.

The first thing she did after arriving home was take a nice hot bath. Then she listened to the messages on her answering machine. Apart from the calls from her father, the only message of importance was from Zara, saying she needed to talk. Lina returned the call, but Zara was with a client. She came on the line long enough to ask if she could drop by that evening after work. Lina said sure, and they agreed Zara would be there at six.

Lina wondered if she'd heard something ominous in Zara's voice or if it was her imagination. She hadn't been able to ask if there was a problem, but she had no doubt something was up. She couldn't brood about it, though.

By the time she'd gotten dressed it was too late to go to the shop. She saw no point in opening up for a couple of hours. She was expecting her father to come by and was surprised when five o'clock rolled around and she hadn't heard from him. Maybe he was angry with her for stomping off. If so, that was tough. She was determined to continue with her righteous indignation awhile longer, though she did worry that she might have been unfair to Webb. After mulling it over, she tried calling him, but his phone still seemed to be out of order.

Lina had just settled down with a mug of herbal tea when she heard a vehicle out front. Not knowing whom to expect, she peeked out the window, only to see it was a delivery truck. The doorbell rang and she was greeted by a kid from a florist shop with a huge bouquet of flowers. She took it inside, curious about who had sent them. She was betting on her father.

Opening the card, she discovered she was right. "Sorry, Lina," he'd written. "In retrospect I see I was wrong. Good intentions weren't enough. Hope you'll forgive me. Love, Dad."

She was touched and immediately felt bad, which of course was his intent. If he was contrite, she told herself, he had good reason to be. However, it still left unanswered the question of what had happened after she left. Maybe Webb wasn't feeling as apologetic as Morgan. On the contrary, he might even feel angry. And maybe he had good reason. Well, she couldn't help that.

Lina had put the flowers in a vase on a table in the sitting area when the phone rang. She went to answer it.

"Lina, it's Webb. You all right?"

He sounded concerned, which was a relief. It also pleased her. But she was terribly embarrassed, too. "Yes, I'm fine."

"I was worried. The phone just got fixed and I wanted to give you a call."

"I'm sure you were blindsided by my walking out the way I did. I was so angry with my father that I was in no mood to be civil to anyone. I'm sorry. You deserved better."

"No need to apologize. I was afraid I'd done something."

"No, it was me. I guess I sort of started feeling like a Ping-Pong ball. But I'm fine now."

"That's good." He hesitated. "I found your earrings in the bathroom, by the way. I didn't want you worrying that you'd lost them."

"Thank you, Webb. To be honest, I'd forgotten about them."

"Do you want me to bring them to you?"

He was being solicitous and she was grateful. He could just as easily have been miffed. It embarrassed her to think she'd acted like a child. "It's not necessary to make a special trip. The next time you're up this way would be soon enough. Or you could give them to Mary. She'll be coming to Aspen regularly."

The silence on the line told her he was disappointed.

"Lina," he said after several moments, "having you stay with me was very special. Turns out I lost a couple head of cattle, but I still consider the storm to have been one of the best things that's ever happened to me."

She chuckled. "That's one of the more unusual compliments I've had."

"I guess it didn't come out quite right," he said. "Point is, I liked being with you a whole lot, and I hope it was mutual."

"It was."

"I'm glad, because after you took off, I wasn't sure what to think."

"My father would have said it was just hormones, I'm sure."

Webb chuckled. "That's sort of what he did say."

"Did the two of you talk about me?"

"Briefly."

Lina wasn't sure if he was being evasive or diplomatic.

"I suppose it's a comment on your maturity that the two of you were civil to each other. I'm assuming you were."

"Politely distant."

She was getting curious. "So what was said?"

"You know how guys are. We talked about the weather—everything except what we were thinking. Neither of us wanted to blow it and incur your wrath."

"You see, women have their uses," she said. "Besides keeping house and bearing children."

"I hope I didn't offend you, Lina, because I do have a great deal of respect for you. I've known one or two women who ranch, and I've met a few others who were strong and capable, but I admit to being a little green when it comes to independent-minded businesswomen who…"

"Chose to have children without the help of a man?"

"Well, that, too," he said with a laugh.

Webb was being sweet and she felt a great warmth toward him. She also realized she wanted to see him. She was sorry now she'd been so quick to turn down his offer to bring her earrings to her. What he really wanted was to see her, she could tell. Lina toyed with the idea of inviting him over.

"As long as you're okay and not mad at me, I feel better," he said.

"No, I'm not mad at you."

"I'll drop your earrings by the next time I'm in Aspen."

She could see he was fixing to end the conversation, and she was suddenly flooded with regret. "That would be fine," she said.

"I'll let you go, then," he said. "Take care."

"You, too."

Webb ended the call and Lina was left with an empty feeling. She had probably been wanting to see him all day, but it wasn't until then that it struck home. Webb Harper, she realized, had gotten to her in a big way. She couldn't think about making love with him without getting shivers.

However, that couldn't change the fact that they were mixed up in a very complicated situation—one that had them on opposing sides. And whether what had happened between them would change things remained to be seen. It certainly wasn't up to her alone.

While she waited for Zara to arrive, Lina brooded, worried about the baby and dared to hope a little. Surely two people with so many positive feelings for each other would find a way to work things out. What she couldn't be sure of was whether time was on her side or his. She did decide a separation would be good for them. If Webb wanted her as much as she wanted him, then several lonely days with nothing to do but tending to his cattle and reading would make him think.

ZARA ARRIVED A FEW minutes late, her cheeks rosy but an unhappy expression on her face. "I've got less than stellar news," she said, getting right down to business. "It's beginning to look as if our position isn't strong."

"What do you mean?" Lina said, taking Zara's coat.

They went into the sitting area and sat side by side on the sofa.

"I'm talking about the relative merit of your claim on the baby," Zara said, crossing one booted leg over the other.

The words were like a knife in Lina's heart. "Are you saying I wouldn't win if it came down to a fight?"

"As I told you, there's no case law and certainly no statutes or regulations. We're in unknown territory. That means both sides have to make their arguments based on analogy to similar situations. The opinions of experts become more important in cases like this. I found an article in a law journal today on the matter of parental rights in connection with artificial reproduction. The author, a woman named Gwen McAllister, is a family law attorney known for her expertise in custody matters. Although the article didn't deal with our precise situation, the author's conclusion was that a natural parent would have a favored position in the law.''

"Meaning Webb."

"Meaning Webb, yes."

"So that means if we go to court, I lose?"

"It means the experts would favor that outcome. The argument set out in the article was a cogent one, Lina. What I'm saying is, legally speaking, Webb has a lot of good ammo.''

"You aren't suggesting I surrender, are you, Zara?"

"No, of course not. And we could still win if it came to that. But I want you to have a realistic view of what we're up against. I'm trying to tell you we have an uphill battle on our hands.''

"Zara, this is the cap on an absolutely wretched day. I can't tell you how good this makes me feel."

"I hate bringing bad news, believe me, but I know you wouldn't want to be blindsided.''

"No, of course not. And I know you're doing your job. Don't worry, I'm not going to blame the messenger.''

Zara took her hand. "We'll do our best."

Lina sighed woefully.

"What did you mean, you've had a wretched day?" Zara asked.

Lina told her the story of her weekend, starting with Mary Carson's dinner party and ending with her father's arrival at Webb's. She also told her about the flowers from her father and Webb's call.

"That doesn't sound too terrible," Zara said. "Not considering the way it ended, anyway. In fact, I'm encouraged.''

"You're *encouraged?*"

"The strength of your case doesn't matter if you never get into a lawsuit. It sounds to me as if Webb's more likely to propose than consult an attorney."

"Zara, you're crazy. We're a long way from anything like that. Anyway, there's much too much going on between us to even think about getting serious."

"I'm not saying he's shopping for rings, but as the months go by and you keep seeing each other, who knows where things could wind up? After all, Lina, stranger things have happened."

CHAPTER FOURTEEN

WEBB HARPER WAS NOT a man to play games, but he realized that sometimes discretion was the better part of valor. The way he figured it, Lina had to know how he felt about her, because there was only one way to interpret what had happened while they were holed up during the storm—unless she considered him a womanizing cad, and he had no reason to think she did.

He'd decided what she needed most was some time to think, to get things into perspective. And so he'd given her space. At the end of the week he'd find an excuse to drive over to Aspen and, while he was there, he'd take her earrings to her.

Years earlier, when Karen had entered that Miss Colorado beauty contest, Webb thought he'd learned the truth of the old saw that "absence makes the heart grow fonder." But he didn't recall that the time away from Karen had been any more painful than this. Actually, in many ways, this was worse. The difference probably had something to do with the fact that, with Lina, he wasn't a hundred percent sure where he stood.

But he also knew it wouldn't do him any good to dwell on it, so he tried to keep busy. It wasn't as if he didn't have things to do. Getting adequate feed to his herd was plenty of challenge. The second heifer that calved had had a rough time, and he'd spent the better part of an afternoon playing midwife. Then on Wednesday Harv Cooper called to say he wanted Webb to drop by the next time he was in

Glenwood Springs. Webb told him he'd be there the next afternoon.

Though he was curious about what the lawyer had to say, Webb knew that whatever it was, it was meaningless aside from what he might learn from Lina herself. He was sorely tempted to drive into Aspen and see her, but then he recalled his decision to give her space. He'd stick to his plan and wait until Friday.

Since the storm, the weather had been beautiful, if cold. The roads were in good shape except for ice here and there. The ski lift operators were in seventh heaven, as the skiers were already making their way to the mountains. It seemed as if every third car he encountered on the way to Glenwood Springs had skis on the roof.

Webb always tried to accomplish several things whenever he went into town. It saved time, gas and wear and tear on his truck, which, to his surprise, had weathered the first cold snap without a breakdown. After visiting the attorney's office, he planned to swing by the supermarket and lay in a couple of weeks' supply of grub. He also wanted to talk to the vet about one of the heifers he thought might have an infection. He couldn't afford to have the vet make an official visit to the ranch, but Ernie was pretty good about dispensing free advice to the indigent.

Webb found Harv Cooper in good spirits.

"I talked to my niece, Gwen," he said. "She feels we've got a pretty damned good case."

"A good enough case that I'd get the baby?"

"Yes, sir. I can't make any promises, of course, but Gwen was positive. It turns out she's been researching the field and recently wrote an article on the subject for a law review, which is a fancy way of saying she's well-informed."

Webb was taken by surprise. He'd assumed all along he'd have a tough fight on his hands. "I'll be damned," he said.

"That's only the first bit of news," Harv said. "It seems Miss Prescott's attorney has been over the same ground as me."

"Oh, yeah?"

"I first talked to Gwen Monday morning. She called me yesterday to say in the interim she'd had an inquiry from an attorney in Aspen with the same hypothetical questions I was asking. I don't think there'd be more than one woman in Aspen inseminated with a stolen embryo from a Denver clinic, do you?"

"You're saying Lina knows that I have a strong case if it became a court battle."

"Her attorney knows, so my guess is she does, too."

That bit of information gave Webb pause. What would Lina be thinking now? he wondered. Thus far they'd both been dancing in the dark. And on equal ground, more or less.

"I don't expect this to turn into a lawsuit," Webb said, "so I don't know if it makes all that much difference."

"Yes, but don't forget it gives you leverage when it comes time to negotiate a settlement."

"I'm hoping it'll be a lot friendlier than that. You see, Harv, Lina and I are on good terms, and I hope to keep it that way."

"You're saying you won't need that war chest we talked about to go up against the Prescotts."

"I hope not."

"Then maybe you can use the money to buy back that ranch of yours."

"Money?" Webb said. "You talking about the settlement with the clinic?"

Harv Cooper leaned back in his chair, a big grin on his face. "Sure am."

"You mean they offered a million?"

"Not yet, but they came up to eight hundred thousand. I'd suggested a million five. I think they see it's headed for a million, but they can't bring themselves to jump at it. I tossed it back to them and will probably hear something in a week or so."

"Well," Webb said, "I see why you were beaming when I walked in."

"There's nothing as pleasant for a lawyer as giving a client good news."

"Not even getting your cut of a settlement check?"

"That's a close second," Harv Cooper said with a grin.

MARY LOOKED AT HIM from the other side of the booth in Eldridge's Café, shaking her head. "Webb, maybe you're in for a turn of good luck after all."

He nodded, but he wasn't feeling as good about it as everybody else. After leaving Glenwood Springs he'd stopped off at Mary's and told her he was taking her to lunch. They'd talked on the phone only once since the storm, and he wanted her to know what he'd heard from Harv Cooper. He also wanted her advice.

"The way this thing is shaping up, my good luck is Lina's bad luck," he said. "That's what kind of worries me."

"It doesn't have to be that way," she said. "You can always come to an accommodation that's pleasing to you both."

"I'd like that, but I'm not sure how to get from here to there."

"First of all, I'd go see her," Mary said. "You've given her some breathing room, and that's fine, but don't keep her wondering forever. You've got an excuse for going to Aspen with the earrings, not that you need one. Seems to me your feelings for each other aren't a secret. I'd say take up right where you let off."

Webb appraised her. Mary had a good heart, there'd never been any doubt in his mind about that. But sometimes he thought she put others first, without regard to her own needs and feelings.

"Mary," he said, "isn't there a part of you that's a little sad at the thought of Lina and me getting together?"

"If you mean because of Karen, no, Webb. I've been encouraging you to find someone for a long time. You know that. And you also know I like Lina a whole lot. The truth is, your friendship with Lina couldn't please me more."

The waitress, a woman named June whom Webb had known as far back as high school, came and cleared away their dishes. "Coffee, folks?"

"Please," Mary said.

Webb nodded. "Make it two."

When she'd gone, he said to Mary, "I don't want to rush Lina. In fact, I think if anything, it's gone a little too fast."

"Then slow things up. Take your lead from her. She'll let you know what feels right and what doesn't. Lord, I can't believe Webb Harper is asking advice about courtin' a lady."

"I'm not asking how to get her to bed. I know how to do that. It's the next phase I haven't had much experience with. In the old days, I'd be hightailing it in the other direction about now."

"Just be honest with her, Webb. That's the best policy."

June came with a pot of coffee. She filled their cups and left. Webb took a sip and watched Mary put a packet of artificial sweetener in hers.

"I think I'll mosey on up to Aspen tomorrow afternoon," he said.

"Good idea. I've finished my first sweater for Lina. Maybe you'd be so kind as to deliver it for me."

"Sure, I'd be glad to."

Mary smiled. "Somehow I thought you would."

Webb tapped his thumb against his coffee cup and shook his head, his expression as wistful as his thoughts. "You know, Mary," he said, "I honestly never thought I'd care for anybody again."

"You and Karen had a wonderful marriage. But you didn't die with her, son. This is meant to be."

"I hope so."

"If you have doubts, it's only natural, Webb. You've got some history to get past."

What Mary was saying was true. But if he did have doubts, it wasn't so much because of the past as the future. Webb wanted to be sure he was loving Lina for the right reasons.

AS THE WEEK PROGRESSED, Lina found herself busier than she had been in a couple of months. It was an early ski season, which meant more people and therefore more sales. By Friday she was beginning to think she'd hire another salesperson now, rather than waiting until Thanksgiving week.

Despite the preoccupation of her work, the challenges Lina faced in her personal life were never very far from her mind. She couldn't help worrying that she'd offended Webb and that he was hurt more than he'd let on. She'd expected that he'd somehow show up on her doorstep before now. It might even be incumbent on her to make the first overture since he'd called last.

A customer who had been browsing for the better part of half an hour finally left the shop, so Lina decided to give Webb a call. She dialed his number but didn't get an answer. Since it was nearly dark, it could be he was out with his cattle or in the barn. She decided she'd try later, after she got home.

Strangely enough, she wasn't quite sure what she would say when they did talk. Maybe she should have something particular in mind, like inviting him to dinner. She'd had several meals at his house. It was definitely his turn to be her guest.

Feeling better for having made up her mind, Lina started closing out the cash register, eager to get home. Why had she been waiting for Webb to make the next move anyway? She was a modern woman and, even if Webb still clung to some anachronistic notions, he was open-minded and reasonable. And from everything she knew about him, his heart was in the right place.

As she worked on the day's receipts, the front door opened and she was surprised to see Kyle Girard come in the door. He was in his ski clothes and looked as though he'd spent the day on the slopes.

"Kyle," she said. "What a surprise." She wasn't pleased to see him but saw no reason to be unpleasant.

"I came to Aspen to take advantage of this early opportunity to ski, and since I was in the neighborhood, I thought the polite thing would be to drop by to pay my respects."

"At my father's suggestion?" she said suspiciously.

"No, actually not. I didn't even mention it to Morgan. To be frank, I'd planned to go to Vail, but I couldn't get into my favorite place. So I rang up the Hotel Jerome and they could accommodate me, so here I am, getting in a bit of skiing before popping off to London. I leave Tuesday."

"Sounds as if you've had a nice visit," she said, making conversation.

"It was good to be back. I've decided to come a little more regularly."

"How nice."

Kyle leaned on the counter across from her. "Lina, I know our friendship is tentative at best, and the last thing I want to do is foist myself on you, but I come with news and thought I might share it with you over a drink."

"What sort of news, Kyle?"

"It concerns your...dispute with Mr. Harper over the baby."

Lina gave him a wary look. "You have news concerning that?"

"I do indeed."

"What?"

He gave her his semicharming, semismug grin. "Ah, but you'll have to join me for a drink to find out."

"Kyle, you aren't playing games with me, are you?"

"No, I promise not."

Lina wasn't sure whether to trust him or not, though she'd never known Kyle to be dishonorable. This couldn't be a ruse to get her attention, because he was smart enough to know she wasn't interested in him. She checked her watch.

"It is closing time," she said. "I suppose I could have a cup of coffee with you before heading home." He looked sufficiently pleased that it made her suspicious. Still, she couldn't imagine what he had to gain by deceiving her. "Just let me get my coat and close up."

WEBB WAS SO MAD at his damned truck that if there was a cliff at hand, he'd have gladly pushed it off without a second thought. Halfway to Aspen the distributor had gone haywire and the electrical system failed. He'd had to abandon it on the side of the road and hitch a ride the rest of the way.

His plan had been to get to Lina's shop late afternoon so that he could take her to dinner, but now it looked as if he'd be lucky to catch her before she left. The framing contractor he'd gotten a ride with had been talking his ear off, but Webb had hardly heard a word. Fortunately the guy didn't require much more feedback than an occasional grunt.

As they made their way along West Main Street, the guy said, "Where was it you wanted to be let off?"

"Middle of town," Webb replied. "Anywhere's fine."

"How about at the light at Mill Street?"

"That'd be great."

They only had a few blocks to go. Webb checked his

watch. It was just past closing time, but if he hustled he might still catch Lina before she got out the door.

From the seat he picked up the department store box Mary had packed the baby sweater in and set it on his knees. They passed the Sardy House on the north side of the street. The next cross street was Monarch. The contractor, who'd just lit his third cigarette of the drive, mumbled something about hating the ski crowd even if they put food on his table. The traffic light a block ahead changed to red and they slowed, finally rolling to a stop in front of the Legends of Aspen Sports Pub.

"Here you are, pal," the driver said.

"I appreciate the ride," Webb replied. "I really do."

"Any time."

As Webb reached for the door handle, he looked up to see a woman in a red coat stepping off the curb in front of them and start across the street. It only took a second for him to realize it was Lina and that she was with the man beside her. The guy had on a ski parka and stocking cap, but Webb recognized him, too. It was Kyle Girard. His mouth agape, Webb watched them make their way to the north side of the street, Lina taking Girard's arm as they approached the curb.

"Light's about to change, amigo," the contractor said. "You'd better hop out."

Webb opened the truck door and stepped down into the street, thanking the guy again. As soon as he slammed the door, the pickup took off up East Main, leaving him standing at the side of the street. Across the way Lina was going into the Hotel Jerome with Kyle Girard. Webb felt his blood begin to boil. What was with this woman? Was it a different guy each weekend, or had her father convinced her that Girard was a better escort than a threadbare cowpoke with three nickels in his pocket?

Webb stared at the building, incensed, jealous. God knows what foolishness he might have uttered had he not arrived late and caught her in an unguarded moment with Kyle. Had she been playing him for a fool all along? Maybe her interest in him didn't have anything to do with *him* at all. Maybe it was really all about the baby.

A car came by, making a turn in front of him and splashing the front of his pants with slush. Webb cursed and stepped up on the curb, brushing himself off. He wasn't sure what to do—confront her or walk away. He had to deliver the sweater for Mary and give Lina back her earrings. If she wasn't in Girard's room, he'd find her, hand over the stuff, then get the hell out of Dodge.

"ALL RIGHT, KYLE," Lina said when the barmaid set his Scotch and her Diet Pepsi on the table in front of them, "what's your news?"

He slowly turned his glass. "I happen to know that the insurance company for the Denver clinic is negotiating with your friend, Mr. Harper. And it looks as if he may be collecting into the seven-figure range, a million dollars anyway."

"Webb is settling with the clinic?" she asked, astounded.

"That's my understanding."

"How do you know?"

"I have a friend from college who's an insurance defense counsel. We had dinner the other night and the conversation turned to a bizarre case he had concerning a fertility clinic. He mentioned no names, but when he said that some cowboy stood to make a million without suffering any real pain, and all because some doctor decided to take a shortcut, I knew whom he was talking about."

"My God!" Lina gasped, disbelieving. "No wonder I haven't heard from Webb." A sharp twinge of disappointment went through her, followed by an empty feeling in the pit of her stomach.

"I did share this bit of information with your father,"

Kyle said. "He seemed to think Harper's motive was clear.
By settling with the clinic, he has the money to fight you
for custody of the baby."

Lina hardly heard Kyle's words. "I suppose that's the
smart thing to do," she said.

"War is hell."

And victory goes to the shrewd, she thought. Lina was
embarrassed to think Webb had been playing her along,
lulling her into a sense of complacency when his real intent
was to fight it out in court. Even if he cared for her some,
it was clear that he had been hedging his bet. She, on the
other hand, had taken the high road—refused to crush him
when she had the chance. And what had Webb done in
response? Used the opportunity to arm himself. That hurt.
It hurt a lot.

"Sorry to be the bearer of bad tidings, Lina," Kyle said.

"I appreciate your thoughtfulness," she replied, patting
his hand. "It's especially generous considering you don't
owe me a thing."

Kyle took her hand and kissed her fingers. "We may be
divorced, Lina, but I still consider you a friend. And letting
you get away I now see as one of the bigger mistakes of
my life."

Just then she glanced up and saw Webb himself standing
at the entrance to the bar. He was wearing his hat and
sheepskin coat and had a box under his arm. He was glaring
in her direction. Lina pulled her hand free of Kyle's grasp.
When Webb saw that she'd seen him, he strode over to the
table, his face a mask of anger.

He dropped the box on the corner of the table as Kyle
glanced up, seeing him for the first time. "Mary asked me
to give this to you," he said, his eyes hard. Then he dug
into his pants pocket, taking out the earrings she'd left at
his place. He put them on the table in front of her. "And
I believe you mislaid these." Tipping his hat, he muttered,
"Good evening, folks," and walked out of the bar.

By the time Lina got home she wasn't sure whether she was more angry or hurt. Webb was clearly incensed that she'd had a drink with Kyle, never mind the fact that it was innocent and he himself had been duplicitous. That was so typical of a man. It was just fine if *he* played both sides of the street, but if she were to look out for her interests, she was a conniving, two-timing harlot, or whatever it was he thought.

She also wondered just how he'd happened to find her at the Hotel Jerome. Had he been spying on her, or was it pure chance?

But then, as she thought more about it, Lina realized Webb could easily have misconstrued what was going on. Kyle had been putting on a show in that affected manner of his, and Webb had obviously assumed the hand kissing meant something. Well, if he wasn't mature enough to be sure of what he was seeing before jumping to conclusions, then he deserved to suffer. On the other hand, more was at stake than pride and dignity. The baby's future depended on the state of their relationship. Lina realized she didn't have the luxury of righteous indignation.

But what to do? She wasn't going to go crawling to Webb on her hands and knees, but she had to get things back on track. If there was to be understanding between them, someone would have to make the first move. Time, it seemed, was no longer on her side. Webb could wait her out, then come get his baby.

It made her sick to think that things had come to that. Webb had her right where he wanted her. So maybe she was wrong—maybe she did have to go crawling to him after all.

The one thing she knew for sure was that she wasn't going to allow stupidity—either his *or* hers—to get in the way of her happiness and well-being. Accordingly, she'd do the intelligent, mature thing, even if it meant giving in, even if it meant eating humble pie—whatever it took to disabuse Webb of his mistaken impressions.

At first she thought she'd phone him, but on reflection decided a bolder statement was called for. She'd go to his place and look him right in the eye. And while she was at it, she'd find out what his intentions were about the baby. If he'd decided on fighting it out with her, she might as well know it now.

Lina left the house and got into her car. She knew she was taking a chance by not calling first, but the odds of him going somewhere else didn't seem that great. He'd most likely head home to stew because it wasn't his style to go to a bar to drown his sorrows or pick up some tart to prove his manhood. No, she'd find him at home alone and he'd be surprised to see her. She'd have her say, then leave him enlightened and, hopefully, contrite.

Fortunately it was a clear night and there was no threat of adverse weather. At least she didn't have to worry about getting trapped at his ranch this time. Of course, she wouldn't stay under any circumstances, though she'd like it if he asked her. She wanted to be able to tell him she wouldn't. Webb might have the upper hand, but she saw no reason to make things easy for him.

Once she left town, the traffic wasn't bad. She passed the Aspen Cross-Country Center, Maroon Creek and then the country club. As she approached the intersection of Route 82 and Owl Creek Road, she saw a man hitchhiking. He had on a cowboy hat and a sheepskin coat. It wasn't until she zipped past that she realized it was Webb!

Lina immediately pulled to the side of the road. Looking back, she saw Webb had turned and was staring at her car. Putting the transmission in Reverse, she backed toward the intersection. Webb started toward her. When he got alongside the car, she lowered the power window.

"Webb, what are you doing hitchhiking?"

He leaned over and peered in, resting his gloved hand on the door. "I'm trying to hitch a ride back to my truck."

"Where is it?"

"It broke down on my way to town." He glanced around the interior of the car. "What are *you* doing out here, Lina?"

"As a matter of fact, I was on my way to your place."

"Alone?"

"Yes, alone. What did you think?"

"You and Girard looked pretty cozy back at the hotel. I assumed he was your new guardian angel."

"Well, you assumed wrong."

A semi went by, blasting its air horn. She was off the pavement and wasn't blocking the road but was apparently causing offense.

"Come on and get in," she said. "I'll give you a ride."

Webb opened the car door and climbed in but didn't close the door right away. "You sure you want to do this?"

"You're not exactly a stranger, Webb. And all I'm offering is to give you a ride."

"Why were you headed to my place?"

"Close the door and we'll discuss it on the way," she replied.

He closed the car door. Lina looked back to make sure it was clear before pulling back onto the pavement. They were soon headed toward Carbondale.

"Put on your seat belt," she said.

Webb looked over at her. "You certainly seem to be in an order-giving mood tonight. Does it come with being a Prescott or driving a BMW?"

"You aren't as attractive with a chip on your shoulder," she commented dryly.

"I don't take kindly to being ordered around," he said, buckling the seat belt, "even if a person's intentions are good."

"I didn't mean to be bossy. But if my voice had an edge, it's because I'm pissed at you."

"*You're* pissed at *me?*" he asked incredulously.

"You were very rude at the bar."

"It's rude if I don't want to stand around watching some jerk slobber all over your hand? Thanks, but I'm not into that kind of indulgence."

"Well," she said, "if you had hung around long enough, you might have found out it was completely innocent. Kyle is affected and pretentious. I had no idea he was going to do that."

"What were you doing with him, anyway? Checking to see if there were still any sparks?"

"Webb," she said, seeing an opportunity, "you're jealous."

His response was stony silence.

After a while she continued, "On the one hand I'm flattered, on the other I'm disappointed in you."

"I notice you didn't answer my question."

"What question?"

"I asked what you were doing, flitting around with Prince Charles."

"If you must know, Kyle was in town for some skiing before he heads back to Europe. He came by and invited me to have a drink with him. The only reason I accepted was because he said he had news about you that I might be interested in."

"News about *me?*"

"That's right."

"What kind of news?" he asked.

"Kyle told me that you're negotiating a settlement with the clinic."

Webb hesitated, taking a moment before responding. "My lawyer is."

She looked over at him, sorry they weren't in the light

and sitting face-to-face so she could see his expression. "Why didn't you tell me?"

"I don't know. Maybe I didn't want to break the mood. Maybe I'm gun-shy. Maybe it's hard for me to trust anyone or anything."

"So what was last weekend?" she demanded. "Fraternization with the enemy?"

"I wasn't thinking in those terms."

"No?"

"Listen, that was a very special thing we shared."

"The sex was good, in other words," she said dryly.

"What is it you want me to say?"

She realized she was being peevish and that it wouldn't serve her. On the contrary, the whole point in coming was to make peace. "I guess I want to think we're working together on this, Webb. I agree that last weekend was special, and I want things to continue being good between us. What happened this evening was a misunderstanding. I'd like to put it behind us."

"I'd like that, too. But you're right about one thing—I owe you an apology," he said. "I was an ass. And, yes, I suppose I *was* jealous. Maybe that says as much as anything about my feelings for you."

She smiled, delighted. "You might as well know I tried calling you this afternoon to invite you to my place for dinner."

"Did you really?"

"Yes. I felt it was my turn to show a little hospitality. I guess I felt bad about the way the weekend ended and I wanted to get things moving in a positive direction."

"Sounds like we're thinking along the same lines," he said. "Bringing your stuff to you was only one reason I came. I was hoping you'd have a bite with me."

"And instead you found me holding hands with Kyle."

"It did tend to dampen my enthusiasm."

"It's not too late, is it?" she said. "I haven't eaten, have you?"

"No, but I've got to get that truck of mine fixed. I need a way to get hay to my cattle. They wouldn't take too kindly to missing chow call."

"Is there anything I can do to help?"

"Just drop me off at my truck. I called a friend who's a mechanic. Wally's getting a tow truck and meeting me where I broke down. He might even be there already."

"How far is it?" she asked.

"Just a mile or so down the road. We're almost there."

Lina reached over and touched his hand. "Will you come to my place for dinner next week, then?"

"Sure."

"Friday evening okay?"

"Friday's good."

"Come as soon as you can after six."

"I'll be there with bells on my toes," he replied, sounding pleased.

They came to Webb's pickup. His friend was already there and was in the process of hitching it to the tow truck.

"Perfect timing," he said as she pulled over. "I appreciate the ride. You salvaged my evening. In more ways than one."

"I'm sorry we didn't get to have dinner."

Webb nodded. "Me, too."

"But I'll see you next Friday."

"Count on it," he told her. "There's no point in you sitting here now. Get on back to your warm house."

"Okay," she said, reluctant to leave him.

Taking off his hat, he leaned over and kissed her lightly on the lips. "It's going to be a long week, sugar," he murmured, nuzzling her neck.

She threw her arms around him and hugged him. "Too long, Webb. Too long."

He gave her a regretful look, but smiled. Then he climbed out of the car.

CHAPTER FIFTEEN

ON THURSDAY MORNING of the following week Lina was scheduled to have her checkup. Ironically she was hunched over the toilet, having a bout of morning sickness, when she got a call from the doctor's office.

"Dr. Radford's delivering a baby and is tied up for a few hours," the receptionist told her. "Any chance you could come in this afternoon around one instead?"

"Sure, one's fine," she replied, dabbing her face with a damp cloth.

Lina hung up the phone before she remembered that she was scheduled to have lunch with her father. Morgan had called the previous evening, saying he'd be flying to the ranch and could swing by Aspen if she'd have lunch with him. They'd only had one brief conversation since the rescue with the snowplow, and they both knew a little more talk was needed to clear the air, so she'd readily agreed. But now she had the checkup to contend with.

She was about to call the doctor's office back to reschedule when she decided it would be good for her father to go with her. He'd admitted to being pretty remote from the action when she was born, having spent most of her mother's pregnancy battling weather, creditors and a livestock virus to save his ranch. "You can have the experience of fatherhood with your grandchild," she'd told him in an earlier conversation. He'd laughed and said he knew her mother would be pleased at the notion.

After her shower, Lina checked her body out thoroughly

in the mirror. For the first time she could see noticeable changes. Her stomach had begun to swell. It wasn't exactly protruding yet, but her soft flesh had become fuller and her stomach was no longer flat. In clothes it didn't show, but naked, there was no question.

Webb, she suspected, would be pleased. Pregnant women, he'd said, were sexy. Lina was happy with the progression of her pregnancy, but she had to admit to gnawing doubts about where things were headed. Her up-and-down relationship with Webb was up right now, and she was convinced he was sincere in his feelings for her, but she also sensed there were things he himself wasn't sure about. Her proposal of sharing the baby fifty-fifty hadn't been mentioned again, though technically the two weeks he'd asked for weren't up. If he didn't raise the issue tomorrow night, she decided, then she would. Lina was convinced their main problem was that things were still up in the air. If they could just come to a firm agreement on the baby, everything else would probably fall into place.

After breakfast she drove to her shop. There'd been more snow at the beginning of the week and more lifts were open, which of course meant more customers. Darlene Mason, the young woman who had worked for her during the season the past two years had agreed to start early and had been there all week. It was a good thing, too. They'd done more business the first three days of the week than in the first three weeks of October.

Lina was especially glad that Mary Carson's needlework had been a success. She'd already sold a third of the embroidered smocked dresses, and on Wednesday Darlene had sold the sweater Webb brought. Lina had called Mary that night to tell her how well things were going.

"I couldn't be more pleased," Mary had said. "You'll be happy to know I've finished another sweater, and the light blue one you wanted with the hood is three-quarters done."

"You keep that up, Mary, and we'll both be rich by Christmas."

Lina had asked her if she could get the sweaters to Webb so he could bring them on Friday, but Mary said she had business in Aspen and would drop them off Thursday if that was all right. Lina told her that was even better.

Around eleven-thirty her father called from his plane, saying he'd be arriving soon and that he had a car arranged so she didn't have to pick him up. Lina didn't mention her doctor's appointment, figuring she'd tell him when he got there.

After a slow start, it had turned into a busy morning. Lina and Darlene were each helping customers when her father arrived. Lina sent him in back to get his own coffee, then, when Darlene finished with her customers, Lina told her to go to lunch so she could cover while Lina went to the doctor's at one.

"So, how's the old bear?" she said to Morgan when she had a spare minute.

He was sitting on the stool behind the counter, sipping his coffee. "The old bear's fine. How're the young mother and her cub?"

"Cub's going to get checked by the doctor in about an hour. And you're coming with me, Grandpa."

"Me?"

"You."

An older woman and her very pregnant daughter had been browsing for the last several minutes. They came to the counter with a little jumper. Lina rang up the sale. When they'd gone, she and Morgan were alone in the shop.

"Let me give you my news," her father said. "My people tell me Harper's settled with the clinic's insurance company."

"Oh, really?"

"He got a million-one out of them."

"Good for Webb."

Morgan's brows rose. "He's no longer at a disadvantage, Lina. He's got the money to fight us."

"There won't be a fight, Daddy. One way or another we're going to work this thing out."

"I hope you've got a plan, because I've been told that the fact that he's a natural parent and you're not gives him all the trumps."

"Yes, legally I'm on shaky ground."

"But you aren't worried?" her father said.

"The past few days I've been giving it a lot of thought, and I think I've come up with a solution."

Morgan sipped his coffee. "What's that?"

"I'll tell you after I get everything in place. There are details to be worked out."

There was admiration in Morgan's smile. "Carolina, you're getting cagier by the hour. One of these days you're going to start sounding like your old man."

"You obviously intend that as a compliment."

Her father chuckled. "What else?"

The front door jangled, and Lina looked up to see Mary Carson enter the shop with a box under her arm. Lina went to greet her.

"Two more sweaters and I crocheted a little blanket," Mary said.

"My, but you've been busy. Let's have a look."

They went back to the counter, where Morgan was waiting. He stood and Lina introduced him.

"Mary, this is my father, Morgan Prescott. Daddy, meet Mary Carson, the grandmother of my baby."

Morgan looked surprised. "Grandmother?" he said.

"Mary is Karen's mom, Webb's mother-in-law."

"Oh, I see." Morgan gave a courtly little bow. "It's a pleasure meeting you, ma'am."

"Likewise, Mr. Prescott." Mary smiled pleasantly.

Lina noticed her father's antennae perk up as he subtly checked Mary out.

"This is Daddy's first shot at grandparenthood," Lina explained. "So if you have any suggestions, I'm sure he'll be all ears."

Mary laughed. "The main rule, Mr. Prescott, is to leap at all the fun things and drag your feet when they try to get you to help out with the dirty work."

"Mary!" Lina protested. "Not that kind of advice!"

"Now you hush, Carolina," Morgan said. "This is exactly the kind of unbiased information I need to hear."

Lina took the box from Mary. "Just remember, Dad, I expect you to be fully versed in the art of diaper changing. Mama always complained how easily you'd gotten off. I think it's time you made your contribution."

"Listen to this, Mrs. Carson—an heir on the way and she suddenly thinks she's queen," Morgan joked, giving Mary a wink.

"You'll be a soft touch," Mary said. "I can see that just looking at you."

"Is that a fact."

"My guess is we'll be competing to see who's the first to spoil the little tyke rotten."

"Is that a challenge, Mrs. Carson?"

"No, Mr. Prescott, more like a warning."

Lina opened the box and took out the little sweaters. They were adorable. Lina oohed and aahed. "Daddy, aren't these the most precious things you've ever seen? Isn't Mary's work exquisite?"

"This is the lady you told me about," Morgan said, realizing. He checked Mary out again.

"You told your father about me?" Mary asked Lina.

"Yes, Mrs. Carson," Morgan interjected. "Lina said I had to take you to lunch sometime when I'm in town."

"Lina," Mary admonished, "what a terrible burden to place on your poor, unsuspecting father."

"Oh, no," he said. "She meant it as a treat for me. And

I can see why. As grandparents to this baby, we have a lot to discuss.''

Lina shook her head, bemused. ''I know he sounds charming,'' she told Mary, ''but it could be that he's angling to get out of going to the doctor's with me. You can't jump to any conclusions when it comes to Morgan Prescott.''

''Listen to this!'' he protested. ''My own daughter fouling my reputation. Now you'll *have* to come to lunch with me, Mary, if only so I can clear my name.''

''Lunch?'' Mary said with a glance at Lina.

''You don't have other plans, do you?'' Morgan asked.

''No, but I don't want to interfere, Mr. Prescott.''

''First, you have to call me Morgan,'' he said, picking up his coat and hat. ''Second, you have to promise never to listen to a thing this girl says about me.'' He came around the counter. ''And third, I sure hope you like good old steak and potatoes and not this prissy European and California cuisine the restaurants are pushing these days.''

''Mary makes the most heavenly apple pie you've ever eaten, Daddy,'' Lina told him. ''Even better than Aunt Sue's.''

''You see how tricky the girl is?'' Morgan said. ''She knows my weakness and doesn't blush at cutting me off at the knees.''

''You two go have a nice lunch,'' Lina urged, giving Mary a conspiratorial look. ''I'll have your check ready for you when you get back.''

''Sure you don't mind, sweetheart?'' her father asked.

''No, Darlene will be back soon and I'll go on over to the doctor's. You two have a good time.''

Morgan and Mary went off, talking happily before they were out the door. Lina grinned with amusement as she watched them go. Knowing her father, there was no telling what might happen. But she knew Mary Carson well enough to know the woman was not only sweet, but had steel in her backbone. She'd be able to handle him.

Lina didn't worry much about either of them; she had enough of her own problems to fret over. First, there was her doctor's appointment and then there was Webb. As time passed and the baby continued to grow, Webb had been quietly shoring up his position. If Morgan was to be believed, Webb would soon have a million dollars in the bank. In the course of a few short weeks he'd gone from being on the verge of annihilation to sitting in the catbird seat. As her mother had once said, if hardship tested a man, so, too, did success. Sometimes the latter was more difficult to deal with than the former. As for Webb, time, she realized, would tell.

WEBB WAS SMART ENOUGH to know his new wealth was of tactical significance but that in the long run it wasn't money that mattered, it was people's attitudes. Lina seemed to want things to work out—not just with the baby, but between them, as well—and that meant a lot to him. As he dressed to go to her place for dinner that night, he thought again about what he would say to her.

They hadn't known each other long, and worse, they had been adversaries from the first. Yet, despite that, he had fallen for Lina in a big way. What held him back wasn't so much his feelings for Karen as his uncertainty about Lina's motives. For that matter, he didn't completely trust his *own* motives. It was damned hard to separate his emotions from the situation he was in. Would they care for each other if Lina weren't carrying his child? That was the real test.

Webb had given the matter a great deal of thought and decided that was what they needed to talk about—how she'd feel about him if he were just Webb Harper, no baby, no million bucks, just a guy with a few head of cattle and a horse.

Unfortunately, there were problems with that approach. First, it wouldn't be easy to ignore the baby. Second, Webb was no longer a dirt-poor cowboy. When Wally had told him it would take three or four days and five hundred bucks to bring his truck back to life, Webb knew he was in danger of losing cattle. So, he'd gone into the Chevy dealership in Glenwood Springs and bought a new pickup. Even though it would be a while before he got his million from the insurance company, a call to Harv Cooper was enough to satisfy the sales manager that the money would be coming.

Buying the truck gave him a new appreciation of what it meant to be able to write a check. There'd been a time when he'd been able to write small checks without having to worry, but it had been a while. This was a whole new ball game. The question was, what would it do to Lina's thinking?

Webb got into his new pickup and drove to Aspen. Strangely, he wasn't as happy as he should have been. At first he wasn't sure why. Then it occurred to him—he felt like a fraud. He hadn't earned the truck. It was the payoff for the doctor stealing Karen's and his baby. Karen's hopes and dreams had been reduced to a truck and some money in the bank.

The one thing that gave him solace was that their baby was still in the picture—growing inside Lina's body. That was the next order of business. He had to come to an accommodation with Lina. He wanted that badly. Oddly, he didn't want it so much for the sake of the baby as for Lina and himself.

He arrived in Aspen early so that he could swing by the florist's and buy some roses. He also picked up a box of chocolates. By the time he pulled into Lina's drive in his new truck, loaded down with gifts, he felt like a phony instead of an admiring suitor. This wasn't a Webb Harper of his own making; this was the cowboy version of Kyle

Girard. He silently vowed that if he kissed her hand, he'd shoot himself.

Lina greeted him at the door in black jeans and a red silk shirt. It seemed as though every time she opened a door he was left dumbstruck. Her smile immediately dispelled his doubts and angst.

"Lordy, do you look beautiful," he mumbled.

"Come on in, Webb," she said cheerily as she eyed the flowers in his hand.

Her beauty and upbeat manner made him feel better instantly. "These are for you," he said, handing her the flowers as he stepped inside.

"Oh, they're gorgeous, Webb."

She gave him a big kiss, and he luxuriated in her sweet scent and her softness as he held her. Why he'd doubted, he didn't understand. A man tended to know when something was right, and Webb knew his feelings for Lina could no longer be denied.

He gave her the chocolates.

"Just what I need—temptation. I saw the doctor yesterday, and he said my weight is right on target. If I have many of these, I'll be a blimp in no time."

"You look perfect to me," he said, taking off his coat and hat.

"Then you'll have to eat the chocolates so I stay that way."

She took him by the hand and led him to the kitchen, where she trimmed the stems of the roses and put them in a big crystal vase. Then she fixed him a drink and they went to the sitting area, where they sat side by side on the sofa. Lina took his hand and rested it on her knee.

"So," he began, "the baby's okay?"

"The doctor said it couldn't be better."

"That's good."

"Yes, I'm pleased."

Webb rubbed the back of her hand with his thumb. He

realized the uneasiness he was feeling wouldn't pass until he'd told her. "I've got news," he said. "I've settled with the insurance company."

"Yes, I heard," she replied. "For a million, wasn't it?"

"A little more, actually."

"Good for you, Webb."

He wasn't surprised that she might be pleased for him, but considering the implications, he wondered why her joy wasn't somewhat qualified. "I have mixed feelings," he confessed. "I didn't earn it."

"You were wronged, though. This is compensation."

"I know the theory," he said. "But money isn't what this is all about. The baby is the issue."

Lina was silent for a moment. "That's certainly true, isn't it?"

Webb took a long drink of bourbon and water.

"It's important that you and I are positive, Webb," she said. "Everything else is secondary."

He could certainly subscribe to that.

"In fact, yesterday at the doctor's, I was thinking you really ought to be involved—assuming you want to be."

"Oh, I'd like that a lot."

Lina squeezed his hand. "There were important questions about the natural parents I couldn't answer, and nowadays they like to know as much as possible about the baby's genetic makeup."

"Karen and I went through that," he said. "And so far as I know, there's nothing to be concerned about."

"I thought that was probably the case, but I wasn't sure."

Webb glanced over at Lina, and it dawned on him that they were skirting the issue. They were making nice, but what they were eventually going to do still hung over them like some sort of Damoclean sword. That might explain the nervousness he sensed beneath Lina's cheerfulness.

"I made a lobster bisque for the first course," she told

him, evidently not quite ready to tackle the hard issue. "I hope that's all right."

"I hate to sound like a hick," he said, "but I don't think I've ever had it before."

"If you like lobster, you're in for a treat. It's rich and decadent but really good."

"I'm looking forward to it," he replied.

"I hope you like it."

He could hear the tentativeness in her voice. There was uncertainty, yes, but maybe also fear. They both knew the evening would be a pivotal one, and Lina had to feel less confident knowing she no longer held the stronger hand.

"I hate to suggest we eat the minute you walk in the door," she said, "but I'm just famished. Would you mind if we started? The notion of crackers and cheese just doesn't do it for me."

"I can eat anytime, Lina."

"Oh, good," she said, jumping up. "I'll get the soup, you go to the table."

Webb watched her go, his eyes taking in her slender figure. She hadn't lost any of her appeal. He ached for her. It muddled things, he knew, making an already complicated situation more so.

They had the lobster bisque. Lina sat at the opposite end of the table, her cheeks rosy in the candlelight, her eyes shining. He sensed her anxiousness. What was wrong? He decided it was time to get to the bottom of things.

"Lina," he began, "something's bothering you. What's the matter?"

She hesitated. "I guess it shows, doesn't it?" Lina folded her hands in front of her and looked down, as though gathering her courage. "I've been thinking, Webb," she said tentatively. "Until we resolve what to do about the baby, both our lives are going to be in limbo."

"I agree."

"Well, I've come up with a solution," she said. "It's a

radical solution, but I've given it a lot of thought and I think it makes good sense.''

"What's that?''

Lina took a breath, holding it for a moment, her face filled with anxiety. "That we marry.''

Webb was stunned. In fact, he was incredulous. "You want to marry me?''

"Yes,'' she replied. "If you think about it, Webb, it's a good solution. We both care about this baby more than anything, and we both want it. Well, why pull it apart? Even if we worked out some sharing arrangement, there'd still be tension and frustration. But if we married, the baby would have both of us. You wouldn't be giving up anything and neither would I.''

Lina chewed on her lip as she gazed at him, trying to read his reaction. He was speechless.

"I know this is a bolt out of the blue,'' she said. "I hope you understand that I couldn't have suggested it if I didn't respect and admire you. You're a special man, and I know you'll be a wonderful father.''

"And so you want to marry me?''

"I know we haven't known each other long, but these are hardly normal circumstances.''

"You can say that again.''

Her anxiety grew. "It isn't an easy thing, asking a guy to marry you, but I figured it was easier for me than it would have been for you.''

He contemplated her silently.

"Webb, you don't have some old-fashioned notion that the man has to be the one to ask, do you?''

He shook his head.

"Then what's wrong?''

"You really don't see, do you?'' he said.

She frowned. "I don't see what?''

"Lina, you just asked me to marry you, but you didn't say a word about the way you feel about me—except that you respect me and think I'd be a good father. Doesn't it occur to you that something's missing from that statement?''

"You must know how I feel about you," she returned defensively.

"Why? Because you went to bed with me? How do I know that wasn't all part of the plan?"

"Webb!"

"Don't get me wrong, Lina. I'm sure you have good intentions. To your eye, marriage is a workable solution. It's just that I'm not so sure. Not under these circumstances.''

Lina put her face in her hands. "Oh, my God," she mumbled. "I guess I made some assumptions.... I thought I knew...how you felt about me.''

"Seems to me the problem is how *you* feel about *me*," he said. "Hey, I'm flattered. I truly am. Marrying a guy for the sake of expediency is a pretty big pill to swallow.''

"Webb, it's not like that!"

He pointed an accusing finger. "Be honest, Lina. Would proposing marriage to me even have crossed your mind if you weren't pregnant with my kid?"

She closed her eyes, biting her lip.

"Well?" he prompted.

"No, but that doesn't mean I don't have feelings for you."

"Let's examine those feelings," he said. "So far we've got respect and the potential for being a good father. What about the potential for being a good husband?"

"That goes without saying," she said, her eyes glistening.

"You didn't mention it, did you?"

"Well, you haven't said anything about your feelings for me, either. Oh, I knew you wanted to go to bed with me, you made that clear." She wiped her cheek with the back of her hand. "Don't you see how hard it is for me to do this? I had to take a chance that you had the right kind of feelings for me. And I took the chance because I knew you were in an even tougher position. You would have looked like an opportunist if you'd asked me to marry you, so I put myself on the line.''

"You don't lack courage, Lina," he said. "Nobody can accuse you of a failure of nerve.''

"So what are you saying? That I'm insensitive? That I don't care about you? That the practical considerations are all that matter? Or is it that *I'm* the opportunist, Mr. Harper?''

"Your timing is rather curious," he replied. "You have to admit that.''

Her eyes rounded. "Oh?''

"A couple of weeks ago you were willing to go fifty-fifty on the baby. Now it's marriage. I'm not questioning your motives," he explained, "but I would like to understand your thinking.''

"All right, Webb," she said, her eyes narrowing, "I'm going to tell you exactly what I was thinking. When I heard you got your money in the settlement with the clinic, I was glad. I figured it put us on an equal plane and any deal we worked out would be fair. Neither of us had to go to the other with hat in hand.''

"That's all well and good, Lina, but it's still no reason to marry.''

"If you think I proposed out of fear, you're dead wrong. Sure, it looks as if you've got the law on your side. If we fight this in court, you might even have a better chance of winning, but I'm not so desperate that I'd marry you just to salvage what I could.''

"Well, I'm glad to hear that.''

She got to her feet, her eyes narrowing again. "You are a bastard, a heartless bastard. I hope you realize that, Webb.''

"I'm sorry. I didn't mean to offend you.''

"You didn't mean to offend me?" she exclaimed. "I've just done the hardest thing a woman can do. You impugn my motives, all but call me a liar and an opportunist, and then you say you didn't mean to offend me? I can't believe this."

"I didn't mean to do any of those things, Lina."

Tears were running down her cheeks now. "Well, you somehow succeeded."

"Listen," he said, "I've had a happy marriage. I know what it's like for two people to be together for the right reasons. Karen and I loved each other. She wanted children, but that isn't why she pulled me out of the line."

"No, and she wasn't already carrying your baby when you met, either."

"That's true."

Lina picked up the linen napkin and wiped her eyes. "You know what? This is an impossible situation. If I told you I loved you, you'd never believe me. Not completely. If my proposal sounded like a business offer, maybe it's because deep down neither of us can be sure of anything. Maybe I should have tried to express my feelings for you, but I was scared. Don't forget, you've never expressed yours for me. From my point of view, this was a shot in the dark. I thought you cared for me as a person, but maybe I was mistaken about that, too."

"Lina, you weren't mistaken. It *is* a tough situation."

"Not tough," she returned. "Impossible."

"Nothing's impossible."

"We don't agree on that," she said, shaking her head. "You can't believe how foolish I feel. I sold myself a bill of goods. How can I possibly know how I feel about you? And if I'd stopped to think about it, how could I have known how *you* really feel about me? You're still in love with your wife, Webb. Your passion about this is due to the fact that this baby is hers. You have feelings for me, sure, but they're confused, just like mine are for you. And the funny thing is, none of this comes as a surprise. We both knew it from day one.''

"Now I think you're overreacting," he stated.

"No, what this has done is open my eyes."

"I still say you're overreacting."

"You feel bad about it and so do I," she said. "If nothing else, that says we're decent human beings."

"Of course we are. And nothing that's been said here this evening changes anything."

She shook her head. "No, you're wrong about that. Everything has changed."

He could see she'd dug in her heels. She was trying to save face—for which he could hardly blame her—but she was rejecting everything. Obviously he'd bungled things. His instinct for candor had gotten him into trouble again.

"Look, Lina," he said, "why don't we start this conversation over?"

She continued to shake her head, her jaw set. "There's no point. I've humiliated myself enough for one evening. Please don't make it any worse than it already is."

"You didn't make a mistake. If anyone did, I did!"

"Please don't argue with me," she responded. "Just go quietly. Don't apologize. Don't say anything. Just go."

"I can't do that, Lina. Not without telling you how I feel. You are not just the woman who happens to be carrying Karen's and my baby. You're a lot more than that. A whole lot more."

"All right," she snapped. "Now you've said it."

"But it's true!" he insisted.

"Fine, it's true. But in the greater scheme of things, it's not enough. I think it would be best if you left."

"Is that what you really want?"

"Yes. I've got a blinding headache and I've lost my appetite. I can send the rest of the dinner home with you. Someone might as well enjoy it."

"Lina, the food doesn't matter. It's you I care about."

"Please, Webb, I've suffered enough."

He got up with exasperation. They stared at each other. He didn't know what to think. The warm feelings between them seemed to have evaporated in one gut-wrenching moment of misunderstanding, mistrust and misjudgment. Everything was suddenly wrong.

"Let me get the leftovers," she offered.

"No, I don't care about that," he replied. "You'll get your appetite back tomorrow. Eat them then."

Leaving the dining area, he went to the front door, taking his hat and coat from the chair where he'd tossed them. Lina followed, but at a distance. She looked stiff, afraid. Webb faced her as he put on his coat and hat. She was unconsciously wringing her hands, avoiding his eyes.

"Lina," he said when he was ready to go, "I have one question for you. The answer is all that matters out of everything you've said this evening, so please tell me the truth."

"What is it?"

"Do you love me?" he asked.

She didn't answer immediately. Her eyes filled and tears began overflowing. After a long minute she shook her head. "No," she murmured, "maybe not."

"No?"

"I wanted to. I guess I might have convinced myself I did so I could propose. But it was the baby, Webb, for me as much as for you. It probably isn't possible to love anyone under these circumstances, and I think we both know it."

He stared at her, asking himself if she was being honest. In the end, he decided she was, painful as that was for him to admit. It was no accident that she'd spoken of marriage without the word *love* once crossing her lips.

"Thank you for your candor, Lina," he said. "I've always respected honesty."

He turned then and went into the icy night. The wind made his eyes tear, but that wasn't the real reason he was crying. It was only an excuse. She'd asked him to marry her and still had managed to break his heart.

CHAPTER SIXTEEN

SATURDAY WAS MISERABLE. Lina'd had a terrible night, awakening early. With nothing else to do, she'd gone to the shop and worked on the books until opening time. The customers seemed to come in droves, which was good for business, as well as keeping her mind off her troubles. That was a blessing, since whenever recollections of the previous evening did seep into her subconscious, she got sick.

Zara telephoned toward the end of the day. Lina was glad. She knew that after her fiasco with Webb, one of the first things she'd have to do was get hold of her attorney.

But Zara had other things in mind. "Is your doctor encouraging you to exercise?" she asked.

"Yeah. Annoyed with me, actually, for not getting enough."

"How would you like to do a little cross-country skiing tomorrow? I've gained three pounds since Alec left and I refuse to be fat when he gets back," Zara said.

"When's he due?"

"He's going to try to be here for Thanksgiving, but he won't know for a while."

"That's only twelve days," Lina said.

"Only? Twelve days seems like forever, especially since I think he's going to surprise me with a ring."

"What makes you think so?"

"At the beginning of the week, when we talked on the phone, he asked about my ring size. And last night he asked if I liked emeralds."

"Emeralds, huh?"

"Don't you think that's a pretty good clue?" Zara said.

"I would say there's an engagement in the offing," Lina volunteered.

"I've been so excited all day that I can't think about anything but getting this weight off me."

"Zara, three pounds?"

"When you're five-two, you have no place to hide it, believe me."

"I'm sure Alec would love you if you gained twenty."

Zara laughed. "He's so wonderful, Lina, he really is. But it's been a while since we've talked about you. Any developments with Webb?"

That, of course, was the opening she needed, but Lina still found it hard to talk. "Things aren't going well. The chances of us cooperating on a settlement don't look good," she said.

"What happened?"

"It's a long story. Why don't I tell you tomorrow?"

"You'll go skiing with me, then?"

"Yes, I definitely can use the exercise, and the air would be nice."

"I'll pick you up," Zara offered. "What time?"

"Not too early. I've been sleeping in...when I sleep at all."

"How about ten?"

"Ten's fine."

Lina hung up, feeling a little better for having talked to her friend. She hadn't shared the story of her aborted proposal, but that was all right. Lina wanted a bit more time to process what had happened anyway.

Several customers came into the shop just before closing time, and Lina ended up staying open an extra twenty minutes to take care of them. Darlene sold four pieces of the Italian baby furniture to a woman from Chicago, so the day turned out to be the best of the season so far.

Lina dreaded going home because she figured she'd mope around, crying as she had the night before, after Webb left. Of course, she couldn't blame him for rejecting her. He owed her nothing—certainly not marriage for the sake of expediency. And that, she'd decided on reflection, was what she'd had in mind—solving the problem in the cleanest, least painful manner possible. She hadn't exactly pictured it that way before they'd talked, but Webb had honed right in on what she was doing. Her marriage idea had a lot more to do with the baby than with them. His skepticism had probably been a blessing to them both.

Not that it still didn't hurt.

Lina was glad that Zara had called, because she knew the time for fooling around had passed. She needed to come up with a legal strategy pronto—which was what her father had been saying all along. Webb was used to dealing with survival challenges, to capitalizing on his advantages and cutting his losses. Now, with Zara's help, she would have to do the same.

After locking up Bébé, Lina walked through town looking in the shop windows, killing time before deciding on a place to eat. It almost felt as though the longer she managed to stay out in the world, the longer she could defer facing her personal misery. It was one of those rare times when home was not so much a safe haven as a reminder of her humiliation.

The Century Room at the Hotel Jerome was not the sort of place a person would go to eat alone, but Lina did anyway. It was an act of defiance of sorts—an in-your-face response to fate. Had Webb leapt at her offer of marriage, they could happily be celebrating at the Century Room together that evening, rather than her eating alone, a woman scorned, pregnant and without a husband.

Lina wondered why she was feeling sorry for herself. After all, she hadn't had marriage in mind when she'd begun this adventure. The answer, of course, was rejection.

Nor did it do a lot of good to tell herself she was lucky, that Webb had saved her from a horrible mistake. A pregnancy was only a moment in time. Even the rearing of a child was just several years. But marriage, in theory, encompassed a lifetime. What had she been thinking?

Thus fortified, Lina went home, built a fire, fixed herself a cup of herbal tea and sat watching the flames. When she finally went off to bed, she felt that the worst of the hurt and humiliation was behind her. Though there would still be tears and sorrow ahead, Lina convinced herself that Webb Harper's time as her lover was over. From here on, he was just a legal problem.

THEY MOVED DOWN the trail along the valley bottom, the field of snow glistening in the morning sun. Lina's heart was beating at an even pace. Her breathing was steady and rhythmic as she moved skis and poles in concert. It felt good to get some exercise—to be out in the air, to think of her body in terms of how it was moving and how it felt, rather than how it looked and what was happening inside it.

She had never been much of an athlete but she'd always enjoyed cross-country skiing, probably because it was pure locomotion. Walking, jogging, swimming, horseback riding were all agreeable pastimes.

Zara, on the other hand, was more practical. To her, exercise was something you did because it was good for you. In the summer they sometimes jogged together, finding their levels of skill and enthusiasm pretty much complementary.

Lina wasn't pushing herself, because she wanted to err on the side of caution. The idea wasn't to enter a marathon, but to have an easier birth. She and Zara hadn't talked much once they'd gotten on their skis, and during the drive they'd mostly discussed Alec. Finding that their present pace was easy enough for conversation, Lina decided to tell her friend what had happened with Webb.

Zara listened without comment, though her face did register surprise and dismay as Lina related the sorry tale. As they came to the top of a rise, they stopped so that Lina, who'd been talking continually, could catch her breath.

"It took courage to do what you did," Zara said. "I could never have done it. Even now, knowing the way Alec feels about me, I'm not so sure I could pop the question."

"The issue wasn't courage, Zara," Lina said, leaning on her poles. "It was stupidity."

"I think that's unfair. Your plan wasn't unreasonable. It might even have worked out all right."

"Well, it was a mistake and it didn't work out. But I don't want to waste energy on what might have been. I've got to come up with a strategy. You're my lawyer, Zara. What do you recommend?"

Zara took off her glove and got a handkerchief from her pocket, then wiped her nose. The two of them stared at the traffic moving along the highway in the distance. Zara put her glove back on, then stamped the snow with her pole.

"In the law," she replied, "sometimes the best defense is a good offense."

"Meaning?"

"Webb's got the upper hand, and I haven't come up with any brilliant legal arguments that are likely to turn the tide. But right now there's no case unless and until Webb contests the fact that the baby's yours. In other words, if he wants it, he's going to have to go to court and say to the judge, 'This lady's got my kid. Take it away from her and give it to me.' One option is to wait until he acts. The other is to take the initiative. We can go to the court and ask for a declaratory judgment that the baby to which you give birth is yours."

"Is there an advantage to that?"

"Well," Zara said with a shrug, "we stake our claim

and force Webb to dispute it. We get the ball rolling, put him in a defensive posture.''

''I like that,'' Lina stated, staring off at the mountains. ''It sounds a whole lot better than waiting for the ax to fall.''

''You want me to get on it, then?''

''Yes,'' Lina said decisively. ''I might lose this, but it won't be lying down.''

''And there's always the chance that the judge might feel compassion and give you visitation rights, if not some kind of joint custody arrangement. Or, who knows, lightning could strike and we could win.''

Lina patted her friend on the arm. ''I like having a fighter on my team,'' she said. ''Let's file the suit and see what happens.''

''Right.''

Lina took a deep breath and glanced up at the cloudless sky. She couldn't exactly say she felt good, but it did feel better to be taking action. If she wasn't lucky in love, maybe she'd be lucky in court. ''Come on, Counselor,'' she said, feeling a burst of energy. ''Race you to that little tree up the trail.''

WEBB SAT WATCHING Mary turn the chops on the broiler pan before pushing it back in the oven and closing the door. She put the fork down on the counter and turned to face him. ''I have no idea what she was thinking,'' she said, ''but I can guarantee you this, it wasn't easy for her to do what she did.''

''But how could she want to marry me if she didn't love me, Mary? Are women that mercenary?''

''I don't know about mercenary,'' Mary replied, ''but they've got survival instincts that men don't necessarily understand.''

''Survival instincts? Hell, she tried to sell herself to me just to make sure she'd get to keep the baby.''

"Oh, Webb, Lina did no such thing!"

"She admitted that her marriage proposal was about the baby and had nothing to do with us."

Mary cocked her head and gave him a skeptical look. "Are you sure you aren't exaggerating a tad? It's obvious to anyone who's seen the two of you together that she has feelings for you, Webb. That couldn't have been irrelevant."

"Oh, she had feelings for me, all right—feelings for what I could do for her."

"That really is unfair," she objected. "And I think you know it."

Webb scratched his head and groaned. "I suppose I am being unfair, but it's because I'm hurt by what she did. I really thought there was more between us than that. I know now it was all in my mind, but I thought it was love, I really did."

"Did you tell her that?"

"No, I didn't. We never got that far. What difference did it make how I felt about her if she had only one thing on her mind—the baby?"

Webb got up from Mary's kitchen table and rotated his sore shoulder and stretched his back. He'd been so upset the night he'd gotten home from Lina's place that he'd saddled Jake and gone for a ride in the moonlight, thinking it would clear his head. But Jake had slipped on an icy trail and they'd both taken a tumble. At least Jake was fine, and Webb was lucky he hadn't been hurt worse. As it was, he'd spent the better part of the next day stretched out on the sofa because standing and sitting were both painful.

"If nothing else, telling how you felt might have made her feel better," Mary said.

"I don't know that she needed any consoling. I didn't leap at her offer, true, but that wasn't a marriage proposal so much as it was a ploy. She as much as admitted it."

Mary removed the pot of potatoes from the stove and

carried it to the sink. "Admittedly I wasn't there, but you might have misread the situation. The girl's pride had to be wounded. It isn't every day you ask a guy to marry you, whatever your reasons. And as for professions of love, they aren't easy to make, especially if you haven't heard them coming the other way. No girl wants to say 'I love you' without being pretty sure she's going to hear it back."

"Sorry, Mary, but you're just making excuses for her. I'm not saying Lina's a bad person. And I'm pretty sure she does have feelings for me...or did. I think she tried to do what she figured was best for everybody, but that's no reason to marry. And that's just what I told her."

"The poor thing must have been thrilled to hear that," she said, taking a milk carton and some butter from the refrigerator.

"Well, dammit, Mary, what was I supposed to do?" Webb asked, pacing back and forth across the tiny kitchen. "I had to be honest."

She turned to face him again, crossing her arms under her breasts. "Let me ask you a couple of questions, Webb Harper," she said sternly.

He was a bit taken aback by her tone. "All right."

"First, do you love Lina?"

He thought for a moment, rubbing his chin. "I thought I did."

"Are you saying you were wrong before or that what happened changed your feelings?"

"I'm saying it's a little more complicated than that."

"Well, maybe Lina found it a little complicated, too. Did that ever occur to you?"

"Complicated or not, she wanted to marry me so she could keep that baby."

Mary rolled her eyes. "You're so damned stubborn, Webb. I'm only now realizing what a saint my daughter was to make it work with you."

"Thanks a lot, Mary."

"If I've told you once, I've told you a hundred times, you're your own worst enemy."

"What's your other question?"

"I'm wondering if you've figured out what you're going to do. Seems to me Lina made the last move."

Webb sat down again. "I reckon I have given it a lot of thought the past few days."

"And?"

"I'm not sure I'm going to do anything."

"What do you mean?"

Webb rotated his shoulder again, rubbing it. "Eventually she's going to have that baby. I figure I'm going to wait and see what happens then."

"You're not going to do anything? Just let nature take its course?"

"For the time being."

"Why?" Mary demanded.

"Seems to me time's more my friend than hers. Anyway, I don't want to rush in with both guns blazing just because the advantage's mine. There's nothing to be gained by handing her reasons to hate me. I might be stubborn, but that doesn't mean I'm a jackass."

Mary gave him a look, then turned to the counter and started preparing the mashed potatoes. Webb waited, but she said nothing.

"You obviously don't approve," he said.

"All due respect, Webb, but you've still got a lot to learn about women."

LINA HADN'T EXPECTED to hear from Webb anytime soon, and she didn't. Things had pretty well settled down to where they'd probably been destined to go from the very beginning.

Zara worked diligently and got the petition to the court together by the Tuesday before Thanksgiving and dropped it off at Bébé for Lina to look over. Lina told her there was no big rush and asked Zara to let her mull it over until the following week. She hadn't told her friend, but Lina had been thinking about going to her father for advice, despite her vow to the contrary.

"It's your decision," Zara told her. "The main thing is for you to feel comfortable about it."

Lina might have talked to Morgan sooner, but he'd spent most of the past few weeks in Houston and New Orleans, working on some big real estate deal. After that, he'd gone to his place in Saint Croix for a week. The one conversation they'd had was when he was in Denver briefly and called to make arrangements for Thanksgiving dinner. "I'd say come on down to Denver," Morgan said, "but then I thought if I went to Aspen, I might be lucky enough to run into your friend Mary Carson."

That had amused her. "You kind of liked her, didn't you, Daddy?"

"Mary's a real fine lady. Not the kind I tend to socialize with, I grant you, but real comfortable to be with."

"Nice for a change not to worry that your hair might be too gray or that your paunch is showing, isn't it?"

"You could have gone all day without mentioning that, young lady." He'd laughed. "Mary *is* my kind of people," her father conceded. "The kind I used to be, anyway."

But Lina didn't see any chance of Mary coming to a Thanksgiving dinner, so she gave her father no encouragement in that regard, saying she'd come to Denver instead. Besides, she didn't have much of a maternity wardrobe yet and wanted to do some shopping in the big city.

Lina and her dad spent a quiet Thanksgiving day, just the two of them. His cook and housekeeper, Maddy Brown, made dinner, but Lina sent her home early to be with her family, saying she could serve it herself. Morgan was talkative during the meal, taking the burden of conversation off her. Lina kept formulating silent entrées into a discussion about her marriage proposal to Webb and Zara's petition for a declaratory judgment, but couldn't quite bring herself to say anything.

Toward the end of the meal Morgan gave her the perfect opening when he said, "You haven't mentioned Webb Harper once, Lina. What's happening with him?"

Lina started to tell him what had happened but lost her nerve. "Things have cooled off and we're both lying low and accessing," she replied somewhat disingenuously.

Morgan didn't press her on the subject, but he did seem pleased when she admitted that she'd talked to Zara and was seriously considering asking the court for a declaratory judgment on her rights to the baby. He sipped his wine and said, "I've always felt if you're going to err, err on the side of being too aggressive." Lina didn't know if it was good advice, but it certainly served her present need.

When she returned home, Lina found a nice note from Mary in the mail. They'd only seen each other once since the proposal fiasco. The Saturday before Thanksgiving Mary had come to the shop with a couple more sweaters, two stocking caps and another crocheted blanket. Lina had scarcely had a chance to talk to her, because there were a half dozen customers in the shop and Darlene had called in sick. They'd both smiled warmly, but Lina could tell Mary had heard the whole story from Webb and was a little uneasy. If Lina had to guess, Mary probably felt sick about the situation.

Lina didn't even get to look at Mary's work before she left the shop, but she did say she'd call. That evening she phoned Mary and was surprised to get an answering machine. She didn't think Mary had one and assumed it was a gift from Webb. In any case, she left a message saying the pieces were lovely, as always, and that she'd pop a check in the mail.

The Monday after Thanksgiving Lina called Zara at her office and told her to file the petition. "No point in procrastinating any longer."

Zara said she'd take care of it and suggested Lina try to relax and put the whole business from her mind.

"The die has long been cast," Lina told her. "God knows, I ought to be prepared."

"But you can never predict what will happen," Zara said.

Lina didn't want to dwell on it and switched the conversation to a happier topic. "So, how are things with Alec?"

"You'll never guess what's on my finger," Zara said, sounding almost giddy.

"Probably an emerald engagement ring."

"The most beautiful one I've ever seen, Lina! It's just gorgeous!"

"Then it's official?"

"Semi. We're having a little dinner party around Christmas to announce it. You'll be invited."

"Congratulations, Zara. It couldn't happen to a nicer, more deserving person."

A few days later Lina came down with a cold, which was of concern only because of her pregnancy. The doctor said there was nothing to worry about, but suggested that she take it easy for a few days. Fortunately, her other seasonal clerk, a young woman named Eloise, had started at the beginning of the week, and she and Darlene were able to keep the ship afloat.

It was difficult to be at home with so much time to think. She knew that Webb would soon be served with the legal papers—if he hadn't been already. Lina couldn't decide if he'd give her some kind of direct reaction or if his response would come through his lawyer.

Lina wondered if perhaps she'd owed him some sort of courtesy call, warning him of what was coming, but decided in the end she had no obligation. The issues were no longer personal. They were legal. Besides, it was too late now.

There was no response from Webb of any kind, either direct or indirect. No calls. He didn't drop by. Nothing. The following Monday Lina returned to work and, as the days went by, the silence from the Harper ranch became deafening. Lina saw Mary, but neither of them brought up the lawsuit. Mary was not by any means unfriendly, but she was cautious, keeping all conversation to subjects relating to the two of them. Lina would have liked to ask her what was happening with Webb, but she didn't want to put the woman on the spot.

As the days passed, Lina often worried that she'd done the wrong thing by taking their differences to court. Webb had left her house that fateful night thinking she was a scheming opportunist, bent on winning at any cost. And when he'd rejected her, no doubt he thought she had fallen back on the courts, hoping she could wring a little mercy out of some judge.

Well, that wasn't entirely false. But all along, her intentions had been good. Her marriage proposal had been sincere. Maybe she'd bungled things, but if Webb thought her cynical, he was dead wrong. She had cared for the man—more than cared for him—but it didn't matter now. It was all water over the dam.

As she waited warily for Webb's attorney to reply to her petition, Lina tried to keep her mind on her work, but it wasn't easy—her growing stomach was a constant reminder of her situation. The morning she discovered she could no longer fit into her jeans was a rude awakening. She still looked all right in loose-fitting clothes, but much of her normal wardrobe was no longer usable.

The day she first decided to wear a maternity dress to work, she stared at herself in the mirror. Seeing that she looked as she had with that pillow the maternity shop gave her to strap to her stomach, she broke into tears. She didn't know why—because she'd been watching herself swell for weeks—but something about seeing herself that way sent her over the edge.

At her bedroom window she watched the snow falling over Aspen and thought of Webb out in that snowy pasture, feeding his cattle. Maybe she hadn't fully appreciated how idyllic those few days had been when she was snowbound at his ranch, the two of them holding each other by the fire, happy to forget the world and all its problems. How had she gone from there to here? Had she deceived herself? Or had she misunderstood Webb?

Lina was plagued with such thoughts day and night— wondering what might have been, second-guessing herself, regretting. She tended to blame herself more than Webb, because he'd really done nothing to bring this on either of them. The one thing he might have done was be a little more understanding when she'd made her clumsy effort to find a solution. If he'd shown some compassion, rather than rebuking her for focusing on the baby's needs, they might have worked things out more amicably. But he hadn't, so here they were, preparing to settle the matter legally, irrevocably.

Though she knew it was coming, Lina was nevertheless stunned when Zara called to say they'd gotten the response from Webb's attorney to their petition for a declaratory judgment. "Nothing surprising in it," Zara said. "Essentially, they deny the validity of our claim and assert that Webb is entitled to the baby. They've asked the court to declare Webb the sole custodial parent."

Though her own petition used practically the same phrase, coming from the other direction the words sounded harsh and hostile. "So now the court decides," Lina murmured.

"There'll be a hearing," Zara informed her. "Probably in February or March."

Lina hated the thought of going to court, but she was the one who had set the wheels of justice in motion. "Just so it's before May,'' she said. ''I want this over before I go into labor.'' She paused, almost afraid to ask the question that was in her heart. ''Zara,'' she said, ''do you think they'll let me see the baby after it's born? Or will they take it right away?''

There was a silence on the line, then Zara replied, ''This isn't over yet, Lina. I haven't even made my case to the judge.''

''I know that,'' Lina said. But she also noticed Zara hadn't answered her question.

CHAPTER SEVENTEEN

LINA HAD INTENDED to ignore Valentine's Day altogether, but her father insisted that as long as he was alive, she'd always have a valentine, a man who loved her. And he told her that whether she liked it or not, he was coming to Aspen to take her to dinner.

The invitation had come in a conversation the previous weekend when Morgan had called from Denver, though initially he'd had another subject in mind—the hearing that was set for February sixteenth. "Are you sure you don't want me to fly up and be with you?" he'd asked.

"No, Daddy. It's sweet of you to offer, but Zara and I can handle it. I'll be fine."

Morgan Prescott had already tried to offer his moral support, if not his actual resources, but Lina had insisted on going it alone. Over the past few months she'd become rather stoic about her troubles. The big hurdles remaining now were to get through the legal entanglements and the pregnancy. Zara had been very frank with her, and not only to make sure she didn't have unrealistic expectations. It was also a gesture of respect.

"All right," her father had said, "I'll stay out of your legal affairs, but unless you've got a beau I don't know about, there's no way you can keep me from taking you out on Valentine's Day. Hell, I've already got dinner reservations!"

"Me, a boyfriend?" She'd laughed. "Daddy, if you

could see my stomach. I'm definitely not dating material. Not unless Aspen gets its first beached whale.''

Though most women wouldn't consider a Valentine's Day date with their father much of a treat, Lina was glad for the attention. After the hectic holiday season, January had been pretty quiet. They'd had a lot of snow and the town's part-time residents were back en masse for the winter season. Business at the shop was steady, but without the preholiday frenzy.

Zara had been preparing for the hearing and had conferred with her occasionally, but the only lengthy conversation they'd had was over the possibility of a lawsuit against the clinic. Lina had no great enthusiasm for the project, but another letter had come from the clinic's insurance company, offering to settle any legal claims for a quarter of a million. Zara advised that they wait to see the outcome of their suit with Webb. "Depending on what happens, your damages resulting from the clinic's fraud could be greater or smaller," she'd said.

One of the few bright moments was Zara and Alec's engagement party. Lina had gone alone, but Zara's twin, Arianna, had showed up after a mysterious disappearance involving a book she'd been editing. She looked absolutely fabulous. Zara was truly happy Arianna had come, and she'd been radiant that evening, glowing like her emerald ring.

There were three other couples at the party. Two were Zara's friends from Aspen. Laura Lacen, a longtime friend of the twins, and Laura's fiancé, a doctor, flew in from Vegas. Arianna was the only one there—other than Lina—who'd come alone, but of course Lina had the better excuse: she was already in maternity clothes. Arianna never did explain why she'd come solo—she simply gave an enigmatic smile and mumbled something about fate and fortune cookies and James Bond.

If there was anything other than the dismal outlook of

her lawsuit that saddened Lina, it was the fact that her friendship with Mary Carson had become a little uneasy. They'd maintained a good working relationship, but once the suit was in full swing, it became tough for them to ignore it. Neither lost her affection for the other, however.

For Christmas, Mary gave Lina an antique quilt that her grandmother had made. "It would have gone to Karen," Mary said when they'd had their Christmas lunch, "but since I've got no one else to leave it to, I wanted you to have it."

Lina had been touched. Her present to Mary had a sentimental note as well. In addition to a bottle of White Shoulders perfume, she'd given her a silver picture frame. "I thought maybe a picture of the baby would look nice in it," she said.

It was the most direct reference to the baby either had made in weeks. Mary had gotten misty-eyed. "You know, I really hate what's happening," she'd said.

Lina had patted her hand. "I know you do."

"I love you and Webb both, and that makes it twice as hard."

All Lina could do was nod.

"The thing is," Mary said, "both of you are doing the best you can, and you both mean well. And I can't say anybody's to blame."

Lina hadn't intended to talk about Webb, but this had been an opportunity to say something she'd been thinking for weeks. "I have no hard feelings toward him," she'd said. "I'm sure it's as difficult for him as it is for me. I hope he doesn't hate me."

"He doesn't. I know that, Lina."

"I wish there were a way we all could get what we wanted."

Mary had brooded for a while before she told Lina that Webb had started dating someone. Lina assumed she'd told her so she wouldn't get caught by surprise. "A gal from

Glenwood Springs named Holly Barker. She's a hostess in a restaurant and sings at the Roundup Club Friday and Saturday nights. Holly's pretty enough, I suppose," Mary said. "A flashy redhead, but I'm sure Webb's goin' with her just to keep his mind off his troubles. Wouldn't make anything of it if I was you, Lina."

Lina was taken aback by the news but managed a gracious reply. "I'm glad he's found someone, Mary. I'm happy for him. Honest. He's better off with somebody in his life. And it could be he'll be needing some help."

Mary looked pained by Lina's response, but she withheld comment. They both knew it was time to let the subject drop.

With Zara pretty much occupied with Alec, Lina had spent some time with her other friends, though everybody was busy during ski season. Just before Christmas she'd gotten a call from Kyle in London. "I've cleared four or five days on my calendar between Christmas and New Year's," he'd said. "I've got an invitation to visit friends in Gstaad, but I could make it to Aspen if you have some time, Lina."

"Kyle," she'd told him, "a pregnant woman isn't much fun in ski country. I'd go to Switzerland if I were you."

Lina wasn't sure what her ex was thinking, unless he'd become fascinated with the fact that she was both available and pregnant. In any case, she wasn't ever going to be lonely or desperate enough to give Kyle any encouragement.

But her father was a different matter altogether. Ever since he'd called to invite her to dinner, she'd been looking forward to the evening. Morgan had been very sweet and supportive since his last intrusion. It seemed he'd learned his lesson. Besides, her father was all she had in the world, except for her friends. She had already begun to emotionally distance herself from the baby to lessen the hurt when the blow finally came. That was the only way Lina knew how to survive.

When the doorbell rang, Lina hurried to the door, finding her father standing on the porch in a black topcoat and with a wide grin on his face. In his hand there were a dozen long-stemmed red roses. "Happy Valentine's Day, sweetheart," he greeted her. "And aren't you the most beautiful thing I've ever seen."

"Thank you, Daddy," she said, giving him a kiss on his rosy cheek and a big hug. "Of course, your objectivity is completely suspect."

"For you," he said, handing her the flowers.

"They're beautiful." Giving the flowers a quick sniff, she remembered the last time she'd seen Webb, back in November. He, too, had come with roses. The perfume of the blossoms brought the moment back vividly, making her shiver. It had been one of the most disastrous evenings of her life, and she couldn't think about it without cringing.

After closing the door, Morgan took off his topcoat. Under it, he wore a dark business suit and red tie. No Western wear this evening.

She put down the flowers on a chair and hung up his coat in the closet. When she turned, he was admiring her. "Carolina, there's not a man alive who wouldn't say you're the picture of beauty itself. Did you get that pretty red dress just for Valentine's Day?"

"When you've got a date with the most sought-after bachelor in Colorado, you gotta look your best!" she teased.

Morgan put an arm around her full waist, bumping his hip playfully against hers. "Suppose we've puffed each other up enough to believe what we're hearing?"

"It's nice to pretend, I guess," she replied a bit sadly.

"Lina, honey, you're everything I said and more. You couldn't be more lovely."

Her father's compliments brought tears to her eyes. She

gave him another hug. As he rubbed her back, tears ran down her cheeks. She wiped her eyes and said, "Come on, Daddy. I'm going to put these roses in water. You can supervise."

"I'll need a drink if you want top-rate supervision."

"You've got it."

"When you've got two Prescotts working together on a thing, you can be sure it'll be done right," he said, following her.

"How long do we have? What time's our reservation?"

"We've got half an hour before we have to leave."

"That's time for two drinks."

"It is if I'm drinking 'em," Morgan agreed.

"So, where are you taking me to dinner?"

"I know you'd prefer one of those fancy French places, but I just have to have myself a good steak, sweetheart. I thought we could go to Piñons."

"I like Piñons," she replied. "Besides, I've had this big craving for a steak myself."

"See, baby, you're going to dinner with the right guy!"

WEBB STARED MINDLESSLY at the highway. The snowflakes swirling at him out of the blackness could be mesmerizing, but Holly's voice kept his mind from slipping too far away. Even so, from time to time it wandered back to the last time he'd made this drive. He hadn't been able to get to Aspen fast enough that night. But afterward, he couldn't wait to get away.

Webb hadn't ventured up this highway since, though Mary had tried to get him to drive her to Aspen after a moderately heavy snowfall. "If it's to help you, I'll be glad to do it, Mary," he'd told her. "If your intent is to get me and Lina together, I'm not interested." She'd grumbled in response and withdrawn her request for a ride. And that was the last he'd heard about Lina from Mary.

It had been a bit of a jolt when Webb had asked Holly

where she wanted him to take her for dinner on Valentine's Day and she'd said, "To Piñons." He'd already said he'd take her anyplace she wanted, but he hadn't expected her to say Aspen. But what did he have to be afraid of? The chances of running into Lina weren't all that great. Even if he did, so what? They'd be seeing each other in court in two days anyway.

The real trouble was that he'd suffered over her mightily the past few months. If Lina Prescott had succeeded at anything, it had been to jolt him out of the past and into the present. But when they'd parted, she'd left a huge vacuum. By the time December had rolled around, he'd come to realize that his solitary life was no longer enough. With Lina he'd been reborn, but she'd also broken his heart, even though that hadn't been her intent.

"Why're you being so quiet tonight, sweet pea?" Holly said, reaching over and putting her hand on his thigh. "If a girl can't keep a fella's attention on Saint Valentine's Day, then she's in *big* trouble."

Webb took Holly's hand, pulled it to his lips and kissed her fingers. "Sorry, sugar," he said. "I'm kind of tired. Had a rough day. Finally lost that sick calf."

"Oh," she said. "That's a darned shame. You had the vet out a couple of times, didn't you?"

"Yep. And I spent a night in the barn with the critter."

"I should be so lucky," Holly said.

"Well, if you didn't work practically every damned night of the week, it wouldn't be so hard for us to see each other," he chided.

Holly scooted closer. She rested her head on his shoulder so that her fluffy red hair tickled his cheek. "Webb, darlin', all due respect, but I don't think it's my work schedule that keeps us from seein' much of each other."

"Holly, it's not easy when you work nights and I work days…and sometimes nights, too."

She turned her face and kissed his neck. "Let's not argue

about seein' each other, sweet pea. I've got tonight off and not a thing to do between now and five o'clock tomorrow evening.''

Webb inhaled the sweet scent of her perfume, finding it arousing, the same way the scent of the girls at those country dances used to arouse him. When a man spent his days in places like barns and pickup trucks, a sweet-smellin' gal could do things to the libido.

"Webb, if I ask you somethin', will you give me an honest answer?'' she said, her tone becoming dead serious.

"I don't lie as a rule, Holly.''

"Then tell me, were you thinkin' about that woman who's carryin' your baby just now?''

Webb sort of gulped, realizing he should have seen that coming. "Some,'' he replied. "But it's only because I've got to drive back up here to Aspen in a couple of days to meet her in court.''

"Is that really why?''

"Yes,'' he snarled, getting irritated. "But what in tarnation are you bringing up her for?''

"Well, you were the one thinkin' about her,'' Holly said, bristling.

"Yes, but you were the one who had to talk about her!''

Holly grew very quiet.

"Sorry,'' he said, "I didn't mean to snap.''

"Webb, I got to be honest. I think you still got a thing for her. Tell me the truth, now. Do you or don't you?''

"For God's sake, Holly, why are we discussing Lina? Do you think that's why I'm taking you out to dinner—so we can talk about her?''

"We're having a fight over her, aren't we?''

"No, we aren't having a fight over *her*. We're having a fight over the topic of conversation.''

"I don't see no difference, Webb.''

"Look, Holly, could you just think about the flowers I

brought you and the dinner we're going to have? That's what this evening's about, not some damned lawsuit.''

"That what you really want?" she asked.

"Definitely," he said.

"And will you take me to your place and make beautiful love to me after?"

"What man could say no to a question like that, considering it's coming from the most beautiful chanteuse in all of Colorado?"

"The most beautiful what?"

"Chanteuse."

"What's that?" she asked, wrinkling her nose.

"It's French for female singer."

"How do you know that, Webb?"

"Because I'm taking a correspondence course in French."

"But why?"

"Who knows?" he said with a chuckle. "Maybe because I can. Hell, maybe I'll up and go to Paris one of these days."

"Paris? Why not just come to Glenwood Springs and see me?"

Webb smiled sadly at the night. Yeah, he thought, why not indeed?

PIÑONS WAS ON South Mill Street in Aspen, an elegantly casual place with the feel of the West. There were large oil landscapes of the Rockies on the walls, lots of wood and leather, palms and wicker. Lina and her father were shown to a booth against the side wall, with high leather banquettes. A shaded lamp came out from the wall, casting a warm glow over the mauve tablecloth set with crystal.

Except for lunch during the workday, Lina rarely went out anymore. Her friends Zara and Kimberly were both involved with somebody, and Jordanna had gotten married in August. There weren't any girls' nights out anymore and, considering her condition, Lina didn't date, so tonight was a real treat. And Morgan seemed pleased to be taking her. She wouldn't have liked it if it had seemed like grim duty.

Her father ordered a bourbon and branch, and she asked for mineral water to sip on as they studied the menus. Morgan, who had a knack for telling a story while reading a menu, recounted his first Valentine's Day dinner with her mother, glancing up at Lina from time to time over his bifocals. "Lordy, Carol was beautiful that night," he said. "Just like you. And she wore a red dress, too. I fell in love, just lookin' at her."

Lina smiled as she listened to her father talk about her mother. That was when Morgan Prescott was the most sentimental. Gruffness was part of his nature, but it was one thing he couldn't be when he talked about his wife.

As he recounted that evening a long time ago, Lina glanced over at the hostess, who was taking a couple to their table against the back wall of the dining room. The woman was a redhead of about Lina's age, maybe a few years older. And the man...her mouth sagged open as she recognized Webb Harper.

Lina's stomach clenched as the couple was seated not fifteen feet from them. Webb was on the side of the booth facing the corner of the room, which meant they only had to turn their heads forty-five degrees to look right into each other's eyes.

Morgan had stopped talking when he heard her mumble, "My God."

"Lina," he said, "what's the matter?"

She turned as red as her dress and stared down at the menu lying on the table in front of her. Risking a quick peek, she confirmed that Webb hadn't yet noticed her.

"Sweetheart?" her father prompted.

"Daddy," she said under her breath, "Webb Harper just came in and he's sitting right over there."

"Harper?"

Morgan had to lean forward, look back over his left shoulder to see him. As he did, Webb who was in midsmile, happened to glance up and saw the two of them. Surprise, even shock, flitted across his face. Lina and Morgan regarded each other.

"Wouldn't you know," Morgan muttered, sounding annoyed.

Lina folded her hands and smiled self-consciously. "Small world," she said with a nervous laugh. Her heart began pounding so hard, it was a bit alarming.

"I'm sorry, Lina," her father lamented. "You want to change places? Or tables? I'll ask for a different table."

"No, that's all right, Daddy. I'm not going to make a big deal of this. What difference does it make? He's not going to bite me."

"Yeah, but why spoil your evening, having him looking at you?"

"I'm sure Webb will ignore me, just as I will ignore him," she replied softly. "He's well occupied."

"Who's he with, anyway?"

Lina risked a glance at the other table, just catching Webb look away and turn his attention back to his companion. "He's with his girlfriend, I'm sure."

"Harper has a girlfriend?"

"According to Mary."

Lina had only gotten a superficial impression of the woman. Her green dress was more flashy than stylish. From where they were seated, Lina couldn't really see her—a cloud of red curls, slender arms and hands that seemed chalk white. Lina's impression of her when she'd walked across the room was that she was of medium height and had a nice figure. She'd hardly seen her face.

"So much the better," Morgan said. "Maybe we can count on him leaving us alone."

"I'm sure Webb has no desire to see us. Less, probably, than we want to see him."

"Still, it's a shame."

"Don't be silly, Daddy. If it doesn't bother me, it shouldn't bother you."

The waiter brought their drinks and Lina picked up her menu. She'd regained her composure, and a curious serenity settled over her. She hadn't chanced another glance in Webb's direction, sensing that he was watching her. Better, she told herself, that she rise above it.

Gazing at the menu, she picked up her glass of mineral water and took a sip. She imagined his eyes boring into her. She fought the temptation to find out if he was looking, setting down her glass and turning the page of the menu. She tried to recall how he was dressed, knowing it wasn't in his usual Western attire. He had on a sport coat, she was pretty sure, and a turtleneck sweater. Beyond that, she wasn't certain. She kept her eyes on the page before her, only occasionally able to focus on what was written there.

"Well, I see the steak I want," Morgan said. "How about you, sweetheart?"

"I'm thinking of sole," she said, noting the first dish her eyes fell on.

"Sole? I thought you were hungry for a steak, too."

"I'm hungry for everything. That is, *we're* hungry for everything," she added with a laugh.

As she said the words, her eyes rose spontaneously, meeting Webb's. He was gazing at her intensely. It was that moment when recognition and awareness could no longer be ignored. But the smile on her face was not reciprocated. Webb didn't look angry—more concerned or confused or bewildered. The waiter walked up to his table and stood between them, cutting off her view. Lina returned to her menu, not knowing what to make of the expression on Webb's face.

Their waiter arrived just then, and Lina told her father she was having what he was having, knowing that was easier than figuring something out. As Morgan ordered, she chanced another peek at Webb. This time he was talking to his lady friend. Accordingly, she was able to study him. In addition to his clothes, which were obviously new—a brown tweedy jacket and moss green cashmere sweater— he'd had his hair cut and looked very nice. She was able to sustain her candid appraisal of him for several moments. The man seemed terribly familiar, despite his makeover, evoking a twinge of remembrance, a very sad one.

Lina remembered him sitting with her at his little kitchen table, that earnest expression on his face as he gazed at her. His eyes were all for…what was her name?…Holly, yes, that was it. His eyes were all for Holly now. But, even as she thought it, Webb turned and stared directly at her. Lina immediately looked away, but she'd been caught.

Their waiter, having gotten their orders, went away and she smiled at her dad, a terrible sadness going through her. Here she was in the prime of her life, at the height of her beauty, pregnant and spending Valentine's Day with her father, while the one man she'd cared the most for in her life was sitting a few feet away with another woman. It was bitter irony.

Morgan seemed to understand her torment, which was a little surprising, since he was normally oblivious to such things. There was compassion in his eyes. The smile on his lips was soft. "You all right, sweetheart?"

"I'm fine, just fine," she replied, tears welling up, despite her best intentions.

It was then, out of the corner of her eye, that she saw Webb rise from his table and make his way slowly toward them. It wasn't until he was at their table, standing next to her, that she actually lifted her eyes to his.

"Hello, Lina," he said.

"Hi, Webb."

"Mr. Prescott," he said, turning to her father.

"Harper," Morgan said, acknowledging him with a nod.

"Please forgive the intrusion, folks, but I saw you sitting here and wanted to pay my respects."

"Yes, I saw you," Lina said as cheerily as she was able. "I almost didn't recognize you."

"I guess there've been some changes," he agreed. Then, glancing at her stomach, he added, "You're looking well, Lina. Radiant."

This was the man whom she'd so grossly offended that he'd rejected her, humiliated her, but now he was all courtesy. She couldn't hate him, though. Any bitterness she'd felt was long since past, but she didn't understand what he was doing. "Your baby's fine, Webb," she said, "if that's what you're wondering."

Lina noticed her father shifting uncomfortably. She knew he had to be biting his tongue.

"No," Webb answered, "I was thinking of you, Lina. How good you look."

"Well, thank you. You're looking well yourself."

"I don't expect my intrusion is much appreciated, so I'll be getting back to my table," Webb said, "but I didn't want any tension or ill feelings because of past problems."

"Seems that our outstanding differences are going to be resolved in court," Lina commented.

"And I regret that," Webb stated. "I truly do."

"Let's hope the judge is fair," she said, looking up at him.

He didn't seem happy with the direction the conversation had taken. "Whatever," he replied. "Oh, Mr. Prescott, if I may, I'd like to thank you for releasing the option you held on my place. It was damned decent of you, and I appreciate the courtesy."

"I tried to emulate my daughter's constructive attitude toward any differences we might have, Harper. I'm not one to hurt a man just for the sake of it."

"Thank you for that, sir."

Webb offered his hand to Morgan, who, though not looking too eager, shook it. Then Webb turned back to Lina, surprisingly offering *her* his hand, as well.

"Good seeing you, Lina."

She put her hand in his and he squeezed her fingers. Then, after a long and penetrating look into her eyes, he turned and went back to his table. Lina watched him sit down. And she saw Holly lean forward to peer around the banquette at her.

"What the hell was that?" Morgan asked, sounding thoroughly perplexed.

"I don't know. A peace offering of some sort, I guess."

"Suppose the guy feels guilty?"

Lina glanced over at Webb, who was looking her way, a brooding expression on his face. "I guess he's just sentimental," she said.

Lina had done her best to maintain her dignity, but seeing Webb this way had opened up all the wounds she'd struggled so hard these past months to heal. If he'd accomplished anything by his little gesture of friendship, it was to convince her that she was not the only victim—they both were.

CHAPTER EIGHTEEN

LINA DREAMED ABOUT Webb that night, and she awoke the next day as confused as she'd been when she and her father had left Piñons. She hadn't made eye contact with Webb as they'd gotten up from the table, but her father had told her he stared at her like a man possessed. Whatever was in his mind, it was a mystery.

She put in a full day at the shop, her mind frequently turning back to the strange events of the previous evening. Webb had seemed bedazzled, much like the very first day she'd seen him. It was a little like meeting all over again, except that now there was history between them—some pretty heavy history.

About four that afternoon Lina got a call from Zara.

"I just got the strangest telephone call of my professional career," Zara said. "It was from Harvey Cooper, Webb's attorney."

"What did he want?"

"Webb wants to know if you'd be willing to drop the lawsuit."

"Drop it?" Lina said. "What do you mean, give in?"

"No, he asked if you'd be willing to withdraw it without prejudice. That means we'd withdraw our pleadings and they'd withdraw theirs, cancel it as though it had never happened."

"Why? For what purpose?"

"That's just it," Zara said, "I don't know. And Mr. Cooper was at a loss to explain it himself. The poor man seemed completely bewildered. He said his client told him he didn't want to go to court and that if you'd agree to terminate the proceedings, Webb would, too."

"Zara, I'm confused. Is this good or bad?"

"It depends on whether you want to go back to where we were before I filed the petition. It would mean that if nothing more were to occur in the future, you'd have your baby and that would be that. If the court isn't asked to determine rights, it won't."

"Then I've won?"

"Unless Webb chose to sue you down the line and claim custody. Remember, Lina, you didn't want to wait for him to sue you, so we asked the court to make a determination as to who should get the baby. Webb's asking that you back away from that. Maybe he lost his nerve. I don't know what's happening."

"Oh, God, it sounds like more crazy-making to me," Lina said. "That man is going to drive me nuts."

"You don't have to agree. I can call Mr. Cooper back and tell him we want the court to decide. The advantage to that, of course, is that you won't be kept in limbo."

"Yeah. What does Webb think? That I'd want to live with the possibility of a lawsuit coming down on my head at any moment?"

"He's probably the only one who can answer that, Lina."

She squeezed the bridge of her nose, anguishing. What was he doing? Trying to force her to deal with him directly? She could call him, true. But if he wanted to talk to her, why didn't he just call *her*? This made no sense.

"The strange part about it," Zara mused, "is that he's the one with the better case. If you were in the driver's seat, I could see him asking you to back off."

"I think he wants to test my resolve," Lina said. "But why should I play chicken with him? Even if I lose, I want this over with. The worst part has been not knowing. Tell them no. I want this thing settled.''

"Okay."

"That's the right thing to do, isn't it, Zara?"

"None of it makes any sense to me, so how can you be wrong to stay the course? I'll tell Mr. Cooper no dice. At worst we might get another offer or a better explanation."

Lina hung up. An hour later Zara called again to say the hearing was still on and proceeding as originally scheduled. Lina was disappointed, though she didn't know what else she might have expected, unless it was surrender. And that, she knew, was impossible. Webb would never walk away from this baby.

WHEN LINA NERVOUSLY walked into Judge Ellman's court-room in the Pitkin County Courthouse with Zara the next day, Webb was already at the respondent's table with his attorney, Mr. Cooper. He glanced at her perfunctorily, a gloomy expression on his face, then turned to stare ahead. He seemed so unhappy that Lina wondered if the whole thing wasn't about fear, but decided Webb had too much courage and had faced too much hardship to allow something like this to defeat him.

After they'd been seated for several minutes, with Webb sitting as still as a statue the whole time, the clerk called for everyone to rise. Judge Ellman, a gray-haired man with a thin jawline beard, entered and took his place behind the bench. He proceeded to call the case.

Zara handled everything smoothly and professionally. Lina, her stomach in a knot, slowly sank into a stupor of her own. She tried to follow what was being said. Some of it made sense, the rest was legalese. Zara's voice faded in and out. From time to time Lina looked over at Webb, but he continued to sit motionless, staring straight ahead.

After Zara had finished her statement, the judge began asking questions. Lina had never been involved in a hearing like this before, but the questioning seemed sharp to her, and not particularly friendly. She read in Zara's body language a similar reaction. Lina's heart sank.

Next Harvey Cooper got up and made a statement to the court in support of Webb's position. The lawyer's manner was more folksy than Zara's, but to Lina's untrained ear, no less astute. The questions from the judge that followed struck her as less pointed, perhaps more sympathetic. If her judgment was correct, it was not a good sign. Lina felt sick.

After the respondent's case was finished, Judge Ellman addressed both parties. "Miss Prescott, Mr. Harper," he said, "I won't be issuing a formal order on the petition before me until next week, but I'd like to say something to both of you while you're here. I haven't heard any evidence in this case, and the only facts I'm aware of are those that have been stipulated. Essentially, I'm to render a decision based on the legal argument presented by your counsels, not the facts. What that means is, I won't be deciding who's a fit parent and who is not, but rather if the rules of law would tend to support the rights of either of you over the other. As I'm sure your attorneys have told you, this case is without clear precedent. We've never had to face it before. What that means, in short, is that my decision on the petition will not be about you as individuals, but rather about anyone standing in your shoes.

"I'll be blunt," he continued. "I'd rather the future of that unborn child be decided on the basis of a custody action. For that we'd have to have a trial with evidence presented. In such a setting, the well-being of the child is the primary issue. I would have experts in child welfare and custody matters assisting me. All that will come of this action is a declaration of rights, which would not prejudice any future legal action based on a cause of action not before me today."

Lina sensed the ax was about to fall, and her eyes filled.

"Miss Prescott," the judge said, "I can see how you

might want to know that you have parental rights to the baby you're carrying. I'm sure this is a very emotional issue for you, as it undoubtedly is for Mr. Harper. While I haven't yet made my decision, I must say that, as a matter of law, I would be inclined to find for the respondent, only because the weight of law tends to fall on the side of a natural parent as opposed to a person who is unrelated to the child.''

Lina gasped and Zara put her hand on hers.

''I know that must sound strange to you, Miss Prescott, sitting there as you are, the child in question in your body, but this is a result of a state of medical science that runs ahead of the social and legal principles that order our society. It appears that the law would not permit me to grant you rights, Miss Prescott, in contravention of those of Mr. Harper and his late wife. Whether other equities might come into play, say, in a custody hearing where the issue of the child's well-being is paramount, I cannot say. But it would not be inconceivable to me that a birth mother may have much to offer a newborn that could be taken into consideration in a custody setting. Whether visitation rights or some sort of joint custody arrangement would be appropriate, it would seem to me, would depend on the facts in evidence.'' He addressed the attorneys. ''Counsels, you may expect my formal decision next Friday.''

''Thank you, Your Honor,'' Zara said.

''Now, unless there's anything else from either of you,'' the judge concluded, ''this hearing is closed.''

Lina sank back in her chair. ''We lost, didn't we?'' she whispered, unconsciously letting her hands rest on her swollen stomach.

''In effect,'' Zara said. ''Come on, let's go outside and talk.''

Lina didn't want to burst into tears. She'd tried to prepare herself for this, but it still hit her hard—the formality, the definitiveness. Zara got up and so did Lina, feeling shaky.

She glanced at Webb, who sat slowly shaking his head. Zara stuffed some papers into her briefcase. Harvey Cooper patted Webb's shoulder.

"Come on, son," Lina heard him say.

Lina watched Webb rise. She felt numb and disoriented. When he turned toward her, his eyes fell on her. He momentarily froze.

Zara took Lina's arm. "Come on, Lina."

But Lina was frozen, too, staring at Webb. Her eyes glistened and so did his.

"That's why I didn't want to come here," he said, his voice a hoarse whisper.

Lina didn't understand what he meant. He didn't want to come because he knew it would be painful? Zara was tugging on her arm. Lina went off with her, leaving Webb in the courtroom. As they went out, the clerk was calling the next case.

Zara led her to the end of the hall, where she stopped by a window. "What the judge said," she began, "was that we lose on the law, but if we go into court in a custody battle and present evidence that you're important to the baby's welfare, we might get something—visitation rights, some form of limited custody, whatever. He was offering us a little hope, was what it amounted to."

"But that's assuming Webb wasn't a very good father or couldn't take care of the baby properly, right?"

"We'd need some facts, maybe some help from the child welfare people."

"Oh, Zara," Lina said, shivering, "I want a baby, not a legal battle. Hope isn't enough. How can I decorate a nursery on the basis of a thin chance that a judge may let me see my baby part time? This isn't right, it isn't right!"

Unable to help herself, Lina began to sob. Zara put her arms around her and held her, rubbing her back. "I'm so sorry."

"It's not your fault," Lina said, sniffling. After a few moments she recovered, wiping her eyes with a tissue.

"Let's go someplace and get a cup of tea," Zara said.

Lina took a deep breath, her body shaking. "I think I just want to go home."

"I'll walk you to your car, then."

They put on their coats and headed for the entrance. As Lina looked up, she saw Webb standing near the door with his lawyer. She and Zara walked toward them. Webb looked so dour, one would have thought that *he'd* lost the case.

"Lina," he said as they moved past him, "can we talk?"

She glanced at him but shook her head. "There's nothing to say," she replied, "except congratulations. You won." Then she and Zara went out into the cold, crisp air.

LINA STARED AT HER TEACUP, mesmerized by the reflection of the lights off the glimmering liquid. She was oblivious to what was going on around her, the chatter of people at other tables, the laughter, the rattle of dishes in the kitchen. She was practically oblivious to Zara, who was sitting right across from her.

After she'd sat there for five minutes or so, she glanced up at her friend, her eyes liquid. "I'm giving up, Zara."

"What?"

"I'm calling it quits. Throwing in the towel."

"But Judge Ellman as good as said we can get something if we're willing to press for it."

"I'm not willing to press. That's not fair to the baby. This is Webb and Karen's child, and it has been all along. When they were unknown, it was different. This baby's not mine. I see that now. Webb was right. The clinic stole his baby. I might have been innocent, but what I have isn't mine."

"Oh, Lina, you're just upset. You don't have to make any decisions now."

"I have decided, Zara. As of this moment I'm carrying this baby for Webb and Karen. Once I've given birth, it's theirs, his." She drew in a ragged breath. "I wish I'd come to this realization sooner. It would have been easier on everyone."

"You're being rash," Zara insisted.

"No, this is for the baby and it's for me, too. Not just Webb. My only regret is that I can't give it to him right now."

Zara took her hands and looked as if she were going to burst into tears.

"This has been rough for both of us," Lina acknowledged. "Thanks for sticking by me."

Zara began to cry softly. Wiping her eyes, she said, "I think they told us in law school we weren't supposed to do this."

"I'm glad you're crying. You're not supposed to be superwoman. Everybody's got to let go every once in a while, even a lawyer."

Zara laughed, then blew her nose.

"There's something I have to do at the shop," Lina said. "I'm going to run."

"Want me to come with you?"

"No, I'm fine now. Really." Lina started to open her purse to get some money.

"I've got it, Lina," Zara told her, getting up from the table. "Don't worry about it. You go on."

The two of them hugged and Lina left the espresso bar. She headed for her shop. It was snowing lightly as she made her way up Galena Street. She felt a deep sadness, but also a curious feeling of relief.

When she reached Bébé, Lina found Darlene and Eloise occupied with customers. Lina went into her office in back and closed the door. She took off her coat and hung it on the coatrack. Then she sat down at her desk, took a piece of paper from the drawer and began to write the words that had been forming in her heart for weeks. Just how and when they were destined to appear she hadn't known until minutes ago when she'd sat in the espresso bar with Zara.

Dear Little Baby Harper,

As I write this letter I don't know whether you are a little girl or a little boy. I don't know your name or what you will look like. All I know is that for more than six months now you have been growing in my womb. I have felt like your mother because I have made you grow, but today the judge said you belong to your father, not me.

I must give you away, but it's not because I don't love you. It was my dream to have a baby and I'd hoped you'd be mine. I fought to keep you, but now that I've lost, I want you to know I'm letting go because I love you. Your father loves you, too, of course, but you will hear him tell you that many times. This is my chance, and so I am telling you how I feel.

Someday you will understand what it means that I am not your biological parent. But I will always be the one who gave you life, who brought you into the world. No one can ever take that special relationship from us. And whether we ever see each other again or not, I want you to know I was not some faceless machine. I was a woman with a heart full of love for you. Dear Little Baby Harper, in that way you will always be my child, and I will always love you. Always.

                                        Carolina Prescott

Lina read over the letter, then put it in an envelope. On it she wrote, "For Webb Harper's child." Then she put it inside a larger envelope and addressed it to Mary Carson in Carbondale. After affixing a stamp, Lina slipped it into her purse, put on her coat and went back into the shop.

"I'm going to the post office," she told Darlene. "Then I'm headed home. Will you lock up, please?"

"Sure."

Lina left the shop, headed down Mill Street. The snow had gotten heavier and the sky had darkened, though there was no wind. The snowflakes were large and dropped from the sky like tiny parachutes, sticking to her hair and lashes.

Lina had a strange empty feeling, an odd sort of detachment. Her pregnant body suddenly seemed alien. For the next couple of months it would be on loan to Webb and his baby. Maybe that was why she felt detached from it.

As she moved along the sidewalk, Lina felt the baby move inside her. For the past month or so it had been kicking her. Baby Harper was becoming its own little person. Soon it would be on its own and need her no more.

By the time she came to the light on East Main, Lina's eyes were filled with tears. The past hour had been a long goodbye to the baby. Never had she experienced such a painful parting. It seemed ironic, but that's exactly what this was.

The light changed and Lina started across the street. She was just past the middle of the wide boulevard when she looked up through the heavy snow and saw a familiar figure standing on the corner in front of the Hotel Jerome. It was Webb.

Lina stopped dead in her tracks. She didn't want to speak to him. She didn't ever want to see him again if she could help it. The snowfall was so heavy that she could barely make out his expression, but it looked pained. He, too, stood mute and frozen.

She couldn't talk to him. She just couldn't! Turning on her heel, she started back the way she'd come.

"Lina!" he called to her. "Marry me! I love you! I want you to marry me!"

She stopped and spun around again. "What?"

Webb had started toward her, but suddenly his eyes

rounded and he threw up his arms and shouted, "Lina! Watch out!"

There was no screech, because the pavement was covered with snow and ice. The sound coming from the side was the low roar of the truck's engine and the hiss of the tires on the icy surface of the street. The vehicle wasn't going fast, but it came upon her very suddenly and knocked her to the pavement.

Lina was momentarily aware of the icy wetness of the ground against her face and the stuttering throb of the beast's engine as the bumper shook above her head. And then she became aware of the pain—the searing pain in her stomach. Her last thought before she passed out was of the baby.

LINA AWOKE TO THE sensation of somebody rubbing her hand. She opened her eyes and found Zara Hamilton staring at her, an anxious, teary expression on her face. Lina looked around the semidarkness of her surroundings and realized she was in a hospital room. Then bits and pieces of what had happened started to come back to her.

They'd pulled her from under the truck and there'd been Webb's voice. "Lina, Lina," he kept saying over and over. "I love you, I love you." She had a vague recollection of her head in his lap and snow swirling lightly around his hat and into her face. Her memories faded then. There was something about an ambulance, a siren, blood.

And there was the pain, the terrible pain. Lina looked into Zara's eyes, but everything was numb. She felt as if her brain were packed with cotton. Everything was wooly—her thoughts, sensation. Her entire midsection seemed to be throbbing. It wasn't a sharp pain. It was dull. And her head hurt. It hurt a lot. Her right cheek was badly swollen and she was having trouble seeing out of that eye.

"Zara..." she murmured.

Her friend bit her lip and gave an anguished little cry. "Oh, Lina."

Lina tried to understand what was happening. Closing her eyes, she took stock of herself again. The dull pain in her stomach. Her baby! Her poor baby!

Lina's eyes popped open. With difficulty she lifted her head and looked down at herself. Her middle was swollen, but not so swollen as before. The little mound that had been growing was flatter.

"What happened to the baby?" she mumbled.

Zara squeezed her hands tightly. "They had to take it," she said in a shaky voice. "They did a caesarian right after you got here."

"Oh, God, is it all right?"

The expression on Zara's face was pained to the point of desperate. "Oh, Lina, she's very tiny. And she was hurt in the accident." Zara choked back a sob. "They're operating now."

"It's a girl?"

"Yes, a little girl."

Lina closed her eyes and began to sob. Zara stroked her head.

"What have I done? What have I done?"

"It was an accident" came a man's voice from behind Zara.

Lina recognized it. She opened her eyes and saw his face approaching from the shadows.

"Lina," Webb said, "I'm so sorry."

Zara got up and slipped away, leaving her to face Webb alone. His eyes were red, his face pinched, the furrows in his handsome brow deep. Moving closer, he reached out to her and touched her fingers.

"She's fighting, Lina, but she might not make it."

Lina gazed up at him, the tears brimming and running down her cheeks. "I should have been more careful."

"No, it was my fault. I wanted you to know my feelings,

that I wanted us to be together, that you didn't have to give up the baby.''

"She's yours. Yours and Karen's.''

"No,'' he said, touching her cheek. "She's yours and mine. Don't you remember what I yelled to you just before you got hit?''

She turned her head away from him. "You were feeling sorry for me,'' she said in a whisper. "You didn't mean it.''

"Lina, I've wanted you all along, but I was afraid it was the baby you really cared about. And the other night, when I saw you at the restaurant with your father, my heart just broke at the sight of you. I hated it that you didn't love me, that you'd asked me to marry you just to get the baby.''

"I know I said that,'' she sobbed, "but it wasn't true. I wanted to salvage my pride after you turned me down. But I do love you, Webb. I do.''

"Really?''

"Yes. I was embarrassed and afraid. And I guess resentful. I thought the baby was all that mattered to you.''

"No,'' he said. "No, Lina.''

She began to cry again and he bent down and kissed away her tears. He kissed her lips and repeated that he loved her.

"The baby's going to die. What have I done. Oh, what have I done?'' she sobbed.

"Lina, the important thing is that we have each other. Whether our little girl makes it or not, I have you and you have me.''

A nurse entered the room and told Webb to leave so that Lina could rest. Webb kissed her again and told her to sleep so she'd get better. "I'll go and be with our little girl,'' he said. "We'll fight as hard as we can. She's a Harper, she'll do her best.''

"Give her my love, too," she said in a quavering voice.

"I will, sweetheart. I'll tell her that her mommy loves her."

LINA AWOKE SUDDENLY, her mind clearer than before. She moved gingerly, rolling to her side to check the clock on the table by her bed. It was five-thirty in the morning. She was sore, but not in as much pain as before. Not that it mattered. The important thing was how the baby was doing.

She rang for the nurse, and as she waited she recalled Webb coming to her the night before to say that the baby had made it through surgery and was hanging on. Poor Webb was exhausted. Lina had told him to get her house keys from her purse and go to her place for the night. He hadn't wanted to leave her and the baby, but she had made him promise he'd go.

"What can I do for you, Ms. Prescott?" It was the nurse.

Lina said, "How's my baby doing? I need to know."

"She's recovering from surgery. She's awfully tiny, but she seems to be a fighter. Would you like to see her?"

Lina felt a surge of pure joy. "Oh, yes."

"I'll get a wheelchair and someone to help you." Then she left.

Lina had waited for this moment for more than six months—ever since the pregnancy had been confirmed. Never had she envisioned it happening like this. A thousand times she'd pictured a nurse handing her a squalling baby to hold in her arms. She had looked forward to that for so long. It would have been the happiest moment of her life.

Of course, it wasn't important how the baby was born. What truly mattered, she told herself, was that she live. Webb had said that being a fighter was in her genes. She prayed to God he was right.

An orderly knocked on the open door to her room. He was pushing a wheelchair. "The nurse said I should take you to the intensive care nursery. Is that right, ma'am?"

"It sure is. I want to see my daughter." Lina's heart skipped a beat at the sound of those words—*my daughter.*

The orderly put the chair by the bed and locked it so it wouldn't move. Then he helped her swing her legs over the side and sit up. Lina felt a little dizzy, so she just sat there for a moment until it passed. Then he eased her into the wheelchair and they went off down the corridor. Despite the hour, the hospital was bustling. A woman with a cart full of food trays was coming out of the elevator as they went past.

As they neared the intensive care nursery, she felt her heart beat faster. Her little girl was in there. Her baby.

The orderly opened the door to the nursery and let her into the room. The nurse, an older woman with short dark hair, graying at the temples, was reading a chart. She glanced up when Lina entered and smiled. "Mr. Harper said you wouldn't be able to wait until he got back." She checked her watch. "He went home a little over an hour ago to get cleaned up. He should be back any time now."

"How is the baby doing?" Lina asked.

"Holding her own. She tolerated the surgery better than we'd hoped. It's a matter of keeping her lungs clear and giving her a chance to get strong."

"Can I hold her?"

"Not yet. She's asleep. But you can touch her."

The nurse moved behind the wheelchair and pushed her over to the incubator. Lina gasped. Inside was a tiny baby with a pink knit cap on her head. Her little chest rose and fell with each breath. She looked like a newborn kitten, sweet and small and very delicate.

"Oh, she's so beautiful," Lina said.

The nurse showed her an opening in the side of the incubator. Lina slipped her hand in and touched her daughter's hand. The skin was so velvety. She lightly rubbed the baby's wrist and fingers. Then she turned to the nurse as tears streamed down her cheeks.

"When can I hold her?"

"Probably later today. After the doctor checks her. It is important that you and Mr. Harper bond with her. The more you are around her, the better it will be for the baby."

Lina wiped the tears from her cheeks with the back of her free hand. "You don't have to worry, my little darling. I'm going to be right here, and so will your daddy. We can hardly wait to take you home."

To her surprise, the baby opened her eyes and grasped Lina's finger. A surge of joy shot through her. All the months of waiting, all the planning and pain and heartache and fear melted into this singular moment.

"Oh, sweetheart, I've waited so long for you. And I love you so much. Just as soon as I can I'm going to hold you in my arms and rock you. And I'm going to give you a name."

Lina turned to the nurse. "You know, even though I've been thinking about names for months, I still haven't settled on one."

The nurse blinked. "Oh. Mr. Harper said a name had already been chosen. I assumed he meant both of you had picked it."

"What name did he choose?"

"He said she was to be named after her grandmother and her mother."

Lina bit her lip. Mary and Karen. She wasn't unhappy but she was surprised. "I didn't know," she murmured. She turned to the baby again. "So, how do you do, Mary Karen?"

"It's not Mary Karen" came a voice from behind her. Turning, she saw it was Webb. "I named her Mary Carolina. I thought we'd call her Caroline…just so as not to confuse her with her mother."

Lina's lip trembled as she looked up at him. Webb leaned over and kissed her temple. The baby was still holding her finger; her eyes were open and she was kicking. Happy tears began streaming down Lina's cheeks. She pressed Webb's hand to her face. "Webb," she said, "I love her so much."

"She's yours, sweetheart. Your baby."

She looked up at him, her eyes shimmering. "No, Webb, she's *ours.*"

Webb Harper knelt down beside her and took her in his arms. He shed a few happy tears of his own. After a moment they looked into the incubator at their daughter. Little Caroline was still clinging to her finger. And Lina knew then that Webb was right. This child was truly theirs.

EPILOGUE

MARY HADN'T FIXED a meal in Webb's kitchen in ages. Since Lina had gotten her hands on it, the place was well stocked and organized, but Mary still couldn't find a thing. At least the apple pie was done.

"That pie smells so good, Mary, there wouldn't be an extra piece for an old grandfather to sample, would there?" Morgan Prescott was standing at the door, a big grin on his face.

"Grandpa is going to have to wait for dinner like everybody else," she replied.

"But that'll be hours from now."

Mary glanced at the clock. "Judgin' by the way I've seen you eat, I don't suppose a little sliver would ruin your appetite."

"The way you cook? Mary, I could eat the whole pie and dinner besides."

"All right, sit down," she said, gesturing toward the table. "But you're certainly not setting a very good example for that little granddaughter of yours."

"Hell, the little thing's not half the size of a shoe box, and until today she's never been outside that hospital. Besides, if there was ever a little critter who deserved to be spoiled, it's Mary Carolina."

"What are you saying, Morgan—that I should save this sliver of pie for her?" Mary laughed. She cut a medium-size slice of pie, put it on a plate and carried it over to

Morgan. "Want some coffee to go with it?" she asked. "There's a pot on the stove."

"If you'll join me, Mary."

She got them each a mug of coffee and sat with him at the table. Morgan took a bite of pie and glanced at the clock. "I'd say the kids ought to be arriving any time now. After we finish our coffee, what say we stroll on down the drive to meet 'em?"

"It is a lovely day."

"Mary, for a rancher, every day during calving season's a lovely day. Webb's future's being born out in those fields as we speak."

"No, Morgan, his future was born last February in Aspen Valley Hospital."

Morgan sipped his coffee and nodded. "You're right about that, Mary. And the same with Lina. I've never seen two kids transformed by something the way they were."

"These past few months have been good for them. It's been hard with the baby in the hospital, and him having to put in so much time here at the ranch, but they've really gotten to know each other. Webb's just bloomed. He adores Lina. There's joy in his heart. You can see it."

"He's not the only one. I think Lina's truly happy for the first time in her life," Morgan said. "Not that she didn't have a good life before. She was content, I believe, but Webb fulfilled a dream. When you're with someone special, it's hard not to feel joy."

"It's remarkable that a father can say something like that about his future son-in-law and actually sound like he means it," Mary teased.

"My daughter's a clever young lady. She conditioned me pretty well."

"Oh?"

"She told me why Webb's such a special guy."

"I'm listening."

Morgan grinned, his jowls turning red. "Mary, she told me he's a lot like me."

She laughed.

"You don't agree?"

"Lina did tell me you can be pretty bullheaded, too."

Morgan shook his head with mock disgust. "Women! It's amazing we put up with 'em the way we do. If it wasn't for things like this confounded apple pie, we wouldn't."

"Apple pie, Mr. Prescott? Is that all it takes to turn your eye?"

He reached over and put his hand on hers. "Mary, there are a few other things."

"Such as what?"

"Well…"

"Yes?"

"Well, I've been thinkin', Mary. You know how after the wedding the kids are going down to spend a couple of weeks at my place in Saint Croix?"

"Yes."

"In the summer, when things aren't so crowded, I try to get down to the Caribbean to do a little sport fishing. So I was thinking maybe you'd like to come along. I mean, how long has it been since you've had a real vacation?"

She looked him in the eye, seeing that she wasn't just hearing idle conversation. "Quite a while, Morgan."

"You see, it's something you need about as bad as me."

Mary gave him a smile. "Let me give that some thought, Mr. Prescott."

He grinned. "You're a coy little filly, aren't you, Mary Carson?"

"Never claimed otherwise." She glanced at the clock. "Unless you're going to insist on another piece of pie, how about we take that stroll?"

"Capital idea!" he agreed.

They left the kitchen and went into the front room, which was all festooned with balloons and streamers and a big banner that read, Welcome Home, Mary Carolina Harper! We Love You!

"Lina doesn't know Webb did this?" Morgan said.

"No, he wanted to surprise them both."

They put on their jackets and went out into the April sun. Standing on the porch, they both looked out across the valley at Snowmass Mountain.

"This is a nice spot," he acknowledged, "but I think that new spread he picked out, the one up the valley toward Aspen, will be even nicer for them."

"Lina loves the idea of them building a place of their own," Mary said. "And I don't blame her. I would in her shoes. Plus, it'll be closer to town and she'll be able to supervise things at her shop easier."

"And the nice thing is that they can still keep this place. And if he adds the adjacent thousand acres that's come on the market, this'll be a viable spread."

"Oh, Webb's going to own most of this valley before he's through," Mary said. "Mark my words."

Morgan shook his head and smiled. "I remember years ago a young cowboy down Montrose way who set out to do the same thing."

"Did he succeed?"

"Yep, but it took him a little longer to figure out what's really important. Come on, Grandma, let's stretch our legs."

They went down the steps and as they did, Lina's BMW came over the rise. By the time it stopped at the top of the drive, they could see that Webb was driving and Lina was in back with the baby.

"He's not going to let a thing happen to those two," Morgan said with a smile as they watched them get out of the car.

"You can bet your life on that."

Webb was helping Lina, who was wearing a pretty red dress and carrying a tiny bundle wrapped in one of Mary's crocheted blankets. The two of them waved; Morgan and Mary waved back.

"There's a happy young family," Morgan observed, sounding pleased.

Mary could only marvel at all those three had been through. Nobody'd ever said life was easy. And they were certainly proof. But if you loved enough and cared enough, often as not a silver lining would come along one day. She took Morgan's arm.

"I don't know about you, Grandpa, but I'm feeling pretty good."

"Mary," he said, putting his arm around her, "I've got a hunch this day has been destined for a long, long time."

Down at the car, Webb gave Lina a kiss. Then the two of them, with their baby in her arms, started walking toward the house.

"You a betting man, Mr. Prescott?" Mary asked.

"I've been known to take a wager now and again."

"I'll give you odds that within two years there'll be another little Harper in the family."

"You got inside information, Mary Carson?"

Mary chuckled. "A couple of weeks ago Lina said something to me I'll never forget."

"What was that?"

"She said, 'Mary, I want you to know something. Every night I say a little prayer to Karen, thanking her for being the person she was and leaving me the legacy she did. I didn't know her, but I still think of her as a sister and a dear friend. She meant a lot to Webb and she means a lot to me. You and he will always love her, and I want you to know that I will, too.'"

"That's my girl," Morgan said.

"My girl, too," Mary said, wiping her eye. "My girl, too."

Cameron
by Beverly Barton

Prologue

With one hand Britt Cameron gripped the steering wheel of his truck and with the other he tilted the half-empty cola can up to his mouth.

At first he hadn't even noticed that it was raining, but when his visibility through the windshield of the mud-splattered old Chevy became completely obscured, he'd turned on the windshield wipers. The scraping beat of the wipers swishing away the heavy raindrops blended with Clint Black's country drawl belting out his latest hit tune. The radio's high volume didn't bother Britt, nor did the loud booms of thunder blasting overhead. The more noise, the better. Perhaps it would block out the memories—the pain—the *fear*.

He took another deep swig from the can, then tossed the empty container onto the floorboard. Wiping his mouth with the back of his hand, he felt the heavy scars that covered his flesh. Quickly he glanced down at his hands. Both were covered with puckered skin and the fingers on his left hand were gnarled, the two middle fingers braided together like a knot.

He ran his deformed hand up the side of his face, the left side. From his left cheekbone to his neck, strips of torn flesh had healed into scars. Scars that he had refused to let a plastic surgeon touch.

For three years after the accident that had killed his best friend and changed his own life forever, Britt had thought that nothing worse could ever happen to him.

He'd been wrong.

For endless weeks he had sat in that courtroom and felt the curious stares of the jurors, and had wondered if they would believe him capable of murder. Tortured weeks when he hadn't known if they would convict him or set him free. Finally he'd reached the point where the verdict no longer mattered. His life became meaningless. He had already lost everything but his freedom.

The past eighteen months of his life had been a nightmare from which he didn't think he would ever awaken. From the day his wife had run off with Reverend Charles, fate had set Britt on a path of destruction.

Now that the trial was over, he didn't know where he was going or what he was going to do. He didn't care anymore. Nothing mattered.

The 10:00 p.m. news report came on the radio. Britt longed for a drink, something much stronger than the sugary, caffeinated cola he'd just consumed. But he never drank when he drove, not even before the accident, and certainly not afterward.

"Today in Riverton, Mississippi, accused murderer Britt Cameron was acquitted of all charges in the tragic death of his estranged wife. Tanya Cameron, who had left her husband six months prior to her death, was found dead in his trailer over a year ago. Ms. Cameron died from a severe head wound. The prosecution claimed that, in a fit of jeal-

ous rage, Cameron had followed through on his threat to
kill—''

Britt flipped off the radio. The rain was getting progres-
sively heavier. He considered pulling off to the side of the
road, but didn't want to stop. He had to keep going, keep
moving. He had to get away from Riverton, and all those
accusing stares, all the whispered innuendos.

He crossed the Mississippi line over into Alabama, his
foot light on the gas pedal as he slowed the truck's speed
down to a crawl. Paying little attention to where he was
driving, and not caring a hoot about his destination, Britt
turned off the main highway onto a side road. As the rain
fell in never ending rivulets, the road ahead curved into the
hills outside of Cherokee. Houses became few and far between. Cultivated farmland, dense woods and a black sky
rioting with a thunderstorm surrounded Britt.

Suddenly a deer dashed across the road in front of him.
His only thought to avoid colliding with the animal, Britt
slammed on his brakes. The truck swerved, hitting a dan-
gerously slick spot on the pavement, then slid across the
road and into a deep ditch. The last coherent thought Britt
had before his head hit the windshield was that, as long as
he lived, he'd never love and trust another woman.

One

A crackle of earsplitting thunder shook the old farmhouse moments before a blaze of brilliant lightning zigzagged through the night sky. Nestling more snugly into the softness of the plump, chintz-covered sofa, Anna Rose pressed her open book against her breasts. Lying at her feet on a hand-braided rug, Lord Byron growled as if the threatening rumble from his massive chest would frighten away the storm. Anna Rose dropped her hand to the rottweiler's head, patting him tenderly as she whispered baby-talk words of comfort.

Bringing the book away from her body, Anna Rose adjusted herself and her treasured volume of verse and prose so that she could see better in the dim light from the kerosene lamp. Thunderstorms had ravaged the state this spring, and even now, in late May, seemed determined to add more destruction to the flood conditions in Alabama. Thankfully tomorrow was Saturday, so, even though the road into Cherokee was blocked from the night's deluge, she wouldn't have to worry about making it in to school.

Centering her attention on the printed word, Anna Rose read the poem, silently at first and then aloud. Marlowe's "The Passionate Shepherd to his Love" was one of her favorites. How many years had she spent longing to hear a man speak such words to her? To ask her to come with him and be his love?

Flipping through the pages, she paused at a section entitled "Unrequited Love". She took a deep breath, releasing it slowly as she ran the tip of her tongue over the edges of her teeth. Willing herself not to cry again, she tightened her throat, trapping the tears. As Anna Rose began to read, it seemed that Lord Alfred Douglas's "Two Loves" was printed in large bold type, so poignant were the words.

Slamming the book closed, she tossed it to the other end of the sofa. "Tarnation! Double, triple tarnation!"

She had to stop this—and now. No more feeling sorry for herself. No more condemning herself for acting like an idiot. After all, she wasn't the first woman who'd made a fool of herself over a man.

"But did you have to lie to the whole town?" she asked herself aloud, shaking her head in disgust.

When Kyle had announced his engagement to his college sweetheart, Anna Rose had become the object of everyone's pity. And pity was one thing she couldn't abide. She'd received far too much of that misplaced emotion in her twenty-seven years. Poor Anna Rose, whose teenage, unwed mother had committed suicide at the age of seventeen. Poor Anna Rose, such a plain, plump wallflower. Poor Anna Rose, who'd had total responsibility for the care of her aging grandparents before their deaths. Poor Anna Rose would make such a good wife and mother, but no man wanted her. It wasn't just because she was no great beauty. Plainer women had married. No. Anna Rose knew that she intimidated most men. Not only was she fiercely independent and a trifle too bossy, but folks in Cherokee said she was too smart, far smarter than any of the men in town. And no man wanted a wife smarter than he was.

Anna Rose stood, stretched her arms above her head and looked down at Lord Byron, who was staring up at her. "I'm hungry. How about you?" Rounding the couch, she picked up the kerosene lamp from the long library table that flanked the back wall and started toward the hallway. "There's some fried chicken left. How about a drumstick all your own?"

The enormous dog came quickly to his feet, following his mistress out into the long, wide hallway that spanned the length of the house from front to back.

After entering the kitchen, Anna Rose placed the lamp in the center of the blue-gingham-covered table. "You know what I need, Lord Byron?" She watched as the big animal slumbered over toward the refrigerator and flopped down, waiting for her to open the door. "I need a man."

Lord Byron stared up at her, his brown eyes bright and alert. Anna Rose opened the refrigerator, retrieved a plate of cold chicken and placed it on the table before seating herself in the straight-back wooden chair. "I made a total fool of myself over Kyle when he first came to town last year. Of course, all the unmarried teachers did. Not just me."

She removed the aluminum foil from the plate, picked up a drumstick and took a bite. Lord Byron moaned. "Oh, all right. Here you go." When she handed him his own piece of chicken, the dog's enormous mouth opened to accept the late-night treat. "Don't you dare leave the kitchen with that," she warned.

Anna Rose munched on the cold chicken as she listened to the torrential downpour and the occasional roar of thunder that seemed to be moving farther and farther away. "I should have had better sense. After all, I'm so darn smart. I'm a school principal, aren't I? I'm practically going on thirty. I should have known that Kyle thought of me as nothing more than a good friend.''

Lord Byron wasn't paying much attention to his mistress's ramblings. He was far too busy devouring his treat.

Anna Rose scooted her chair over to the cabinet, removed a dish towel from a drawer and wiped her hands and mouth. "What I need, Lord Byron, is a fiancé. A temporary fiancé.''

Licking his lips, the rottweiler cocked his head to one side as if recognizing the word *fiancé*. Anna Rose laughed. "Yeah, I've been saying that word a lot lately, haven't I?''

If only she hadn't overreacted when Kyle had married and the whole town began whispering behind her back. If only she hadn't told her friend Edith Hendricks that people were silly to think she'd been seriously interested in Kyle Ross. After all, she, too, had a secret fiancé, a man she'd met on vacation the previous year who'd been writing and phoning her on a regular basis.

"Me and my big mouth,'' Anna Rose said. "That was nearly two months ago, and folks are wondering why my mysterious fiancé hasn't shown up.''

Suddenly Lord Byron stood, his big body tense, his nose pointing in the air and his ears set back as he listened. Like a small, galloping horse, the rottweiler ran from the kitchen, his loud, leonine bark echoing in the long hallway.

"What in tarnation's the matter with you?'' Anna Rose picked up the lamp and followed quickly, wondering just what had upset Lord Byron.

The dog stood at the front door, one big paw scratching—his signal for wanting outside. As Anna Rose neared, she set the lamp on the seat of a massive oak hall tree. "What's the matter, boy? Did you hear something?'' She seriously doubted that she had late visitors, especially on a night like this.

Opening the front door, Anna Rose braced herself for the blast of damp air. The high wind whipped through the trees and blew rain across the wide front porch. Peering outside through the screen door, she saw nothing but the black night sky and heard only the wind and the rain.

"There's nothing there, boy. See?" The minute she eased the screen door open slightly, Lord Byron lunged, pushing past Anna Rose and out onto the porch. He emitted several loud howls, galloped out into the yard, then disappeared down the driveway.

Something was wrong. Terribly wrong. Lord Byron never acted irrationally. His keen animal instincts had alerted him to danger—a danger of which Anna Rose was unaware. But she trusted the rottweiler's innate ability to sense trouble. Her own intuition told her that someone needed her help—that out there in the dark, stormy night, a fellow human being was alone and in pain.

Without giving the weather or her own safety another thought, Anna Rose rushed back inside her warm, dry home. Reaching into the hall closet, she grabbed her raincoat and cap. Slipping the tan, water-resistant jacket over her shirt and jeans, she fastened the top two buttons, then settled the wool-felt beret on her head, pulling down one side so that it almost covered her eye. She jerked her purse off the shelf and dug inside for her keys.

Once outside, she quickly became drenched, damp strands of wispy hair clinging to her face, the wetness adding weight to the already heavy braid that hung down her back. As she ran toward the driveway, she sidestepped several deep puddles of muddy water, only to lose her footing and step directly into one of the deepest holes. Water covered her foot and wet her jeans to mid-calf. Inside her leather sneaker and squishy sock, Anna Rose flexed her toes.

She jumped into her dark blue Blazer and slammed the door. Feeling her way, she inserted the key into the ignition. Within seconds after starting the motor, she backed out of her drive and searched desperately to find Lord Byron. The

Blazer's bright headlights illuminated the paved road that ran north and south in front of Anna Rose's farm-house. She had no sooner turned out of her drive than she saw her rottweiler running ahead of her, then suddenly jumping off the the road and down an embankment.

Parking the four-wheel drive on the side of the road, Anna Rose opened the door and hopped out, her feet marring up in the thick mud. Reaching inside, she picked up the flashlight lying in the back floorboard, then gave the door a hard shove with the side of her hip. Turning her attention to where Lord Byron had exited the road in such a hurry, she cast the flashlight's beam down the steep ravine. With his heavy body braced against the side of the old Chevy truck, the dog pawed at the door.

Dear God, someone had run off the road. She didn't recognize the truck, so it had to belong to a stranger. Anna Rose knew the entire populace of Cherokee and just about everybody in the surrounding areas of Mt. Hester, Margerum, and Allsboro.

Making her way cautiously down the rain-slick embankment, Anna Rose called out to Lord Byron, who was moaning plaintively. Just as she reached the bottom of the ditch, her foot caught on the far-reaching roots of a nearby tree. Trying to steady herself, she lost her balance and fell flat on her behind. Her hand holding the flashlight plunged into thick, gooey mud while the other flattened against a growth of wet moss and grass.

"Tarnation," she grumbled as she struggled to stand.

Once at the truck, she shoved Lord Byron aside. "Down, big boy. Stay." Wiping off the flashlight on her wet jeans, she cast the beam through the window and into the cab.

He was slumped over the steering wheel. A big man with a heavy dark beard and thick, tousled black hair. He was wearing jeans and a long-sleeved gray shirt. The best she could make out through the dirty widow, whoever he was, he was unconscious.

She eased the door open, but since the truck leaned slightly to the side, she found it difficult to keep the door from closing on her. Finally she crawled into the cab and allowed the door to slam behind her, shutting her inside with the stranger. She clutched the flashlight, running the bright beam slowly over the unmoving body of the man who was now only inches from her. She'd never seen him before, so if he lived hereabouts, he was a newcomer.

Reaching out, she touched his shoulder. He didn't move. She edged closer and closer until she was sitting directly beside him. She ran her fingers over his forehead and felt a sticky wetness. When she pulled her hand away, the man moaned.

Anna Rose jumped. "Are you hurt?" she asked, then cursed herself for voicing such an inane question. Of course he was hurt. He'd wrecked his truck, he was barely conscious and his forehead was bleeding.

He made no reply, not even another moan. She touched the back of his neck, her fingers encountering the overly long hair that curled about his collar. As if on cue at the touch of her hand, he moaned again, a deeper grunting sound. She didn't flinch or pull away, but allowed her hand to travel down his back and across to his shoulder, her arm draping about his massive width.

Slowly he turned his head, but didn't try to lift it from the steering wheel. He opened his eyes, gazing up at her. For one tiny instant, one delicate moment, Anna Rose looked into the stranger's topaz-flecked brown eyes and felt as if she had met her destiny. Quickly she brushed aside the foolishly romantic notion.

"It's going to be all right," she said, wanting desperately to reassure him. He kept staring at her, not moving, not speaking, just staring.

"Are you badly hurt?" she asked. The agonized look in his eyes told her that he was in great pain and yet she saw no evidence of any physical injuries other than the cut on his forehead, where the oozing blood was already beginning to congeal. "My phone's out, so there's no way I can call for an ambulance or help of any kind."

When he closed his eyes, Anna Rose felt an irrational fear surge through her. This man couldn't die. He couldn't! She didn't understand why her concern for this stranger was more than one human being's care for another, but it was.

"We've got to get you out of here," she told him, squeezing his shoulder. "Do you think you can help?"

He opened his eyes again, lifting his head slightly and turning to face her. Inside the darkness of the truck cab, the only illumination came from the small flashlight Anna Rose still held in her hand.

"Get that damned light out of my eyes." His voice was a deep, deadly rumble.

Anna Rose gulped in surprise, heat rising to her face. Shocked by his angry command, she didn't immediately remove the source of his irritation, allowing the light to remain on his face long enough to make a thorough inspection of his hairy appearance. He wasn't handsome, but he was totally masculine. And he was badly scarred, at least on the left side of his face and neck. The heavy beard and mustache concealed a great deal of the scarring, but not across his forehead or along the flesh exposed by the open collar of his shirt.

A sudden chill racked her body. She wasn't repulsed by the man's scars. She was deeply saddened. What pain he must have known, must still endure, if no longer physical, then emotional. Instinctively she knew the agony she'd seen in his eyes only moments ago came from the past, not the present.

Realizing that she hadn't moved the flashlight, she turned it off and stuck it in her pocket. "Do you think you can walk?"

"I can try." He raised his head and leaned back against the seat, trapping Anna Rose's arm.

She slipped her arm out from beneath his broad shoulders. "My Blazer is parked up on the road. It's a steep climb and the ground is slick from all the rain."

"Were you driving along and saw the truck down here?" he asked, running his big hands over his face, as if trying to awaken himself from a bad dream.

"No, I live back off the road a piece. My dog heard something and I followed him." She thought it rather odd that she and a perfect stranger were sitting inside his wrecked truck having a normal conversation while outside the wind and rain ravaged the earth, and Lord Byron howled as he pawed at the door.

The man moved, brushing up against her. She stared at him, open-mouthed and wide-eyed. "I can't get out of the truck until you do," he said. "This door is jammed against the side of the embankment." He nodded toward the driver's side of the truck.

Hurriedly Anna Rose slid across the seat and opened the door. The rain blew inside. The strong wind fought with her as she struggled to keep the door open. He reached across her, bracing the door with his powerful hand while she stepped out of the truck. She turned to assist him, but he brushed her hands away, stepped out and grabbed the rim of the truck bed to brace his unsteady legs.

"Don't try to be so macho." She slipped her arm around his waist. "Lean on me. I'm not some fragile little female who's going to break in two."

She felt his compliance, and wondered if she had spoken too hastily. Merciful heavens, he was heavy. And tall. She wasn't short herself, standing five-foot-nine in her bare feet, but this man towered over her a good five or six inches.

"I'm too heavy," he said, easing away from her. "I'm hurting you."

She tightened her hold about his waist, refusing to release him. "Don't be an idiot. You can't make it up to the road without help."

Off in the distance, a low roll of thunder sounded, followed by a brilliant flash of lightning that momentarily illuminated their faces. She noted a spark of amusement in his eyes while he saw the look of determination in hers.

"Are you by any chance a marine corps drill instructor?" he asked as she guided him toward the steep incline of slippery rocks, mud and grass.

"Very funny." She felt her feet mar up in the mud. They seemed to have heavy weights attached, slowing her progress. And it didn't help that the man at her side halted momentarily. "Don't you dare pass out. It's not much farther. Just hang on."

"You're a prison warden?" He held on to her, following her lead as she guided him onward and upward toward the road.

"You have a very warped sense of humor. Here I am trying to rescue you and all you can do is insult me." She was beginning to wonder if she were dreaming all this and that any minute she'd awaken to find herself all warm and dry inside her house.

Finally they reached the top of the embankment. The bright glare from the Blazer's headlights struck them boldly as they moved along the roadside. Lord Byron followed, and when Anna Rose opened the passenger door, the dog, all muddy feet and dripping wet fur, jumped in the back seat.

"Tarnation, Lord Byron. Double, triple tarnation. I ought to paddle your backside." She stood beside the open door, hands on her hips, the wind whipping loose strands of hair into her mouth as she scolded her disobedient pet. A slow, steady rainfall pelted her robust body.

Britt Cameron watched her, wondering what the hell it was about this strange woman that amused him so much. He'd known her for all of ten minutes and she'd already made him smile more than he'd smiled in a couple of years. "I've got it," he said. "You're a schoolteacher."

She turned, giving him a startled then condemning look. "Get in. I'll take you back to the house with me. The phone was out when I left, but we'll check and see of it's working now."

Man, she was bossy, he thought. As bossy as his mother. Maybe that was the reason he liked her, the reason he didn't feel threatened by the fact that she was a woman. She reminded him of his mother. Hell, how could a woman like that give him any trouble?

"Yes, ma'am." He got inside, slammed the door and watched while she circled the vehicle, getting in on the other side.

Suddenly he felt the nuzzle of the rottweiler's damp nose against his shoulder. Turning slightly, he came face-to-face with the biggest dog he'd ever seen. "Does he bite?" Britt asked.

Anna Rose started the Blazer and began backing up. "Only if I tell him to." Even in the darkness, Britt knew she was smiling—could almost see the corners of her wide, full mouth turning up.

He was surprised at how well she maneuvered the four-wheel drive on the dark country road in a storm, and how unemotionally she had handled his rescue from the truck. She wasn't like the women he'd known, certainly nothing like the type of woman he preferred—petite and blonde and utterly feminine in their helplessness. Tanya had been like that. Tanya, the girl he'd adored since childhood. The girl who'd married his best friend and who had been widowed at twenty-two when Paul had died in the accident that, even now, Britt blamed on himself.

"If the phone's still out, you'll be stuck here till morning." Anna Rose pulled the Blazer into the drive beside her house.

"Why can't you take me into the nearest town for a wrecker?" he asked.

"The road into town is flooded. That happens whenever

it rains a lot. The only way out would be back the way you came.''

''I see.'' He had no intention of going back to Mississippi. Certainly not tonight or tomorrow. Not for a long, long time.

''Can you make a dash for the house or do you need help?'' She shut off the motor and turned toward him, sensing more than seeing his large hulking frame in the darkness.

''I think I can make it.''

''Wait until I get to the house.'' Without hesitation she flung open the door on the driver's side, jumped out, then waited a couple of seconds for Lord Byron to hurl himself over the seat and into the yard before she slammed the door.

Britt could barely see the house, so he waited as long as he thought it would take for her to get inside before he threw open the door and made a mad dash up the front steps.

She stood in the doorway, a soft rosy light illuminating the entrance. She looked like a very large drowned rat, he thought. When he stepped over the threshold and entered the warm, dry hallway, he felt a sudden sense of peace— almost of homecoming. When he shook his head to dislodge such ridiculous notions, droplets of moisture jetted off his hair. Realizing he was making a muddy mess in her foyer, he started to apologize when he noticed that Lord Byron was shaking off far more water and had left wet, dirty paw prints on the wooden floor.

He watched while she removed her raincoat and beret and hung them in the hall closet. Underneath she wore a large, billowy blouse. He thought it looked like a man's shirt. Her jeans were baggy, damp all over and soaking wet from the knees down. He wasn't certain if she was a bit on the plump side or if a trim figure was hidden beneath the overly loose clothing.

Anna Rose caught him giving her a thorough appraisal and had the oddest feeling, as if she should try to cover herself because this man could see straight through her clothes. What a silly thought, she told herself.

"Look, just go into the living room. I'm going to get out of these wet clothes and I'll see if I can't find something of my grandfather's that will fit you." She smiled at him and was disappointed when he didn't return the smile.

"You live here with your grandfather?" he asked, glancing around the hallway and through the open door into the the dark living room.

"He died several years ago. I live here alone, except for Lord Byron and a few stray animals that come and go." She picked up the kerosene lamp from the hall tree and handed it to him.

"Won't you need this to see where you're going?" Their hands touched briefly when the lamp went from her possession into his.

She couldn't help but notice his left hand. It was all she could do to stop herself from gasping out loud. The skin was badly scarred, obviously from a severe wound, and two fingers were twined together like knotted tree roots.

"There's another lamp lit in my bedroom." She nodded down the hall and to the right, praying that he hadn't noticed the shock on her face or the slight hesitation in her voice.

When she started to walk away, he reached out and touched her on the shoulder with his crippled hand. "Aren't you afraid to be alone in your home with a stranger? For all you know I could be some maniac, an escapee from the looney bin...a murderer."

"I'm Anna Rose Palmer," she said. "Introduce yourself and we won't be strangers."

There it was again, he thought. That irresistible urge to laugh. But he didn't even smile, except inside his mind. "Britt Cameron." He watched her closely for a reaction.

After all, he couldn't be more than forty or fifty miles out-side Riverton. It was possible that she'd heard about the trial.

"Pleased to meet you, Britt Cameron." Her gaze trav-eled over him slowly, measuring him up the way he'd as-sessed her a few minutes ago. "When I helped you up out of the ditch, I didn't see or feel any weapons on you. No gun or knife. So unless you can figure out some way to kill Lord Byron with your bare hands, there's no way he'll allow you to hurt me."

Britt was glad she hadn't recognized his name, relieved that he wouldn't be sent back out into the dark, rainy night...alone. "I promise to be on my best behavior." He turned and went into the living room.

Anna Rose rushed down the hall and into her bedroom. With nervous fingers, she removed her soggy shoes and socks, then stripped out of her wet clothes and slipped into a fresh pair of slacks and an oversize cotton sweater. All the while she was unbraiding her damp hair, she kept think-ing about the man in her living room—the man who had wrecked his truck in front of her house. She didn't think he'd been drinking. She hadn't smelled anything on his breath, and they'd been close enough that their lips could have touched if either of them had moved a fraction closer.

She picked up the kerosene lamp from her nightstand and went into the bedroom that had once belonged to her grandparents. It had remained unchanged since her child-hood. As she searched through the contents of the cedar chest that sat at the foot of the bed, she wondered about Britt Cameron. Odd—wasn't it?—that she'd been thinking about needing a temporary man in her life, someone she could pass off as her mystery fiancé, and then, *poof,* out of nowhere, a tall, dark stranger had appeared.

"I hope these fit," she said aloud as she pulled out a pair of faded jeans and a khaki, cotton work shirt. Gramps had been a big man, probably a bit heavier than Britt Cameron, but Anna Rose didn't think he'd been quite as tall. Oh, well, these clothes would just have to do until her houseguest's own clothes dried.

Feeling her way more than seeing, she made a quick stop by the bathroom before going back up the hall. She found Britt standing at the windows, watching the storm outside. The minute she entered the living room, he turned and faced her.

He noticed that she had her arms full. Sitting atop a pile of clothes was what appeared to be a first-aid kit. "Can I help you with some of that?"

She laid the kit on the sofa beside her book of poetry, then handed him Gramps's old clothes. "You can change in here. I'll go in the kitchen and fix us some coffee." She took several tentative steps, then stopped. "Are you hungry?" she asked. "I could fix you a sandwich or…I've got some cold fried chicken."

"Thanks. A sandwich would be great." He'd never met a woman like Anna Rose Palmer. She seemed to be bossy and independent and yet at the same time she possessed an old-fashioned sense of hospitality and friendliness. He couldn't figure her out.

"I'll knock before I come back in here. Feel free to check the phone, but I doubt it's working. We've had rain for over a week and the phone's been out for a couple of days. The roads are in a terrible mess. I barely made it home from school this afternoon."

"You *are* a schoolteacher." He smiled then, despite all his efforts not to. He didn't want to like this woman. Hell, he never wanted to like another woman as long as he lived. But Anna Rose didn't pose a threat to him. He wasn't attracted to her. Not that way. She was tall and plump and rather plain. And bossier than his mother. Good God, there was no way he could ever be physically attracted to a woman like that.

"I'm the principal of Cherokee's elementary school."

She liked his smile. It softened his harsh face and put a warm sparkle in his sad topaz eyes. "Change clothes. Just lay your wet things in the hall. I'll have you some coffee and a sandwich ready in a few minutes."

"How about some coffee first?" He could use something warm in his stomach. The rain had drenched him down to his briefs, chilling him to the bone.

"Sure thing."

"Won't you need the lamp?" he asked.

"You'll need it. I can feel my way, then light a couple of candles I keep on the kitchen counter for occasions like this."

Britt took his time stripping. He noticed she hadn't bothered to bring him any underwear. It didn't make any difference. He'd just do without. He had no intention of wearing his soaked briefs. The clothes were old, faded and a bit worn, but damn comfortable. The shirt was a fairly good fit, but the pants were a couple of inches too short and at least three inches too big in the waist. He looped his own belt through the loose jeans.

Should I tell her who I am? he wondered. *She has a right to know that I was an accused murderer and that half my hometown still thinks I killed my wife.*

He hadn't murdered Tanya. Hell, he'd loved the girl...loved her since they'd been kids when she'd tagged along after him and Paul. But she'd never loved him as anything but a friend, even though she'd married him after Paul's death. No, Tanya had never loved anyone but Paul Rogers. Certainly not that pretty-boy minister, Timothy Charles—the guy she'd run off with six months before her death.

A loud knock on the door brought Britt back from thoughts of the past. "Come on in," he said. "I'm decent."

Anna Rose eyed her guest, then smiled at the way he looked in Gramps's clothes. "Oh, my. I was afraid the pants wouldn't fit. Come on over here and sit down on the couch and drink your coffee while I clean that cut on your head.''

"Ms. Palmer, are you always so bossy?'' Although he questioned her orders, he followed them, seating himself on the large, colorful sofa.

"Bossiness is one of my many shortcomings. And call me Anna Rose.'' Seating herself beside Britt, she handed him the mug of steaming black coffee. "No sugar or cream.''

He nodded that she had guessed his preference correctly.

Placing her book on an end table and the first-aid kit in her lap, she ran her fingers through his hair, pulling the long, damp strands off his forehead. "Doesn't look like more than a scratch, but you've got a nasty bruise. Weren't you wearing your seat belt?''

"My truck is a classic and not equipped with seat belts.'' He studied her while she cleaned his wound. Her eyes were a very dark blue. Like sapphires, he thought, then wondered where that comparison had come from.

"What happened?'' she asked, replacing everything in the kit. "Were you driving too fast and just lost control?''

"Nope. I was creeping along. Couldn't see more than a few feet in front of me. A deer dashed across the road. I missed the deer, but hit a wet spot and skidded into the ditch.''

"Well, this far out, you're likely to see deer crossing the road pretty often. There's a hunting lodge a few miles from here.'' She watched as he raised the mug to his lips and drank, slowly but steadily.

"Good coffee. Thanks.''

"You're welcome.'' She couldn't seem to pull her gaze away from his left hand. What on earth could have happened? Surely the doctors could repair it, could do plastic surgery and remove the scars on his face and neck. Why would a man as young and vitally attractive leave such reminders of an experience that must have been agonizingly painful? She longed to ask him, longed to tell him that he could share his pain with her, that she understood the loneliness she saw in his eyes.

Britt tried not to let the way she was staring at his hand bother him. Tightening the hold on the mug, he averted her questioning eyes. He knew she was wondering what had happened to him. Was she feeling sorry for him? Or was she simply repulsed by the sight of his scars and deformed hand?

He could have had the scars removed, even allowed the doctors to perform some experimental surgery in the hopes of partially restoring life back into his useless fingers. But he didn't want the reminders erased. Paul had died in the accident, and he had lived. He'd been driving. Too fast, maybe, even though the police said the accident had been no one's fault. A tire had blown. The car had swerved and hit a tree, then exploded into flames. He'd been thrown free. Paul had been trapped inside. He'd received the burns, the damage to his hand when he'd tried to rescue Paul. He'd passed out from the pain, and Paul had burned to death. He would never forget. And he would never forgive himself.

Anna Rose knew that he'd noticed her staring at his hand. She'd seen the pain, the anger, and then the glazed look of a man remembering…remembering something that haunted him.

"I'll go fix that sandwich for you now," she said. "Make yourself at home. I'll prepare a bed for you after you eat."

She couldn't get out of the living room fast enough. She had to get away from Britt Cameron, away from her overwhelming need to comfort him. Her feminine instincts told her that he wouldn't welcome her pity or her comfort.

Britt finished his coffee, set the cup on the end table and stretched out on the big, comfortable sofa. The soft, golden glow from the lone kerosene lamp cast flickering shadows across the room. It was a warm, welcoming room, he thought. A room filled with contentment. Anna Rose Palmer reminded him of just such an emotion. Contentment. She was the kind of woman that made a man feel comfortable. The kind of woman a man could talk to, share things with. A strong woman a man could lean on if he needed to.

"Hell, Cameron, what's the matter with you? You'll be leaving here in the morning and you'll never see the woman again."

A few minutes later Anna Rose came back into the living room carrying a tray. She'd fixed him a chicken sandwich, thick and piled high with sliced meat, tomatoes and lettuce. She'd opened a bag of potato chips, poured him a fresh cup of coffee and added one of her homemade dill pickles to his plate.

"Here we are," she said, then hushed immediately when she saw his big body lying on the sofa, his eyes closed and his breathing deep and even. He was asleep.

Setting the tray on the library table, she gazed down at Britt Cameron. He didn't look quite as ferocious, quite as threatening, asleep, she thought, then trembled when she realized that, subconsciously, she'd been thinking of this man as dangerous. But sleep took nothing away from his size, the breadth of his shoulders, the hard muscles in his arms and long legs. Nor did sleep diminish his dark, mysterious looks.

Anna Rose picked up a hand-crocheted afghan and laid it over Britt. Even though it was late May in Alabama, the nights after a heavy rain could still be chilly. Without thinking, she ran her fingers across the scars on his forehead. When he grunted, she jerked her hand away.

Before leaving, she took one last look. "Well, Lord," she whispered. "I prayed for a man, but I'm afraid you might have given me just a little bit more than I can handle."

Two

Anna Rose awoke at a little after six. Years of getting up early had set her internal clock and it refused to allow her extra sleep even on weekends. She sat up in the half-canopy bed that had been passed down in the Palmer family for generations. The ornately carved mahogany bed matched the chest and armoire that decorated her room, a room that looked as if it had been plucked from the pages of history. Anna Rose loved the antiques that filled her home, and she cared for them with adoration and pride.

She noticed bright sunshine pushing against the curtained windows and French door, seeping through the fabric and around the corners to lighten the cool darkness inside. A soft morning breeze was blowing. She could hear the gentle scrape of the weeping willow branches against the side of the house.

Stretching her arms over her head, she sighed, feeling an undeniable soreness in her limbs and back. Helping Britt Cameron climb the steep embankment onto the road had exercised unused muscles, leaving her body aching. Wondering how her visitor had fared the night, she got out of bed, slipping on her floor-length cotton robe over her gown. If she hurried, she might have breakfast finished before he awoke. The thought of sharing breakfast with a man gave Anna Rose a rush of delight.

She opened her bedroom door and stepped into the hall. Just as she was chastising herself for being a silly romantic fool, Britt walked out of the bathroom across the corridor. She opened her mouth on a startled gasp, then sucked in an awed breath. He stood only a few feet from her, tall and dark and overwhelmingly big, wearing nothing but her grandfather's too short jeans.

Although she'd seen men in shorts and swim trunks, she'd never realized how erotic a man's partially naked body could be, but then, few men looked like Britt Cameron. His black hair was worn a bit too long for fashion. Thick and wavy, it curled about his neck and a few loose strands fell across his forehead. His heavy beard and mustache gave him a look of mystery, the appearance of a rugged warrior, of a saddle-weary cowboy, of a ruthless pirate.

"Good...good morning." She forced the words, her breath caught in her lungs, creating an ache in her chest.

"Morning." He didn't move. He simply stared back at her.

Anna Rose tried to stop looking at him, but seemed powerless to end her perusal of his totally male physique. His shoulders were unbelievably broad and sculptured with large, smooth muscles. His big arms were covered with a smattering of dark hair, as was his thick chest, where a dense swirl of blackness centered between his bulging pectoral muscles and arrowed down his belly and into his jeans.

In the dimly lit hallway, the scars that marred his otherwise perfect appearance took little away from his devastatingly masculine appeal—indeed their very existence seemed to add to his powerful macho aura.

"I hope it's all right that I went ahead and took a shower," he said, noting the oddly dazed look in her eyes, the peculiar way she was staring at him. "I tried the phone already. It's still out."

"Oh…I—I'm not surprised." She willed herself to act rationally, not like some sex-starved old maid. Tarnation, how she hated that term—*old maid.* It was an antiquated term, but one still widely used in the rural South, and most definitely overused in Cherokee, Alabama.

"Thanks for drying my clothes." He plunged his hands into his pockets, the gesture tugging on the overly loose waistband and lowering it to hip level. "I found them on the rocking chair in the living room. I was just fixing to put them on."

She swallowed—swallowed hard. His hips were lean and narrow. She couldn't take her eyes off that line of black hair that thickened at his navel. "You're welcome," she gulped the words.

"Do you suppose the road is clear so you can take me into town for a wrecker?" he asked, his gaze traveling leisurely over her sleep-tousled appearance. In the soft lighting, she was almost pretty, a fact he tried to dismiss from his mind.

"If it's still flooded, I can drive you back into Mississippi to the first town over the state line, or we can go the long way around into Cherokee. It'll take forever."

Britt's attention was caught by the way her breasts lifted when she breathed deeply, as if she were nervous and trying desperately to calm herself. Her faded housecoat hung open from shoulders to hem, and her thin, slightly worn cotton gown did little to conceal the lush fullness of her breasts or the curve of her wide hips and the shadowed cleft between her long legs.

Unwanted and completely unexpected, Britt's body responded in a natural way to the feminine allure of the woman standing so close to him. He cursed his arousal, and since he didn't find her attractive, he couldn't understand his reaction.

"Won't you stay for breakfast?" she asked, hoping beyond hope that he would stay.

"Sure...sure. Breakfast would be nice. If it wouldn't be too much trouble." He looked directly at her. That was a mistake. There was something gentle, almost lovely about her features. The wide mouth and full lips. The long, slightly large nose. The heavy-lidded, sapphire-blue eyes. And a mane of ash-brown hair that hung over her shoulders and down her back halfway to her waist. Britt's body tightened, his masculinity threatening to embarrass him. Luckily she didn't seem to notice his blatant state of arousal.

"You can change clothes, then go out back to the patio. I'll get dressed and fix breakfast and we'll eat outside." She had always dreamed of sharing breakfast on the rock patio with a man—a special man with whom she'd shared an unforgettable night. Well, she laughed to herself, she most certainly would never forget last night.

"Yeah, well...yeah. Fine." With his hands still in his pockets, he turned and went down the hall, grateful that Anna Rose Palmer had either not noticed his condition or was too much of a lady to mention it.

He swept the fallen leaves, small sticks and pieces of debris from the patio, all the while breathing in the fresh, after-rain smell of the world, and occasionally stealing glances at Anna Rose as she dried off the wooden table and chairs with a ragged towel. She had changed out of her revealing nightgown into some rather dowdy, beige twill slacks and a long-sleeved white blouse that hung below her hips. She'd pulled her hair into a loose ponytail, and not a smidgen of makeup adorned her pale face or covered the delicate splattering of freckles across her nose.

"Isn't everything beautiful after a rain?" She hugged her arms tightly across her chest as she looked up at the sky. "So fresh and clean. Almost new."

"Yeah. Like the world's starting all over." He watched her, noting the way she seemed to absorb the simple beauty of the day into her, as if she were able to draw strength from the natural wonders surrounding her. She's like this morning, he thought. Anna Rose is fresh and clean. He knew nothing about her life, and yet whatever she had experienced hadn't erased the facade of innocence she projected.

"Breakfast will be ready as soon as the biscuits are done," she told him. "I'll set the table."

When she turned to go back inside the house, he called out, "Where's Lord Byron this morning?"

"Oh, he ate in the kitchen and now he's out exploring in the woods with CoCo and Snowball."

"Friends of his?"

"They're a couple of strays that I've been feeding."

Britt sat down in one of the enormous redwood chairs, stretching his long legs out and crossing them at the ankles. Anna Rose's house reminded him a lot of home, now that his brother Wade's wife Lydia had redecorated the run-down Victorian structure. The furniture at home was mostly new, except for the few antique pieces Lydia had found at estate sales. But Anna Rose's well-kept house was filled with old furniture, polished to a gleaming shine. Her yard was neatly manicured, spring flowers blooming in abundance, their rain-and-wind-battered petals strewn hither and yon.

From the patio he could see endless acres of land, cultivated crops as far as the eye could see to the north and south on each side of the house and verdant forest to the west behind the house. The house itself, painted a pristine white, boasted a dark green roof and matching shutters. Delicately carved gingerbread trim created a fancy lace edging on the two-story structure and the one small third-story turret room.

Anna Rose returned with blue gingham place mats, matching napkins and glistening silverware. "The biscuits are ready." She smiled at him when he turned to face her. "I have homemade strawberry jam, pear preserves and grape jelly. Which do you prefer?"

"Pear preserves." Ma always canned several extra pints for him every year. They were his favorite. Nothing tasted quite as good on hot buttered biscuits. Although she'd been raised in the country, Tanya had never learned how to can fresh fruits and vegetables.

"I'll be right back," Anna Rose said.

"Need any help?"

"No, thanks. I've got everything on a serving cart."

He looked at the neat, homey setting she'd spread out on the redwood picnic table. All it needed, besides food, to be perfect was a bouquet of flowers in the center. Wade's wife Lydia loved flowers, and had filled the old homeplace with them after she'd redecorated and made the house truly hers. Britt figured Anna Rose probably liked flowers as much as Lydia did. Maybe it was a female thing. Without thinking, he got up, walked into the yard and began searching. Finally, near the barn he saw something that looked like white daisies growing in profusion. After picking a handful of the wildflowers, he started back toward the patio.

Anna Rose rolled a wooden cart filled with food to the table, looked around in search of Britt, and sighed with relief when she saw him coming toward her. Narrowing her eyes, she squinted against the hazy sunshine and tried to figure out what he carried in one hand. When he neared, she realized that he held a huge bouquet of daisies.

She stood there staring at him, smiling back and forth from him to the flowers. He shifted uncomfortably and grunted. "You fixed everything up so fancy, I thought you'd probably want a centerpiece." Damn, he felt like an idiot. What the hell had prompted him to go running off to pick flowers? He'd never done anything so...so unmanly in all his life.

"Oh, Britt, what a sweet thought." She reached out and took the bouquet when he thrust it at her. "They're beautiful. Sit down and eat. I'll go put these in a vase and be right back."

"Hey, there's no need—" He tried to tell her that she didn't need to stick the damn weeds in a vase. They weren't anything but wildflowers. They were more suited to being stuck in a tin can, he thought. But before he could protest, she whirled around and went back inside.

His feelings of discomfort soon vanished when he sat down at the table and breathed in the succulent aroma of ham and redeye gravy, scrambled eggs, crisp hash browns and hot coffee. If everything tasted half as good as it looked, Anna Rose Palmer was a whiz in the kitchen. He picked up the china cup, noting the blue flowered pattern just as his lips touched the rim. Delicious. The best damn coffee he'd ever drunk. Even better than Ma's, and that was saying a lot.

Savoring the heavenly taste of the morning's first cup of coffee, he glanced up to see Anna Rose bending over and placing the vase of daises in the center of the table. The vase matched the dishes—a crisp white, edged with tiny blue flowers.

"This is just perfect," she said as she sat down across from him.

Her face glowed with health and vitality and some inner happiness he didn't even try to discern. In the brutal light of day, he couldn't help but notice that Anna Rose was no great beauty. Her features were too strong, too vibrant. And yet, that very strength plus the Amazon proportions of her body combined to make a rather striking woman. But, dear God, her taste in clothes was awful. He wondered if she had anything in her wardrobe that actually fit her body, or if all her attire had been purchased at least one size larger than she needed.

"Eat up," she told him. "Enjoy everything while it's hot." She began by breaking open a fluffy biscuit and spreading a thick layer of pear preserves on each half.

For several minutes they each ate in silence. Britt thought that if the way to a man's heart was through his stomach, Anna Rose Palmer would have men lined up from her front porch into the next county.

"More coffee?" she asked, and, when he nodded, she poured from the sterling-silver pot.

Amazed by her healthy appetite, he thought about the other women he'd known over the years. None of them would have indulged in eating so heartily in front of a man they barely knew. As a matter of fact, most women of his acquaintance were always dieting. "How much of this land belongs to you?" he asked, nodding his head from left to right.

"About five hundred acres altogether." She finished off her second cup of coffee and poured a third, lacing it liberally with cream and sugar.

"You don't farm it yourself, do you?"

"I rent out some of it, but there are acres just sitting idle since Gramps died. A place this size needs a full-time farmer and I'm afraid my job in town pretty well fills my life." She thought about the offers she'd had for her land, and knew she'd never sell. She didn't need the money. Her salary was sufficient for her needs and what she collected in rent more than covered the cost of upkeep on the house and the farm itself. No, this land had been in her family since before the Civil War, and someday, God willing, she'd pass it down to her own children.

"I grew up on a farm something like this." He sipped his coffee as he leaned back in the redwood chair. It had been a long time since he'd enjoyed a meal so much.

"Is there…someone…anyone that you need to call? I

mean is there someone who'd be worried about you?''
What if Britt were married? she thought. It would be impossible to ask a married man to pose as her fiancé.

"My folks aren't expecting me back for a while.'' His
conscience urged him to tell her the truth. After all, didn't
her generous hospitality afford her that much?

"No wife and children?'' she asked, not caring if he
might take her inquisition the wrong way.

"I've never had a child...and I don't have a wife.'' He
had wanted children, longed to see Tanya pregnant, had
hoped a baby would save their doomed marriage. But she
hadn't wanted a child. Not his, anyway.

The poignantly sweet smell of honeysuckle wafted
through the mild spring breeze while Anna Rose sat on her
patio sharing a fantasy breakfast with an unmarried man
who just might be the answer to her prayers. If only there
was some way to persuade Britt Cameron to hang around
a few more days, she could tell everyone that he was her
fiancé. Then when he left, she'd simply explain that they'd
had a quarrel and had broken the engagement. There was
no reason why anyone had to know the truth about her
foolish lie.

While they continued enjoying the peaceful morning and
savoring the last of the fresh coffee, Anna Rose studied
Britt as discreetly as possible. Through most of the meal,
he'd seemed peaceful and relaxed, as if he were thoroughly
enjoying himself. But when she'd asked him about a wife
and children, his mood had altered. After responding to her
question, he'd become quiet and withdrawn, and she'd felt
a deep sorrow within him. It made her want to reach out
and put her arms around him. Instinctively knowing he
needed comfort, she longed to share his pain, ease his loneliness with all the stored-up love in her heart.

But Britt didn't look like a man who'd readily accept a
woman's tenderness. Certainly not from her, a plain Jane
whose forceful personality kept most men at arm's length.

In the bright, clear light of day, Britt's scars were vividly apparent. Puckered burn scars spread in thin, prominent lines across the left side of his forehead and into the density of his dark beard. Along his neck the scarring grew wider. Remembering him without a shirt, she knew the scars tapered off into nothingness as they approached his left arm.

She watched while he clutched the delicate china cup with his right hand, totally encompassing it. His left hand, which she'd noticed he seldom used, lay in his lap. She wondered again, what horrible event had marred this man for life, and why with the miracles of modern medicine he hadn't undergone reconstructive surgery. Then, perhaps he had, she thought. No, surely not. Unless…

Two tiny brown sparrows played in a nearby puddle of standing rainwater, dipping low, flapping their wings, relishing in the cleansing spray from their private pool. In three backyard trees, wooden bird feeders swayed in the breeze, and a lone gray squirrel scurried about from branch to branch, springing effortlessly from tree to tree like an accomplished highwire performer.

"Do you need a job?" she asked.

Snapping his head around, Britt glared at her, uncertain he'd heard her question correctly. "What?"

Anna Rose's cheeks flushed with embarrassment. She hadn't meant to blurt out her offer without some preamble, but, as usual, her forthright manner had taken precedence over better judgment. "I'm sorry. I should explain. You see, Corey Randall, my sort of…well, handyman around the place, had an accident and broke his leg several days ago."

"Handyman, huh?"

"Well, he keeps the house, the yard, the barn in good repair. Also, he checks the fences, makes sure no one is on my land without permission. Those sorts of things." She couldn't tell by the blank expression on Britt's face what his reaction was to her explanation.

"Are you offering me the job?" he asked, his topaz eyes narrowing to oval slits.

"Yes, on a temporary basis. The doctor said Corey probably wouldn't be able to work for about six weeks."

"Six weeks?" He ran his fingers over the short, neatly trimmed beard that spread across his chin and jawline. "How much does it pay?"

"The pay is minimum wage, but I could throw in room and board."

"You'd want me to stay here, with you?" He gave her an amused look.

"No, of course not." She emitted an exasperated huff. "There's an old sharecropper's shack about a quarter of a mile down the road. You'd need to clean it up and air it out, but it has electricity, indoor plumbing and the essentials in furniture. Bed, chairs, stuff like that."

"You'd provide groceries or would I take my meals with you?"

"The shack doesn't have a stove, just an old hot plate…no real kitchen. You'd have to come up to the house for meals." She desperately wanted him to take this job. His presence around the farm, even for a few weeks, could solve her mystery fiancé problem. "There's no air-conditioning, but the job won't last into much of July, and the house is in a grove of trees."

Britt didn't know why her offer was so appealing, why he was even considering accepting it. "How do you know you can trust me? What makes you so sure I'm not just some shiftless, lazy bum?"

"Instinct tells me you're trustworthy. And if you don't earn your salary, I'll fire you." She didn't want to sound too eager, push too hard, but she uttered up a silent prayer that he would accept her offer. She told herself that she simply needed his assistance to get herself out of a sticky social situation. Although the thought that she was taking in yet another stray, hoping to the heal the wounds of one more of God's injured creatures appealed to her sense of reason, she refused to acknowledge the way Britt Cameron made her feel every time she looked at him.

Britt considered his options. He was a man with no place to go...a man who badly needed a sanctuary, a place to hide away and lick his wounds. Anna Rose didn't know who he was, had no idea the trauma he'd lived through. Should he tell her? Did he dare to be totally honest with her? "I can't promise I'll stay the entire six weeks," he said, his gaze meeting hers. "Would you hire me on a week-to-week basis?"

Obviously he didn't want to be committed. Whatever he was running from, he wanted to be able to flee again if it caught up with him. Anna Rose knew she would take him on any terms. "Today's Saturday. How about a Saturday-to-Saturday basis?"

"Deal," he said.

"Deal." She smiled, certain that Britt Cameron's arrival the night before hadn't been a mere accident. He'd been sent to her—a gift from on high.

He stuck out his right hand. She accepted his strong, brisk handshake. The touch of his flesh against hers shook her slightly, giving her a breathless, nervous feeling. She hoped he hadn't noticed how she'd quivered just as he'd pulled his hand away.

"Why don't you take a look around the place while I clean up these dishes?" She began clearing away the table, stacking everything onto the cart. "Check out the barn. I don't have any cattle or horses now, but I expect you to keep it clean. The barn's open to stray animals. Dogs, cats, any animal in need of some food and a dry place to sleep."

Britt stood, then set his empty plate and cup on the cart. "You sound like my sister, Lily. She was always bringing home strays. Biggest fool over animals I ever saw."

Anna Rose laughed, and the sweet, honest sound touched Britt, making him want to respond in kind. He didn't like the idea that he was enjoying a woman's company. But what harm could this woman's presence cause him? Her plain looks didn't tempt him, and her bossiness certainly wasn't an inducement. And somehow he knew she wasn't the nosy kind, so she wouldn't be prying into his life, trying to discover his secrets. No, Anna Rose was the type of woman who'd leave a man alone.

"Need some help with these dishes?" he asked.

"You mean you're not too macho to do dishes?"

"Around our house, chores were chores. My brother and I mopped floors, washed dishes and made beds just like our sisters, and they had to milk cows, drive a tractor and pitch hay. Believe me, Ruthie Cameron was an equal opportunity mother. She made all four of her children, regardless of sex, work their butts off."

"I like your mother."

"She'd like you," he said without thinking. But it was true. He wondered if everyone liked Anna Rose. She seemed to be the kind of person who could easily endear herself to others. He certainly liked her, despite trying so hard not to.

"You go on and look around. I'll take you over so you can see the sharecropper shack in a little while, then we'll find some way to get to a garage. You'll need your truck. I let Corey keep the farm truck. He doesn't own a vehicle of his own."

Fifteen minutes later, Britt decided that running his truck into a ditch in front of Anna Rose Palmer's house had been a blessing in disguise. Her job offered him a temporary safe haven from the world, from his overly compassionate family, from the vicious suspicions that bombarded him in Riverton, and, if he were lucky, he would stay busy enough to keep the memories at bay.

He felt guilty for not telling Anna Rose that he'd been an accused murderer, only yesterday acquitted of a crime he had not committed. Oh, there had been a time when he'd wanted to kill Tanya. Hell, he'd spouted off for weeks after she left him, telling anyone who'd listen that if she and that holier-than-thou minister ever showed their faces back in Riverton, he'd kill them both. But by the time Tanya had come back, he hadn't wanted to harm her. He hadn't even wanted to see her.

He couldn't remember a time in his life when he hadn't loved Tanya. Ever since they'd been kids. But she'd never seen him as anything but a friend. She'd loved Paul, had married Paul, and had been pregnant with Paul's baby when...

Damn, he'd been a fool to marry her knowing she was still in love with her dead husband. But after Paul's death and her miscarriage, Tanya had tried to commit suicide. He had wanted to give her a reason to live, and had, stupidly, thought that offering her a new life with him would make her as happy as it did him. But his happiness had been short-lived. Their two-year marriage had been a disaster.

In retrospect, he couldn't blame Tanya. He'd practically forced her into the marriage. It hadn't been her fault that desperation drove her away, that she turned to the most sympathetic man in town—Reverend Timothy Charles. Young, handsome, charismatic. A man who, even after having committed adultery, had been forgiven by the people of Riverton, while those same people, unjustly, condemned Britt as a murderer.

If he'd thought for one minute he could have proven them wrong, he'd have stayed in Riverton. But what difference did it make? His own life wasn't worth a damn and neither was his reputation. Besides, he had no proof to substantiate his suspicions, and not even Sheriff Leonard Jett, who'd known Britt all his life, would listen to his accusations when he'd tried to tell Jett that he knew who had really killed Tanya. Hell, his own mother had looked at him with shocked disbelief when he'd told her that he thought the town's beloved Reverend Charles had killed Tanya.

No, he was better off trying to put the past behind him. There were some things a man couldn't change, some things not worth the effort. Maybe a few weeks spent as Anna Rose's handyman would serve as a stopgap between his past and his uncertain future. A few weeks of blessed anonymity. Days spent working to the point of exhaustion, seeing no one except Anna Rose—a woman whose laughter reminded him that there was still some good left in the world.

Three

Anna Rose placed her beige heels in the shoe rack, then hung up her suit in the closet before stripping out of her slip and panty hose. Rummaging around in the bottom drawer of the oak chest, she found her blue bathing suit. It was a modest-cut one-piece she'd had for years. It did nothing to enhance her large-boned physique, but its simple lines weren't unflattering to her generously proportioned body.

All during church, much to her shame, she'd thought of nothing except Britt Cameron. He'd been her replacement handyman for a week and, with each passing day, she liked him more and more. As she peeled off her bra and panties, she wondered if *like* was too mild a word for the emotion Britt had stirred to life within her. She pulled on her bathing suit, reached into her closet for a wraparound cotton skirt, put it on and tied the string belt.

While she had sung hymns this morning, she'd been planning a picnic lunch with Britt down by the pond. And all the while Brother Sherman had admonished the congregation to be on guard against sin, she had been thinking about the past week, all the breakfasts and lunches she had shared with her new employee.

She had another ten days to go before her summer vacation officially began, but for her students, school had ended last Friday. The final days were always hectic, especially for the principal, but she'd made time to prepare breakfast every morning. Britt had been punctual, knocking on her door at six-thirty. And she had taken special pleasure in fixing a large, hardy supper every night. Although their evening meal usually lasted nearly two hours and they enjoyed each other's company, as soon as he'd helped her with the dishes, Britt always left. They discussed her job, the farm and how their individual days had gone, but he seemed reluctant to talk about himself or his life before the night he'd wrecked his truck in front of her house. Occasionally he'd mention his mother, brother or sisters. From bits and pieces of conversation, she'd learned his brother was married and had children.

She had longed to explain her problem to him, to ask if he would be willing to share in the solution, but finding herself growing more and more attracted to him each day made it difficult for her to ask him to pose as her fiancé. She didn't know what to make of Britt Cameron and the way he made her feel. Not once had he been anything but a perfect gentleman. He never touched her, never intimated that he was the least interested in her as a woman, and yet Anna Rose found herself daydreaming about him, fantasizing about what it would be like to kiss him, to be in his arms.

What would it take for her to finally learn? she asked herself. Men weren't attracted to her. She was big and tall and plain. Men liked smaller women. Of course, she was smaller, a lot smaller, than Britt. Her keen intellect often intimidated men and her aggressive, take-charge attitude scared them away. But Britt Cameron, though not formally educated, seemed highly intelligent, and he acted more amused than offended by her bossiness.

Don't do this to yourself, she chided. *Enjoy Britt's company, work up enough courage to ask him to pose as your fiancé, but don't be stupid enough to imagine you're falling in love with him. You would have had a better chance of snagging Kyle Ross than you'll ever have of enticing a man like Britt Cameron. An inexperienced virgin like you wouldn't have a prayer of attracting a man as virile as Britt.*

During the time it took her to prepare a huge picnic lunch and pack it, Anna Rose had convinced herself that what she felt for Britt was a growing friendship. And as she walked over to the sharecropper's shack, she told herself that hiring him had been a stroke of genius on her part. Not only did he work tirelessly all day, he provided companionship at meals, and might, if she could work up the courage to proposition him, solve her *mystery* fiancé problem.

The sun was at its afternoon high, radiating warmth and light over everything within sight. Overhead a clear blue sky spread from horizon to horizon like an enormous azure canopy, and a gentle spring wind rippled through the trees, so light as to be almost indiscernible. The day was so perfect it defied description, Anna Rose thought as she made her way along the path from her home to the old shack. With heavy picnic basket in one hand and folded towels and quilt in the other, she felt God's presence as much here in her woods, on this piece of earth that she had inherited from generations of Palmers, as she had today sitting in church.

She stopped short when she saw Britt sitting on the porch, his back propped up against the house. Anna Rose swallowed, heat rising within her as she gazed at his big, hairy body clad only in a pair of cutoff jeans. He seemed to be relaxing and totally unaware of her presence. She knew she should say something to him, but all she could do was stare.

What was it about this man that stirred such primitive emotions within her? she wondered. No man, not even the handsome and charming Kyle Ross, had ever created such chaos in her mind and heart. And in her body. Every time she looked at Britt, she felt ashamed of her body's traitorous reaction. She had never been with a man, but she wasn't so ignorant of human nature that she didn't recognize desire, especially when she was consumed by it.

Tarnation. Double, triple tarnation. She didn't need this, certainly didn't want this complication in her life. Maybe she should just turn around and go back home.

Too late. He'd spotted her, was looking directly at her.

"Hey there." He stood up slowly, then took a step in her direction, stopping just as his bare feet touched the first wooden step. "Sorry about the way I'm dressed. I wasn't expecting company."

"Don't apologize." She tried to smile, but the effort proved useless. She was too caught up in her own emotions to sympathize with his apparent embarrassment at her finding him partially undressed. "I—I thought we might go over to the pond and have a picnic for lunch today."

"I, er, was going to change into jeans and a shirt before coming up to the house for lunch. You said two o'clock." He turned around, took several steps, then grasped the handle on the screen door.

"Change of plans," she said, praying her voice didn't give away her nervousness. "Since it's such a beautiful day, I thought… Well, there's no need for you to change… unless you have swim trunks."

"Nope." He released the door handle, turned halfway around, and gave her a tentative smile. "Are you sure it's all right? I could at least put on a shirt."

"No need, unless you're worried about sunburn."

He glanced down at his darkly tanned torso and shook his head.

"Forget it," she said, feeling more a fool with each passing minute. Of course he wasn't worried about sunburn. His naturally dark complexion had taken on an almost bronze hue in the week he'd been working for her. She knew he went without a shirt some days. But never once had he come to her house without one. "Let's go. I'm starving." She tried for a light, friendly tone, knowing that if Britt even suspected she wanted him, he'd run as far and fast as he could.

"Just let me put this up," he said, reaching down to where he'd been sitting to pick up an open paperback book lying on the porch. "I've enjoyed reading the other two, and started this one about an hour ago."

She saw that he held one of the Dick Francis novels she'd loaned him earlier in the week. She had seen him looking at her huge collection of books and had asked if he enjoyed reading. He'd eyed her most recent purchase, a romance novel, lying on her desk, and told her his taste in reading material didn't run to romance or to poetry. That was when she'd gone to the shelf and retrieved three of her favorite Dick Francis mysteries, and was surprised that Britt was familiar with the author.

When he came back out of the house, he was wearing an unbuttoned, short-sleeved shirt. Neither of them mentioned his apparel. He took the heavy picnic basket and load of towels, leaving her to carry only the quilt.

"Lead the way," he said, following.

"An underground spring feeds the pond, you know," she told him as they walked along the narrow path that meandered through the woods.

"There's one on our property at home like that. We used to swim in it all the time when we were kids. Ma always made sure there were at least two of us together. She didn't take chances with our safety."

"I used to slip out here and just sit by the pond. My grandmother was very strict. She never allowed me to own a bathing suit, but Gramps taught me how to swim, anyway. I just wore loose pants." Anna Rose didn't like to remember the unpleasant things about her childhood, the horrible lectures Grandma had given her about the evils that lurked everywhere. Indeed Grandma had thought that anything that gave a person too much pleasure had to be a sin.

"Overly religious, huh?" Britt asked. "I had an aunt like that. My father's aunt, actually. Ma despised Aunt Methel. Said she committed more sins in her fanaticism than most folks did just living life the best they knew how."

"Here we are," she said, thankful that they had arrived at the pond. She never discussed the details of her restricted upbringing with anyone, and doing so with Britt made her feel uncomfortable. Even she and Gramps had never really talked about the situation. Her grandfather had just accepted his wife as if he had no other choice, telling Anna Rose that her grandmother meant well. She had never understood what the outgoing, fun-loving David Palmer had had in common with his taciturn, sour-faced wife.

"This is nice," Britt said, glancing around at the tree-shaded pond, appreciating the peacefulness and solitude. "It's a lot like our pond."

"In Mississippi?" she asked as she spread the quilt on the ground.

"Yeah, in Mississippi." It was the first time she'd asked him about where he'd come from, and he didn't think, even now, she was being nosy. "I grew up on a farm in Riverton. My mother still lives there with my brother and his family. My sisters moved away as soon as they finished high school, but they visit from time to time."

"Riverton?" Anna Rose had been to Riverton, or rather, had ridden through Riverton on her way to Memphis. But that had been years ago, before the four-lane highway came

through and bypassed all the small towns between Cherokee, Alabama and Corinth, Mississippi.

"You've been there?"

"Through there. Years ago. It's in Tishomingo County,
isn't it?"

Britt stacked the towels at the edge of the quilt and set
the basket in the center. "Yeah. Do you want me help you
unpack?"

"No, no. Just sit down. I'll fix everything. Are you hungry?"

"Starving." He sat, stretching his long legs out in front
of him. "Did your grandmother teach you how to cook?"

"Yes, as a matter of fact she did." Anna Rose sat down
and began lifting out parcels covered in aluminum foil and
clear plastic wrap. "Grandma was an excellent cook, and
she thought every woman should know how. She considered it a duty."

"But you like to do it, don't you? It's a pleasure for
you."

Amazing, she thought, that he understood. She did indeed like to cook, loved to, as a matter of fact. "It's been
fun having someone to cook for besides myself," she said,
then stole a glance at him to see if he might have misin-
terpreted her admission.

"Believe me, the pleasure has been mine."

He watched while she prepared them both a plate. By
the time she poured the iced tea into tall, blue plastic cups,
he was drooling. Fried chicken, potato salad, deviled eggs,
baked beans and big, fluffy yeast rolls covered the large
paper plate she handed him. When he took the plate, she
delved into the basket and brought out blue paper napkins,
along with plastic forks and spoons.

"What a feast," he said, setting the plate in his lap and
situating the cup between his knees. Eyeing the napkin she
laid at his side, he nodded his thanks. "You must like
blue."

"You noticed."

"Yeah. A blue kitchen. A blue bathroom. Touches of blue in your living room. And you even wear a lot of blue."

"It's my favorite color." She glanced down at the blue bathing suit she wore and the blue flowered skirt that covered her from waist to mid-calf.

Britt's gaze followed hers, hesitating at the top edge of her bathing suit where her breasts swelled invitingly, then his gaze traveled the long length of her body and finally stopped at her feet, clad in a pair of slip-on white sandals. Unwillingly his thoughts filled with images of Anna Rose the way she had looked in her thin cotton nightgown the morning after he'd spent the night on her couch. What would she look like naked? he wondered. Would the rest of her body be as pale and smooth as her arms and legs, her long neck and broad shoulders?

"Let's eat," he said, his voice a harsh grumble.

She eyed him with a questioning glare. "Is something wrong?"

"No. I'm just hungry." The last thing he needed was to become embroiled in a relationship with Anna Rose. She wasn't the type of woman with whom a man could share a brief, meaningless affair. And God knew, he never again wanted to try to have a lasting relationship with a woman.

They ate in silence for endless minutes, neither looking up from their plates. Suddenly Lord Byron came bounding through the woods, rushing headlong into the middle of their picnic. Both Britt and Anna Rose held tightly to their plates, but the big rottweiler slammed into Anna Rose's side, knocking her tea out of her hand. The cool liquid spread quickly into the quilt and over Anna Rose's skirt.

"Oh, Lord Byron, you big baby. Where have you been?" she asked. "Out courting Murphy?" She glanced over at Britt, who held his plate in one hand and a drumstick in the other. "Murphy is my nearest neighbor's Labrador retriever."

"Is Lord Byron a ladies' man?"

"I'm afraid he's a regular Don Juan." Anna Rose laid her plate on the quilt, put two pieces of chicken on another plate and placed it at the edge of the quilt. Lord Byron, knowing from experience that the dish had been set aside for him, stretched out in the grass and began devouring his meager feast. "He's also a glutton. I can't fill him up. He not only looks like a small horse, he eats like one, too."

"We had a couple of German Shepherds when we were kids. Lily was only about three and she'd ride Wolf around like he was a pony."

"Lily is your baby sister, right?"

"Yeah. Wade's the oldest. He's thirty-four. Then me, two years younger, then Amy, three years younger than me, and finally Lily, who's just turned twenty-six."

"Are either of your sisters married?" Anna Rose nibbled on a roll.

"Not now. Amy married right after high school and left home. The marriage only lasted a couple of years." Britt didn't like to think about what bad luck the Cameron bunch had had in their marriages. The eldest three had all been divorced. Of course, Wade was happily married now. "Lily's still single."

"It must be wonderful to have brothers and sisters."

"You were an only child?"

"Yes."

"You told me that you were raised by your grandparents, that your grandmother was very religious and very strict, but you've never mentioned your parents."

"I never knew my father. He and my mother were just kids when she got pregnant. His parents sent him off to college and my sixteen-year-old mother gave birth to an illegitimate child and shamed her parents. I don't think my grandmother ever forgave my mother or...or me."

"Anna Rose..."

"It's all right. There's no more pain. I put it aside years

ago. I've never even met my father. He and his family moved to California when he was still in college.''

"Your mother—''

"Committed suicide when I was ten months old.''

He laid his plate and cup aside, reached out and pulled her toward him. She hesitated momentarily, uncertain and afraid. Knowing that he intended to comfort her, Anna Rose wasn't sure she could go into his arms and not want more than sympathy.

"Please don't feel sorry for me,'' she said.

"Oh, Annie Rosie.'' He pulled her closer as he leaned over to take her in his arms, cradling her head in the curve of his shoulder. "Did your grandmother teach you to hide your feelings?''

"Grandma was Grandma. Gramps kept me sane, made me feel as if I were worthy of being alive.'' She couldn't bear to think about all the times her grandmother had ridiculed her, had scolded and punished her for crimes so infinitesimal that other parents would have dismissed them without a thought. Everything had been a sin. Parties. School dances. Dating. Kissing. Bathing suits. Shorts. Movies. Grandma had taken away every possible pleasure from her life, except her books. Anna Rose had kept them hidden in her room.

"When did she die?'' he asked, wondering how many years Anna Rose had been forced to endure the old woman's mental cruelties.

"When I was eighteen and away at college. I had graduated from high school at sixteen and earned a full scholarship to the University of Alabama. When Grandma died, I came home and went to U.N.A. so I could be here to help Gramps.''

"A full scholarship at sixteen?'' She'd told him she was an elementary school principal, so he'd assumed she was college educated. He knew she was very intelligent, but suspected her intellect had often been more of a curse than a blessing. "What's your IQ, Annie Rosie? Are you a genius?"

She flushed, embarrassed instead of proud. Well-meaning friends and relatives had told her often enough that most men didn't like women who were smarter than they. Her cousin Tammy had cautioned her when she'd been dating Kyle Ross. But he hadn't seemed to object to the fact that she was intelligent, and it hadn't seemed to bother him that she was the principal and he a teacher. But then, he had never been seriously interested in her. They'd dated numerous times, and she had allowed her infatuation to cloud her vision, had seen love when only friendship had existed.

"No, I'm not a genius," she said, relaxing against Britt when he began to run his hand up and down her back in a soothing gesture. "But I am intelligent."

"And a good cook."

"What?" She raised her head from his shoulder.

"I said not only are you intelligent, but you're a good cook." He knew he'd said the right thing when she smiled, then started laughing.

Her laughter warmed his cold heart, the sound sweet to his ears. He refused to examine too closely the reasons why it was important to him to see her smile, to ease her pain and try to erase the bad memories.

"You're good for me, Britt Cameron," she said, looking him squarely in the eye. Her breath caught in her throat at the intense way he was staring at her. It was as if he could see straight through to her soul. Confused and a little frightened, she pulled away from him. "Why don't we go for a swim?"

"So soon after eating? I'm afraid I'd sink to the bottom of the pond." He tried to make the tone of his voice light and teasing. He'd seen that look of confusion in her eyes, had felt her hesitation. Had she realized that, for one split second, the thought of making love to her had crossed his mind? Hell, he didn't want to make love to Anna Rose. She wasn't his type. Besides, she was becoming his friend, and he'd never had a female friend before. He didn't want to louse up the easy companionship they shared when all he needed was a quick tumble. Any woman would do for that. Any woman except Anna Rose.

"Well, you sit here and let your lunch settle." She patted him on his flat stomach, then jerked her hand away. "I'm going for a swim."

He watched her jump up, discarding her skirt before running to the pond. She dived in, swimming with swift even strokes. Her touch had been innocent, a teasing gesture, but he could still feel the imprint of her long fingers, their warmth spreading through him like a slowly growing flame. She'd felt it, too. That was why she'd jerked her hand away.

Something was wrong, damned wrong when a woman like Anna Rose could arouse him. Hell, what he needed was a couple of nights in some sexy little blonde's bed.

Anna Rose simply wasn't the kind of woman a man fantasized about. But she sure was the type to comfort a man, to give his heart and mind ease. She seemed to know instinctively when he needed to be alone and exactly when he needed her company. For eight days he'd shared meals with her as well as good conversation and genuine companionship. She never pried, but he knew she'd listen if he wanted to talk. The funny thing was that all during the day when he was working, he'd think about her. At odd times, something she'd said would pop into his mind—the way she blushed when she was embarrassed—the sound of her laughter.

He stood up and walked over to lean against an enormous maple tree. Folding his arms across his chest, he stared out at the pond, his gaze riveted to Anna Rose. She had stopped swimming and stood near the water's edge, her body visible from the knees up. She'd turned her face toward the sun, allowing her long hair to fall in a wet, tangled mass down her back. For such a large woman, she wasn't built half bad, he thought. A couple of generations ago, her generous proportions would have been considered perfect.

The sunlight glistened off the moisture coating her skin and it turned her hair to a silvery tan. Drops of water clung to her face. For one split second, Britt looked at her and thought she was lovely.

As if drawn by a force he was powerless to resist, Britt flung his unbuttoned shirt on the ground, ran up behind Anna Rose and grabbed her around the waist, flinging them both into the pond. They went under, then resurfaced quickly.

Wiping the water from her eyes as she coughed several times, Anna Rose faced him. "What were you trying to do, drown me?" she asked, unable to mask her smile.

"Why didn't you tell me the water was this cold?" Giving a mock shudder, he ran his hands up and down his arms, as if trying to warm himself.

"It's not cold, just cool." She scooped up water in both hands and flung it at him, laughing when he spluttered.

"You're going to be sorry for that, Annie Rosie." When he reached out for her, she swam away toward the opposite side of the pond.

He followed suit, catching up with her just as she made a mad scramble onto dry ground. He swung her up in his arms, spinning her around and around before tossing her back into the pond. She hit the water with a resounding splash. Standing on the bank, he broke into peals of laughter. While watching her swim back to the other side, the thought struck him that only a week ago he'd been sure he'd never laugh again. Tanya's betrayal, her subsequent death and then the nightmare trial had taken all the laughter from his life—what little there had been since Paul's death almost five years ago.

Britt walked around the edge of the pond, making his way back to the quilt where Anna Rose sat, drying herself off with a huge blue-and-white striped towel.

"We never did eat dessert," he said, slumping down beside her as he reached for a towel.

"You're a bottomless pit."

His gaze settled on her mouth, still damp from her swim. A single drop of water fell from her lips onto her chin. The sunlight caught on that one transparent particle, creating a tiny pastel rainbow inside. Britt had the strangest urge to lick away that magic touch of moisture.

While he dried off, she brought out a bundle of fried pies, placing one on a napkin. "Here. I made fried peach pies."

Tossing his damp towel aside, he accepted the treat, immediately taking a huge bite. After swallowing, he said, "I can't believe some man hasn't married you just for your cooking." The moment he looked at her face, he regretted his choice of words. Her stunned expression was enough to make him wish he'd bitten his tongue. "Ah, you're probably one of those career women who doesn't want to be tied down to a man. I mean considering your education and career."

Well, it's time to tell him, she decided. *He's given you the perfect opening to ask him the big question.* "I'd like to get married and have children, but I seem to scare men."

"Look, you don't have to—"

"Last fall I made a complete fool of myself over a new male teacher. His name is Kyle Ross, and I misunderstood the friendly attention he paid me. We dated several times, and I thought I was in love. Everyone in Cherokee thought that, finally, poor Anna Rose had found herself a man." Once started, she couldn't stop talking, but when he grabbed her by the shoulders, she ceased her incessant babbling. "What?"

He didn't like to see her this way, baring her soul. He

could actually feel her pain. "There's no need for you to tell me about this."

"Yes, there is." With more courage than she knew she possessed, she looked him squarely in the eye. "I need your help."

"What sort of help?"

"Let me explain." She swallowed hard and took a deep breath before continuing. "Kyle didn't really lead me on. He didn't need to, I was so infatuated with him. But he never once told me that there was someone else. Just when I and the whole town thought he was ready to pop the question, he married his college sweetheart. He just went home for Spring Break in March and came back married."

"My God. What a bastard." Britt thought that if he could get hold of this Kyle Ross, he'd give him a much needed lesson in the right way to treat a woman like Anna Rose.

"Not really. I simply read more into our relationship than was there." *The same way I'm doing now—with you,* she reminded herself. Only the way she had felt about Kyle was nothing compared to her feelings for Britt. She had never wanted Kyle, not in that basic, sexually hungry way she wanted Britt. She'd never been with a man, but every time she got near Britt, she started thinking about what it would be like if he made love to her.

"Did he kiss you?" Britt asked, releasing his tight hold on her arms. "Embrace you? Whisper sweet nothings in your ear?"

"Ah, er, yes." Kyle had been smooth, a practiced ladies' man. He'd had every female teacher at Cherokee Elementary swooning over him.

"Did he ever…?" Britt wanted to ask her if she'd ever allowed Kyle Ross to make love to her, hating the very thought of another man touching her. Not that he cared, personally, he told himself. It's just that he'd hate to think the guy had seduced her. "Just how serious was your relationship?"

"He did ask me to sleep with him, if that's what you're asking." Anna Rose remembered how tempted she'd been to have sex with Kyle, not because she'd wanted him so desperately, but because she longed to know what it was all about, longed to lose her virginity and become a real woman.

Suddenly Britt felt like smashing his fist into something, and wished Kyle Ross's face was handy. "Damn him."

"I didn't," she said, her voice delicately soft and filled with vulnerability.

"You didn't have sex with him?"

"No. I considered it, but while I was trying to make up my mind, he married someone else."

"You're better off without him."

"I've come to that conclusion on my own, but I still have a problem to deal with." She braced herself, hoping her courage wouldn't fail her now.

"What problem?"

"After Kyle's unexpected marriage, all my friends and relatives…well, practically the whole town felt sorry for me." She almost let her gaze falter when she saw a glimmer of sympathy in his eyes. "People have felt sorry for me my whole life. Poor Anna Rose, born out of wedlock. Poor Anna Rose's mother killed herself. Poor Anna Rose who took care of her elderly grandparents. Poor Anna Rose, with her plain looks and bossy personality, she'll never get a man."

"People can be cruel," he said, thinking of himself as much as her. She couldn't bear her townspeople's pity; he couldn't bear his townspeople's distrust.

"I did a stupid thing. I told my friend Edith that everyone had been mistaken about my feelings for Kyle…that all the while he'd had a secret lover, so had I."

"What?"

"I told Edith that I had met a man on my vacation last summer and we'd been corresponding ever since, and…well…that he'd asked me to marry him and I'd accepted."

"But there is no man, no fiancé?" he asked, knowing full well that she'd concocted the lie to protect herself.

"That was a couple of months ago, and people are asking when my mystery fiancé is going to show up." She wanted to ask him to pose as that fiancé, but somehow she couldn't make the words form on her lips.

"You have boxed yourself into a corner, haven't you?"

"If I don't come up with a fiancé, and soon, I'm going to wind up looking like more of a fool than I would have if I'd just gone ahead and let everyone feel sorry for me." *Please, Britt, don't you realize that you're the solution to my problem?*

He understood her predicament and realized that she was trying to ask him to pose as her fiancé. Without even thinking, he said, "Would it help if you passed me off as your mystery man?"

The smile that spread across her face overrode the shock he felt by his own words. He hadn't meant to volunteer, but he had allowed his emotions to overrule his common sense. It was a habit he needed to break, one for which he'd already paid dearly.

"Would you? Oh, Britt, would you really?"

"I don't want to be paraded around, go to parties or church or whatever, but I'm sure if I stay another few weeks, sooner or later someone is going to notice I'm here. When they do, just say I'm your fiancé." What the hell, he thought, what harm would it do to help out a nice lady like Anna Rose? It seemed to him she'd had too many tough breaks in her life. Even if he couldn't make his own life any easier, maybe he could hers.

"No, no, you won't have to do anything," she assured him. "When you leave, I'll simply say that we had a serious quarrel and I asked you to go…that I decided you were the wrong man for me.''

''Okay. Sounds like something we can both handle.''

''Then you will? You'll pretend to be my fiancé for a few weeks?''

''Sure, why not?''

Not expecting what happened next, Britt was caught totally off guard when she threw her arms around him and kissed him soundly on the mouth. As if sensing that she'd made a serious faux pas, Anna Rose jerked away from him. ''Oh, Britt, I'm sorry. I didn't mean to do that. Really. It's just that I'm so grateful. Tarnation, Britt, say something.''

Instead of saying anything, he reacted on a purely instinctive level. Pulling her into his arms, he gave her a quick, hard kiss. ''That's to seal our bargain.''

''Oh.'' Her lips formed a soft, moist oval.

Kissing her had been a mistake. She'd been so warm and compliant. He hadn't kissed a woman in a long time, too long a time, he thought as he again covered her mouth with his. Damn, she was sweet. Her lips parted, eagerly accepting the thrust of his tongue as he deepened the kiss, turning it from a gentle invasion into a thorough ravaging. She moaned when his arms encircled her, hauling her up against him, crushing her breasts into his chest.

Anna Rose had never been kissed so completely in all her life. She felt as if her bones were dissolving, that if Britt didn't hold on to her, she would melt away. As abruptly as he'd taken her mouth, he released it.

''Hey, hey, Annie Rosie, we're unofficially, officially engaged.'' He couldn't—wouldn't—allow himself to use this woman, he thought, looking at her, seeing the passion so evident in her eyes. He was aroused. She was needy. What he felt was lust, but a woman like Anna Rose would call it love. No way in hell was he going to hurt her. She'd been hurt enough. He could never love her, so he had no right to take from her when he had nothing to give in return.

"Thanks, Britt," she said, glancing down at her long, full thighs, hating herself for not being little and slim and desirable.

Jumping up, he grabbed both of her hands and helped her to her feet. "Come on, let's take another swim before heading back."

Without giving her time to reply, he scooped her up in his arms and ran into the cool water, not releasing her until they were in the middle of the pond. Slowly, ever so slowly, he eased her down his body. She gasped when she felt his arousal.

She swam away from him before he could see the tears in her eyes. He was aroused and yet he didn't want her, she thought. *Am I so undesirable? He needs a woman and yet he'd rather do without than to make love to me.*

Anna Rose knew now that she'd never been in love before, most definitely not with Kyle Ross. But she suspected that she was falling in love with Britt and realized there was little hope of his ever returning her affections.

Knowing that, she dreaded the next few weeks. She would see him every day and would eventually be introducing him as her fiancé. How was she going to be able to live a lie when, with every beat of her heart, she'd be wishing it was true?

Four

The setting sun's warmth was spread by the wind's gentle breath as it floated through the trees and grass and flowers. The fragrance of honeysuckle wafted in the breeze, combining with the smell of freshly plowed earth and the refreshing, natural aroma of country air. Britt loved the land, and couldn't imagine living in the city. The never-ending noise, the constant commotion, the filth of so many people crammed together in a small area, not to mention the odor, the smog and the high crime rate. No, some people might enjoy a more hectic life-style, might actually prefer the hustle and bustle associated with city living, but not Britt Cameron. His sisters seemed happy enough living away from the farm, but he knew he would never be content anywhere but in the country. Four years in the marines had proven that fact to him years ago.

Britt checked his watch. He'd taken time to shower and change clothes as he did every evening before walking from the sharecropper's shack over to Anna Rose's house for supper. After their picnic by the pond four days ago, they had both been careful not to allow their emotions to over-rule their common sense. The next morning at breakfast, Britt had felt her uncertainty, her uncharacteristic shyness, and he'd tried to act as if nothing of any importance had transpired between them. Hell, all they'd done was kiss, he told himself. That *wasn't* anything important. At least it wouldn't have been to most women. But Anna Rose wasn't most women. The longer Britt knew her, the more he understood what an insecure and inexperienced woman she was. He suspected that she didn't know a damn thing about men.

He wasn't sure why, but concentrating on Anna Rose's problems seemed to divert his attention from his own. But that only made him feel all the more guilty for not telling her the complete truth about himself. If she was going to pass him off as her fiancé, she had a right to know that he'd been accused of his wife's murder, that half his home-town still thought he was guilty.

He didn't want Anna Rose to know that Tanya had been murdered, and that he'd gone to trial and only the lack of hard evidence freed him from a prison sentence. He didn't want to take the risk that she would turn from him and ask him to leave before he was ready to go. He'd found the first real peace he'd known in years here in Alabama, living in a shack, working as a handyman and sharing meals with a woman who looked at him with adoration in her eyes. He couldn't bear the thought of seeing that adoration turn to suspicion.

He liked Anna Rose. She was genuine and honest and didn't know the first thing about using feminine wiles to trap a man into making a fool of himself. She was the type of person who made a good friend, a congenial companion whose intelligent conversation was never boring. What surprised him the most about his relationship with Anna Rose was that, despite the fact she wasn't the type of woman who usually attracted him, he wanted her. And if she wasn't so damned inexperienced, he would pursue an affair with her. They were both lonely people dealing with a past neither of them could change. He had no doubts that they'd be as good for each other as lovers as they were as friends. The only problem was that when his temporary job ended, he'd have no problem saying goodbye and going on his way. But Anna Rose was the kind of woman who'd have sex and love all mixed up. She probably thought she couldn't have one without the other. He wouldn't risk letting her fall in love with him when he had no love left to give anyone.

Deep in thought, Britt emerged from the path onto Anna Rose's driveway, not noticing the big white Cadillac parked behind Anna Rose's Blazer. The petite blonde wearing skin-tight jeans and a hot-pink halter top caught his attention. She was stepping onto the porch, her small hips swaying seductively.

Damn, who is she? he wondered. Anna Rose hadn't mentioned expecting any company. Hoping he could make his way back along the path before the woman noticed him, Britt started to turn. Too late. She'd seen him.

''Hi, there.'' Her voice held a high-pitched, childlike quality.

Gritting his teeth and muttering imprecations, Britt stopped dead still. He didn't want to have to face this stranger, whoever she was, but it looked as if he had no choice. She was walking straight toward him.

Britt guessed she was in her late twenties. She was very attractive in a rather gaudy way. Her figure was good, but she wasn't really pretty. Perhaps that was the reason she wore too much makeup. Her pale blond hair was cut short. A pair of half-dollar-size gold hoops hung in her ears, three strands of gold chains draped her neck, a pair of gold bracelets circled each wrist and every finger was adorned with a ring.

"I'm Tammy Spires," she said, as if her name should mean something to him.

"Britt Cameron, ma'am." He could smell her perfume. Something heavy and spicy and liberally applied.

"My, oh, my, you must be Anna Rose's mystery man. I've just been dying to meet you." She giggled like a junior high cheerleader making a pass at a senior quarterback. "As a matter of fact, half the town's been wanting to get a glimpse of you. Edith Hendricks said she'd driven by five times hoping you'd be outside in the yard."

Tammy laid her hand on his arm, her long, hot-pink nails scraping his skin. He looked down into her big blue eyes. Smiling, she giggled again, and he thought of Tanya. This woman reminded him of his dead wife. She was about the same size, had the same coloring, the same childish laugh and the same coquettish way of flirting with a man. Just as he started to move away from Tammy, he heard the front door open and looked across the yard. Anna Rose walked out onto the front porch.

"I see you've met Britt," Anna Rose said.

"Your fiancé." Tammy sighed. "Who would ever have believed it." Tightening her hold on Britt, she laced her nails through the curly hair on his forearm. "I must say, he isn't quite what I expected."

Not caring if he appeared rude, Britt pulled away from the blonde's tenacious grasp. When he did, she gave him an amused look, then walked away. Britt watched her join Anna Rose on the porch, wishing he could escape, but knowing Anna Rose was counting on his cooperation. He'd promised that he'd pose as her fiancé, and he was a man of his word.

Anna Rose hated the old feelings of jealousy she'd always secretly harbored against her cousin Tammy, and had thought she'd long since overcome such a fruitless emotion. But seeing Tammy practically drooling all over Britt had given new life to the old green-eyed monster within her.

"How nice to see you, Tammy," Anna Rose said, forcing a smile. "What brings you out this way?"

"Nothing special. Just thought I'd drop by and see how you're doing. Of course, word's all over Cherokee that you've got a man staying in the old shack over in the woods."

"Britt, come on in. Supper's almost ready." Anna Rose opened the front door, looking over Tammy's shoulder to where Britt stood, silent and unmoving.

"Yeah," he finally said. "Sure thing."

Anna Rose didn't want to issue her cousin an invitation, but years of having hospitable Southern manners drilled into her superceded her own personal desire. "Won't you join us?"

Tammy couldn't seem to stop looking at Britt. Anna Rose didn't like the way she was sizing him up, as if she were measuring to see if he'd fit in her bed. "I'd love to stay, but I'm afraid Roy Dean's expecting me. We're driving up to Florence to eat at the Renaissance Tower."

Anna Rose watched while Britt walked slowly toward the house. She knew he wasn't pleased about Tammy's visit, about having to actually begin the pretense. "Well, come on in and stay a few minutes. I'll get us all some tea."

Anna Rose held the door open for Tammy to enter, then waited until Britt came up behind her before taking a step. Unexpectedly he put his arm around her waist and led her inside. His arm was big and warm and strong. She loved the feel of it about her, the gentle power in his embrace. She knew he was acting affectionate for Tammy's sake, but even a pretense of caring was more than Anna Rose had expected.

"Who is she?" he asked, his mouth at Anna Rose's ear.

"My cousin." Her reply came on a whispered sigh.

He nuzzled her neck. She trembled. "Loosen up," he said under his breath. "We're engaged. Remember?"

Tammy eyed Britt's arm about Anna Rose's waist, then flashed him her most seductive smile. "Now, tell me, just what on earth do you and our Anna Rose have in common?"

"Besides love?" he asked, deciding in that one moment that he didn't much care for Cousin Tammy. It was obvious the conceited little bitch didn't think Anna Rose could attract a man.

Tammy giggled again, but this time the sound had a false ring to it. "Yes, of course. Love, hmm?"

Standing in the middle of her living room, Anna Rose was thankful for Britt's arm about her, giving her support and encouragement. She had always felt so plain and plump and tall beside her colorful, petite cousin. "Well, Britt and I love the land since we both grew up on a farm. He grew up in Mississippi. We both appreciate the simple pleasures."

"Honey, why don't you sit down and have a visit with Tammy while I go fix us all some tea," Britt said, just before he kissed her on the cheek and gave her an affectionate squeeze.

Open-mouthed and wide-eyed, Anna Rose stared at Britt. He smiled at her. She released a breath she hadn't even realized she was holding and smiled back at him. "Thank you...sweetheart. That would be nice."

The minute Britt left the room, Tammy grabbed Anna Rose by the arm. "Honey? Sweetheart? My, my, how lovey-dovey y'all are."

"Sit down, Tammy." Anna Rose hadn't dreaded a visit from her cousin in years, but she did this evening.

"What's he like in bed?" Tammy asked, and laughed loudly when Anna Rose blushed. "Good God, how on earth do you think you can hold on to someone like that? There's a lot of man there, cousin. More than you can handle, I'd say."

Anna Rose closed her eyes for a brief second, praying

for the patience to live through the next few minutes without giving Tammy a proper tongue-lashing. The two had locked horns before, years ago, and although Anna Rose could out-think and out-talk Tammy, her own insecurities always gave her cousin the upper hand.

Opening her eyes, Anna Rose smiled at Tammy. "You'd better not stay for tea. Roy Dean's probably waiting on you right now. Besides, supper is ready and I was looking forward to sharing a romantic meal with my fiancé."

"Getting all huffy, are we?" Tammy gave Anna Rose a long, critical appraisal. "What's the matter? Afraid Britt likes my looks better than yours? You ought to be used to that by now. I can't help being cute any more than you can help being plain."

Britt carried a tray of tall frosty glasses when he walked into the room. "Well, I'll admit that you're all right for a skinny little girl," he said, setting the tray down on the coffee table, then raising his eyes to meet Anna Rose's startled gaze. "But I prefer tall, bosomy women. I've never known a woman that I find more appealing than my Annie Rosie."

Later, Anna Rose decided that she would have given a year's pay to have had a camera handy and taken a snapshot of Tammy's face. Dazed. Shocked. Total disbelief. It was one of the absolutely best moments of Anna Rose's life.

Her cousin had muttered something about being late and having to leave, then she'd walked briskly out of the room. As if hoping to attract Britt's attention, she slowed to a leisurely saunter as she swayed her hips on the way to the front door.

"Thank you," Anna Rose said as she wiped the happy tears from her eyes, bursting into laughter as she fell backward onto the couch.

Laughing almost as hard, Britt slumped down beside her. God, how he loved the sound of Anna Rose's laughter.

*   *   *

Britt spooned the last bite of blackberry cobbler into his mouth, savoring the lush sweetness of the berries and the rich buttery taste of the delicious crust. Moaning as he rested his spoon in the empty bowl, he shoved his chair back as he looked across the table at Anna Rose, who was finishing off her own generous helping of dessert.

"You're the only woman I've ever known who is a better cook than Ma."

"Never, ever, tell your mother that," Anna Rose advised.

"Hey, I may not have a college degree, but I'm not stupid."

"Does it bother you, not having a college education?" she asked, wondering if the fact that she did would prove to be an obstacle to the romantic relationship she longed for them to share. Her education and a man's lack of one had proven to be a strike against her when it came to finding a husband.

"Hell, no." Britt picked up his glass of iced tea. "If I'd wanted to go to college I could have used the GI bill when I got out of the marines." He swallowed the remainder of his tea, then set the glass back on the table. "I'm a country boy, with farming in my blood, rich black earth under my fingernails and manure on my boots."

Anna Rose smiled at his self-analysis. "Well, I'm just as much of a country girl as you are a country boy. But I never did excel at being a girl or a woman, so I realized that being a farmer's wife with a passel of kids running around probably wasn't in my future."

"Did you ever try?" he asked, running his big hand up and down the moist tea glass.

"Ever try what?"

"To excel at being a woman?" The thought that someone, probably her grandmother, had stunted Anna Rose's natural feminine growth made him wish that he could do something to help her reach her full potential as a woman.

She felt the flush begin at the back of her neck and knew her cheeks were turning pink. "I'm sure you noticed that Tammy excels at being a woman. I found that out when we were teenagers."

"Tammy excels at flaunting herself," Britt said, tightening his hold on the glass, angered at Anna Rose's lack of self-esteem. Didn't she realize that she was twice the woman her cousin was? "You're not the type, honey. You wouldn't even begin to know how to seduce a man, would you?"

"No." Tarnation. Double, triple tarnation! What was the matter with her? Here she was admitting to Britt, the man she was falling in love with, what a failure she was as a woman. And he was feeling sorry for her.

"Your grandmother really did a number on you, didn't she?" When he heard her gasp and saw the stricken look on her face, he almost regretted his rash question. Almost. If Anna Rose had never dealt with the emotional abuse he suspected she'd suffered as a child, then she would never be free from the past. He'd learned that the hard way. He had never allowed himself to come to terms with Paul's death, with his own guilt over the accident, so he'd married Paul's widow as some blind act of contrition.

"Grandmother was very moral. Nothing was more important to her that what other people thought of her, how they perceived her, and…and what sort of impression her family made. I don't think she ever completely recovered from my mother's unwed pregnancy and subsequent suicide."

"Did she blame herself?" He watched the subtle change in Anna Rose's blue eyes, a hint of moisture glazing the surface, a delicate narrowing as if preparing to close and blot out the truth.

"No. She blamed me." Anna Rose's breath came in quick, jerky gulps. Clutching the edge of the dining-room table with her fingers, she tried to control her erratic heartbeat.

Britt scooted his chair farther from the table and stood, never once removing his gaze from Anna Rose. Had he pushed her too far with such a blunt question? Facing the truth wasn't easy, and he suspected this was the first time she'd ever said the words aloud. "It's all right, honey. Don't hold back." He rounded the table in a swift but smooth move.

When he knelt down, squatting beside her chair, she looked at him, large crystal drops of moisture caught in the corners of her eyes. "Everything was always my fault." She gulped down the first onslaught of tears. "I was always doing something wrong. I was too noisy, too messy, too tall, too big, too plain." She felt his hands lifting hers, encompassing them within his gentle grasp.

"Go on. What else?" He encouraged her to release all the repressed anger and pain within her. He knew what guilt felt like, no matter how senseless. He'd lived with it every day of his life since Paul's death.

"Gramps was a good man, but he wasn't strong enough to stand up to Grandmother. Maybe…maybe he was dealing with guilt of his own. I don't know." Anna Rose bit her bottom lip in a effort to keep from crying. The hurt inside her had spread from her heart into her chest and throat and stomach. Her emotional pain had become a physical ache. "Gramps was kindhearted, and so gentle. Too gentle to cope with Grandmother. He loved animals. We used to have horses. And he kept pigs and cattle… and…and there were always dogs and cats and…"

"You got your love of animals from your grandfather." Britt tried to summon up some sympathy for the old man whose life had probably been made a living hell by his wife, but all Britt could think about was how badly Anna Rose must have needed her gramps's support and care. Maybe he'd given her all he was capable of giving. God knew, no one could make another person feel something that wasn't in them to feel. He'd learned that lesson all too well with Tanya. He'd thought that if he loved her enough, she would eventually love him, too.

"When I started school, I found that I was smart, despite the fact that Grandmother often told me I wasn't as smart as my mother had been." She pulled her hands free from his, wiping the tears from her cheeks with her fingertips. "No matter what I did, how hard I tried, I could never please her. But she was proud of my accomplishments at school. I found that making good grades met with her approval."

"So you excelled at schoolwork—"

"I couldn't excel at anything else. I was big for my age, quite plain, and I found that, despite the fact that I hated it in her, I had inherited my grandmother's bossy personality. It drove the other kids crazy. I always acted like a mother or a big sister instead of a playmate."

"What happened when you got old enough to date?" He reached out and ran the forefinger of each hand under her damp eyes. He had become so accustomed to the way Anna Rose ignored his deformed hand that he didn't feel the least uncomfortable in caressing her with it.

"When was that?" she asked, laughing, the sound tight and dry and anguished.

"Didn't you date in high school?" He framed her face with his hands, and felt a sudden jolt of adrenaline shoot through his body. This face wasn't plain, he realized. It was a strong face. A face with character. Anna Rose would look the same forty years from now as she did today. Just a bit older with a few wrinkles, but her bone structure would do her proud in old age. Her eyes were the most incredible shade of blue—as pure as she. And her lips were so full and pouty and irresistible.

"No one ever asked me, except..."

"Except?" he asked.

"Howard Gene Dowdy."

"Did Howard Gene match his name?" Britt ran his hands down her neck and across her shoulders.

"Oh, yes." Anna Rose smiled, surprised that the memory wasn't so unpleasant anymore. "Pure redneck. He drove a truck with a Rebel flag on the back window. He was shorter and fatter than I was and so full of it you had to wear knee-high boots for protection."

"What happened with good ol' Howard Gene?" Taking her by the shoulders, Britt urged her to stand. "While you tell me about your first date, I'll help you clean up the dishes."

She smiled, nodding agreement, then began helping him clear away the table. "There was no first date. At least, not with Howard Gene Dowdy. Grandmother found out from Aunt Hattie that Tammy had engineered the date, had promised Howard Gene that if he'd take me to the senior prom, she'd go out on a date with him."

"And your grandmother told you?" Pushing open the kitchen door with his hip, he allowed her to enter first.

"Yes." She placed the dishes on the counter. "Grandmother didn't approve of dancing, but hadn't forbidden me to attend the prom because she didn't think anyone would ask me. She knew telling me the truth about what Tammy had done was the easiest way to keep me from going." Anna Rose opened the dishwasher, stacking the dishes inside as she continued talking. "Now, I wish I'd gone. I never attended a school dance. That was my only chance. And I was so angry with Tammy. I shouldn't have been. She meant well."

Reaching down, Britt took her by the hands and pulled her up to face him. Holding her at arm's length, he smiled. "Leave the dishes until later."

"Why?" She didn't hesitate to follow when, tugging on her hands, he led her out of the kitchen, down the hall and into the living room. He took her in his arms, spinning her around and around as if they were moving to some silent rhythm that only they could hear.

Twirling her back into his arms, Britt watched her face as it became vibrant with life, flushed with color, glowing with laughter. Her eyes sparkled with astonishment as she stared at him. "What on earth are you doing?" she asked, a hint of amused wonder in her question.

His gaze wandered over the room, lingering on the arrangement of fresh flowers that graced the mantel, their beauty reflected in the gold-framed mirror above the fireplace. With his hands at her waist, he pushed her backward. "Close your eyes, and stay right there while you think about being sixteen again. Picture yourself in a blue satin evening gown."

"What?" With amazed uncertainty she watched while he walked over to the stereo situated beneath the double windows. Opening the lid on her stash of cassettes, he flipped through them, then pulled out a tape and dropped it into the open slot.

Before moving from the stereo to the mantel, he turned, frowned at Anna Rose and shook his head. "I told you to close your eyes." He smiled when she obeyed.

He lifted a white rose from the flower arrangement. Since spending the past couple of weeks around Anna Rose, he'd found that she loved flowers and cut arrangements from her own flower beds to keep the house filled with springtime color, even on the darkest night or gloomiest day.

When he came near, she shivered. "Keep your eyes closed," he told her again, not stopping to ask himself why he was doing what he was doing.

Britt lifted the long tan strands of her hair away from her face, then slipped the thornless stem behind her ear, allowing the rose to lie nestled against her cheekbone.

"Britt?"

"What?" He took her in his arms just as the music began. The song was "Unchained Melody." Bill Medley's sensuous baritone voice filled every corner of the room.

"May I open my eyes now?" she asked as Britt moved his hand to rest slightly above her hip.

"Are you sixteen?"

"Am I...?" She suspected what he was trying to do, and loved him all the more for being so kind, but it broke her heart, just a little, to think that his motivation was pity. "Yes, I'm sixteen."

"Are you wearing a blue satin gown?"

She knew full well that she was wearing an old pair of loose-fitting blue slacks and a matching cotton sweater. "Yes, I'm wearing blue satin, and I'm ready for the prom." She opened her eyes just in time to catch him watching her intently. In that one timeless moment, she knew she loved Britt Cameron. Loved his rough, scarred face. Loved his big, lean body. Loved his tender, caring heart.

"Good," he said, dancing with her to the hauntingly sweet tune that had enchanted more than one pair of lovers.

Without any words between them except the lyrics of the songs that played off the cassette tape, Britt danced with Anna Rose. Gradually their bodies drew closer and closer. She rested her head on his shoulder as she draped her arms around his neck. He lowered his left hand to her back while easing the right one down her hip.

When the music ended, their movements were already so languid that neither of them stopped. With her feet still shuffling as they followed his, Anna Rose raised her head and stared into his half-closed eyes.

"Why did you do this for me?"

It wasn't a question with an easy answer. The complete truth was a mystery to him. How could he explain that the weeks he'd spent as her handyman had saved his sanity, had given him solace when he'd thought he'd never find any, that he had felt more comfortable, more relaxed and at home here with her than he'd felt in years?

He couldn't remember the last time he'd met someone he liked as much as Anna Rose, and it seemed ages since he'd truly wanted to make love to a woman. But he couldn't—*wouldn't*—take advantage of Anna Rose's vulnerability. If he'd ever known a woman in need of loving, it was Anna Rose Palmer. But she deserved a man who'd be around for the long haul. A man capable of returning all the love she could give him. He wasn't that man.

"I'm sorry," she said, averting his intent stare. "I didn't realize the question would be so difficult for you to answer."

"You're a special lady, Annie Rosie. A lady who should have sweet memories of her senior prom." He lifted her downcast chin.

She refused to meet his gaze. "You feel sorry for me, don't you?"

He forced her chin higher, clutching her jaw in his forceful grasp. "I resent like hell what your grandmother did to you, what you keep doing to yourself, but I don't feel sorry for you."

Her eyes flew wide open. She glared at him. "Then why—"

"Look, you took in a stranger, gave him a job, a place to live. You took a risk allowing me to stay—"

"You're trying to repay me?" she asked.

"In a way." When she tried to pull away from him, he dropped his hand from her chin, but grabbed her by the waist. "Don't run away from me. Let me help you."

"Help me?" She stared at him, her eyes questioning as she struggled to free herself from his tenacious hold.

"I know I owe you a complete explanation, but... I...there are things about myself I'd rather not discuss. At least not tonight. Let's just say that having you trust me, care about me, share your life with me has meant more to me than you'll ever know."

"Oh, Britt."

He saw her eyes soften, her whole face brighten to what she considered a promise in his words. She relaxed against him, no longer struggling to escape. God, he couldn't let her misinterpret what he'd said. He couldn't let her think, not for one minute, that he could give her what she so desperately needed.

He released her. She swayed toward him, her eyes dreamy. "Look, honey, I realize that you don't know much about men."

"Is that a problem?" she asked.

"For you it is. You're the kind of woman who'd make some man a good wife, but, well—"

"What makes you think I want a husband?"

"Well, you do, don't you? Something tells me that you're the type of woman who needs a family."

"My career is very important. I love working with the children and their parents, with other teachers." She paused momentarily, surveying his face for a clue to where their conversation was headed. "You're right, I do want to marry and have a family."

"What you need are some lessons in how to excel at being a woman."

She felt a jolt of mixed emotions. Exactly what was he trying to say? she wondered. For a few ecstatic moments she had hoped he was going to tell her that he loved her, but now she realized that the idea had been wishful thinking on her part. "I've never known how to flirt or act helpless or any of the things that seem to attract a man."

"A man likes for a woman to respond to him. He likes to know she enjoys his advances, that she wants him."

"I always scare off any and all potential husbands."

"I could teach you how to attract men instead of scaring them off. I could teach you what men like and want from a woman." God, was he out of his mind making such an offer? How could he hold her and touch her, instruct her in the art of pleasing a man and then call a halt before actually taking her? How could he give her lessons in love-making and then turn her over to another man?

"Are you saying...saying that..."

"You need to know a lot more about men and women and...and sex. You're too innocent, Anna Rose. Some man might take advantage of that, and probably already would have if you weren't such a damned bossy butt."

Placing her hands on her hips, she scowled at him, then in her best authoritarian schoolteacher voice asked, "Are you offering to give me a few lessons? Is that what this is all about? I've done you a favor by letting you stay here and you'd like to repay me by giving me some free instructions on how to snare a husband. Well, thanks, but no thanks. I'd rather die an old maid than accept... charity...from...from you, Britt Cameron."

Oh, she was angry, he thought. He'd never seen her this way. So, the sweet rose had a few thorns. "I certainly didn't mean for you to take the suggestion as an insult."

"Well, I did. I appreciate the fantasy." She opened her arms in a mock gesture of gratitude. "The music, the dancing, the flower." She jerked the rose from behind her ear and flung it at him. It landed at his feet.

"What the hell's the matter with you?"

"I want you to leave."

"Leave the house tonight or leave the farm altogether?" he asked, shocked by how much her answer mattered to him. He didn't want to leave the farm. He didn't want to lose her as a friend.

"Just tonight." She backed away from him when she saw the stormy intent in his eyes. "You can...can stay on until Corey's able to come back to work."

He walked toward her. She took several steps backward. He moved again, shoving her gently until he forced her up against the wall. Determined not to allow him to intimidate her, she stared him directly in the eye, but when he lowered his head, his lips almost touching hers, she drew in a deep breath.

With his mouth hovering over hers, Britt said, "If you change your mind about the lessons, you know where I'll be. Otherwise, I'll see you at breakfast in the morning."

She didn't move until he'd turned and walked away. The moment she heard the door slam, she sighed and slumped down to her knees. She looked across the room to where a single white rose lay, several loose petals scattered on the floor. Dropping her chin to her chest, she started crying.

Five

Anna Rose gave herself a thorough appraisal in the mirror attached to the back of the bathroom door. She had bought the new blue dress yesterday, telling herself that she really needed a new Sunday outfit. But this evening, she admitted that she'd bought the dress hoping to impress Britt.

Well, she didn't look too bad. At least he couldn't accuse her of wearing something a size too large. Indeed this slender-skirted, padded-shouldered linen dress was an exact fit. Perhaps a little shorter than she usually wore her dresses, but the salesclerk had assured her that the trend was leaning more to above-the-knee styles. Anna Rose wasn't sure what the current fashion was, but did suspect that the dress ended just above her knees due to her five feet nine inch height.

In the ten days since she and Britt had quarreled, she had longed to return to the easy-going friendship they had shared before she had overreacted to his offer. In retrospect, she supposed she'd been hurt because she had fantasized that Britt was beginning to love her the way she loved him.

Why had she allowed herself, once again, to want something—someone—she knew she couldn't have? Would she
never learn? A man like Britt Cameron, despite his scars
and deformed hand, could probably have any woman he
wanted. He was so utterly male, so totally, unashamedly
masculine. And he was mysterious. She knew little more
about him now than she had when she and Lord Byron had
rescued him from his wrecked truck.

She had to admit that he wasn't a man to hold a grudge,
and he *was* one who kept his promises. When he'd shown
up for breakfast the morning after their quarrel, he'd acted
as if nothing had happened the night before, but she hadn't
been able to pick up where they'd left off. She, not he, had
caused the rift in their friendship. She never asked him to
stay and talk after meals, and though he tried to be pleasant
whenever they were together, she found it difficult not to
resent his unemotional attitude.

True to his word, he allowed her to pass him off as her
fiancé, backing up her brief, sketchy stories of how they'd
met and fallen in love. Whenever they encountered her
friends and acquaintances, he let her do all the talking while
he simply acted the part of an attentive lover. Those moments proved difficult for her. When he would put his arm
around her or give her a hug or plant an affectionate kiss
on her cheek, she had to remind herself that it was all for
show, that Britt didn't love her and that no power on earth
could persuade him to marry her.

People were stopping by the farm, on any pretense, just
to meet Anna Rose's fiancé, and whenever she drove into
town, to the Piggly Wiggly or the bank or to check on
things at school, someone was bound to corner her and ask
dozens of questions about her upcoming nuptials. Even
Tammy, once over her astonishment that a man like Britt
could actually be in love with poor Anna Rose, had stopped
by again, offering to give Anna Rose a bridal shower and

hinting that she'd be delighted to serve as matron of honor at the wedding.

Anna Rose knew now that she would have been better off if she'd never made up a farfetched tale about having a mystery lover. She supposed she could defend her stupidity by saying that she simply didn't want to look like a fool in front of the whole town. She'd spent her entire life the recipient of everyone's pity. Poor Anna Rose. God, how she hated pity.

But here she was, passing off a stranger as her future husband. A man who'd only be around a couple more weeks. Then what was she going to do? Well, having asked herself that question more than once every day for the past week, she had come to one conclusion. If she couldn't have Britt's love, could never be his wife, then she'd be smart to agree to his offer. Who better to teach her how to be a woman than the man she loved?

Checking her appearance in the mirror one final time, Anna Rose forced a smile on her face. She'd stopped by the store and bought some new lipstick, along with eye shadow and blush. She'd applied all three, then seeing the ghastly sight reflected in the mirror, she'd washed her face and started all over again. Now she wore only the pink lipstick, and a hint of matching blush colored her cheeks.

With a quick detour through the kitchen to pick up the sack of homemade brownies she'd made for Britt as a peace offering, Anna Rose said a silent prayer for strength. If her courage didn't fail her, she was going to walk down to the sharecropper's shack and ask Britt Cameron for a date.

Leaving the top button of his shirt undone, Britt straightened his collar, then ran his hand over his freshly trimmed beard. Taking a long, studious look at himself in the cracked bathroom mirror, he decided he'd done all he could do to make himself presentable. He hadn't really worried about his appearance since Tanya had left him, and he hadn't had a real date with another woman since the car accident more than five years ago.

Well, old son, you don't know that you've got a date tonight. Anna Rose may well tell you to get lost. After all, she'd been less than friendly since he'd made his magnanimous offer to coach her on how to trap a man. Damn, he still couldn't believe he'd been that insensitive. He'd meant the offer as a thank-you for giving him food and shelter and a part-time job, as a sign of appreciation because she'd taken him on face value, never prying into his past, never bombarding him with questions he didn't want to answer. But what he'd done was hurt the one person on earth he didn't want to hurt. She'd taken his offer as an insult. Women! Go figure them.

But he was sick and tired of this armed truce. He wanted things back the way they'd been. He needed Anna Rose's friendship. Despite the fact that he'd sworn he'd never trust another woman as long as he lived, he knew he trusted Anna Rose. She was a rare woman, indeed, and far prettier than she gave herself credit for being. What the hell was wrong with the men in Cherokee? Couldn't they see past the superficial to the beauty that lay beneath?

Well, if Anna Rose didn't want lessons from him about…men and women…about sex, then maybe she would allow him to repay her many kindnesses by letting him show her what it felt like to be courted. From what she'd told him about her past, she'd dated very little before Kyle Ross came into her life and their relationship had never gone beyond hand holding and a few kisses.

Damnation! That was as far as he could let *their* relationship go. But, unlike Ross, he wouldn't lead her on and let her think they might have a future together. In a couple of weeks, Corey Randall would be able to take over his duties around the farm, and Britt knew there would be no reason for him to stay on. He didn't like the idea of leaving, of going back out into a lonely world where the nightmares from his past awaited him. Sooner or later he'd have to return to Riverton, to the accusatory stares and whispers—and to the truth. Someone else had killed Tanya. And Britt knew that that someone was Reverend Timothy Charles. But could he ever prove it?

If Anna Rose were a different type of woman, Britt knew that he would have already bedded her. Hell, they'd be in the middle of a raging affair right now. He hadn't had a woman in a long time, and he needed one badly. But the last thing he wanted was an insecure, inexperienced lover who was sure to think that sex and love were synonymous. Another woman he could take and leave without sharing any more of himself than his physical release. Unfortunately he could never make love to Anna Rose without telling her the truth about his past. He could never have sex with her, and then walk away from her in a few weeks.

But he didn't want to leave things the way they were between them. He wanted their friendship intact when he said goodbye. Who knew, he might want to keep in touch with Anna Rose, make sure she was all right and even keep tabs on the men in her life. Sooner or later some smart man was going to come along and marry her.

With a disgusted grunt, Britt reached down on the sink, picked up a bottle of after-shave and shook a small amount into the palm of his hand. He slapped his hands together to distribute the liquid, then patted it into his beard. He didn't like the way he felt when he thought about Anna Rose with another man. Hell, he couldn't be jealous. He didn't love her. He was just concerned. That's all. She'd been hurt enough in her life. He didn't want to see anyone else cause her pain. Anna Rose deserved happiness, and if some other man could give it to her, then he should be glad.

He'd been thinking about telling Anna Rose the truth, the complete truth. But why should he burden her with his problems when he'd soon be gone? What if she didn't understand? What if she suspected he'd killed Tanya? He couldn't take that chance. When so many people had turned against him, he had survived despite how much it had hurt. But Anna Rose's distrust would destroy what little faith he had left in the human race. He knew she thought of him as someone special, a sort of rugged gentleman, maybe even a knight in shining armor. Or least she had before he'd opened his big mouth and ruined the unique bond they'd shared.

Well, old son, nothing ventured, nothing gained. In the room he used as both living room and bedroom, Britt removed his jacket from the back of a wooden chair. He slipped on the tan sport coat, wondering if he looked ridiculous wearing it with jeans and Western boots. But he'd packed light when he'd left home nearly a month ago, not ever thinking he'd need a suit.

He headed straight for the front door, stopping just long enough to pull the bouquet of wildflowers from a glass jar filled with water. He'd picked the flowers less than an hour ago, wanting them fresh when he gave them to Anna Rose. She loved flowers, and she was the kind of woman who'd appreciate the gift itself and never the cost.

He had considered buying her a book of poetry, but thought better of the idea. First of all, it would have meant a trip to either Iuka, back in Mississippi, or a twenty-mile drive up to the Shoals area. And second, and more important, he didn't know a damned thing about poetry.

With bouquet in hand, Britt opened the door and stepped out onto the porch. If he were lucky, Anna Rose would accept both the flowers and his invitation out to dinner. And if he were really lucky, she might even forgive him and be his friend again.

They met on the path halfway between her house and the sharecropper's shack. She carried a white sack tied with a red ribbon, a dozen walnut brownies nestled inside. He held a huge bouquet of wildflowers—daisies and tiny pink roses and Queen Anne's lace.

Lord Byron and his friends trailed along behind Anna Rose. The big rottweiler nuzzled Britt's leg. Instinctively, Britt rubbed the dog's head, paying special attention to the spots behind Lord Byron's ears. But all the while he was petting her dog, he was looking at Anna Rose.

They were both utterly surprised by the other's unexpected appearance on the pathway. For endless moments neither spoke. They simply stared at each other.

"Hello." His voice was strong and steady, unlike his nervous stomach and accelerated heartbeat. Anna Rose looked...pretty. And she was smiling at him. Well, at least the corners of her mouth were curled and her eyes were smiling.

"Hello, yourself," she replied, then cleared her throat. "How are you?" She'd never felt so quivery inside, and prayed the trembling wasn't outwardly visible.

"I'm fine." He glanced down at the ribbon-tied white sack she carried. "Were you coming to see me?"

Holding out the sack to him, she nodded affirmatively. "I—I made some of those walnut brownies you like so much and...and I thought you might want some."

"Thanks. I love 'em. I've never tasted any as good."

The bouquet he held in his right hand caught her attention. "Were you on your way up to the house?"

He thrust the flowers at her. She accepted them with a warm smile. "These are for you. I know they're not much, but—"

"They're beautiful. Thank you."

"Look, Anna Rose—"

"Britt, I'd like—"

Having spoken simultaneously, they both stopped abruptly and laughed. Suddenly neither of them could speak. Only the sounds of Lord Byron and his playmates running through the woods and the rustle of a late evening breeze disturbed the tender quiet. Later, when the sun began to set and the night creatures stirred, the sounds of katydids and frogs and hoot owls would awaken the stillness.

"You first," she said.

"No, ladies first."

"The brownies are a peace offering," she admitted. "I want to apologize for overreacting to your suggestion to tutor me. I'm not used to being the student."

"You don't owe me an apology. I'm the one who's sorry. I like you, Annie Rosie, and I thought that if I could repay you for your kindness by giving you a few pointers on—"

"I know, I know." She took several small, tentative steps toward him. "That's one of the reasons I was coming to see you. I—I've reconsidered your offer."

"You have?"

"Yes. I'd like to invite you to dinner and the movies, and…afterward…well, I'd like to start my lessons." There, she'd said it. The ball was in his court now. The rest was up to him.

"A date?" he asked, moving toward her, never once averting his intense gaze from her face.

"Uh-huh…"

"Would you believe that I was on my way to ask you for a date?"

"You were?"

"I'll drive if you don't mind riding in my old truck. And I'm paying for dinner and the movies."

"Britt, that really isn't necessary. After all, my Blazer is in better condition and I realize you don't have much money. Besides, I know my way around the Shoals. We'll have to go to Florence to the movies, and—"

He hadn't meant to grab her and kiss her, so when he did, it surprised him as much as it did her. It was one of those hard, quick kisses that left both participants breathless.

Holding her close, he rubbed his nose against hers and smiled. "Lesson number one. Don't be so bossy. When a man asks you for a date, assume he's driving and he's paying. Most Southern men are still old-fashioned about stuff like that."

With her heart racing, her knees weak and her breath caught in her throat, all Anna Rose could do was nod meekly. If lesson number two was anything like lesson number one, she wasn't sure she'd live through it.

By eleven o'clock, they had returned from Florence where they'd eaten at the Court Street Café and later laughed themselves silly at the current comedy hit showing at the Hickory Hills Cinema. They'd run into Tammy and Roy Dean at the movies, and had politely declined their offer to join them at the current adult hot spot in Muscle Shoals. Anna Rose had never been inside a *club,* one of those places her grandmother's generation had referred to as honky-tonks. On the long drive home, she asked Britt about what those places were like, and he'd seemed surprised that she'd never been in one, especially during her college days. She had explained her grandmother's aversion to alcohol and tobacco as well as to music and dancing. Britt's reply had made her laugh.

"Well, to have been such a pious woman, your grandmother certainly did know a lot about honky-tonks. If she'd never been in one, how'd she know that the places are filled with smoke, loud music and slightly drunk men and women rubbing all over each other on the dance floor?"

Though the interior of his truck had been dark, she was certain he'd winked at her.

Lord Byron, asleep on the front porch, raised his head and gave Anna Rose and Britt a sleepy look, then put his head back down and closed his eyes.

"Won't you come in?" she asked, hoping he remembered that she'd asked for a lesson after their *date.*

"It's such a beautiful night, why don't we sit out here in the swing." He nodded toward the cushioned oak swing hanging at the end of the front porch.

"If you're going to instruct me on men-women relationships, we'd have more privacy inside." She wasn't sure what lesson number two would be, but she certainly hoped it would involve more kissing. Britt Cameron had a knack for kissing.

"Hey, lesson number two isn't going to involve anything that we can't do out here." Not that he didn't want to do a lot more than kiss her, he thought, but he'd promised himself that he wouldn't let things get out of hand. "Besides, your nearest neighbor is at least half a mile away. Nobody would know if we stripped off buck naked and chased each other around the house."

Giggling, she punched him on the arm. "Good Lord, Britt, do people actually do stuff like that?"

Slipping his arm around her and guiding her toward the swing, he snarled his lip in imitation of a sinister leer. "People do worse than that, and love every minute of it."

They sat down in the swing, side by side, their bodies touching from shoulder to knee. Anna Rose breathed in the sweet honeysuckle-scented air—pure, Alabama nighttime, country air.

"I'm really going to miss you when you leave," she said, wishing she had the right to ask him to stay.

"I'll miss you, too, Annie Rosie. You're the first woman I've ever been friends with." He squeezed her shoulder.

"You've never been friends with a woman?" *Of course not, you ninny,* she told herself. *A man like Britt would have lovers, not friends, and you're the type a man thinks of as a friend.* She'd had a lot of male friends over the years, but not one lover.

"I'm afraid I've always been a bit macho when it comes to male-female relationships. I tend to think of women as sex objects." He hoped she wouldn't fly off the handle and preach him a sermon on his antiquated, sexist notions.

"In other words, all the women with whom you've had relationships have been lovers and not friends."

"Look, before you get the wrong idea, there haven't been that many women…and there hasn't been anyone in a long time. Not since my wife died."

She spun around so quickly that the movement shook the swing. "You were married?"

"For a couple of years. She, uh, died eighteen months ago." He wasn't sure why, but for some reason, he wanted to share a part of his past with Anna Rose. Even if he couldn't bring himself to tell her about the way Tanya had died, he wanted to tell her about his marriage, about his family and his home in Mississippi.

"I'm sorry, Britt. I had no idea you'd lost someone you loved." Had his wife died in the accident that had left Britt physically scarred and emotionally injured? Anna Rose wondered. And to have gone well over a year without a woman must mean that he had loved his wife a great deal. Perhaps he still loved her.

"I'd known Tanya all my life. Her folks rented and farmed some land in Tishomingo County not far from my parents' farm. We went to school together from first grade through high school." He'd never forget the way just looking at Tanya Berryman had made him feel. She'd been so cute, so perky, so irresistibly helpless and feminine.

"So, you were childhood sweethearts?" Anna Rose hated herself for the jealousy that ate away at her insides. How could she be jealous of a dead woman?

"No, just childhood buddies. She was my best friend Paul's girl, not mine." He'd loved Paul like a brother, had in some ways been closer to Paul Rogers than he'd been to Wade. He'd been careful not to let either Paul or Tanya know the way he felt about her. He'd dated dozens of other girls in school, had learned the earth-shattering pleasures of sex with other women, but he'd never loved anyone except Tanya.

"Oh, well, she must have changed her mind if she married you instead of Paul."

"She married him first."

"She...I don't understand."

He'd never talked about his unrequited love for Tanya, not even to Ma or Wade. They'd known, of course, but it hadn't been something they'd discussed. "Tanya and Paul married straight out of high school. I went into the marines. Partly to get away from having to see them so happy and in love—"

"Oh, Britt." She turned to him, overcome by feelings of sympathy, hurting for him, sharing the pain he must have felt in loving someone who loved another. Reaching out, she covered the scarred side of his face with her hand.

He pulled her hand to his lips, caressing the palm with his mouth. "That wasn't the only reason I joined the marines. Pa had died when I was fourteen, and Wade had to take over and keep things running. It was all we could do not to lose the farm. We had two sisters still in school. We needed money bad. I sent home as much as I could. All I didn't have to have."

"What happened to...to Tanya and Paul? Did they get a divorce?" Just saying the other woman's name proved painful. Anna Rose had never known such intense jealousy.

He placed her hand against his scarred forehead and held it there. "Five years ago Paul and I had been to a cattle sale and were on our way home. I was driving. We were both stone sober, but tired and eager to get home. I suppose I was driving a little over the speed limit. We had a blowout, skidded, hit a tree...."

When she heard his voice crack with emotion, she wanted, more than anything, to take him in her arms and comfort him, to tell him that she loved him and would always be there to share his sorrows. "You and Paul were in a car wreck," she said, realizing that Paul had not survived the accident. "That's how you got the scars, isn't it?"

"Yeah, but I was lucky compared to Paul. He lost his life." It had been years since he'd cried, and the one time he'd allowed his emotions to overwhelm him, he'd been alone. But right now, with Anna Rose's caring blue eyes devouring him with her love, he had to fight the urge to go into her arms and cry like a baby.

"It must have been so difficult for you...afterward."

"I've never gotten over the guilt. I was driving. I lived. Intellectually, I know it was no one's fault, but emotionally I've never forgiven myself for living, for—"

"For finally getting Tanya?"

Britt grabbed Anna Rose, enclosing her within his big, strong arms. She'd never felt as needed, as essential to another person's well-being as she did this very minute.

"You understand, don't you? God, I'd wanted her all my life and the only way I could get her was—" He couldn't say more. Angry tears lodged in his throat, emotions never truly faced before surfaced to torment him.

Anna Rose stroked his back, hoping her touch would ease the tenseness she felt in his tight muscles. "But Tanya must have loved you, too, to have married you."

He held on to Anna Rose, absorbing her gentle strength, comforted by her tenderness. "She was pregnant when Paul died. She miscarried and a few months later tried to kill herself."

"Oh, my God!" Anna Rose tightened her hold on Britt when she felt him trying to pull away. She wasn't going to let him suffer alone. He needed her.

"I married her because I loved her, because I wanted to give her a reason to live. I thought that she'd learn to love me. She didn't." His two year marriage had been a living hell for both of them. He had wanted and expected too much. She'd tried, but she'd never been able to forget Paul. At least not with him.

"How did you lose her?"

"An accident," he said, not wanting to lie to Anna Rose, but afraid to tell her the complete truth. After all, if his suspicions weren't correct, Tanya's death could well have been an accident. Reverend Charles probably hadn't meant to kill her.

She held him in her arms, one hand stroking his back, the other cradling his head where it rested against her breast. His body trembled, and she knew he was fighting the need to cry. Why was it that men were so afraid to cry? Was it really a learned restraint, she wondered, or was it some primitive masculine trait that kept getting passed down in the genes? They sat there in silence, their hearts beating steadily, their breaths coming slowly while the June night surrounded them like a soft, diamond-studded, black blanket. A mild breeze stirred through the trees, issuing a barely discernible melody that somehow wasn't lost in the mélange of woodland music. Nocturnal animals and insects created a symphony heard only in the wild, in the undisturbed, unspoiled places of nature. And a lover's moon floated in the sky, a full moon, lighting the dark night.

She didn't know how long they stayed there, a man and a woman, alone in the world, undisturbed by any living creature. A man in pain, and the woman who comforted him.

She felt him stir and released her protective hold when he raised his head and looked at her. Her heart plummeted to the pit of her stomach. He was staring at her with such hunger, such desperate need.

"Do my scars repulse you?" he asked, but before she could reply he went on. "Or my crippled hand? The scars go down my neck, across my shoulder and over my arm, you know. You've seen them. Tanya hated the sight of me like this. She said my scars reminded her of Paul's death, but I think it was more than that. We never made love with the lights on. We never—''

Anna Rose covered his mouth with the tips of her fingers as warm, heartfelt tears streamed down her face. ''I think you are the handsomest man I've ever known. If…if you were mine…''

''If I were yours, what?''

''If you were my lover, I'd kiss every scarred inch and weep for the pain you must have endured. I'd love you all the more for not being perfect.'' She reached up and kissed his forehead where the ugly scars marred his skin.

Britt couldn't bear the tumultuous emotions brewing within him. It was as if all his feelings for Paul and Tanya—the sorrow over their deaths, the hatred he harbored for Reverend Charles and the misery he'd endured during the trial—collided, and only the sweet, giving entity that held him in her arms could offer him salvation from his torment.

With quick and accurate force, he shot out his right hand, grabbing her by the back of her head, bringing her lips to meet his. His kiss was hard and hot and demanding. As if on command, she opened her mouth to his plunder. And he devoured her. The hunger for a woman had been building inside him, but not for just any woman. He'd been starving for the response of a woman who cared, genuinely cared about him, a woman who wanted him as much as he wanted her.

He couldn't seem to control himself, though reasonable thought kept trying to break through the wild and all-consuming desire that was riding him. While he deepened the kiss, thrusting forcefully into her, he ran his hands over her body…a body so soft and warm and inviting. Taking her hip in one hand, he kneaded her firm flesh with urgent fingers.

She became a willing participant, holding on to him, returning the wild passion of his kisses, longing to do whatever he wanted, but unsure because of her inexperience. Guided solely by feminine instinct, she cuddled closer as a moist heat began to form in the apex between her thighs. When she felt his fingers slowly opening her neck-to-hem buttoned dress, she didn't even consider refusing him.

Her lace-covered breast swelled in his hand the moment he cupped it. Running his other hand up and down her hip and over her tight bottom, he longed to strip away all the barriers between them. When he felt her fingers trembling as she tried to undo his shirt, he released her breast long enough to unbutton several buttons.

"Do you want to touch me?" he asked, his lips on hers, his breath hot and coffee-laced as it mixed with hers.

"Yes." Her answer was part moan and part sigh. The moment he released the buttons, she slipped her hand inside his shirt, curling her fingers through his thick, dark chest hair.

He couldn't hold back the groan that exploded from his throat. Her intimate, yet oh-so-innocent touch ignited a fire of desire within him, a raging inferno of passion. His hand returned to her breast, pinching at the nipple, using his forefinger and thumb to rotate it into pebble hardness. With desperate need eating away at his insides, he pulled her onto his lap and thrust himself up against her as he began again the assault on her mouth.

Anna Rose had never known desire, but she knew exactly what was happening to her. She might be inexperienced, but she wasn't stupid. She had thought this would never happen to her, that she would never feel such raw, primitive hunger. What ecstasy, she thought, to learn what lust was in the arms of the man she loved.

Breaking away, he lowered his head to her shoulder and gave his lips free rein to explore her neck. "I want you, Annie Rosie. I want to make love to you. I want to take you inside and lay you down in that big old antique bed of yours and teach you what it's all about."

"Oh, Britt, Britt, I want that, too." Her heart was so full that she couldn't begin to tell him all that she was feeling.

"Oh, honey. Sweet, sweet, Annie Rosie." No matter how much he wanted her, needed her, he couldn't let her think that he was offering more than a night of passion. She was too fine a lady, too dear a friend.

"Britt, I lo—"

He covered her mouth with the palm of his hand. "Hush. Don't say any more." He lowered his hand, and saw the questioning look in her blue eyes. "I ache with wanting you. But...but I'm not what you need. I can give you tonight and a few other nights, but I can't give you forever, and that's what you want, isn't it?"

He let her draw away from him and reseat herself on the swing. It broke his heart knowing that he had hurt her, but, by being honest, he'd done her a favor in the long run. When she sat there, not moving, not speaking, he wondered what she was thinking. "It's my fault," he said. "I never should have let things go this far. It's just that you're so sweet, so tempting. I'm sorry, honey."

"What if I said tonight and a few more nights would be enough? That if that's all you can give me, then I'll take it?"

"You don't mean that, Annie Rosie. You don't want an affair. You want marriage and children and all that happily-ever-after stuff."

"I want you, Britt Cameron." She looked at him when she said it, dry-eyed and filled with determination.

He cupped her face in his hands, not feeling the least self-conscious about his crippled hand, not with her, not with his Annie Rosie. "And if I could love you, could give you what you really want and need, I'd carry you to bed and make you mine forever." God, how he wished he'd met Anna Rose years ago. Before he'd married Tanya. Before a part of him had died. Before his heart had been buried beneath a layer of pain and bitterness.

"You still love her?" The words were part question, part statement.

"No," he replied truthfully. He kissed Anna Rose softly, tenderly, as if her lips were fragile porcelain and could withstand only the lightest, most delicate pressure. "I don't love Tanya anymore, but she…she made it impossible for me to love anyone else…ever again."

Releasing her, Britt stood and, with one final farewell glance, walked away. He didn't dare look back. If she was crying, he didn't want to know. It was taking every ounce of strength, every particle of willpower he had to leave her. But she'd be better off without him. He was doing the right thing.

Anna Rose sat in the swing for a long time. She didn't cry. She hurt too much to cry. It was the same way she'd felt when Gramps died. She hadn't shed a tear for weeks.

All she could give Britt was her love, and he'd made it perfectly clear that it wasn't enough, would never be enough, to mend his broken heart.

Six

Anna Rose dumped the remainder of her food in the garbage, scraped off the plate and placed it in the dishwasher. She threw her iced tea in the sink. Sunday lunch had been a lonely affair. Her naturally healthy appetite had been spoiled by Britt's absence. She was half tempted to run over to the shack to see if he was still there, but her pride wouldn't allow her to go to him. Surely, she told herself, he'd come say goodbye before he left. No doubt, last night had affected him as much as it had her, albeit in a different way. Being such an honorable man, Britt was probably feeling guilty about what happened.

Anna Rose walked down the hall and entered her bedroom. After Sunday church services, she had come home, thrown off her clothes and slipped into a pair of baggy cotton trousers and a loose-fitting, gauzy top. With meticulous care she now hung up her dress, placed her heels on the shoe tree and put her panty hose and slip in the clothes hamper.

Trying desperately to come to terms with her feelings for Britt, she hadn't slept much last night and had been little more than a zombie at church. Thankfully the lesson she'd prepared to teach the pre-school class was one she'd used in the past. When Tammy and Roy Dean had mentioned stopping by later in the day, Anna Rose had reluctantly agreed. Now she wished she had invented some excuse to prevent their visit. She simply wasn't in the mood to listen to Tammy's prattle.

I wonder what Britt's doing? she thought. And what did he eat for breakfast and lunch? Had he driven down to Cherokee and picked up some canned goods at the Piggly Wiggly? Maybe he'd left during the night. Maybe he'd thought it best not to say goodbye. *Stop it!* she scolded herself. *Stop tormenting yourself. If he's gone, he's gone and there's nothing you can do about it.*

Restless and sick with worry, Anna Rose prowled around the house, looking for something—anything—that would take her mind off Britt Cameron and the way he'd made her feel last night. She loved him, loved him more than she'd thought possible to love someone. But he didn't love her. He had loved his wife, and her inability to return his love had hardened his heart and paralyzed his emotions.

Anna Rose picked up the book of poetry she'd been reading the night Britt had wrecked his truck in front of her house. Slumping down on the couch, she held the book in the palm of her hand. It opened automatically to the page on which Marlowe's poem was printed.

She read aloud the first verse. *"'Come live with me, and be my love, and we will all the pleasures prove.'"* As she continued reading silently, tears formed in her eyes. By the time she neared the last verse, her vision was completely obscured. Closing the book, she quoted aloud from memory the last two lines. *"'If these delights thy mind may move, then live with me and be my love.'"*

So absorbed in the beauty of the words, the depth of the

poet's feelings as well as her own, Anna Rose jumped at the sound of loud knocking at her front door. Wiping away the tears from the corners of her eyes, she laid the book aside and went out into the hall.

Praying that her visitor was Britt, she rushed to the door and flung it open. Her anticipation changed to disappointment when she saw Tammy and Roy Dean standing on the porch.

"Are you all right?" Tammy asked. "I was beginning to wonder if something had happened to you. I've been knocking and knocking."

"I—I'm fine. You two come on in." Anna Rose escorted her relatives into the living room. Husband and wife sat side by side on the sofa.

"Where's your fiancé?" Roy Dean asked, turning his round head this way and that. "You should have brought him to church, or ain't he a religious man?"

"Hush up, Roy Dean," Tammy scolded.

"Can I get y'all some iced tea or some coffee?" Acutely aware of the tension coming from her relatives, Anna Rose knew something was wrong. Her cousins weren't paying her a friendly social call. She was sure of that.

"Tea would be real nice." Roy Dean removed his Atlanta Braves ball cap and ran a meaty hand across his partially bald head.

"Don't bother, Anna Rose." Tammy gave her husband a condemning stare. "We...well, we didn't come for a Sunday visit."

"No?" Anna Rose watched the color rise in Roy Dean's fat face. His normal pink-tinted complexion turned a splotchy red. "Then, to what do I owe the honor of this visit?"

"Sweetie, you'd better sit down." Unshed tears misted Tammy's eyes.

Without reply or question, Anna Rose sat in the big rocker near the front windows. Although a virtual kaleidoscope of possibilities raced through her mind, she refused to focus on one specific suspicion.

"It ain't like we want to be the ones to tell you," Roy Dean said. "Hellfire, we're your family. We care about you, and don't want to see you hurt any more than you've already been."

"How much do you know about Britt Cameron?" Tammy stood up and began to pace back and forth in front of the couch, not once looking in Anna Rose's direction.

"What's this all about?" Anna Rose asked, tension rushing through her like floodwaters from a broken dam.

"Where did you meet him? Really?" Tammy asked.

"I told you that we met on vacation last year, that we—"

"You're lying, girlie." Roy Dean's small brown eyes widened to the point where they looked like round shiny marbles set in his face. "We know where Britt Cameron was last year when you were on vacation, and it wasn't with you."

"Hush up, Roy Dean. She probably has no idea what kind of man she's gotten herself involved with." Tammy finally faced her cousin. Lacing together her ring-covered fingers in a prayerful gesture, she gave a theatrical sigh. "I hope you haven't gone and done something stupid, like getting yourself really engaged to him. Tell me that it's all a sham. Tell me you lied about a fiancé to save face after what happened with Kyle."

Anna Rose widened her eyes, her mouth parting in a silent gasp. How had Tammy discovered the truth? And what on earth did she mean about the kind of man Britt was? "You're confusing me. I don't have any idea what you're talking about."

"Me and Tammy both thought the name Britt Cameron sounded familiar." Roy Dean leaned back on the sofa, adjusting his short, heavy body as he buried his wide butt in the cushions. "We didn't figure it out until I was talking to Henry Moss over in Iuka yesterday."

"If Britt Cameron is still around, you'll have to send him packing. As a matter of fact, you probably ought to let Roy Dean ask him to leave. It might not be safe for you to do it. When I think that the two of you have been alone out here for weeks…" Tammy covered her cheeks with the palms of her hands and shook her head. "No telling what could have happened."

"Hellfire, girlie, you're lucky to still be alive." Roy Dean flopped his flabby arm across the back of the couch.

Anna Rose jumped up, every nerve in her body bow-string tight. "Stop it!" she screamed. "What are you trying to tell me about Britt?"

Tammy grabbed Anna Rose by the shoulders, the shorter woman looking up at her cousin with pity in her eyes. "Britt Cameron killed his wife and they put him on trial for her murder down in Riverton."

Tammy continued talking, but to Anna Rose the words became a blurred buzzing in her ears. The room spun around and around.

"Good Lord, Tammy, she's going to faint," Roy Dean said as he came up off the sofa with rapid speed for a man so heavy. "Move out of the way and let me catch her."

Anna Rose reached out, grabbing the arm of the rocking chair to steady herself. Closing her eyes, she took several deep, calming breaths. Over and over she heard Tammy's words…*Britt Cameron killed his wife…Britt Cameron killed his wife.*

"You all right, girlie?" Roy Dean asked. He stood on one side of Anna Rose while Tammy stood on the other.

"If…if Britt was accused of his wife's murder, why is he free? Are you saying he's an escaped convict?"

"He ain't no convict," Roy Dean said. "Seems the jury acquitted him for lack of evidence."

"But the whole town knows he's guilty," Tammy said. "Henry Moss told Roy Dean that when Britt's wife ran off with the preacher, Britt told anybody who'd listen that if they ever came back to Riverton he'd kill 'em both.''

"He was acquitted?" Anna Rose asked.

"That don't mean nothing," Roy Dean said. "The fact is you've been passing off a murderer as your fiancé. Folks in Cherokee are already talking."

"How do they know about Britt?"

"Well, er, that is, I wasn't the only one down at the gas station who heard what Henry had to say. Steve Hendricks was with me." Stuffing his hands into his pockets, Roy Dean looked down at his feet.

"I don't know how you met that man or what possessed you to take in a stranger, but your life has been in danger. Heaven help us, Anna Rose, the man could have killed you in your sleep." Tammy threw her arms around her cousin, giving her a protective hug.

Anna Rose stepped out of Tammy's embrace. "I know y'all came here to tell me this out of real concern for my welfare. Thank you. I'll…I'll take care of things myself."

"Oh, sweetie, don't you think you ought to let Roy Dean—"

"No. I'd appreciate it if y'all would go on home. I'm…I'm not afraid of Britt. I can handle things in my own way."

"Do you think that wise, girlie?"

It took her ten minutes to finally persuade Tammy and Roy Dean to leave. By the time she heard their Cadillac pull out of the driveway, she was ready to scream.

Britt's wife had been murdered. He had been accused of the crime. No wonder he was so bitter, so determined not to ever love again. His wife had betrayed him with another man—a minister.

In that moment, Anna Rose hated Tanya Cameron. She hated her for not loving Britt, for betraying him with another man, and, as irrational as it was, she hated her for getting killed and putting Britt through the tortures of the

damned. The whole town of Riverton still thought he was
guilty, even though a jury had acquitted him. How did that
make Britt feel? she wondered. Dear God, she had to go to
him, comfort him, tell him that she believed he was innocent. In her heart, she knew that Britt Cameron was not a
murderer.

Britt sponged the soapy rag across the hood of his old
Chevy, adding more muscle to the job than was actually
necessary. The truck wasn't muddy, just slightly dusty, with
a sprinkling of dead insects across the front windshield. He
needed to keep busy, keep moving, keep his mind off Anna
Rose and what had happened between them. Damn it all,
how had he allowed himself to get so out of control? The
last thing he'd wanted to do was hurt her.

He'd been acting like a coward today, not going up to
the house for breakfast or lunch. But he couldn't face her.
He couldn't bear to see the pain in her eyes, that soft sad
expression. He'd stayed around Cherokee too long as it
was, enjoying the friendship, the innocent adoration of a
woman who allowed him to keep his secrets, who didn't
pry or question him at every turn. He'd taken a lot from
Anna Rose—her hospitality, her trust, her friendship—and
he had given very little in return. He'd known how vulnerable she was, how needy, and yet he hadn't been able
to resist the comfort she so freely offered him.

Grabbing the water hose that lay on the ground at his
feet, Britt sprayed the soapy residue off the truck. He knew
he'd have to face her, sooner or later. No, he'd have to face
her today, he told himself. He had already packed his duffel
bag. A man on the run traveled light. But he couldn't just
get in his clean truck and drive away. He had to say goodbye. He owed her that much, at least.

He should have gone over for breakfast this morning,
gotten all the goodbyes over with, but he'd stayed at the
shack and feasted on walnut brownies and strong, bitter

coffee he'd brewed on the antiquated hot plate. For lunch he'd opened a can of Vienna sausages and unwrapped some crackers, washing it all down with reheated coffee. Damn, but a man could get used to Anna Rose's cooking. She had a talent for cooking that put even Ma to shame. Hell of waste, a woman who could cook like that with no one to cook for...no man of her own, no kids.

Britt shut off the water at the outside hydrant beside the porch and wrapped the hose into a compact circle before laying it on the front steps. Picking up several rags from where he'd placed them in the bed of the truck, he began rubbing down the metal surface, giving it as much care as he would a prized stallion.

He wanted to postpone the inevitable. He had no idea what Anna Rose would say when he told her he was leaving. Would she be glad to see the last of him, or would she beg him to stay? He had to admit that he wasn't sure which reaction he would prefer.

Anna Rose stood just inside the wooded area along the pathway. The sun hung in the sky like a fiery cinnamon ball casting translucent yellowish light over the earth, brightening the green of the trees and shrubs and thick wild grass, spotlighting the glorious colors of the blue sky and the pink wild roses that grew around the tree trunks and climbed their way upward toward the branches. Honeysuckle, subtly sweet and bucolic rich in its aroma, wafted through the hot summer air. The earlier breeze had died away, leaving a heavy humidity that promised rain by nightfall.

Her mind filled with unanswered questions and her heart bursting with love and compassion, Anna Rose stood, silently and out of sight, while she watched Britt. He was wearing only a ragged pair of cutoff jeans. His bare feet were covered with a light coating of red clay dust. His hair was mussed, as if he hadn't bothered to even run a comb through it. Rivulets of sweat ran down his neck, then through his thick, black chest hair, cascading downward to catch in and be absorbed by the waistband of his jeans where they circled his lean hips.

She wanted to run and throw her arms around him, to tell him that she loved him. She had to face him with the truth he'd been too ashamed to tell her. She understood why he had omitted the past eighteen months of his life when he'd told her about his past. He'd been afraid she'd think he was guilty of murder.

With all the courage she could muster, Anna Rose continued along the path, moving slowly but surely toward Britt.

He heard the crackle of footsteps as they touched the decomposing grass and leaves and broken twigs that cluttered the pathway. Before turning around, he knew who stood behind him. Anna Rose.

What he saw when he faced her wasn't what he'd been expecting. She wasn't smiling, exactly, but she certainly wasn't crying. Her face seemed...serene. Yeah, he thought, she looked as if she were at peace with herself and God on high. And there was something in her eyes—a hint of knowledge that he'd never seen there before.

"Hi." He threw the wet rag on the ground, wiped his hands off on his jeans and gestured toward the house with a nod of his head and a jerk of his wrist. "Care for a glass of water? I could offer you some coffee, but you'd probably take one sip and pour it out."

"I, uh, missed you at breakfast." She forced herself to look directly at him. It hurt. They were making small talk, trying to exchange pleasantries when he was obviously ill-at-ease, and she was dying inside.

"And lunch, too, huh?"

She smiled, but the expression faded as quickly as it had sprung to life. "Britt...I...last night—"

"Damn, Anna Rose, I'm sorry about what happened. It

was all my fault. I never should have let things get out of hand that way.''

"It's all right. Really. I don't regret last night. It was special, and...and I'll always cherish the memory that you wanted me...even if you can't love me.''

He couldn't keep himself from moving toward her, from reaching out and touching her. He took her finger-entwined hands that she held in front of her into his strong, steady grasp. "If I were capable of loving...anyone...I wish it could be you.''

"You don't have to say that.'' His words ripped through her, slicing away her strong resolve not to cry. Powerful, aching tears threatened to cut off her breath.

Bringing her hands to his lips, he placed a kiss atop her folded fingers. "You know I'm going to have to leave.''

"Don't...don't go because of my foolishness.'' The words cost her a high price. She lost the battle to remain unemotional and calm. Tears formed in her eyes. "Stay on, at least another week until Corey comes back.''

"I don't want to hurt you. I don't want you to think that there's a chance—''

"No, no, I understand. More than you think I do.''

Something in the way she spoke alerted him to the deeper meaning hidden in her statement. Dropping her hands, he took her by the shoulders, his gaze intent on her upturned face. "What do you know?''

"Tammy and Roy Dean paid me a visit after church today. It seems Roy Dean ran into an old buddy of his from Iuka yesterday.''

Dread—cold, gut-wrenching dread—spread through him. "And?'' He prayed she wasn't about to tell him the one thing he never wanted her to know.

"They told me that your wife had been murdered, and...you had been accused of the crime, put on trial and acquitted.'' Unchecked tears streamed down her face like the downpour from a slow, steady rainfall.

His grip on her shoulders tightened painfully. He muttered a string of searing obscenities. His topaz eyes turned darker and darker, until they were the color of burnt gold. "I didn't kill her, Anna Rose. You've got to believe me. I hated her for not loving me. I hated her for leaving me. And God help me, I threatened to kill her, but I didn't."

"I know you didn't. Oh, Britt I know you didn't."

He pulled her against him, encompassing her with his strong embrace. She slipped her arms around his waist and hugged herself closer and closer to him. Laying her head on his chest, she began to kiss his naked flesh.

He held her, stroking her hair, anointing the side of her face with his lips. He hadn't realized how much her trust meant to him, how important it was for her to believe him. "She...she left me. Ran off with a preacher. Reverend Timothy Charles. But then, I suppose Tammy's already told you all about it."

She hugged Britt tighter, trying to convey her feelings by her touch, wanting him to know that he could share his pain with her. "You don't have to tell me anything you don't want to. If it's too painful, if—"

He held her as close to him as he could, feeling as if she were his lifeline and without her he would drown in the dark and deadly waters of the past. "I was so angry when she left. I went around spouting off some nonsense about killing her and the good reverend if they ever showed their faces back in Riverton."

"You reacted the way any normal man would have."

"I acted like an idiot." He ran his hand up and underneath the fall of her thick, tan hair, gripping her neck, threading his fingers through the long, loose strands. "When Tanya came back to town, she called and asked to see me. I refused. I told her that we had nothing to talk about. She said that she'd made a mistake and she was sorry. I hung up on her."

"Did you ever see her again?" Anna Rose knew that,

even now, on some deeply subconscious level, Britt still cared about Tanya, and that knowledge was like a near-fatal wound to Anna Rose's heart.

"I never saw her alive again." He rested his forehead against Anna Rose's, his breath warm and heavy on her face, his lips trembling above hers. "Damn, I'll never forget the sight of her lying there on the floor in the trailer. I'd been out, down at Hooligans...a roadhouse. I'd been trying to forget about her phone call. I came in, turned on the light and...there she was. Lying in a pool of blood. Her blond hair dyed red with her own blood."

Anna Rose felt the beginnings of a tremor as it racked his body, closely followed by another and then another. She held on to him, praying that she could give him strength and comfort and...love. "Oh, Britt, how horrible for you."

"I touched her. She was already cold." Another shudder gripped his body. "I called Wade. He came over and phoned the police. I don't remember much of what happened. Wade said that he found me sitting on the floor holding Tanya in my arms."

"It's all right that you loved her, that you mourned her death."

"I didn't cry. Not once, and I still haven't shed a tear."

"Sometimes things hurt too much to cry. I understand."

He eased her away from him just enough to look at her, to clearly see the compassion and trust in her eyes. "How is it that you understand me so well? No matter what I tell you, no matter what you find out about me, you understand?"

"I don't know why it is," she said, afraid to tell him that love had a way of giving a person special insight into the beloved. "The same way you understood about me, my life, my past. Not every man would have taken pity on me and allowed me to pass him off as my fiancé."

"And few if any women would have taken in a perfect stranger and offered him friendship as well as a job."

Although tears still dampened her eyes, she managed to smile. "I guess that makes us a couple of very special people, doesn't it?"

Taking her face in his hands, he stared at her, noting every bone, every inch of flesh, every tiny freckle that dusted the top of her nose. He didn't think he'd ever seen anything as beautiful as Anna Rose, her pink lips slightly parted, her cheeks delicately flushed and her big blue eyes gazing at him with complete love and utter trust. God, he didn't deserve such a woman as this. She was far too good for him. He couldn't give her what she needed, no matter how much he wished he could.

"You're one incredible lady, and you have no idea how wonderful you are." If only the past, his past, didn't stand between them, Britt thought. Finally after a lifetime of loving a woman who, even in marriage, had never belonged to him, he'd found a woman who, with her every look, her every touch told him that she was his—a woman who had never belonged to another man.

"You're trying to say goodbye, aren't you?" she asked, wishing she had the power to erase his past and keep him with her forever.

He nodded, then dropped his hands from her face and stuffed them into his pockets. Throwing his head back and stretching the taut muscles in his neck, he groaned in a rage of anger, damning the powers that be for offering him love when it was too late to accept it. "What are you going to do when I'm gone? How are you going to explain getting yourself engaged to an accused murderer?"

When she reached out for him, he stepped away from her caressing hand. She pulled back, her hurt gaze questioning his abrupt move. "You were acquitted."

"But as long as the real killer is never found, folks are going to think that, in a jealous rage, I knocked Tanya in the head and killed her."

"Surely the police haven't closed the case?"

"I was their only suspect." Britt wondered if she would believe him if he told her who he thought had killed his former wife. "I think Reverend Charles killed her." He waited for a shocked gasp or a word of protest and heard neither.

"She came back to you and he didn't want to lose her. Is that what you think?" Anna Rose realized the assumption made sense. Wasn't it logical that, even a minister of the gospel, who was capable of adultery could resort to violence if he thought the woman he loved wanted to return to her estranged husband?

"I think he followed her to the trailer, they got in an argument and he hit her. I don't think he meant to kill her. It could have been an accident. My lawyer tried to point that out in the trial, that Tanya could have struck her head after a fall instead of falling because she'd been struck."

"Why haven't you told the police your theory?"

"I have. More than once. When they first arrested me. While I was awaiting trial. During the trial. And after I was acquitted."

"Why wouldn't they listen?"

"Because Timothy Charles, despite the fact that he stole my wife, is considered a saint in Riverton. Believe me, the man knows how to control and manipulate people. After Tanya's death, he convinced everyone that she'd left me because of my violent temper. He pleaded for forgiveness and the whole town forgave him." Britt couldn't begin to explain the bitterness he felt whenever he thought about the way Tanya's lover, her probable killer, had used his charismatic personality and his silver tongue to worm his way back into the good graces of Riverton's Christian populace.

"When you leave here, will you go back to Riverton and try to prove your theory?" If only he'd let her go with him, she thought. She'd be willing to give up everything for him, to stand by him and support him until he could prove the truth and free himself from the cloud of suspicion that darkened his future.

"I don't think I'll be going home for a long time. Maybe never."

"Then don't leave, Britt. Stay here." She wanted to say *come live with me and be my love.* Instead, when he seemed about to refuse, she said, "Stay the week, anyway, until Corey comes back."

"Folks around Cherokee aren't going to let you forget that you're harboring a murderer. My staying here could cause trouble for you." He wanted to pull her back into his arms and tell her he wanted nothing more than to stay—for another week, another month, indefinitely. He had begun to feel relaxed and almost comfortable these past few weeks he'd spent on the farm with Anna Rose. He didn't want to give that up. It had been too long since he'd felt at home anywhere.

"Why don't you let me worry about that," she said, knowing that she would face the devil himself if it meant keeping Britt in her life, even if only for another few days.

"I'll stay on one condition," he said, not wanting to hurt her, but determined to make her realize that they had no future together.

"When Corey is able to come back to work, I'm going to leave and I don't want you to ask me to stay." When she started to speak, he hushed her with his stern look. "I have nothing to offer you, Anna Rose. Not permanence, not money, not a good name, and certainly not the kind of love a woman like you deserves."

She had known, hadn't she, that her dreams were futile? That what she wanted, she could never have? "Stay the week. Please." She willed herself not to cry. She was a strong woman, a survivor. "I promise not to beg you to stay, no matter how much I'll want to." She stuck out her hand, palm open. "Deal?"

He stared at her hand, noting the long, shapely fingers,

the square short nails, the slight quivering that signified her nervousness. "Deal." He took her hand in his and gave it a hardy shake.

She jerked her hand away. He saw the way her chest rose and fell with her labored breathing. He knew she was struggling not to cry again.

"I'll come up to the house for supper, if you'll invite me," he said.

"You have a standing invitation," she said. "Don't you know that?"

"Thanks." He wanted to say more, but knew that nothing he said could change the situation.

"See you about six-thirty, then."

"Six-thirty."

She turned and walked away, not hurriedly, not as if she were running. She didn't want him to think that she wasn't strong enough to give him the friendship he needed without demanding more.

Once deep into the woods, she broke into a run. Hot, heavy tears spilled from her eyes. Her heart wept with the pain of loss; her soul railed against the injustice of life. By the time she reached her house, she was breathless and all cried out. Slumping down on the back porch steps, she reached out her arms to Lord Byron who'd come running the minute he'd seen her enter the yard.

Cuddling the rottweiler close, she nuzzled the side of his head with her nose. "Looks like you're the only male in my life. I had hoped, maybe this time, things would be different, but I was wrong. I guess it isn't meant for poor Anna Rose to have a man of her own."

Seven

Would he stay the week? she wondered. Would they share their meals together, and, afterward, spend hours talking? They had quite a lot in common. Things such as their love for country living, their shared appreciation of life's simple pleasures—sunsets, rainbows, wildflowers. With every conversation, each of them revealed more and more about themselves, about their childhoods, their teen years, their youthful hopes and dreams.

But they had their differences, too. Anna Rose loved poetry and read voraciously, especially fond of romance novels with their inevitable happy endings that life could never promise. Britt didn't appreciate poetry and the only things he read were newspapers, magazine articles and mysteries. He liked to drink an occasional beer; she was a teetotaler. She seldom missed Sunday church services; he never attended.

Anna Rose wandered through the house, the familiar rooms little comfort to her troubled mind and heart. Open-

ing her bedroom door, she stood on the threshold and
looked inside. Late afternoon sunshine brightened every
corner. Delicate blue-flowered wallpaper created a soft,
feminine background for the heavy antique furniture and
coordinated well with the white Priscilla curtains that hung
at the three long, narrow windows. A blue-and-white quilt,
with matching white pillow shams, graced the half-canopy
bed.

An overwhelming sense of loneliness swept over her.
Would Britt come to the house for supper as he'd said he
would? And would he stay the week until Corey was able
to return to work? Really, what difference did it make in
the long run? Britt Cameron was a temporary man, who'd
soon be gone, and she was a forever woman, who'd once
again be left alone. In the past she had been able to find
solace in her work, her books, and the mundane chores of
everyday living. But it wouldn't be that easy this time. She
was in love, truly in love for the first time in her life, and
nothing could ease the pain of loss she would feel when
Britt left.

She sat down on the edge of her bed, clutching her folded
hands in her lap as she closed her eyes and uttered a silent
prayer for strength. She had so much love to give, yet no
one wanted her love...no one would return it. A book of
poetry lay open on the nightstand. Anna Rose reached out,
picked it up and gazed down at the words through a thin
mist of tears. *Love. Love. Love.* She hated the very word.
Angry at herself for wanting—always wanting—more than
she could ever have, Anna Rose flung the book to the floor,
then threw herself across the bed, burying her face in the
soft, old quilt that smelled of fresh air and sunshine.

Britt knocked on the back door. No answer. For the past
hour he'd moped around the shack trying to forget how
Anna Rose had felt in his arms, wishing he didn't remember the way she had trusted him, had taken him at his word.

There had been no doubt in her eyes, no suspicion in her voice. She had held him, comforted him and listened patiently while he had told her the sordid details of Tanya's death.

He knocked again. Still no answer. Her Blazer was in the driveway, so, unless she'd taken off somewhere on foot, she had to be in the house. He'd met Lord Byron chasing after a stray cat when he'd come through the woods, so he knew she wasn't out strolling with her dog.

Turning the doorknob, he found the back door unlocked. He stepped inside the kitchen, looking around as he made his way across the room.

"Anna Rose."

No answer. Where the hell is she? he wondered. He'd known that she was upset, that she was hurting and had been eager to escape from him. He had wanted to pick her up and carry her inside the shack to the rusty iron bed with the bumpy mattress and threadbare sheets. More than he had needed air to breathe, he had needed the feel of her beneath him, loving and giving and totally accepting. And she would have given him her body, and along with it her heart and soul. But what could he have given her in return except a few stolen hours of physical pleasure? Anna Rose deserved so much more—more than he'd ever be able to give her or any other woman.

Slowly, hesitantly, he entered the hallway, then searched the living room before heading for her bedroom. Had she decided to take an afternoon nap? Had she shut herself off from the world in the privacy of her bedroom and cried herself to sleep?

Just as he reached out, his big hand encompassing the cut-glass doorknob, a loud boom of thunder rumbled overhead. The old Victorian house shook from the force of the impending storm. Opening the door, he glanced inside, and what he saw tore at his heart as much as it aroused every male instinct within him. Primitive urges controlled him.

The need to claim what was his, the need to protect, and the desire to mate.

She lay across the bed, her long hair falling wild and free about her shoulders, her face nestled against a pillow, her blouse rumpled and several buttons undone, her legs curled upward and inward in a childlike position. All the way across the room, he could smell the clean, unperfumed essence that was Anna Rose. Soap and water, country air and Alabama sunshine, baby powder and pure female aura. Although he could see only the side of her face, he knew she was crying. He could hear the soft sniffling, the little gasps for breath.

He stood there, unable to move for endless moments as he watched her. He had no right to be in her house, in her bedroom, a voyeur to her most intimate moments of desperation. But he had caused her misery. Wasn't it right that he should take it away?

"Anna Rose." He took a tentative step inside the room.

She jerked around, half sitting, half lying on the bed. Her overbright eyes glared at him, shock and disbelief clearly evident. Her face was damp, her blue eyes swollen and red. Brushing an errant tear from her cheek, she sat up on the side of the bed.

"Britt? What...what—"

She couldn't believe her eyes. Britt stood just inside her bedroom, his big body casually attired in the same cutoff jeans he'd been wearing earlier. A short-sleeved cotton shirt covered his chest, but only the bottom two buttons held it together. His feet were bare. His hair, damp and tousled, curled around his ears, several stray locks hanging down over his forehead. She could hear his labored breathing. Had he run all the way from the shack? His strong masculine scent filled her senses. There was an aroma of soap and hot air, of clean sweat and springwater clinging to him. Had he taken a swim in the pond? Had he been naked? she wondered.

"I knocked at the back door. I called out." God, he'd never seen anything as soft and vulnerable and feminine as Anna Rose. And he'd never wanted anyone so badly.

"I didn't hear you." She clutched the front of her open blouse, holding it together with trembling fingers.

"The thunder, I guess." He could see the need in her eyes, the female hunger that tensed her body. "Anna Rose—"

"It isn't suppertime, yet, is it?" She wanted to get up, knew she should stand, invite him into the kitchen and start preparations for the evening meal. But she couldn't move.

"No." She had to know that the last thing on his mind was food. He was starving all right, but his insatiable hunger was for her. "I—I got to worrying about you after you left. I wanted to make sure you were all right."

"Thank you." If he didn't turn around and walk out of her bedroom soon, she wouldn't be responsible for her actions. Unless he wanted to hear her beg, he'd better leave. "I'm...okay, I guess. Just...just feeling a bit sorry for myself."

"I think you should know that...if things were different..." How could he say, if you were the type of woman who'd be willing to accept a brief affair, we would already be lovers?

"If I were different." Her voice grew lower and softer, a slight tremor vibrating every word. "If I were pretty and slim and—"

Before she could complete the self-derisive sentence, he had crossed the room, pulled her up off the bed and taken her in his arms, silencing her with his mouth. His lips were hard and moist, his tongue insistent as it plundered, then retreated, only to boldly attack again. She cried out, the sound caught by his mouth as it ravaged hers. No man had ever kissed her this way before—as if he were dying of thirst and she was his oasis in the desert.

She could feel the steady beat of his heart where his chest

crushed her breasts. He held the back of her head in one hand, his fingers speared through her hair. He gripped her waist with the other hand, pressing her closer and closer.

Through the haze of intense desire, she tried to think, tried to make sense of what was happening. But rational thought wasn't possible. Not as long as he kept kissing her. Not as long as she could feel the throbbing heat of his arousal pulsating against her stomach. He wanted her, that much she realized. Britt Cameron wanted her. There was no doubt about it. And she wanted him.

Her acceptance of his predatory claim to her body seemed as instinctive as breathing. Slipping her arms, trapped by his possessive hold, around his waist, she worked her fingers up and underneath his loosely hanging shirt. She ran her nails over his tight skin, and gloried in a heady sense of power when she felt him tremble.

Outside, another loud roar of thunder plummeted the summer day, but inside, Anna Rose barely heard the noise, so loudly was her own heart beating.

Britt released her mouth. They both gasped for air. Lowering his head, he looked down to where her blouse hung open, held together by three buttons. He could see her white lace bra, the swell of her full breasts and her dark pink nipples. He placed his mouth against her throat, then slowly made his way downward, his tongue painting a damp, curling line across her chest and into the shadow between her breasts. Anna Rose clung to him, then prompted by urges she didn't understand, she tossed her head backward and thrust her body toward his marauding lips. She spread her fingers out over his shoulder blades, kneading his powerful muscles.

Britt grabbed her by the hips, holding her steady with both hands. He could tell she was melting, slowly, degree by degree, becoming hotter and hotter. When he removed his hands from her hips, she remained locked to him, as if some invisible glue had bound their bodies. She dropped her arms to her sides. Shedding his shirt, he fumbled with her buttons, freeing them, removing her blouse.

Looking at his chest, she could not resist the urge to touch him. A thick, heavy mat of black hair beckoned her fingers. Her hand hovered over his chest. She glanced up at him.

"Touch me." He covered her hand with his, pressing it against his erratically beating heart.

Of their own accord, her fingers inched through his chest hair. She was utterly fascinated by the way the lush dark strands curled about her fingers. "Is this what you want?" she asked, unsure of how to please him.

"That's just a little of what I want," he told her. "Just the beginning."

She watched his head descend, then closed her eyes when his mouth opened over her lace-covered breast, taking a distended nipple and suckling it until she cried out with pleasure. While he lavished similar attention on her other breast, she whimpered, the sound an irresistible inducement to a man who needed very little prompting.

With manic urgency, he unhooked her bra, tearing it from her body. She gulped in huge swallows of air, then flung her hands over her bare breasts with a sudden burst of modesty. His hands covered hers, gripping them, prizing them away from her body.

"Don't cover yourself. I want to look at you."

She couldn't breathe. Her lungs were frozen, her throat constricted. He held her arms away from her body, gazing at her intently, his yellow-brown eyes alight with amber fire. He studied the feminine beauty of her large breasts, so round and firm and irresistible. When he lowered his head again, she made no move to assist or resist. With his hands holding her waist, he made love to her breasts, teasing the nubs with repeated lapping strokes, then tiny, prickling nips with his teeth and finally an all-consuming suckling. She cried out, consumed with aching pleasure.

"Britt, please…it's too much. I can't bear it." She'd had no idea that a man could create such exquisite pleasure inside a woman by the mere touch of his mouth and tongue and teeth on her breasts.

Raising his head, he smiled at her, pleased by the dazed look of rapture on her face. She was incredibly responsive. Lifting her breasts into his palms, he squeezed them gently and felt an almost uncontrollable yearning rip through him when she sighed. The sound was so soft, so passionate, so utterly feminine.

"There's more…much more," he told her, releasing her breasts. He unbuttoned and unzipped her slacks. She made no protest. "Will you let me look at you, see all of you?"

No one had seen her completely unclothed since she'd been a very small child and had been incapable of bathing herself. She had never seen a naked man, and knew at that precise moment that she longed to see him as much as he did her. With a courage derived from a deep internal well-spring, Anna Rose reached out and, with shaky fingers, unsnapped and unzipped his jeans.

He looked at her. She looked at him. "Oh, yes, baby, yes." Britt lowered his cutoff jeans, pulled them over his feet and tossed them aside.

He stood there, big and hairy and thickly muscled. All man. And undeniably aroused. His manhood filled the front of his white cotton briefs. Anna Rose wanted to touch him there, wanted to strip away the one remaining barrier that held his blatant arousal in check.

Without saying a word, he removed her slacks, but when his fingers slipped beneath the elastic waistband of her lacy panties, she panicked and tried to pull away from him.

"Don't, baby. Don't be afraid. I'm not going to hurt you. All I want to do right now is look at you."

While she stood, pliable if not eager, he eased her panties down her hips and over her legs. She raised one foot and then the other. Britt, on his knees before her, laid the scrap of silk and lace on the floor, then buried his face in the apex between her thighs.

Stunned, Anna Rose cried out and would have run from him had he not clutched her buttocks in his hands and held her to him. He breathed in the sweet, musty aroma of woman. He couldn't remember ever wanting anything as much as he wanted to make love to Anna Rose.

When he dampened the front of her thighs with his tongue, she clutched his shoulders, bracing herself. Myriad emotions ran riot within her—desire, so hot and intense it consumed her, diminishing all other feelings. But a deep sense of wonder mingled with an ever present sense of morality. Was what they were doing wrong? How could it be, she asked herself, when nothing she'd ever done had felt so right?

Tormentingly, he moved his lips upward, over her stomach, around her navel, between her breasts and to her throat. Standing upright, he faced her and could see the hint of doubt in her blue eyes. When he pulled her into his arms, she went willingly, her body trembling when his manhood pulsated against the delta between her thighs.

"Britt, please...please..."

Holding her with one hand at her waist, he ran the inside of his other hand down her cheek, capturing her jaw and chin in his palm. "Do you know what you're asking for?"

"I...yes." She closed her eyes, savoring the delicious agony of desire that radiated from her femininity, spreading like the flames of a uncontrollable fire.

"I want you," he said, running his hand down her throat, tightening his fingers, feeling the throbbing of her pulse. "Do you have any idea what I want to do to you?" When she neither opened her eyes nor replied, he said, "Do you?"

She only groaned, lost to the new and painfully erotic feelings that his passionate loving had created deep within her.

"I want to lay you down on the bed." He heard her moan again, a sound soft, but easily detectable. "I want to come down on top of you. I want to bury myself deep inside you. So deep that you'll think I've become a part of you."

When she swayed toward him, he took her in his arms, lifting her off her feet. She knew she was neither small nor light, but he held her as if her size was nothing to him. And perhaps it wasn't, she thought. Britt Cameron was a very large man, with big arms and broad shoulders bulging with muscles.

He laid her on the bed, and slowly eased himself down beside her, propping himself on one elbow as he turned to her. "Have you ever been with a man, Anna Rose?"

The question panicked her. What answer did he want to hear? Did he prefer an experienced woman or would her virginity be appealing to him? "Does it matter?" she asked, so afraid of making the wrong reply. If he left her, walked away now after bringing her so close to the ultimate act of love, she wasn't sure she would survive.

Did it matter? he asked himself. Yes. No. Hell, if she'd never had a man or had been with a dozen, it wouldn't change the fact that he wanted her to the point of madness. "No," he said truthfully, slipping his leg over hers, lifting himself up as he spread her thighs with his knee.

He loomed over her, big and dark and breathtakingly male. She reached out for him. He lowered himself, careful not to crush her, hoping he could take her slowly and carefully, half certain that she was a virgin or, at least, very inexperienced. But the blood rushed through his body, pounded in his head, throbbed in his manhood.

"I don't want to hurt you." He called upon every ounce of his willpower when he probed the moist entrance to her body.

"You won't," she said, curling her arms around him, lifting herself up to meet him. "I trust you completely."

The sweet compliance of her willing body and her total trust in him dissolved the last remnants of his control. He entered her, a fraction at a time. She was hot and wet and tight. So very, very tight. Suddenly he encountered her maidenhead. His whole body tensed with the knowledge of what she was offering him, of what he was taking from her.

"Annie Rosie…Annie Rosie…" With one commanding thrust, he entered her completely, shattering her innocence as he made her his.

She cried out, as much from the fullness, the incredible feel of having him buried deep inside her, as from the pain.

"Baby, are you all right?" He stopped his movements, waiting for her reply.

"Yes, oh, yes. Please, Britt, don't stop. Love me. Love me." She moved first, her seductive feminine body tempting his maleness with a charm she had never known she possessed.

He took her then, in a frenzy that left no room for gentleness or concern for her inexperience. She writhed beneath him, her body answering the primitive mating call of his. Sensation after sensation washed over her as her whole body tightened into one huge, throbbing need. He could feel his own release nearing, and tried to stem the tide of passion flooding him. Lifting her hips, he shoved her up and into him as he lunged in and out, each consecutive thrust deeper and harder and faster than the one before.

With her nails biting into the flesh of his lower back, Anna Rose groaned, overpowered by an intensified ache at the point where their bodies joined. Suddenly that ache became unbearable. Her body tightened.

"Britt, Britt…I love you." She hung on to him for dear life, knowing surely she must be dying, so great was the pleasure, so compelling the tidal wave of fulfillment that consumed her.

"Let it happen, baby. Just hang on tight and let it happen.'' He could feel her tightening around him, sheathing, stroking.

Ecstasy claimed her. She moaned, then cried out, his name an awed chant on her lips. The sounds of her satisfaction sent him over the edge, triggering the most earth shattering climax he'd ever known.

They stood together in front of the open French doors that led from her bedroom out onto the side porch. Hours ago, the earsplitting thunder and the sizzling lightning had diminished as the heavens opened and rain fell in a hard and furious downpour. Now the rain had turned into a slow, steady shower that would give the earth a deep and thorough soaking.

After they had made love a second time, then slept until twilight, Britt had gotten up and slipped into his cutoff jeans. Understanding her shyness, even after giving herself so unashamedly to him, Britt had retrieved Anna Rose's cotton robe from the closet and turned his back while she slipped it on.

Now she stood in front of him, leaning back against his chest. He draped his arms around her, his big hands lying low on her stomach. He nuzzled the side of her face.

Anna Rose watched the sweet summer rain as it created a sheer haze that covered the earth. ''Thank you,'' she whispered, closing her eyes, savoring the feel of his lips pressing a kiss against her cheek.

''For what?'' he asked, wondering if she was thanking him for bringing her to the peak of physical pleasure.

''For wanting me,'' she said quite honestly.

For wanting her? For wanting her! The loneliness, the emotional deprivation, the low self-esteem came through loud and clear in her words. Had she never been wanted? he wondered. Had that damned old grandmother of hers made her feel so totally unwanted and unworthy that, even now, as an intelligent, successful woman, Anna Rose couldn't imagine someone wanting her? Tightening his hold around her, he buried his face in her long tan hair. God, she smelled good. Sweeter than all the flowers in her garden.

"I've never wanted another woman as much as I wanted you." Although it was the truth, he had been hesitant to tell her. He didn't want her to think that wanting and loving was the same for him as it so obviously was for her.

"Then I...I satisfied you?"

"You know you did." He tried to turn her around to face him, but she struggled against the move. "Ah, Annie Rosie, don't go getting all shy on me now."

"It's just that I...I love you so much. Even more now...now that we've made love. And you didn't say the words...you didn't—"

He allowed her to keep her back to him. Placing his chin atop her head where it rested, slightly tilted, against his chest, Britt hugged her tightly. "I wish I could say the words, but I can't. I'd never lie to you. If I said them I'd mean them."

"You still love her, don't you?"

"No," he said. "It's not that I love her, it's just that I don't think I'll ever be capable of loving another woman." When he felt her body tense, he wanted to comfort her, but wasn't sure what he could say or do that would make any difference.

"Will you still be leaving next week when Corey comes back to work?" She held her breath, waiting anxiously for his reply. More than anything, she wanted him to stay. Maybe, if he stayed, he'd learn to love her just a little.

"I don't think so, Annie Rosie." He sighed deeply, calling himself all kinds of a fool. He wasn't some green kid who didn't know better. He'd had no right to put her at risk the way he had, to make love to her without taking the proper precautions. "You realize, don't you, that I didn't protect you. Either time."

"Oh." She hadn't given it a thought, so lost to the new-found joy of being wanted by the man she loved. How foolish! How completely irresponsible! "Britt, I'm so sorry. I—I…I'm sure it'll be all right. I mean, even if I am…that is, I'd never blame you, and I'd never expect you to—"

He whirled her around so quickly that her loosely tied robe fell open, exposing the inner curve of her breasts and the tawny tan triangle of curls between her legs.

"If you're pregnant, I'll marry you," he told her, his tone commanding, leaving her in no doubt of his intentions.

"But…but it wouldn't be right to ask you to marry me. You don't love me. You just said that you'll never love another woman."

"But you love me, don't you, Annie Rosie?" He slipped his hands inside her robe, placing them on her hips, pulling her to him. "And I want you, and respect you, and admire you, and enjoy being with you."

"But you don't love me?"

"No, I don't love you."

The words hung between them, dark and deadly, like a microscopic virus, waiting, waiting, waiting.

Eight

He wore a navy suit, a pale blue shirt and a striped tie. She was dressed in the new sapphire-blue silk suit that Britt had told her matched her eyes. She held a small bouquet of pink wild roses and baby's breath. He had done everything he could to persuade her to wear white, but she had adamantly refused. Perhaps, if he loved her, she would have worn white and felt, since he was her first and only lover, that she deserved the honor. But he didn't love her, despite the fact that she carried his child.

He had stayed with her after Corey had returned to work. He'd tried to find employment locally, but no one wanted to hire an accused murderer, despite the fact that he'd been acquitted of the crime. Anna Rose had defended both Britt and their relationship, not only to Tammy and Roy Dean, but to numerous relatives, friends and even to the county school board.

The past few months had not been easy. When she'd missed her first period, Britt had insisted she see a doctor,

but she'd assured him that she was often late and occasionally missed a period altogether. In truth, she'd never
missed a period, but she hated the thought that Britt felt
trapped, that he was so noble he would marry her without
loving her, just to protect her and their unborn child. By
the end of the second month, she could no longer deceive
herself or put him off. The doctor had confirmed her pregnancy a week ago. Britt had called his family and invited
them to his wedding.

Anna Rose, despite the fact that they were marrying because of their child, insisted on marrying in church, with
her minister officiating. Britt had balked at the idea, his
bitterness toward religion and ministers of all faiths a by-
product of his hatred for Reverend Timothy Charles.

Although Tammy had tried her best to dissuade Anna
Rose from marrying Britt, she had, once she'd seen how
determined her cousin was to go through with the wedding,
taken charge.

Two enormous flower arrangements flanked Brother
Sherman. Wade Cameron, Britt's older brother, stood at his
side, serving as best man. Tammy had insisted on being
the matron of honor. The large country church was almost
empty, save for Roy Dean, Steve and Edith Hendricks, and
two of Anna Rose's older relatives, Opal Palmer and
Maude Welborn, both ladies first cousins to her grandfather. Britt's family, except for his youngest sibling Lily,
had shown up in full force. His sister Amy had arrived only
this morning, but the rest of the Camerons had been in
residence since the night before.

Anna Rose liked Wade's wife, Lydia, who had openly
discussed her own shotgun wedding, and the happily ever
after results. Ruthie Cameron was as good hearted and caring a woman as Anna Rose had ever met, but it was apparent that she didn't completely approve of her son's marriage.

Anna Rose listened carefully to each word Brother Sherman said, repeating the appropriate phrases when called upon, wanting to scream "He's lying" when Britt said yes to the question, "Will you love her and..."

Within minutes, it was over. Both she and her husband wore plain gold bands on their fingers, symbols of never-ending love. She barely heard Brother Sherman say, "You may kiss the bride." Britt's kiss was thorough, but quick.

As they turned to step down from the raised pulpit, Anna Rose's head began to spin. She clutched Britt's arm to keep her balance. Slipping his arm around her, he braced her against his body.

"What's the matter?" he asked, concern evident in his voice. "Are you going to faint?"

Taking in several deep breaths as she rested against Britt, Anna Rose shook her head. "I just felt light-headed for a minute. All the excitement, I guess. I'm all right now. Really."

"Could be the heat. This is the hottest September I remember in years," Ruthie Cameron said. "What she needs is to get home and take it easy."

"She can just sit and let us wait on her," Tammy said, making her way to Anna Rose's side. "I've got everything set up at the farm for a lovely little reception. You do feel up to that much, don't you?"

"Of course. I'm...I'm looking forward to it. Thanks, Tammy." Anna Rose had been taught, from childhood, that there was a difference in out-and-out lying and telling socially acceptable white lies. Grandmother had been an expert in saying the correct thing, even if she had to stretch, bend or even totally disregard the truth. One never told the complete truth if it injured another's feelings or made one appear foolish in the eyes of others.

When they were outside the church building, Britt helped her into her Blazer. "If you don't feel up to going through with this damned reception, I'll be the bad guy and tell everybody it's off."

"No, don't do that." When she saw the determined look on his face, she smiled and placed her unsteady hand on his arm. "Please."

"Whatever you want, Anna Rose," he said, bending to kiss her on the forehead. "I'm going to try to make life as easy as possible for you. You may not believe this, but I do want you to be happy."

"I know you do." She leaned back against the seat, closing her eyes and willing herself not to cry. Britt Cameron was a good man, the man she loved with all her heart. It wasn't his fault that his own heart was buried so deeply beneath a frozen layer of bitterness and hatred and unrequited love that he was incapable of returning her feelings.

They were married now. For better or worse. They were going to have a child. It was more than Anna Rose had ever hoped to have. But would it be enough—for either of them?

Tammy and Roy Dean had left, taking Opal and Maude with them. The Hendricks had stayed less than ten minutes. Ruthie Cameron had assured Tammy that Amy and Lydia could take care of the cleanup and make sure nothing was left for Anna Rose to worry about.

Anna Rose suspected that her new mother-in-law had been as eager to see the last of the Palmer friends and relatives as she was herself. Opal and Maude had made no pretense of their dislike for Britt, and, although they hadn't been openly rude to him, they had been hostile in their attitude. Roy Dean, a know-it-all big-mouth since childhood, had gotten on everyone's nerves, especially when he'd taken it upon himself to advise Britt to find a way to clear his good name if he ever intended to be accepted in Cherokee.

"Folks around here are going to keep giving Anna Rose a hard time about you," Roy Dean had said. "And when your kid is born, don't think anybody's going to let him forget that his old man was accused of murder.''

Tammy, the consummate hostess, at least in a small-town, amateurish way, had flitted around the house like a hyper butterfly, smiling too much, talking too much, and laughing far too loudly.

The evening sun brightened the western horizon, lying low in the sky like some fat, slowly melting scoop of orange sherbert. Anna Rose hadn't changed clothes, but she had slipped out of her heels and put on a pair of flats. Lydia had coerced Britt and Wade and Amy into helping her clean up, while her daughter Molly took baby brother Lee into the bedroom for a nap. Anna Rose suspected that Lydia had maneuvered events in order to give Ruthie Cameron time alone with her younger son's new wife.

Anna Rose sat in one of the big white rockers on the front porch; Ruthie sat in the other. An afternoon thundershower had cooled things off a bit, but had been so brief it had done little more than settle the dust. A few remaining raindrops clung to the shrubbery and rosebushes that lined the front porch.

"We're going to be leaving tonight," Ruthie said. "As soon as little Lee wakes from his nap."

"Y'all don't have to drive home tonight," Anna Rose said, resting her head against the wooden round of the chair as she rocked back and forth, the gentle rhythm soothing to her overwrought nerves.

"It shouldn't take more than an hour. Amy's got a plane to catch tomorrow and Wade's got a farm to run. Two big chicken houses." Ruthie leaned over, placing her fat hand on Anna Rose's arm. "Besides, you and Britt need to be alone on your wedding night."

"It's not exactly as if…as if we—" The words lodged in her throat. How could she discuss something so private, so completely personal with her husband's mother, a woman she barely knew?

Ruthie patted Anna Rose's arm gently. "Now, there's no need to be embarrassed around me. Regardless of the circumstances, a wedding night should be special."

"I want you to know that I love Britt, and I'm going to do everything in my power to make him a good wife." Anna Rose forced herself to face her mother-in-law. "I didn't trap him into this marriage. We...we didn't mean for me to get pregnant, and I certainly didn't force him to—"

"Hush up that kind of talk, girl. Nobody's ever been able to force Britt Cameron into doing anything he didn't want to do. He's acted foolishly more than once. Done some stupid things, but his motives are good. For a hot-tempered country boy, he's noble. Yep, that's what my Britt is. He's noble." Ruthie's brown eyes clouded with tears as she reached down to take Anna Rose's hand, squeezing it tightly. "I don't want to see either one of you hurt."

"You know, of course, that he doesn't love me." Just saying the words was a painful act. She didn't know if she would ever again have the courage to voice the heartbreaking fact.

"He thinks he doesn't love you." Ruthie reached up and wiped away the tears from the corner of Anna Rose's eye. "He loved Tanya, had loved her since they was kids, but she was the wrong woman for him. Immature. Selfish."

"We don't always love wisely, do we?"

"Britt didn't. Not the first time, but you're very different from Tanya."

"I'm not petite and blonde and cute." She averted her gaze from Ruthie's disapproving stare.

"No, you're not," Ruthie said bluntly. "You're tall and big-boned, with the kind of body made for hard work and childbearing. The perfect farm wife."

Anna Rose was shocked by her mother-in-law's brutal honesty, not accustomed to people being so truthful. Instead of being offended, she felt a sense of relief that Ruthie hadn't pretended, hadn't sugarcoated the obvious. She couldn't refrain from smiling.

Ruthie smiled back at her, then emitted a sound somewhere between a grunt and a laugh. "God knows you're not cute, Anna Rose. Your features are too strong, your personality too serious. But don't sell yourself short. You're far from being the plain Jane you've convinced yourself you are."

"Ruthie Cameron, where were you when I was a teenager and needed someone like you to talk to?"

Ruthie leaned over and took Anna Rose in her arms, both women half sitting, half standing in their respective rockers. "You give that boy of mine some time. Be patient and understanding, and keep on loving him. One of these days, he's bound to realize how much you mean to him."

"Do you honestly believe that?"

"I know my boy better than anyone else does, and you can take my word for it. Britt loves you. He just doesn't know it yet."

Anna Rose hugged her mother-in-law again and said a quick and silent prayer to a loving God that Ruthie Cameron was right.

Anna Rose had changed into the shimmery white and gold peignoir set that Lydia had given her as a wedding gift. She'd never worn anything like it in her life and felt a bit self-conscious. Britt was still in the shower, had been in there for at least twenty minutes. She couldn't help but wonder if it was possible that he was as nervous as she was. After that first time when they'd made love twice, Britt had assured Anna Rose that he would take care of protecting her when they had sex, but she had told him that she didn't think they should be intimate again. After all, he would be leaving as soon as they were certain she wasn't pregnant, and she admitted to him that it would be far easier to let him go if their sexual relationship didn't continue.

So, here they were, a few months later, married. If only the circumstances had been different, she knew this would be the happiest day of her life. She had longed for someone to love, someone to fill her life with happiness and make all her romantic dreams come true. All her life Anna Rose had longed for a man of her own. Simple little things that other women took for granted had taken on a special significance for her. Just to be able to sit beside the man she loved, to hold his hand, to rest her head on his shoulder. How many times had she wanted and needed a comforting arm around her, an encouraging smile, a caring word or two?

For twenty-seven years she had stored up so much love and so much need. And now she had someone. A husband. At long last, she had found him—that special someone. A man for Anna Rose. But that man didn't love her.

Anna Rose opened the French doors and stepped out onto the side porch. The black night sky was star-studded. An almost full moon released a glimmering silvery-gold light. The smell of honeysuckle and roses saturated the warm summer air.

Hearing the bedroom door open, she turned to see Britt entering. His black hair was damp and beads of moisture clung to the curls on his chest. A blue-and-white striped towel covered him from waist to mid-thigh. Anna Rose swallowed hard, realizing that he was naked beneath the towel.

"The rain cooled things off a bit," he said, wondering what the hell he could do to make things easier for her. This had been a difficult day for Anna Rose, far more difficult for her than for him. After all, he was the one getting everything—a wife who loved him, a child he truly wanted, a chance for a new life. And what was she getting? An unplanned pregnancy. The rebuke and pity of her friends and family. The very real possibility that she could lose her job. And a husband who not only didn't love her, but had a tarnished reputation and no money.

"If you think it's too warm with the doors open, I can turn on the air conditioner." Anna Rose stood in the doorway, suddenly quite aware of how sheer her gown and matching robe actually were. Could Britt see through the almost transparent layers of diaphanous silk?

"No, it's fine. I kind of like the nighttime coming into our bedroom." He began walking toward her, slowly, cautiously, uncertain how she would react to him. After all, for the past two months she had been adamant about not continuing their sexual relationship.

"I imagine your folks are home by now." She turned her back to him, her heart beating wildly. The very thought of his coming to her, touching her, sent her nerves into spasms of expectation. "I really did like all of them. Your niece and nephew are darling. And your mother is such a wonderful woman. I—I wish Grandmother could have been more like her."

Britt kept walking toward Anna Rose, despite the fact that she'd turned from him. Even if they had married because of the baby, even if he didn't love her, Anna Rose deserved a special wedding night. Damn it all, he only hoped he was capable of giving her something. Tenderness, passion, friendship and loyalty. If only that would be enough. "Yeah, Ma's something, isn't she?"

Anna Rose felt him standing behind her, his big body only inches away from hers. Why didn't he touch her? she wondered. Didn't he know that he would have to make the first move, that what little pride she had left wouldn't allow her to initiate whatever was going to happen between them tonight?

"I like the gown Lydia gave you," he said, scanning the length of her body encased in the shimmery white silk edged with pale gold lace. "You look beautiful, even more beautiful than you looked at our wedding today." The moment the words left his mouth, he saw her body tense. Damn! She didn't believe him.

"Thank you." Why did he have to lie to her? she wondered. Her heart might long to hear sweet flattery, but she wanted whatever he said to her to be the truth. She didn't want any lies between them. The one thing they did share was trust in each other, and she didn't want that to change. "Britt, I'd rather you didn't say things you don't really mean."

He moved closer, his naked chest brushing against her back. When he slipped his arms around her and drew her to him, she didn't resist. Lowering his head, he whispered in her ear. "You were beautiful today, and you are even more beautiful tonight. I think marriage and motherhood agree with you."

Her breath came in quick, erratic gulps as he nuzzled her neck. "Please, Britt, I know I'm not even pretty. How can you say that—"

Without warning, he lifted her into his arms, her floor-length gown and robe swirling around his bare legs. "I'll never lie to you, Annie Rosie. Never. When I look at you, I see beauty...pure and honest and real."

She couldn't bear to look at him, so overcome by his adamant profession. Laying her head on his shoulder, she shut her eyes and tried to hold back her tears as he carried her across the room and placed her on the bed.

She lay there, her eyes closed, her heart thundering in her ears, her fingers gripping the quilt. Since he hadn't laid down on the bed with her, she knew he must still be standing. The room was very quiet, except for the faraway sounds of nighttime in the country and the noise of their own heartbeats and breathing. She heard something hit the wooden floor with a light thud, and knew he had discarded his towel.

She felt the bed give slightly from the weight of his big body as he lay down beside her. She wished she weren't so afraid, so uncertain. She knew she could hardly be seductive, lying there like a stick of wood, unmoving and unresponsive. When she felt his fingers touch the tiny covered buttons on her robe, she drew in her breath and held it until he had undone the robe and spread it away from her body.

"This thing is gorgeous," he said, running his hand over the fine lace where it covered her breasts. "But I'd much prefer to be touching your skin than silk or lace."

"I...do you...should I..."

He kissed her closed eyelids while he slipped his hand beneath her back, giving her a gentle push. "Sit up a little, honey, and I'll take care of it."

Obeying like a programmed robot, Anna Rose sat upright in bed and did little more than respond to his requests to raise her arms and lift her hips. The warm night breeze coming in the open French doors struck her naked flesh, puckering her nipples and making her shiver.

With her eyes still closed, she sat there while Britt ran the tips of his fingers from her throat to her navel. An ache began inside her, a tingling, insistent yearning throbbing between her thighs. Her breasts felt heavy and full, hurting with a need to be suckled.

"Open your eyes and look at me, Annie Rosie." His voice, deep and husky, echoed the hot, sensuous longing pulsating through his body.

She didn't respond immediately, but when he dropped his hand below her navel, his fingers slipping through the tan curls to find the moist heat of her body, she moaned and opened her eyes to find him staring directly at her. A warm flush crept up her neck and pinkened her cheeks.

"We can make this marriage work, honey." He fondled her, his fingers moving in a circular motion, creating friction against her damp flesh. Reacting instinctively, she arched against his hand. "I want to make love to my wife."

Nothing, not even her mounting desire, could change the

fact that Britt didn't love her, that her whole marriage was based on a pregnancy that neither of them had planned.

"Britt, please…" She grasped his wrist, trying to halt the tantalizing movements of his hand.

Gripping the back of her neck, Britt lowered his face until his lips were almost touching hers. His eyes, bright and glowing with amber brown sparks filled her line of vision. "I know you want me, Anna Rose, so don't try to deny it."

His breath was hot, his lips moist. She gulped down a sob of protest. She wanted to scream, *but you don't love me.* She remained silent, but moved her body toward his, brushing her breasts against his thick chest hair, rubbing her cheek against his beard.

"You don't have any idea how it makes a man feel to know his woman wants him, do you?" He mouthed the question against her lips.

Had his first wife denied him? Anna Rose wondered. Had Tanya Cameron's lack of love extended to a lack of desire? She couldn't bear to think of how much that would have hurt Britt. He was such a proud man, a man of deep and tempestuous passions.

Without giving another thought to denying him, Anna Rose covered his mouth with her own, initiating an intimate kiss. She circled his lips with her tongue, then nipped at his lower lip and finally touched his teeth. He opened his mouth, inviting her entrance.

Like an explosion of the senses, Britt began a frenzy of exploration, moving over Anna Rose, deepening the kiss as one hand continued tormenting her and the other cradled her breast. Placing her hands on his shoulders, she lifted herself upward, inviting him, tempting him. When he nudged her legs with his knee, she opened her thighs to him, offering herself. And all the while she moved her hands over his back, kneading the thick, rippling muscles.

The feelings he created within her kept spiraling, higher

and higher, until she writhed beneath him. Breaking the kiss, she gasped for air. "Please, Britt. I want you."

He took her with one powerful thrust. She shivered from head to toe, crying out from the sheer pleasure of their joining. "You make me feel the way a man wants to feel." His words came from him in a thick, heavy drawl as he plunged in and out of her with quick, deep stabs.

She clung to him, reveling in his complete possession. Britt might not be in love with her, but he was loving her body with total obsession.

Slowing his pace, he ran his lips down her throat and to her breast. She squirmed when he took her nipple between his teeth, nipping, then licking, then nipping again.

She accelerated the rhythm of her upward lunges, intensifying the sizzling friction building between her legs. It hit her, wild and hot and all-consuming. "Britt...Britt...love you..." she screamed out into the stillness of her bedroom.

Her fulfillment sent him over the edge. Her tight body surrounded him, clinching and releasing him as spasm after spasm of release quivered through her. His big body jerked once, twice, and then he groaned, a loud and animalistic roar, signifying his completion.

When he lay down on top of her, she cradled his sweaty body in her arms, loving the feel of his damp hairy chest against her breasts, the earthy manly smell he emitted through every pore of his body, the satisfied grunts he continued to make. And most of all, she loved the feel of him still inside her, a part of her, as surely as the child he'd given her.

Easing off her and onto his side, he cradled her head on his shoulder, then kissed the side of her face. "Thank you."

"Thank you," she said, cuddling closer, knowing that in the future she would never deny Britt her body, that despite the fact that he didn't love her, she did love him.

And maybe, just maybe, Ruthie Cameron had been right. Maybe Britt loved her, but just didn't know it. With that thought uppermost in her mind, Anna Rose closed her eyes and slept until dawn, when her new husband awakened her and took her to heaven once again.

Nine

Anna Rose took her coat out of the hall closet. From where she stood near the front door, she could hear the sound of the Blazer's motor running and the chilling wail of a below-freezing December wind. She slipped into her coat, not surprised that it barely buttoned across her protruding stomach. Some women, she knew, didn't even show at five and a half months, but already her body had expanded, her belly rounded like a big balloon. A large baby, Cousin Opal had said. Too much water retention, Cousin Maude had decided. But Tammy had probably guessed correctly. Anna Rose was just eating too much and would probably be as big as an elephant by the time she delivered.

Anna Rose set her wool-felt beret on her head, tied her scarf around her neck and pulled on her gloves. She didn't want to keep Britt waiting. He'd had the Blazer running for at least ten minutes and was now waiting on the front porch in the windy cold. They'd had another little disagreement, which they always had whenever she asked him to go anywhere in Cherokee with her. She didn't blame him for wanting to avoid the curious stares, the behind-the-back murmurs, and the out-and-out confrontations with the few people brash enough to question him about his first wife's murder.

Tonight was the annual Christmas play followed by the PTA party to honor the school staff. It was one of the most important events of the year for Anna Rose. She wanted her husband to share the night with her, and didn't think it too much to ask that he did. After all, she'd completely given in to his wishes to stay on the farm. He hadn't gone into Cherokee more than four times in the three and half months they'd been married.

Anna Rose opened the door and stepped outside, shutting her eyes momentarily before sucking in her breath as the frigid night air swirled around her.

"Come on," Britt said, taking her by the arm. "Let's get you in the Blazer before icicles form on your nose."

Within seconds she was seated inside the toasty warm four-wheel drive. Britt backed out of the driveway. Neither of them said a word for a couple of miles down the road.

"I appreciate you going with me tonight. It means so much to me." She reached out and touched him on the arm.

He shrugged off her tender gesture. "Folks aren't going to be pleased that you've brought me along." He looked straight ahead at the desolate patch of darkened country road ahead of them. His resistance to attending this event had more to do with his desire to protect Anna Rose than his desperate need to avoid being the center of attention.

She didn't know how to reply. What could she say? She couldn't tell him that he was wrong. The past few months had not been easy for either of them. With each passing day, she became more and more aware of her friends' and relatives' disapproval of her marriage, and the fact that the school board president's wife had implied that Anna Rose's

job could well be in jeopardy hadn't set well with Britt.
He'd threatened to go and have a personal talk with President Davenport. Anna Rose couldn't go anywhere without
having to confront the whispers, the stares, the pointing
fingers and the blatantly rude behavior of people she'd
known all her life. The words *poor Anna Rose* had taken
on new meaning.

And matters had only worsened during the Thanksgiving
holidays when the Cameron clan had come to Cherokee.
Everyone had enjoyed the gathering, and Anna Rose had
been in her element for days ahead, preparing a scrump-
tious feast. But before the Camerons left, Wade had taken
Britt aside to inform him that Timothy Charles had found
a new church in nearby Iuka, Mississippi. Britt had told
Anna Rose that his brother had advised him to quit running
from the past and try to clear his name by proving Reverend
Charles's guilt.

"He's right," Britt had said. "You're suffering because
of my reputation. And our child will suffer even more if
he has to go through life having people think his father is
a murderer."

"But, if the Tishomingo sheriff won't even consider
Reverend Charles as a suspect, what can you do?" she'd
asked him, half afraid that if he did go after Timothy
Charles, he would leave her and never come back.

Britt had admitted he didn't know what to do, but that
soon, he'd have to make a decision.

Anna Rose rested her head on the back of the Blazer's
front seat, wishing that she and Britt could run off to some
deserted island where no one knew either of them, where
they didn't have past lives. When they were together alone
at the farm, life was good. They were quite compatible,
enjoying each other's company and finding shared pleasures in the simplicity of their daily lives. And when they
made love, Anna Rose could almost forget that her husband
didn't really love her.

* * *

Howard Gene Dowdy, in his new crisp overalls, plaid shirt and baseball cap stood by the punch bowl talking to Kyle Ross, who looked his usual debonair self in brown slacks and a camel sport coat.

"Rudolph the Red-Nosed Reindeer" played over the intercom and hordes of costumed youngers milled around the school lunchroom, spilling Kool-Aid punch and dropping cookie crumbs over the shiny linoleum floor. Parents of various ages, sexes and races mixed and mingled while a small group of rather superior mothers, those with *important husbands,* detached themselves from the others. Several of those important husbands were busy ogling Nina Costairs, the curvaceous young kindergarten teacher who had bent over to help tie one of her student's shoelaces.

Anna Rose, trapped between Myra Davenport, the school board president's wife and Tracy Ross, Kyle's skinny blond bride, scanned the room for a glimpse of Britt.

"My dear, it's a pity you're showing so quickly," Myra said. "People are such gossips. They'll be implying all sorts of things. After all, you do look...well...huge."

"I think you look lovely, Mrs. Cameron," Tracy said, smiling pleasantly at Anna Rose. "Pregnancy certainly agrees with you. You're just glowing."

"Thank you, and please call me Anna Rose." She'd tried to dislike Kyle's wife, but it was impossible. Tracy Ross was sweet and friendly and very likable.

"I thought the Christmas play was a huge success, didn't you, Mrs. Davenport?" Tracy asked.

"Well, I have to admit it's the biggest crowd we've ever had." She tilted her salon-coiffured head and stuck her snobbish hawk nose into the air as she surveyed the multitude of Cherokee parents and grandparents as well as numerous aunts and uncles. "No doubt, the possibility of your husband's appearance here tonight prompted the curious to come out in such frigid weather."

Anna Rose had to bite her tongue to keep from making

an acid reply. The word frigid would have been the cornerstone of her comment. Instead, turning to Tracy Ross, she chose to ignore Myra's stinging barb. "I understand that you and Kyle have bought the old Vickery place."

Tracy picked up the conversation and after a few minutes of being completely ignored, Myra Davenport walked off in a huff. "Obnoxious woman," Tracy said, then laughed with Anna Rose.

Britt had tried, unsuccessfully, to disappear into the woodwork, seeking dark corners and spots near exit doors for the past hour. He'd seen Anna Rose scanning the cafeteria more than once looking for him, and hated himself for leaving her on her own. But he figured she was better off if he wasn't by her side gaining them both undue attention.

The after-play party seemed to be winding down a bit, quite a few guests having already left. He noticed Anna Rose talking to Kyle Ross and his wife, and wondered how Anna Rose felt about the couple. Ross was certainly a good-looking devil and his petite wife was the physical antithesis of Anna Rose. Tracy Ross was wide-eyed immaturity packaged in a doll-like body.

Britt decided he'd delayed the inevitable long enough. Making his way across the room, he stopped dead still when he heard Howard Gene Dowdy's loud, nasal voice uttering a comment about Anna Rose.

"Sure never figured an old maid like Anna Rose would go and get herself married to a murderer." Howard Gene hooked his big, fat thumbs beneath the straps of his overalls and stuck out his barrel chest. "Of course, I guess a desperate woman will settle for getting a little anywhere she can."

The group of three men standing around the punch bowl joined the loudmouth in his bellowing laughter. Turning around, Britt accidently ran into a matronly lady who took one look at him, gasped and moved quickly out of his way.

"Now, if I'd known Anna Rose was looking to put out, I'd have offered myself." Howard Gene laughed again, egged on by the receptive response from his listeners, who themselves made a few unflattering remarks about Anna Rose.

"Hell, yeah, I could've had her back when we were in high school, but I didn't figure she was the type, you know." Howard Gene was too absorbed in his ribald comments to notice that his comrades weren't laughing, that they were slowly backing away from him. "We ought to ask ol' Kyle. Bet he could tell us what kinda—"

Howard Gene wasn't able to finish his sentence. A huge hand gripped him by the neck. Another equally strong hand clutched his shoulder. And a pair of fiery amber eyes issued a warning. "You sorry bastard." Britt tightened his hold around Howard Gene's thick neck. "My wife happens to be a lady. And the next time you open your mouth to say anything about her, you'd better remember that fact."

Howard Gene's big round eyes bulged, startling blue in contrast to his bright red face. He tried to pull loose from Britt's tenacious grip.

"Hey, man, you're choking him," one of the other men said. "Give him a chance to apologize, will you. Howard Gene didn't mean no offense. Everybody knows he's full of—"

"Britt!" Anna Rose called out, rushing across the room. The remaining crowd parted, allowing her to pass.

"Do something, Anna Rose. Your husband is going to kill Howard Gene," a bespectacled, red-haired Clayburn Davenport pleaded. "Howard Gene didn't mean those things he said about you. It was just men talk. Nobody meant for your husband to hear."

"Britt, please let him go," Anna Rose said.

Britt hesitated for a few seconds, wanting nothing more

than to beat the living daylights out of the foul-mouthed moron. Slowly he relaxed his hold around the man's neck, then released him altogether. "Remember what I told you."

Britt turned his back on Howard Gene, hoping he could explain his actions to Anna Rose so that she would understand and forgive him for putting her on public display the way he had.

"Britt, look out!" Anna Rose shouted.

Britt whirled around just in time to see Howard Gene draw back his meaty fist. Acting on instinct and the practice he'd gained in more than one roadhouse fistfight, Britt landed a hard blow to Howard Gene's midsection, followed by a solid right cross straight into his jaw. Like a mighty timber, Howard Gene fell to the floor, the loud thump echoing in the deadly stillness of the cafeteria.

Britt glared at the people standing around staring back and forth from him to a horizontal Howard Gene, a mixture of awe and fear in their eyes.

"We're leaving," Britt said, grabbing Anna Rose by the arm and practically dragging her across the room, through the murmuring crowd.

"I can't let things go on this way," Britt said, throwing his shirt on the bed. "We can never have a life here in Cherokee as long as people think I killed Tanya."

Anna Rose sat on the bed, her arms clutched possessively around her expanded waist. What had happened tonight had brought their lives to a turning point. All the months of hoping people would accept Britt, accept their marriage and allow them to live some sort of normal life had vanished. After what Britt had done to Howard Gene, no matter how justified, folks would say that Britt's actions were evidence of his hot temper—the same temper that supposedly led him to kill his first wife.

Stripping off his shoes, socks and jeans, Britt turned out

the overhead light and sat down on the bed by Anna Rose. "I know you're still upset about what I did."

"I could lose my job. One of those calls we had before I took the phone off the hook was from Kyle. He said that after we left, Myra Davenport preached poor old Clayburn a sermon on the kind of example I was setting for the children."

"I'm sorry." Britt reached out, pulling up the cover as he lay down beside Anna Rose. "I did what I had to do."

"I know Howard Gene was going to hit you...and I realize he must have said some pretty awful things about me, but—"

"When we go to Riverton for Christmas, I'm going to talk to the sheriff again, see if I can get him to do more than give lip service to keeping the investigation open." Feeling her withdrawal, Britt wanted to pull her into his arms and tell her that she had no reason to feel threatened by his memories of Tanya. He didn't love Tanya anymore. He didn't even hate her now.

"I'm tired, Britt. I think we should try to get some sleep." She turned over, clutching the covers up to her neck.

He lay there for a long time thinking about what had happened tonight, about how much Anna Rose was having to endure because of him. He couldn't let her go on suffering because he'd been too much of a coward to face the past and finally put it to rest. He owed her more than this, and he damn well wanted his child safe from all the ridicule he and Anna Rose couldn't escape.

His child. Growing inside Anna Rose's body. He reached out and placed his arm around his wife, resting his open palm over her belly. When she tensed, her body tightened and the child gave a sturdy kick.

Britt nuzzled Anna Rose's neck. She lay silent and unmoving. "I'm sorry, honey. I never meant to do anything that would hurt you."

She released a long, deep sigh and covered his hand with her own. "I know."

"I wanted a child with Tanya." He felt Anna Rose go rigid. "No, honey, don't do that. Don't tense up when I mention her name. What I felt for her is no threat to you, to our marriage."

How could he say that? Anna Rose wondered. By his own admission he had loved only one woman in his entire life, and because of that woman's inability to return his love and her subsequent betrayal, he could never love again. Unable to respond verbally, Anna Rose simply squeezed his hand, pressing it down against her stomach.

"You're the best thing that ever happened to me. You know that, don't you? You've given me so much." Slipping his hand out from under hers, he ran the tips of his fingers upward until they encountered her swollen breasts. He circled her nipple through the thin layer of her much-laundered, cotton-flannel nightgown. She sucked in her breath.

She knew he wanted her. He always wanted her. The problems with their marriage didn't lie in their bed. The one constant between them was their unbelievable sexual compatibility. But how long could sex without love keep them together?

"I'm going to find a way to make all this up to you." With one hand caressing her breast and the other easing her gown up her thigh, Britt whispered raw love words into her ear.

By the time his fingers delved beneath her tight curls, Anna Rose dripped with desire. When Britt slid his briefs down his legs and kicked them to the foot of the bed, Anna Rose snuggled backward against his heated arousal. He lifted her leg slightly and positioned himself, easing into her sheathing warmth. With slow, rhythmical motion, he set the pace for a gentle, leisurely lovemaking. All the while he moved in and out of her with such savage tenderness, he stroked her breasts, paying special attention to her overly sensitive nipples. With her neck arched, her heart soaring and her body throbbing, Anna Rose swelled and tightened around him, trembling when his knowledgeable fingers fondled her sex.

On the verge of fulfillment, Anna Rose quivered and reached out, clutching the side of his hairy leg. And then ecstasy claimed her, shivering through her body. While still experiencing climactic aftershocks, Anna Rose cried out her love. Britt accelerated the pace of his thrusts, faster and harder and deeper. Release poured out of him, hot and furious. Shuddering, he hugged her to him, whispering her name.

Hours after Britt fell asleep, Anna Rose lay awake. Easing out of bed as quietly as possible, she reached for her robe lying at the foot of their bed. The house held a wintery nighttime chill. She slipped into her robe and slippers, then walked out into the hall.

When she entered the living room, she felt her way in the dark until she reached the switch Britt had rigged up when they'd put the lights on the Christmas tree. She flipped the switch. Hundreds of miniature white stars sparkled on the eight-foot pine tree.

She stood back, away from the tree, watching the tiny lights flickering on and off in the darkness. Her child moved within her, secure and loved, safe in his mother's womb. More than anything she wanted to give her child the things she had never had. Two parents. Love. Understanding. Self-confidence. Security.

During all the lonely years she had devoted herself to her career, she had dreamed of a husband and child of her own. How strange, she thought, that one's fondest dreams could come true and still not bring happiness.

Lord Byron walked up beside her, nuzzling her leg with his nose. She bent down and rubbed his head. ''Couldn't you sleep, either? What's wrong? Problems with your love life?''

Anna Rose sat down on the couch, curled her feet up beneath her and gazed at the tree, remembering all the Christmases her grandmother had refused to indulge in the foolish luxury of a Christmas tree. After Grandmother died, Anna Rose had put up a tree every year.

Lord Byron opened his enormous mouth in a yawn as he stretched his big body and lay down at Anna Rose's side. "I love him so much," she said. "But you know that, don't you, big boy. And so does he. But no matter how much I love him, I can't make him love me back."

Britt found them at two o'clock in the morning. Anna Rose asleep on the couch, her ever-faithful rottweiler asleep beside her. Tiptoeing across the room, he pulled an afghan from the back of the couch and covered Anna Rose with it. Lord Byron opened his eyes, cocked his head and looked up at Britt.

Britt patted the dog on the head and smiled. "It's all right, buddy, you know I'd never hurt her." The moment he whispered the words, Britt knew them for a lie. The very fact that he'd become a part of Anna Rose's life had hurt her, and as long as he didn't resolve the unsettled issues from his past, he'd go on hurting her.

Ten

Britt whipped the zipper closed on his nylon gym bag, but left it lying on the bed. He crossed the room to where Anna Rose stood by the window, her back to him.

"Maude will be here before dark. She said she was looking forward to taking care of you for a few weeks." Britt placed his hand on Anna Rose's shoulder. She lowered her head, resting it on his hand.

"You can't promise me that you'll come back in a few weeks." *I will not cry,* she told herself. She had already exhausted her supply of tears, as well as patience, the past few days while she'd been pleading with Britt to let her go to Riverton with him.

"You're right, I have no idea how long this will take." He placed his crippled left hand on her other shoulder and nudged her backward.

She pulled away from him, turning slowly to face him. "I know that you're doing what you think is right, what you feel you must do. But...but I need to be with you. Can't you understand how I feel?''

"I don't want to leave you. Especially since you're over six months pregnant." His amber eyes pleaded for understanding. Hesitantly he reached for her, relieved when she allowed him to take her into his arms. "But you know we'll never be able to live a normal life until I can prove, beyond any doubt, that I didn't kill Tanya."

"I understand. I accept the fact that you have to go back to Riverton, but I could go with you." She clung to him, fighting a tremendous battle to hold back the tears that were smothering her.

"You can't afford to take a leave of absence from your job." He stroked the long, plaited braid that rested on her back, easing his hand downward to caress her waist. "That's all Myra Davenport would need to finally badger her husband into asking for your resignation."

"I could speak to Clayburn, explain—"

"No. You know it wouldn't do any good. He could promise you anything, but once you were gone, that viper-tongued wife of his would stay at him night and day. I can't ask you to give up anything else for me. You've spent years building your career. I've already taken your good reputation from you, I won't be responsible for ruining your career, too."

"I know you're doing what you think is best for all of us, you and me and the baby." She gave him a tight hug, then pulled away. "You'd better be on your way if you want to make it to Riverton before dark."

Running his hand down over her large stomach, Britt cradled the bulge that was his child. "I'll call every day to check on you and my little quarterback." He leaned over and kissed her, tenderly, possessively, then released her and turned away.

She watched him put on his heavy sheepskin-lined jacket

and pick up his gym bag. He stopped in the bedroom doorway.

"I'll miss you, Annie Rosie."

She smiled although her heart was breaking. It was all
she could do not to run after him, begging him, one final
time, not to leave. But she simply stood there in the quiet
of the bedroom that had given her sanctuary from the world
since she'd been a child. Gray shadows floated across the
floor, creations of fading afternoon sunshine.

She heard the old Chevy truck's motor start, listening as
Britt backed out of the driveway. Lord Byron's low, plain-
tive howl came from the living room.

Well, that was that, she thought. Nothing she could do
but accept the fact that Britt was gone, for God only knew
how long. His return to Riverton had been brewing since
Thanksgiving, and she was surprised that he had waited this
long.

All of his explanations for leaving her behind were perfectly logical, and her mind accepted them without question. But her heart was another matter. Her emotions told
her that Britt's return to Riverton would renew all his memories of Tanya—the good as well as the bad. Even though
Britt had convinced himself that he no longer loved his
former wife, Anna Rose wasn't so sure. Britt Cameron's
emotions ran deep. He was a passionate man, and once he
loved, he would love forever.

Even if Britt could prove that Reverend Charles killed
Tanya, would that set Britt free to love again? And, even
if it did, who was to say that he would ever love her?

Britt waited in the truck, the lights off and the motor not
running. The cold January wind was beginning to seep inside the cab, and despite the fact that he wore his heavy
coat, his rabbit-fur-lined gloves and his brown Stetson, he
was damned cold. How much longer could choir practice
last? he wondered. Peering down at his expensive lighted

digital watch that Anna Rose had given him for Christmas, he saw that it was almost nine o'clock.

He'd spent the past two weeks in Riverton, talking daily to the sheriff. Hell, not only talking to him, but harassing him. The authorities hadn't seemed the least bit interested in a former accused murderer's suspicions about a beloved minister. Hoping to discover any possible evidence, Britt had sought out people he had once avoided, people who had known Tanya and hated him because they believed him guilty of her murder. But he'd gained nothing except a renewed bitterness and complete frustration. To make matters worse, he missed Anna Rose. He'd gotten so used to her. To her smile, her laughter, her companionship, and the pleasure he found in her body.

Suddenly the church doors opened, flooding the front steps with light. Britt scooted down in the seat, and, peering over the steering wheel watched while members of the Iuka Congregational Church's choir said their farewells, got in their cars and drove away. One man stood alone on the front steps, waving goodbye, a wide, charismatic smile on his handsome face.

Britt flung open the door and jumped out of the truck. Walking at a fast trot, he crossed the street, rushing up the steps just in time to catch Reverend Timothy Charles before he closed the church doors.

Reverend Charles looked at Britt with startled blue eyes, then gave the doors a hard push, trying to close them in Britt's face. Britt reached out, grabbing the door while he inserted his foot over the threshold.

"You wouldn't be trying to shut out a poor sinner on a cold night like this, would you, Reverend?"

Britt gave the door a hard shove with his shoulder. Timothy Charles moved backward when Britt stepped inside the foyer.

"What do you want, Cameron? Why are you here?" Timothy's tall, slender body stood outlined against the darkness of the sanctuary behind him where only the lights illuminating the baptismal were burning.

"I heard you'd found yourself a new church here in Iuka." Britt watched the other man carefully, wondering why he'd never noticed before how much Timothy Charles resembled his one-time best friend Paul Rogers. It wasn't so much that their facial features were identical, although Paul had possessed the same pretty-boy looks. No, it was more in coloring, fair-haired and blue-eyed, and in the long, lean body structure. Was that why Tanya had fallen for the good reverend? Had she seen the resemblance? Had she pretended Timothy was Paul?

"The fine Christian people here, in Iuka, in Riverton, are willing to accept my repentance and give me a second chance." Despite the cold air blowing in from the open doors, sweat dotted Timothy's brow and moistened his upper lip. He twined his long, slender fingers together in front of him in a prayerlike gesture.

"You're a lucky man. You seduced my wife, ran off with her, then killed her, and people are willing to give you a second chance." Britt resisted the overwhelming urge to put his hands around Timothy's neck and choke him until he confessed the truth.

"I didn't kill Tanya! I loved her...and she loved me." Timothy backed into the sanctuary, slowly, one step at a time. "She never loved you, but you wouldn't let her go. She didn't want to hurt you, but she didn't know what else to do."

"Then why did she come back to Riverton? Why did she call and ask to see me?"

"She wanted a divorce."

"Did she? Lawyers could have handled a divorce. No, that wasn't why she came back." Britt reached behind him, slamming the front doors, twisting the heavy metal lock until it clicked.

When Britt turned around, he saw that Timothy had

backed himself halfway down the darkened center aisle in the sanctuary. "If you leave now, Cameron, I won't report this to the police." The man's voice, so strong and commanding in the pulpit, now sounded like the whimper of a frightened little boy.

"There's nothing to report." Britt started walking down the aisle toward Timothy. "You're a minister. Your job is to comfort those in pain, administer to sinners in need of your help. I'm a man whose life has been destroyed, and you're the one person on earth who can help me."

"I'm warning you." Timothy held his arms up in front of him, his palms spread wide as a signal for Britt to stop. "No one is going to believe anything you say when it's your word against mine."

"Tanya was leaving you, wasn't she?" Britt asked, slowing his stride when he was within several feet of Timothy. "It took her six months, but she finally realized you weren't Paul, didn't she?"

"She wasn't coming back to you!"

"No, she probably wasn't, but more than likely she was coming to me for help, the way she'd done all her life. I was her friend a long time before I became her husband." Britt took several tentative steps forward until he stood chest-to-chest with the reverend. "Was it an accident or did you mean to kill her?"

"I didn't...I..."

Just as Timothy started to bolt, Britt grabbed him by the shoulders. "I'm back in Riverton and I'm going to stay until I can prove who really killed Tanya. I'm close by, and I'm going to be watching every step you make. I'm going to be breathing down your neck from now on."

"You're insane. I'll call the police and have you arrested." Timothy struggled to free himself, but found his captor's hold far too strong.

"I don't think you want to stir up trouble, do you, Reverend? I'm the one who wants people to start thinking about

Tanya's murder, to start talking about the hows and whys and whos again. I'm the one who's determined to prove that you killed my wife.''

Britt shoved Timothy Charles backward. The minister hit the red-carpeted floor with a resounding thud. Britt stared down at him. ''Just keep in mind that, not only is God watching you, but so am I.''

Britt turned and walked away, his hands trembling, his heart beating like a trapped beast within his chest. He had to get away from Timothy Charles before he knocked the truth out of him, and that was something he couldn't afford to do. He had to bide his time and wait for the good reverend to make the next move.

Four days after his nighttime encounter with Reverend Charles, Britt was no closer to unearthing the truth than he'd been when he first arrived in Riverton nearly three weeks ago. Although he spent part of his days helping Wade out around the chicken houses, his nights were spent alone.

Britt lay on the bed in the trailer, the bed he had never shared with Tanya. After being gentle and patient and understanding the first few months of their ill-fated marriage, Britt had finally given up trying to give his wife pleasure. She had accepted him into her body, but she had never responded. After the first year, he seldom touched her. He had loved her, but he hadn't been able to bear making love to her knowing she was thinking of Paul.

Being married to Anna Rose had shown him what a farce his first marriage had been. What he had with her was real. She loved him, only him, and accepted him for the man he was. But what had he given her? Did she ever wonder if he thought of Tanya when...

''Hell!'' He sat upright in the bed, appalled that he'd never even considered the possibility that Anna Rose could have thought he compared her to Tanya. Perhaps, when they'd first met, he'd noticed the differences in their looks and personalities, but after getting to know Anna Rose, he realized that she was a woman beyond compare. Every other woman, no matter how beautiful, paled beside Anna Rose. Even his memory of Tanya.

And never once when he'd touched Anna Rose had he thought of his first wife. When he wanted Anna Rose, she filled his senses so completely that she was the only thing in his world.

He had called her thirty minutes ago and had been surprised that there'd been no answer. He'd tried not to worry, telling himself that Maude would have called if anything was the matter. He'd just wait another hour or so and call again. His nightly phone conversation with Anna Rose was the only thing keeping him sane. Being back in Riverton, surrounded by memories, angered by the lack of cooperation he'd received from the sheriff and tormented by the fear that he might not ever be able to prove his innocence, Britt felt overwhelmed by the pain and bitterness that had driven him from his hometown nearly eight months ago.

What he needed was a drink. Maybe he should hop in the truck and run over to Hooligans for a couple of beers. But what would Anna Rose think if she found out, and he'd tell her when he called her. He and his wife didn't keep secrets from each other.

Coffee. Hot and rich and served with a slice of Anna Rose's apple pie. Only he couldn't make coffee that tasted like his wife's and her apple pie was fifty miles away in Cherokee.

Damn, but he missed Anna Rose. Her smile, her laughter, the dreamy expression on her face when she was reading poetry, the way she talked baby talk to Lord Byron—the way she came into his arms whenever he wanted her and filled him with a man's pride.

Just as he took the jar of instant coffee down from the cabinet in his tiny kitchen, he heard the sound of an approaching vehicle. It sounded like a four-wheel drive, Anna Rose's Blazer to be exact. By the time he'd made his way into the living room and flung open the front door, she was standing on the bottom aluminum step.

"Anna Rose." If he didn't know for sure that he was wide awake, he'd swear he was dreaming. He'd wanted her with him so badly, he could easily have conjured her up. "God, woman, get in out of the cold."

He stepped down and practically dragged her inside the trailer, then helped her off with her coat, beret and gloves before taking her in his arms and nearly squeezing the breath out of her.

Her large, rounded belly kept him from acquiring the intimate contact his body craved, but just the feel of her in his arms was more than enough.

"I couldn't stay away any longer, Britt. Three weeks." She threw her arms around his neck and smiled up at him. "I started to call, but I was afraid you'd tell me not to come, so I surprised you."

"You're a wonderful surprise, Annie Rosie." Lowering his head, he kissed her, tenderly, almost reverently. She was the most precious thing in his life, and he just now realized it. "I wouldn't have told you not to come."

"Really?" She hadn't known what kind of reception she'd receive when she arrived, unannounced. Britt had been so adamant about her not coming to Riverton with him that she'd been uncertain how he would feel about a weekend visit.

"Really." He kissed her again, a bit more forcefully, but still couldn't get her body close enough to his. "My son is in the way." Britt covered her stomach with both hands. "Three weeks and he's grown. Are you sure there aren't twins in there?"

"Dr. Middleton says one very big boy."

"Come on, honey, sit down and rest. You must be tired after driving all the way from Cherokee."

"It's only fifty miles." She didn't resist when he led her to the couch. After seating her, he shoved a round ottoman beneath her feet. "Oh, Britt, I need to go get my suitcase. I left it in the Blazer. And there's a sack with some walnut brownies, a half gallon of chicken stew and an apple pie I baked this morning."

"I'll get it all later. It's as cold as an icebox outside so the food won't spoil."

"But I'll need my gown—"

"The trailer is toasty warm. You won't need anything but me to keep you warm." He sat down beside her and drew her into his arms, lifting her onto his lap.

"You've missed me." Sitting sideways, she cuddled against him.

Unzipping her corduroy jumper, Britt ran his hand inside and around to fondle her breast still covered by a turtleneck cotton sweater. "That's the understatement of the century."

Working with hurried but gentle hands, Britt removed her clothing. First the jumper, then the sweater, followed by her stockings and shoes. When she wore nothing but her bra and panties, he picked her up and carried her into his bedroom.

When he laid her down on the unmade bed and began tearing out of his own clothes, Anna Rose sat up and looked around the room. Britt threw his jeans into a nearby chair, then stopped before removing his briefs.

"This is a two-bedroom trailer. This was my room. When I slept with Tanya, I went to her room." He nodded to the wall behind him.

"How…how did you know—"

"Because I used to wonder about Paul all the time." When he saw her flinch, he wished he could rephrase his statement. "Every time I touched Tanya, I knew she was thinking about Paul. That knowledge chipped away at my manhood a little bit at a time. I was a fool for ever marrying her."

"The two of you had separate bedrooms?" Anna Rose asked, surprised by his admission.

"Sex for Tanya and me wasn't very good." He sat down on the bed, taking Anna Rose's chin in his hand, gripping tenderly. "It was never anything like it is between us, so don't think that I've compared you to Tanya or our love-making to... When I make love to you, Annie Rosie, there is no other woman on earth."

"Oh, Britt."

"Hey, now, don't cry."

"I'm sitting here as big as a barrel, overly emotional about everything and feeling so alone and unwanted, then you go and say something like that...and make me feel... feel..."

Still holding her chin, he lifted her face to his and planted a quick, wet kiss squarely on her mouth. "Did it put you in a romantic mood?" he teased.

Easing away from him, Anna Rose unhooked her bra and dropped it on the floor, then lifted herself just enough to remove her maternity panties. "If you're interested in making love to a very pregnant woman, I know one who's available."

While he stripped off his briefs, he never stopped looking at her as he smiled devilishly. "This is going to take some figuring out. I've never had to devise a plan to maneuver lovemaking around a ten-pound tummy."

"I'm open to suggestions," she said, spreading her legs apart as she lay down.

"Oh, you hussy. What am I going to do with you?"

"And here I thought you were a man with vast experience."

"Annie Rosie, with you, every time is a new experience." He had never missed anyone or anything the way he'd missed his wife. Her love had turned his life around, given him hope where he'd had none, joy where he'd only known sorrow, laughter where he'd only known bitterness.

While she touched him and whispered words of love, he began a thorough worship of her body, his hands and lips and tongue learning every inch of satin flesh as he gave back to her a portion of the pleasure she'd given him in the months since he'd first made her his.

Her normally large breasts were very full, the aureoles darker, the nipples bigger and already producing occasional drops of milky white liquid. Soon his son would nurse at her breasts. The thought sent a surge of pure masculine urgency through him. From her neck to her heels, Britt covered her with tender strokes and moist kisses. Aware of her breasts' ultrasensitivity, he took extra care when he caressed them, dying with the need to be inside her when she moaned with pleasure.

"You're so beautiful pregnant," he told her, his lips pressing a series of adoring kisses across her stomach. "I think I should just keep you this way."

She laughed, then sighed, running her fingers through his hair as his lips traveled beyond her navel and anointed the thatch of thick curls. When he spread her legs farther apart, she made no show of protest, only whimpered as his mouth touched her intimately.

"Britt—" she finally managed to say.

"Don't talk. Don't think. Just enjoy."

And she did. With every stroke of his tongue, every tight caress of his lips, Britt brought her closer and closer to the edge. Thrashing her head from side to side, she squirmed as she clutched the bed sheets. He took her breasts in his hands, raking his thumbs back and forth over her nipples until he felt her convulse, once, twice, and then her whole body shook with release. He continued his loving until he knew she was spent.

While Anna Rose came to terms with the tiny ghosts of sensation that still warmed her body like embers left over from a raging fire, Britt eased her onto her side, pulled her back against his chest and slowly entered her. After only a few hard, quick thrusts, fulfillment claimed him.

Turning to gaze lovingly into his warm eyes, Anna Rose cuddled against Britt. "Every time I look at you, I'm glad that I'm a woman."

"Ah, Anna Rose, what a thing to say to a man." He kissed her, then enfolded her in his possessively tender embrace.

They went to sleep that way, both of them naked and sated, Anna Rose wrapped securely in the arms of the man she loved.

Eleven

Britt awoke abruptly. He looked over at Anna Rose, curled against him and sleeping peacefully. Other than his wife's gentle breathing and the thumping of his own heart, the only sounds he heard were the moaning of the icy February wind and the purr of a car's motor.

A car? In his driveway at this time of night? Jumping out of bed, he reached down on the floor for his jeans, slipped into them and headed straight for the front door. He opened the blinds covering the glass door just in time to see several bright red spots disappear into the darkness. A thin layer of frost covering the glass and the pitch blackness of predawn obscured his vision. He couldn't see the make or model of the vehicle leaving his drive, but by the size and shape of the brake lights, he guessed his unexpected visitor drove a late-model car.

But who the hell would have turned off a country road and driven a quarter of a mile up a private drive to simply turn around and leave? It didn't make sense.

A cold chill shivered through Britt, more a result of unwanted suspicions than from the weather. Returning to the bedroom, he checked on Anna Rose, who still slept soundly. He dressed quickly, wanting to check on things outside. The minute he opened the front door, the strong acrid scent of smoke engulfed him. And then he saw the fire. The wooden lattice work that flanked the underpinning of the trailer burned with a quickly spreading flame.

What the hell? Who? Why? Anna Rose! Thinking of nothing but his wife, asleep inside the trailer and totally unaware of the danger that threatened her life and their unborn child's, Britt ran back inside, racing to the bedroom.

Flinging the covers off Anna Rose, he wrapped her in a quilt. She awoke with a start when Britt scooped her up into his arms.

"What's wrong? Britt…"

"You're safe, honey. You're safe," he said as he rushed through the trailer, stopping only long enough to retrieve his truck keys from the coffee table.

Using his booted foot, he kicked open the front door. A gush of wind blew the rising flames into his face. Jerking around to prevent the fire from touching them, he realized that they couldn't escape by this route.

The back door! God, he had to get her out before the rapidly spreading fire reached the heating-oil tanks on the north side of the trailer. He knocked open the door. Although smoke billowed from beneath the back steps and Britt could see orange sparks floating in the black sky, the path was clear.

Running, he made his way to his old Chevy truck, opened the door and shoved Anna Rose inside. He jumped in, slamming the door behind him. With shaky fingers, he inserted the key in the ignition. The motor rumbled, spluttered and coughed.

"Damn it, start you…" Britt let out a stream of obscenities as he pumped the gas pedal.

"Oh, my God, Britt." Anna Rose sat, clutching the quilt around her, feeling the frigid night air that seeped through the cracks in the old truck. "How...how did the trailer...?"

With a few choice words, half curse and half prayer, Britt tried again to start the truck. He realized that Anna Rose had no idea how close they were to death. If he couldn't get the truck started before the fire hit the fuel tanks, the explosion would rip through the truck and... Start! Damn it, start. The motor growled and sputtered. If it didn't start this time, they'd have to make a run for it, out into the fields. But Anna Rose could hardly run in her condition and just how fast could he run carrying her?

Looking out the windshield, he saw the flickering tongues of the orange-gold blaze licking at the fuel tanks.

The motor turned over, starting with a roar of protest. Britt rammed the gearshift into reverse. With lightning speed, he backed the truck up the long drive. Just as they reached the country road exit, a powerful explosion rocked the trailer, sending fire and smoke shooting into the heavens.

Anna Rose screamed. One long, uncontrollable cry. Britt put the truck in park, then pulled Anna Rose's trembling body into his arms.

"It's all right, honey. We're safe." He kissed her forehead, her eyes, her cheeks, her mouth, her chin. He ran his hands over her from neck to hips, stopping to pat her round stomach. "I think all the excitement woke up my little quarterback."

"Oh, God, Britt, how can you joke at a time like this? We could have been killed. Your trailer is gone. My Blazer is on fire. My clothes are in there...and the food I brought you...and..."

He covered her mouth with his, swallowing her words and putting a stop to her lengthy tirade. Anna Rose might be sitting naked and wrapped in a quilt, she might have come within an inch of losing her life, but she certainly hadn't lost her spunk. God love her, she was priceless.

When she began struggling, he released her. She sagged into his arms. "We need to call the fire department," she said.

"I'll take you on over to Wade's place and call from there." He tucked the quilt across her breasts, his big hands gentle as he tightened them on her shoulders, reassuring himself that she was really all right.

"But...but I don't have on any clothes."

"Lydia and Ma will find you something to put on."

"Oh, tarnation. What will your mother think?"

"She'll think you sleep in the buff." Britt couldn't keep from smiling.

Emitting a shrill wail of anger and aggravation, Anna Rose muttered, "Double, triple tarnation."

"Why don't you just go ahead and cuss? No matter how much you'd like to let out with a few hells and damns, all you ever say is—"

"Grandmother never allowed ugly words to be spoken in her presence, so just shut up, Britt Cameron, and take me to Lydia's so I can put on some clothes before I freeze to death."

Mile after mile of four-lane highway stretched ahead of her. The sun had set, leaving less than thirty minutes of daylight, but Anna Rose knew she'd have no problem making it home before dark. She was only a few miles outside of Cherokee, just having passed the Allsboro turnoff.

Her surprise visit to Britt two nights ago had turned into more of a surprise than she could ever have imagined. She hadn't wanted to leave Britt, especially after the fire. But he had insisted that she return to Cherokee, telling her that she would be safer at home, and that he wouldn't have to worry about her while trying to prove Reverend Charles's guilt.

The sheriff and the fire department determined that the fire had been deliberately set. They had spent a big part of Saturday sifting through the debris that had once been Britt's trailer. When Britt suggested they question Timothy Charles concerning his whereabouts, the sheriff gave Britt a skeptical response and even suggested that he might have set the fire himself to try to discredit the good reverend.

Britt's whole family was worried, but they backed him one hundred percent. They all knew that Britt could never lead a normal life until Tanya's real killer had been brought to justice. But everyone was realistic, especially Ruthie Cameron, who'd voiced her opinion to Anna Rose this morning.

"The only way this whole mess can come to an end is if Reverend Charles confesses. It's been over two years since Tanya died and he seems to be able to live with his conscience."

Suddenly, Anna Rose knew what she had to do. Britt's strategy was to shadow Timothy Charles until the man couldn't stand the constant scrutiny, but, if Reverend Charles had set the fire that destroyed Britt's trailer, then who was to say that he would stop short of murder—again?

At the next median crossing, Anna Rose turned her rental car around and headed west. The Sunday evening church services were well under way by the time she pulled up in the Iuka Congregational Church parking lot.

Realizing she might appear a bit conspicuous in the maternity jeans and red flannel shirt she'd borrowed from Lydia, Anna Rose slipped into a back pew and removed the brown wool coat that Ruthie had loaned her.

The choir finished singing "Whispering Hope." Reverend Charles approached the microphone. He was an extremely attractive man, almost femininely beautiful. And the moment he began to speak, utter quiet descended upon the congregation. Even the children and crying babies seemed mesmerized by his strong, authoritarian voice, his theatrical actions and his charismatic presence. No wonder people refused to believe this man capable of murder, Anna Rose thought. One would sooner accuse the angel Gabriel than this man of God.

The contrast between Timothy Charles and Britt Cameron became so evident in Anna Rose's mind that she could easily see why the good people of Riverton had accused the wrong man. Britt's dark, surly looks, his scarred face and crippled hand, combined with his hot temper and bitter attitude, painted a picture of a devilish roughneck.

When the lengthy service ended and people milled about in the vestibule, Anna Rose spoke only when spoken to, informing the friendly church members that she was visiting from Cherokee. Biding her time by looking at the bulletin board, she waited until the last of the crowd had gone outside before speaking to Timothy Charles, who stood just inside the open front doors.

"Reverend Charles?" She paused directly beside him.

"Sister, we're so pleased to have you as a guest tonight." His smile beamed like a three-hundred-watt bulb.

"Reverend, I have a personal problem, one I desperately need to discuss with you."

"Of course, Sister, of course. Just let me close these doors against the cold." His task accomplished he turned back to Anna Rose. "We can talk in the sanctuary or we can go to my office."

"The sanctuary will be fine."

He followed her. She sat down in the last pew in the center row. "Now, my dear, how may I help you?" He sat beside her.

"It's my husband." Anna Rose prayed that she wasn't making a mistake, that by coming here tonight, she wouldn't push Timothy Charles into another violent act.

"Yes, how can I help your husband?" He covered Anna Rose's hand with his own.

It took every ounce of her willpower not to jerk away

from him. Anna Rose thought the man's disarming personality was lethal. How could poor, unhappy Tanya have resisted such practiced charm? "My husband was accused of a crime he didn't commit."

"How terrible for both of you, but I believe a good lawyer would help you far more than I could. Unless, of course, you've come to me for prayers."

"I've come to ask you for the truth."

Timothy's clear blue eyes widened suspiciously. "Who are you?"

"I'm Anna Rose Cameron, Britt's wife."

Dropping her hand abruptly, he stood. "I had no idea Britt had remarried."

"As you can see," Anna Rose said, patting her stomach, "we're going to have a child. Although Britt was acquitted of Tanya's murder, he can't go on with his life while the real murderer goes free."

"I see he's filled your head with all his lies about me." Timothy shrank back against the wall. His voice quivered. His hands shook. He grabbed the back of the bench as he gazed at some invisible point beyond Anna Rose's vision. "If you love your husband, then you must convince him to end his vendetta against me."

Anna Rose saw the fear, raw and ugly, on the reverend's face, and she knew in her heart that Britt was right. This man, for whatever reason, was responsible for Tanya's death.

"Someone set fire to Britt's trailer early Saturday morning. We could have died, Britt and I and our unborn child."

"I had no idea that you—"

"Was it an accident?" Anna Rose asked. Standing, she took a couple of steps toward Timothy. "Tanya's death *was* an accident, wasn't it? You never would have deliberately harmed her."

"I loved Tanya." His eyes glazed over with memories, his voice low and soft, almost a whisper. "She was sunshine and light, truly one of God's perfect creations. We didn't intend to fall in love. I was helping her with problems in her marriage.''

"She never loved Britt." Anna Rose heard the front doors open, but noticed no sign of awareness on Timothy's face.

"No, she never loved him. She didn't want to hurt him. Neither of us did. But life with him became intolerable for her.''

"So, she came to you and you took her away," Anna Rose said.

"Yes. What else could I have done? I loved her and she needed me.''

"But she came back to Riverton after six months and called Britt, begging for him to see her.''

Anna Rose's breath caught in her throat when she looked at the center aisle entrance into the sanctuary. With his hair tousled from the wind and his sheepskin-lined jacket hanging open, Britt stood beside a middle-aged man wearing a uniform. Neither Britt nor the sheriff made a sound.

"I don't suppose you ever knew Paul Rogers, did you?'' Timothy asked, tears forming in his eyes. "He was the only man Tanya ever loved. Not Cameron. Not me. I could have gone on pretending...but she couldn't. She left me."

"Was she coming back to Britt?''

"No, she...she just wanted to talk to him, ask his forgiveness and try to make things right. She didn't want either of us.'' Tears streamed down his face. He gripped the back of the bench so tightly that his knuckles turned white.

"Tanya went to Britt's trailer, but he never saw her alive,'' Anna Rose said. "Tell me what happened.''

Britt took a step into the sanctuary. Anna Rose gave him and the sheriff, who was right behind him, a warning look. They stopped dead still.

"I followed her to Cameron's trailer,'' Timothy said. "She planned to wait for him. We argued. I begged her to come back to me. I told her that I could accept the fact that she loved Paul, that I was willing to act as a substitute for him.''

"But she refused, is that it?''

"Do you have any idea how it feels to love someone who doesn't love you?'' Timothy fell to his knees on the carpeted floor, laid his head on the velvet-cushioned bench and wept like a heartbroken child.

Anna Rose went to him, placing her hand on his head. "Yes, I know,'' she said.

Timothy gazed up at her, his face pale, his eyes swollen and red. "She told me to leave, to go back to the congregation and ask their forgiveness. She told me she was sorry for everything.''

"How did she die, Timothy?'' Anna Rose kept stroking his hair. He turned his face into her belly and clutched the back of her knees. "God knows you didn't mean to hurt Tanya. He understands.''

"I grabbed her by the shoulders, begging her...pleading with her. When...when I tried to kiss her, she slapped me. I reached out...I shook her. She...she fought me...jerked away and fell. She struck her head.''

"It's all right, Timothy, it's all right.'' Anna Rose comforted him, feeling more pity than any other emotion toward the man who had put her husband through a living hell for the past two years.

"It was that antique flat iron she used as a doorstop.'' Timothy released Anna Rose, seating himself on the bench. "There was blood. So much blood. All over the floor and in her hair...her beautiful blond hair.''

Britt stepped forward, taking Anna Rose in his arms. Timothy Charles seemed oblivious to everything and everyone around him. The Tishomingo County sheriff read the reverend his rights, then handed him over to the officer who had been waiting in the vestibule.

"I'll need a statement from both you and your wife, Mr.

Cameron," Sheriff Jett said. "We'll get everything done up nice and legal so we can take care of Reverend Charles. I'd say he's going to need a doctor as well as a lawyer."

"Thanks," Britt said, then turned to Anna Rose, taking her by the shoulders. "What the hell did you think you were doing coming here and confronting Charles alone like that?"

"Why are you here?" she asked, sticking out her chin defiantly.

"Don't answer my question with a question. Do you realize what a stupid thing you did? For all you knew, Timothy Charles could have killed you."

"He didn't. Now, please explain why you and the sheriff showed up?"

"It seems Sheriff Jett finally had to take my accusations seriously when a couple of witnesses came forward to say they'd seen Reverend Charles's white Mazda come barreling out of my drive around three o'clock Saturday morning."

"Who?"

"Jimmy Skinner and Danny Collier, a couple of boys who'd been to Hooligans and were on their way home. They didn't think much about what they'd seen until they heard about my trailer burning down. They heard it from Jimmy's ma, who picked up the gossip at church this morning."

Anna Rose took in a deep breath, then released it slowly. "Thank goodness this is all over. After we make our statements to the police, I just want to go home and sleep for a week. I'm exhausted."

"Exhausted!" Britt reached out for her, but she ducked his grasp.

"I came here tonight hoping that I could—"

Britt captured her upper arms in his viselike grip. "You put your life at risk, and the life of our child. The good reverend is mentally unstable. What do you think would have happened if the sheriff and I hadn't shown up?''

"I don't know. Not for sure. I—I have to admit that I hadn't thought everything out. I just acted on impulse. I wanted to do something to help."

"Woman, you need a keeper."

"I most certainly do not." She yelped when he lifted her into his arms. "Put me down. I'm perfectly capable of walking."

"Shut up, Annie Rosie, before I really lose my temper."

She had slept from the time her head hit the pillow at ten o'clock that night until Ruthie Cameron had awakened her with a breakfast tray at eleven the next morning. The entire Cameron family had treated her as if she were made of spun glass, especially Britt, who had ranted and raved until his fiery temper burned out and he finally lay down beside her and held her through the night.

Facing Britt had proved to be difficult, exceedingly difficult. For she had made a decision that both of them would have to live with for the rest of their lives. After everything that had happened, she realized that, despite how much she loved Britt, if he didn't love her, they had no hope of real happiness.

Britt deserved to be happy. And, tarnation, so did she. His reaction had been exactly what she'd expected. He had not made any sudden confession of undying love. He'd simply pointed out that they were married and expecting a child.

"I'm leaving this afternoon," she'd said. "I'm going home to the farm, to Lord Byron, to my job and… Stay on here until everything's settled with poor Reverend Charles. Take some time to think about your feelings, to decide what you really want."

"But I know what I want. I want a life with you and our child," Britt had said.

"Do you love me?"

"Why now, all of a sudden, is that so damned important? You gave me your virginity...you married me...you're having my child, and you never once had to hear the words."

"And I still don't have to hear the words." She had touched his face, that hard, rough face she so dearly loved. "But I want to know that the man I love, loves me. Maybe it's taken me a lifetime to finally realize that I deserve that much, that I'm worthy of being loved."

"Annie Rosie..."

He hadn't been able to say more. She'd driven the rental car back to Cherokee and left her husband in Riverton. If she were very lucky and God was very generous, the day might come when Britt could admit to himself that he loved her.

Twelve

Britt slammed the truck door, then turned and kicked it with his booted foot. The relentless rain drenched him to the skin. Issuing a few choice words, he stomped around to the back door and entered the kitchen, wiping his muddy feet on the throw rug that lay just inside the entrance. Wade sat at the table, a cup of coffee in one hand and the morning paper in the other.

Britt threw an envelope on the table, then hit it with his fist. Wade eyed his coffee cup, the contents still jostling from the vibration of the table against his elbow. "Bad news?" he asked, giving his brother a warm smile.

"It's the letter I sent to Anna Rose. She sent it back... unopened." Britt dropped down into the chair beside Wade, stretching out his long legs.

"She must want you to deliver any messages in person," Wade said.

"She's being totally irrational about this."

"Women who are nearly eight months pregnant have every right to act any way they want to," Wade said, folding the newspaper and laying it down beside his empty lunch plate. "Besides, I don't think she's asking for so much. All she wants is to be reassured that her husband loves her. Women are funny about stuff like that. Lydia even wants me to say the words when we're not making love. Can you imagine that?"

"Hell, Wade, this is no laughing matter. I will not go to her and say the words if I don't mean them, and how the hell do I know if I really love her or not?" Bracing his elbows on his knees, Britt slumped over and rested his chin on top of his clasped hands. "It seems like I loved Tanya all my life. Since we were kids."

"You had a boyish crush on Tanya that you let get out of hand just because you could never have her." Wade finished off the last drops of his coffee, then set the cup on the table. "You'd have gotten over that infatuation and fallen in love with somebody else if Paul hadn't been killed."

"What are you trying to say?"

"That you married Tanya out of guilt, not love. Because you were driving the car the night Paul was killed, you blamed yourself for his death, for Tanya's miscarriage and her attempted suicide. Maybe you still loved her, but I think, more than anything else, you pitied her."

The truth hurt, but then, maybe it should, Britt thought. Deep down inside, he'd known for a long time that what Wade had just said was the truth. But the feelings of pain and anger and bitterness with which he'd protected himself since Tanya's death were far more easily explainable if he'd loved his wife instead of simply pitied her.

"How the hell does a man know if he loves a woman?"

Britt looked at his brother, hoping for an answer that would solve his problem.

Leaning over and chuckling, Wade slapped his brother on the shoulder. "You want me to go all soft and sloppy on you?"

"Yeah, if that's what it takes to explain."

"All right." Wade took in a deep breath, then ran his hand over his mouth and rubbed the stubble on his jaw. "She stays on your mind a lot. More than anything or anyone else. When you're away from her, you can't wait to be with her again. When she looks at you, you feel ten feet tall."

"Is that it?"

"You want her…hell, you get aroused just thinking about her. And no matter how good looking other women are or how attracted you might be to them, she's the only one you really want. No matter how many times you make love to her, you can never get enough of her."

"Yeah, I know exactly what you mean," Britt said.

"You want to take care of her and protect her and make her happy because she makes your life worth living."

"Damn!" Britt jumped up so quickly that he knocked over his chair.

"Who lit a fire under you?" Wade asked, grinning.

"I need to borrow some money, Wade. A couple of thousand maybe. I'll pay you back if it takes the rest of my life."

"What on earth are you going to do with two thousand bucks?"

"I'm going to buy my wife a ring, a sapphire ring as blue as her eyes."

"Anna Rose isn't the type to expect you to spend money on an expensive ring for her," Wade said.

"I know, but she's the type of woman who deserves it."

* * *

He'd had to take the back road to the farm. Days of pre-spring rain had flooded the only road coming in directly from Cherokee. The detour had cost him precious time. But he was here, finally. Home. He didn't recognize the vehicle in the drive, but assumed the shiny new red Blazer belonged to Anna Rose.

Checking his pocket for the sapphire and diamond ring he'd bought yesterday, he reached down on the seat, picked up the book of poetry that Lydia had helped him pick out and grabbed the huge bouquet of flowers he'd bought at the florist in Riverton.

With flowers in hand, Britt tucked the book under his coat before opening the door. Jumping out of his truck, he made a mad dash for the front porch. Slinging the moisture off his body, he tried the door. Locked. He rang the door-bell. No answer. He rang again. He delved into his pocket for the key, then inserted it in the lock and opened the front door.

"Anna Rose," he called out as he stepped inside the foyer. When he received no reply, he called out her name again.

Well, maybe she was in the kitchen and couldn't hear him for all the thunder. Damn, the electricity must be off again, he thought when he saw the kerosene lamp burning on the table at the end of the hall.

"Anna Rose, where are you?" He checked the living room, then walked through the dining room and into the kitchen. The rooms were empty. He'd started to turn around and head for the bedrooms when he heard Lord Byron's mournful howl. Where was the dog? His howl sounded as if it had come from the back porch.

After placing the bouquet and book of poetry on the kitchen table, Britt swung open the door leading to the porch. Lord Byron lay beside the open screen door, both his big paws resting atop the prone body lying half inside the porch and half outside on the steps. The rottweiler's soulful whine turned Britt's blood to ice.

"Anna Rose," he cried, rushing to her, going down on his knees to take her in his arms.

Her face was damp and stained with mud splatters. Her hair was soaking wet, as were her clothes. "Oh, Britt, I'm so glad to see you."

"What happened, honey? Are you hurt?"

"Help me…please, help me."

When he tried to lift her, she cried out in pain. "Tell me what happened. Did you fall?"

"The phone's dead…the electricity is out. I started having labor pains this morning." She clutched at her belly. "Maude's brother-in-law died yesterday. She left…" Anna Rose pulled her legs up to her stomach, crying out when another pain hit her. "She's in Chattanooga."

"I've got to get you up. Your legs and feet are lying out in the rain." Trying to ignore her moans, Britt lifted her in his arms. "The road's out into Cherokee, but I can take you to the Iuka hospital on the back roads, the way I came in."

Resting her head on his shoulder, she clung to him. "We'll never make it. I tried to get to the car, but…I was in such a hurry, I fell. The pains are every minute, now, and I can feel the baby's head trying to push out."

"Oh, God!" Carrying her inside, he made his way to their bedroom and lowered her to the bed. "Don't worry, Annie Rosie, I'm here and I'll take care of you."

"Have you ever delivered a baby?" she asked, then screamed when yet another labor pain struck.

The sound of her shrill scream and the look of anguish on her face sliced through Britt's heart, creating a shared pain within him. "No, but I've delivered calves and colts."

"Then you should have no problem delivering your own son, should you?"

"Let me help you get out of your clothes, honey. You're soaked to the skin." Without another minute's delay, he stripped her naked, then slipped on her robe, bunching it around her hips. "Better?" he asked.

"Warmer." She began breathing in hard, fast pants. "I'm afraid something might be wrong. I'm not due for another five weeks."

"I've heard first babies are always either late or early." Britt bent over the side of the bed and checked Anna Rose's condition. She was right—the baby's head was already in the birth canal.

Anna Rose felt tired, as if she'd been running a race, but she knew there would be no rest for her until the baby was born. Clutching the quilt on which Britt had laid her, she tried not to scream as pain sliced through her like a hot branding iron. Although the ache was low in her back, spreading to her abdomen, she could feel it all over. A body-racking pain that hurt more than anything she'd ever felt.

"Get some old sheets and a quilt out of the hall closet," she told him between contractions. "We...we can burn them after this is over. And...get some more towels out of the linen closet."

Britt hesitated leaving her. "You shouldn't be alone. What if—"

"Go on! Get the sheets and towels and quilt," she ordered. "And get a sharp knife out of the kitchen and sterilize it with the flame in one of the kerosene lamps."

Just as he left the room, he heard her scream again. Anna Rose wasn't the type of woman who endured pain meekly. He'd have to remember that if they ever decided to have another child. Oh, God, what was he thinking? *Please,*

Lord, just don't let anything happen to Anna Rose and this baby and I won't ask for another thing as long as I live.

Carrying all the items she'd requested, Britt returned to the bedroom to find his wife drenched in sweat and repeating the word *tarnation* over and over again.

"Put that old quilt under me and then the towels. Save the clean sheets for the baby."

She felt an overwhelming need to push, a desperate urge to bear down. Her body arched upward as an enormous pressure built inside her, preparing her body for childbirth. She didn't know how much longer she could endure the pain, and she wondered how much longer Britt was going to be able to stand. He looked as if he were about to faint, and Anna Rose knew that the worst was yet to come.

Britt knelt between her spread thighs, watching, waiting as the baby's head emerged. "I can see the head. Push, honey. Push."

He didn't have to tell her to push! She wanted to tell him to just shut up and quit being so bossy. After all, she was perfectly capable of pushing without his orders.

Suddenly, nothing in the world existed except the life-giving force that controlled her body. Straining, Anna Rose cried out when, with a tremendous push, the pain began to ease as her body expelled its precious burden.

Britt guided the child out and into his arms, holding his son up so his mother could see him. Their son was round and fat and very dirty. Thick, black hair covered his little head.

"He's not crying," Anna Rose said. "What's wrong?"

"It's all right. He'll cry," Britt said, praying.

Laying the child atop Anna Rose's stomach, Britt quickly cut the cord, tied it off, then focused all his attention on his son—his son who wasn't breathing.

"Britt..."

Momentarily ignoring Anna Rose, Britt wiped off the baby's face and tried desperately to clean out his nose and mouth. *Breathe, son. Please breathe.*

"Oh, God, do something, Britt. He's dying." Using what little strength she had left, Anna Rose lifted her head to look down at where her husband was administering artificial respiration to their infant son.

The sound of a shrill, angry cry filled the bedroom. Britt, tears streaming down his face, held his child in his hands. "That's it, little man, cry for your mama. Let her know that you're all right."

When Britt handed their son to Anna Rose, he couldn't even see them, only the blurry outline of their faces and bodies. His vision was marred by tears.

Anna Rose opened her robe and held the squalling infant to her breast. He nuzzled her with his tiny nose. When she took his hand in hers, he curled his little fingers around her thumb.

So in awe of the new life she'd just delivered into the world, Anna Rose didn't even look at Britt until she heard his muffled moans. Turning her head toward the sound, she cried out, so touched by the sight of Britt on his knees beside her bed. He laid his head against her hip. Racked with tears, his big body trembled from the force of his unchecked emotions.

"Britt, it's all right. We're both fine." She placed her hand on his head, running her fingers lovingly through his hair.

Raising his head, he stared at her, then lifted himself enough to reach out and touch her face. "I love you, Anna Rose. More than anything on this earth."

There was something so powerful about a strong man's

tears, Anna Rose thought as she smiled at her husband. "It took you long enough to come to your senses, Britt Cameron."

David Palmer Cameron and his mother came home from the hospital three days later amid the chaos of a family celebration that extended to include Anna Rose's long-time friends and neighbors.

With Grandma Ruthie installed in the guest bedroom for an extended visit, Britt turned over the care of his son to her until David's next feeding. There had never been any question in Anna Rose's mind that she would breast-feed, but she promised Britt that, as soon as David was old enough for fruit juice, he would be allowed to give him his bottle.

"I don't feel the least bit tired, Britt," Anna Rose said when her husband laid her down on their bed. "I just had a baby, you know, I'm not an invalid."

"Humor me." He sat down beside her. "It's not every day a woman gives me a child. So quit trying to boss everybody around and let me run this show."

"You brought me in here for a reason, didn't you?"

"For privacy," he admitted.

"Well, as much as I'd like to indulge in a little lustful lovemaking, I'm afraid there are parts of my body not quite ready for—"

He laughed. God, what a woman. His woman. "Annie Rosie...Annie Rosie." He couldn't stop laughing.

"What's so funny?" She sat up in the bed.

He pushed her back down, hovering over her. "You are."

"I am not."

He pulled a tiny jeweler's box out of his pocket, flipped it open and stuck it in Anna Rose's face.

"What's this?" she asked, trying again to sit up.

"It's your engagement ring."

"But we're married."

"I bought it before I left Riverton." He lifted the jeweled circle from its velvet cushion and held it out to her. "I love you, Anna Rose. Will you marry me? Will you come live with me and be my love...forever?"

Wiping away tears of joy, Anna Rose held out her left hand for him to slip the ring onto her finger. "Yes."

Britt nudged her over. Lying down beside her, he took her in his arms. And that's the way Grandma Ruthie found them an hour later when she brought a hungry David Cameron to his mother.

Epilogue

The Palmer-Cameron farm had played host to an annual Fourth of July picnic for the past five years, and this year was no exception. Friends and family filled the yard. Children of all ages and sizes ran helter-skelter everywhere. Roy Dean and his amateur band filled the hot summer air with the sounds of bluegrass, rich with fiddle music.

Just as she stepped out the back door, a pie in each hand, Anna Rose felt Britt's arm go around her as he took one of the pies. He patted the side of her stomach. "I'll bet no one suspects you're pregnant. Let's make an announcement?"

"Do you really think anyone will be interested in the fact that there's a third little Cameron on the way?"

"The folks in Cherokee, Alabama, are always interested in the latest news. Besides, the birth of my first daughter is going to be a media event."

A dozen picnic tables had been set up beneath a grove

of century-old oak trees. Ruthie Cameron sat wiping ice cream off three-year-old Daniel Cameron's mouth, much to his aggravation, while five-year-old David fed his hot dog to Lord Byron.

Wade and Lydia had taken their children down to the pond where a small crowd was swimming. Cousins Opal and Maude were taking turns giving Kyle Ross instructions on the proper way to crank an ice cream maker, while his pregnant wife Tracy watched with barely concealed amusement.

"There's not a soul in the house right now," Britt said. "Who would know if we slipped away for a little while?"

"Britt Cameron, are you suggesting that you want to make love to me in the middle of the day with at least sixty people visiting?"

"Yeah."

"Don't be silly."

He gave her a little-boy pouty look. "Tired of me already?"

"Quite the contrary." She set the pie down on the table filled with desserts. He did the same. Turning, she threw her arms around his neck, then ran her fingers across his smooth cheek. After his plastic surgery four years ago, he had shaved his beard but left the mustache. "I have definite plans for tonight…down at the pond…a private party."

"Tell me more," he said.

"Well, first we'll take off all our clothes and go skinny-dipping. We'll kiss awhile and play around a bit, and then…"

"And then?"

"And then I'm going to…" She told him in simple, explicit terms exactly what she was going to do to him.

"Annie Rosie…Annie Rosie…wherever did you learn such language?"

*   *   *   *   *

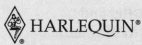

INDULGE IN A QUIET MOMENT
WITH HARLEQUIN

Get a FREE
Quiet Moments
Bath Spa

with just two proofs of purchase from
any of our four special collector's editions in May.

Harlequin® is sure to make your time special this Mother's Day
with four special collector's editions featuring a short story
PLUS a complete novel packaged together in one volume!

Collection #1   Intrigue abounds in a collection featuring *New York Times*
bestselling author Barbara Delinsky and Kelsey Roberts.

Collection #2   Relationships? Weddings? Children? = *New York Times*
bestselling author Debbie Macomber and Tara Taylor Quinn
at their best!

Collection #3   Escape to the past with *New York Times* bestselling author
Heather Graham and Gayle Wilson.

Collection #4   Go West! With *New York Times* bestselling author
Joan Johnston and Vicki Lewis Thompson!

Plus Special Consumer Campaign!
Each of these four collector's editions will feature a
"FREE QUIET MOMENTS BATH SPA" offer.
See inside book in May for details.

Only from

HARLEQUIN®
Makes any time special ®

Don't miss out! Look for this exciting promotion on sale in May 2001,
at your favorite retail outlet.

Visit us at www.eHarlequin.com   PHNCP01